Miracles on the Land

Bestselling Australian Author

FIONA McARTHUR

MILLS & BOON

First Published 2002
Fourth Australian Paperback Edition 2023
ISBN 978 1 867 29167 1

First Published 2003
Fifth Australian Paperback Edition 2023
ISBN 978 1 867 29167 1

First Published 2009
Sixth Australian Paperback Edition 2023
ISBN 978 1 867 29167 1

Published by
Mills & Boon
An imprint of Harlequin Enterprises (Australia) Pty Limited (ABN 47 001 180 918), a subsidiary of HarperCollins Publishers Australia Pty Limited (ABN 36 009 913 517)
Level 19, 201 Elizabeth Street
SYDNEY NSW 2000
AUSTRALIA

FSC www.fsc.org MIX Paper | Supporting responsible forestry FSC® C001695

Printed and bound in Australia by McPherson's Printing Group

CONTENTS

Fiona McArthur is Australian and lives with her husband and five sons on the Mid-North coast of New South Wales. Her interests are writing, reading, playing tennis, e-mail and discovering the fun of computers—of course that's when she's not watching the boys play competition cricket, football or tennis. She loves her work as part-time midwife in a country hospital, facilitates antenatal classes and enjoys the company of young mothers in a teenage pregnancy group. You can read more about Fiona on her website www.fionamcarthur.com.

Emergency In Maternity

To volunteers everywhere

CHAPTER ONE

Tuesday 6 March

NOAH MASTERS PUSHED open the door to Riverbank Hospital and the unmistakable buzz of the internal cardiac arrest alarm sent a bolus of unwanted adrenaline through his body.

He'd sworn he would never work as a doctor in Emergency again, and he hated that staccato buzz. Finally it stopped, and Noah felt the tension ease in his neck as he approached the main office. He could see that the receptionists had returned to whatever had occupied them before the sudden rush of urgent phone calls and he didn't have to wait for their attention.

'My name is Noah Masters, regional CEO. I'm looking for Mr Beamish.' He smiled at the receptionist and the woman blushed and stared up at him. Noah was used to people looking twice at his height but sometimes it irritated him.

She cleared her throat and apologised. 'You're the new chief executive officer? I'm sorry, Mr Masters. Mr Beamish isn't in on Tuesdays, and Miss Glover, the nurse manager, is in a meeting. Perhaps the shift co-ordinator could help you?'

Served him right for not ringing before he came. Noah mentally shrugged and smiled at the woman again. 'If he or she isn't too busy, that would be fine.'

'I'll page her. She shouldn't be long.' The woman seemed to be all fingers and thumbs, so Noah turned away to survey his surroundings. A Gordon Rossiter riverscape painting took pride of place on the wall and unwillingly his eyes widened in appreciation. The foyer was furnished with a cedar china cabinet and matching chairs. He couldn't resist a stroke of the polished wood and it passed like silk beneath his fingers—hand-turned, he guessed. You had to admit it all made the entrance foyer more warm and homey than he was used to.

Probably all donated, he thought cynically, like most of the equipment in these small country hospitals, but his irritation had eased. Community hospitals had their place, but that didn't change the fact that the big money needed to be spent where the greater population was. He glanced at his watch and the receptionist obviously picked up his impatience.

'Sister hasn't answered her page, but if you'd like to continue around to the emergency department, Mr Masters, I'm sure you'll catch her. If she rings back, I'll tell her you're coming.'

Noah couldn't exactly tell the woman he hated Emergency, so he just nodded and followed the direction of her pointed arm. Just his luck.

When he pushed open the sheet-plastic doors the smells and sounds of a typical morning in Casualty crowded his senses. Before he could orientate himself, a militant Valkyrie with spiky blonde hair stopped in front of Noah and barred his way.

'Can I help you?' she said, but it was more of an accusation than an offer of assistance.

Suddenly the sights and sounds of Emergency receded and Noah eyed her quizzically. She must have been outside recently, because rain beaded in her hair and the corridor seemed to vibrate around her like the electricity that flashed across the heavens outside the window.

'This is a restricted area.' She used her well-modulated voice with authority and Noah cynically admired her technique. Perhaps because he did it all the time himself.

She squared her shoulders at him. He outweighed her in muscle by a good twenty kilos, so he wasn't quite sure what she thought she could do if he decided to proceed past. There was something about her that made his day brighten and a smile hovered on the edge of his lips. There could be no mistake she was a hostile native! A magnificent hostile native but definitely hostile.

'Good morning,' he said. 'I'm looking for the shift co-ordinator.' Noah smiled his charming smile but the warrior maiden wasn't like the receptionist and didn't budge. He resisted the almost irresistible temptation to move another step forward to see what she'd do.

She raised her chin, almost as if she'd read his mind, and Noah had to bite back a smile. He returned her appraisal and gained the impression that the mind behind her really quite beautiful blue eyes was as sharp as the creases ironed into her short-sleeved shirt.

Thick lashes came down and hid her thoughts. 'I'm the shift co-ordinator but I'll be busy for the next half-hour. Are you connected with the hospital?'

His mouth curved a little more. She was interrogating him. He nodded and held out his hand. 'Noah Masters, regional CEO, and you are...?'

Cate had known it! The enemy! 'Cate Forrest, the morning shift co-ordinator.' The suit he was wearing had warned her. But that was the only part of his appearance that tied in with her mental image. She'd known he was coming, she'd just expected a weasel with accountant's glasses.

Unfortunately, he was nothing like she'd imagined. He had a smooth, masculine presence that radiated command and Cate had to tilt her head slightly to look up at him. She didn't like the necessity. There weren't that many men taller than Cate and she wasn't used to it. His hand was out in front of her, waiting, and reluctantly Cate took it.

When his fingers closed around hers in a firm clasp, she returned the shake, frowned and then pulled free as soon as possible.

Her fingers still thrummed. She certainly couldn't say his handshake was as furtive as his visit. The man vibrated with energy! She couldn't stand a man with a limp handshake but that buzz between them was ridiculous. Surreptitiously she wiped her hand on the side of her skirt to remove the tingle.

They stood there and eyed each other like opposing generals, and the silence lengthened. Cate had a suspicion it was amusement she could see in his eyes and it stirred her temper, as a breeze lifted a tiny pile of leaves. Yes, he rattled her, she admitted grudgingly. She was usually the one in control. One minute in his company and she could tell he wouldn't be as co-operative as Mr Beamish was to her plans.

She steered Noah Masters around and back out through the plastic doors to the corridor. 'I'm sorry, I don't have the time for a formal tour today. Perhaps you can arrange something later with Mr Beamish?'

Noah's smile was winning but it bounced off Cate. 'This isn't a formal visit, Sister Forrest. I'm not inspecting Riverbank, I'm just gaining a feel for the place.'

Cate raised her eyebrows delicately. 'How interesting.' You can get a feel just by poking around, can you buster? She only just kept the words from her lips. The pager clipped on her belt emitted an insistent beep and she glanced down to see the phone extension displayed on the mini-screen. It was the accident and emergency main desk. 'Excuse me. I must answer this call. The cafeteria is on this floor if you would like some lunch.'

Noah inclined his head. 'Perhaps I'll see you on my travels later?'

You'd better believe it. 'We're a small hospital. I imagine you might,' Cate said dryly, and walked away to answer the page.

Noah watched her stride away, her straight back not apologising for her exceptional height and the gentle sway of her hips more provocative, he guessed with a grin, than she intended. She wasn't a dainty, helpless female like Donna had been—totally the opposite, in fact—but she was arresting.

His lips twitched. She actually looked like she wanted to arrest him!

Noah turned back towards the cafeteria with the smile still tugging on his lips. This visit to Riverbank could be more interesting than he'd anticipated.

Cate's head was high. Big city sleaze. He was a big man all over, most of it muscle. Broad-shouldered and deep-chested, and she wouldn't like to meet him in a dark alley. Cate realised it could be a problem to keep her antipathy towards him under control. There was something about him that made her bristle, apart from his obvious threat to Riverbank. But it was a worry what the snoopy Noah Masters was really doing, and how much of a disadvantage to Riverbank it could be to leave him unsupervised. She looked at her watch and sped her footsteps. Hopefully he'd linger over his lunch and she'd be able to find someone to keep an eye on him.

As Cate entered the emergency department, the activity was centred on an elderly gentleman and her footsteps quickened in concern. Mr Beamish, the present CEO of the hospital, was lying on a trolley, obviously in a lot of pain. Judging by the splint still attached to his leg, the problem would affect the man she'd just left. Hell. When it rained it poured.

Casualty Sister Moore turned to Cate with her usual calm. 'Well, that saves me answering the phone. Thanks for coming. Mr Beamish has just come in. He has severe hypothermia and a probable fractured femur.'

Cate nodded and smiled gently at the older man's pale face as he almost blended in with the white pillowcase. 'Hello, Mr Beamish. You've come to the right place for some tender loving care. We'll get you fixed up as soon as we can.' She didn't mention Noah Masters—it was the last thing the poor man needed to know!

Stella Moore followed her out to the nurses' station. 'The ambulance officers just brought him in. He slipped over on his cattle-grid this morning and his wife didn't realise he was in trouble for at least a couple of hours. Mr Beamish had to lie in the rain until she found him, and he's pretty shocked.'

Cate's face clouded for a moment before she said, 'It must have been horrific. Hopefully he won't get pneumonia.' She picked up the phone and glanced out of the window. Water streamed off the pane as she waited for her call to be answered. 'My dad says we're in for a flood and I wouldn't be surprised.'

Stella winced. 'Don't say that. We've just recarpeted our house.' Cate nodded sympathetically. She thought of her parents' farm and the cattle that would have to be moved if the river rose too far, then shelved that problem for after her shift. The telephone just kept ringing so she dialled the nurse manager's number again and finally Cate's immediate superior answered.

Cate left the notification of Mr Beamish's accident with her, along with the news of Noah Masters's appearance.

Miss Glover's voice was hurried. 'I'm in a meeting. Show Mr Masters around if you have time, Cate, please.'

Cate screwed her nose up at the phone and reluctantly agreed.

Her pager beeped and she glanced at the number on the screen. She looked at Stella. 'Anything else you need for the moment, apart from Mr Beamish's old medical records?'

'No. But a lunch-break wouldn't go amiss when you get a minute.' Stella rubbed her hollow stomach and Cate grinned back at her.

'No problem. I'll get the old records, dash over to Maternity to answer this call and come back as soon as I finish there.'

By the time Cate had procured some out-of-stock drugs for Maternity and relieved emergency staff for their lunch, she was in dire need of sustenance herself.

When she entered the cafeteria Noah Masters was the only person left in the room. On the point of leaving, he hesitated, then walked towards her to refill his cup.

Some people took extended lunch-breaks. Cate chewed her lip. She wished he'd left, which was strange considering her previous decision that someone needed to keep an eye on him and she was supposed to show him around.

'The coffee must be good if it's kept you here this long.' Cate snapped her mouth shut on the you-don't-have-anything-better-to-do implication, but it was clear to both of them what she meant.

He raised his eyebrows at her comment and his smile, devastating as it was, was all on the surface. 'The company was good. Your *staff* are very friendly.' The inference was clear.

She supposed she deserved that but she didn't trust him or his smile. She mentally shrugged. She'd never been good at dissembling so most people knew pretty quickly how she felt.

Obviously her staff hadn't realised this man was a wolf casing the flock. She bristled. 'The nurses who work here are wonderful and it always amazes me how they keep their spirits and standard of care up, considering such low funding and the workload expected of them.' By number-crunchers like you, she almost said.

He accompanied her back to the table and on the surface he still didn't seem particularly ruffled. 'Hmm, maintaining a budget is always going to be difficult in a small establishment.'

As if here at Riverbank they didn't try! Cate narrowed her eyes as she set her cup and plate carefully on the table. 'But less important than actually continuing the service.' She paused to let her words sink in. 'Personally, I don't give a hoot for your budget. My concern is maintaining the standard of care the people of this valley deserve—without having to leave the area to get it—and the sooner money is put in its proper perspective, the better.'

His face remained expressionless and she marked another point against him. The guy probably didn't have emotions—just numbers running around inside his computer brain. And she knew he'd been a doctor before he'd taken up administration, which didn't make any sense to her.

He waited until Cate was seated and then sat down. At least he had manners, she grudgingly acknowledged.

Noah set his cup down. 'Unfortunately budgets are a fact of life.'

'Or you'd be out of a job,' she muttered. He turned his head to look at her fully and his eyes flared briefly at her comment. She became sidetracked by the realisation that his chocolate brown eyes could freeze to almost coal black when he was annoyed. The air temperature dropped about ten degrees. She blinked. 'I'm sorry. You were saying?'

For a moment he looked to be inclined to follow up her previous comment but then, with only a brief cryogenic glare, decided against it and reverted to business mode. 'I was saying that budgets are a fact of life and while it's your job to maintain patient services, it's my job to streamline the process cost effectively. The money should go where the needs are greatest. Perhaps we could agree to the necessity for the other person's job.'

The deep timbre of his voice sent an unwelcome shiver across Cate's shoulders. He could be persuasive and she could just see him at a boardroom table, smiling winningly at weaker individuals. She wasn't fooled, though.

In fact, she wasn't temperamentally suited to this conversation. She was more of an action person. Let the official party chat with him. There was no way she could carry on a rational conversation with this guy and not get indigestion. Cate pushed aside the second half of her sandwich and took a last sip of her coffee.

There were still the orders to show him around. 'Is there any area in particular you'd like to see while I have a spare moment, Dr Masters?'

A tiny crease appeared above his right eyebrow at the title. 'If you've finished…' He glanced down at the meagre lunch left on her plate and then away. 'I'd like to see the maternity ward.'

Grimly Cate rose and carried her crockery back to the dish trolley. 'Do you have a special interest in Maternity, Dr Masters?'

Noah winced again at her calling him 'Doctor'. He wished she wouldn't do that. He was never going back to practising medicine. Then he considered the question. Despite the fact that it was the least offensive thing she'd said to him, he knew the question was loaded. He couldn't believe this woman. He'd met people who'd disliked him before, not often, but none as aggressively against him as she was. And she did aggression well. He'd had to struggle with his temper twice already and he couldn't remember the last time that had happened. He'd been controlled like a machine since Donna had died.

He chose his words carefully. 'I believe Maternity can be the showcase of the hospital. Front-line public relations are an important facet of any hospital's success.' And the most common area of overspending. But he didn't say it.

Public relations led back to the dollar again, Cate correctly deduced, and shrugged.

When they walked into Maternity two of the room buzzer lights were on and the nursery was lined with bassinets in which most of the tiny occupants were crying. Mothers with their babies in their arms, crowded around the sink as they waited for weighings and baths.

Noah frowned. 'Where are all the staff?'

Cate almost snorted. '*Both* midwives are doing fifty things at once.' She felt like saying, Can you see anywhere to save money here? But she didn't. Well done. What control, Cate. She patted herself on the back then moved away from him to punch some numbers into the phone.

'Hi. It's Cate Forrest here. Can you send Trudy over to Maternity to help in the nursery for an hour, please? Yes, they're snowed under.' She smiled into the phone and he realised he hadn't seen her smile before. It lit her face with a sweetness that warmed the ice around his heart. She had a smile that reached the corners of the room and shone up the walls. Noah wondered what it would feel like to have that wattage directed solely at him. It would be a smile worth waiting for. He blinked and refocused on the ward around him.

'Thanks,' she said to whoever was on the phone. 'I owe you one.'

One of the midwives came out of the birthing unit and grinned at Cate. 'Two new admissions, both in established labour, right on bathtime, and four babies are waiting for discharge weighings.'

'Trudy is coming over for the nursery. Have you guys had lunch?'

Noah nodded at the mothers who walked past as Cate rearranged staff. He listened to her acknowledge the good job the midwives were doing with the workload and then she proceeded to address several of the mothers by their first names and enquire about their other children. She seemed to know and have one of those smiles for everyone. Except him.

But, then, he guessed she was a people person. He wondered if he still had that knack after two years in administration. Had he lost the knack of emergency surgery, too? Noah squashed that last thought down ruthlessly, and the guilt that rose with it.

Cate caught him studying her and excused herself from the mother she was speaking to. She moved across to his side with the light of battle in her eye. 'Do you advocate breastfeeding, Dr Masters?'

Under attack, Noah looked around at the mothers watching him. 'If at all possible, of course I do,' he said cautiously.

'So you'd agree it's important that first-time mums in particular have access to help for at least the first few days after the baby is born to establish lactation? Especially if you believe that breastfeeding is best for babies.'

A glimmer of light appeared and Noah narrowed his eyes. Before he could ask if this had to do with his suggestion to shorten postnatal stays, she continued.

'Were you aware that, unlike larger hospitals, Riverbank clients don't have access to early discharge follow-up by midwives? Only overworked early childhood nurses?'

Her blue eyes bored into his and he had to admire her passion, if not her subtlety.

'No, I wasn't aware of that.' He was going to continue but Cate cut him off.

'Or that we have some of the best long-term breastfeeding rates in New South Wales?' She looked justifiably proud about that.

She was like a steamroller and from one steamroller to another he couldn't help admiring her—but a public hallway was unfair. 'No. I wasn't aware of that either, Sister Forrest,' he replied sardonically. He didn't understand why he wasn't more annoyed with her. Perhaps it was the obvious undeniable passion she had for her work.

'Pity!' She'd scored her point and was ready to change the subject. 'Seen enough?'

Before he could answer, her pager went off and she was thinking of something else. 'I'm off to Accident and Emergency, Dr Masters.'

He knew she wanted to get rid of him but he wasn't going to be shaken off that easily. 'I'll tag along, then.'

He lengthened his stride to keep up with her, which was quite a startling change from usually having to slow his pace for women. He found himself smiling again—Cate Forrest was certainly different.

Thunder rumbled outside and Noah shook his head as he glanced out of the window to see the sheets of rain falling even harder. 'This is some storm.'

Cate paused and followed his gaze out of the window. 'It's more than a storm.'

Noah frowned. 'Meaning?'

'My father says we're in for a flood—and when a farmer predicts a disaster, it's a definite worry.'

Farmers predicting weather. He'd heard of that but he didn't believe in it. 'So how often does it flood around here?'

Cate turned from the window and started walking again. 'Nineteen sixty-three was a big flood but 1949 was the biggest in recent history. That flood washed right through the centre of town, killed six people and left others stranded on the roofs that didn't wash away. The locals still talk about that one.'

Her pager shrilled and she glanced down and muttered, 'Outside call.' Then picked up the pace again.

'The staff with creek crossings can have problems getting in when it's like this. That will be the first of those who can't get in.' She smiled sweetly at him. 'They get flooded-in leave.'

He frowned. 'Can't you make them stay in town before they get flooded so the hospital will be staffed properly?'

Cate raised her own sardonic eyebrow. 'Perhaps if that was a permanent rule, we could have our hospital staffed properly at normal times?'

He flicked a questioning glance across at her until he realised she was baiting him—again.

A small frown marred her forehead and he realised that he had only a fraction of her attention. Another thing he wasn't used to. 'I'll leave you to it, Sister Forrest. I can see you have your hands full.'

For the first time she smiled at him, and he couldn't help but smile back. As he turned down the opposite corridor towards his car, he acknowledged wryly that all he had to do was leave her and she'd smile.

CHAPTER TWO

AFTER WORK, Cate tried to concentrate on the road home to her parents' farm in the torrential rain, but it required more attention than she wanted to give. She knew she needed to be less fixated on scoring against Noah Masters and more focused on the rising river and her father's cattle.

Compartmentalising had never been a problem with men before. Even during her engagement she'd been able to parcel Brett up in to one part of her life while she carried on with something else. So why did thoughts of Noah Masters not stay where she told them to? She grimaced. Maybe he was too big.

She couldn't help the image of Noah popping so clearly into her memory. And she couldn't help the awareness of her attraction to him—something she'd been fighting all day—from stealing her concentration.

Cate's utility rattled over the cattle-grid and the sheets of rain made it hard to make out the figure sitting in the wheelchair on the verandah. She waved anyway as she drove past and parked in the garage. Shaking rain off as she came, Cate hurried up the verandah steps to drop a kiss on her father's leathery cheek. 'Hi, Dad.' William Forrest was another big man and her heart ached to see him confined to the wheelchair. Oddly, he'd adapted to being paralysed better than his family had.

'Hello, love. River's rising,' he said, and they both turned to look towards the bottom paddock river flat. The thickened brown snake of the river was spreading slowly across the lowest areas. 'Your mother's trip to town yesterday was in good time. We've enough supplies for a month.'

'Hopefully the rain won't last a month.' Cate grinned wryly at her father and laid her hand on his shoulder. 'I'll change after my coffee and move the cattle up to the house paddock.'

His bushy white eyebrows drew together. 'I thought the fence had snapped up in the house paddock?'

'I fixed it yesterday before I went to work but the gate's only just hanging on.'

He put his hand over hers and gripped it as if to say, Hear me out. 'The farm is too much for you and your mother. I've asked your brother to come home.'

Cate tried not to feel that she'd failed him. Her father shouldn't have had to do that. 'Oh, Dad, there's no point worrying Ben! We can manage. I'll fix the gate this evening.'

William was still very much the head of the family and knew how to be firm. 'It's too much. You're a fine daughter and as good as any man on the farm. But you have your own life. And I'll need him for the flood, if it comes.' There was no doubt her father believed they were in for a big flood.

Cate turned away and tried not to think about the changes that Ben's return would make. Her brother had left home without a backward glance as soon as he'd turned eighteen. He had chosen to work in the Northern Territory on another man's property, leaving her parents to manage with only her. Cate was really proud that she and her mother *had* managed. They still could—but it was her father's choice. This day couldn't get worse.

'That's good, Dad.' The words nearly stuck in her throat. She'd worry about Ben coming home when, and if, he actually did. For the moment there were things to do before the next two days' shifts at the hospital and she was looking forward to some activity for the restlessness that had been eating at her since she'd driven away from the hospital. She left her father watching the rain.

'How were your shifts, darling?' Cate's mother set two coffees on the kitchen table and sat down to listen. Leanore was a tall woman, though not as statuesque as her daughter, and her hair was more silver than blonde.

Cate's thoughts flew to the regional CEO, and strangely she was reluctant to discuss Noah Masters with her mother. She stared down at the cup cradled in her hands. 'Busy.'

Not one to avoid discussing awkward subjects, Leanore went straight to the family issues. 'Your father and I are looking forward to Ben's return. It will be wonderful to see him. Are you upset your father asked him to come home?'

Cate couldn't help the tinge of censure in her voice. 'If he stays long enough.'

'Now, Cate. It's been a hard couple of years but Ben is a man now and he wants to come home. He'll be better for the time away. He was too young to take over the huge job that you've done and too old to take orders from his big sister.'

She patted Cate's hand.

'Your father rose above his disabilities and is still the man of my dreams. We have our life and you have yours. We know you've carried the lion's share of the workload for a long time now. You deserve a break. Sit back and let Ben and your father do the worrying without you. Live a little.'

Leanore pushed a plate of home-made biscuits towards her daughter. 'So tell me some good news from the hospital.'

Cate tried to brighten up. 'My friends Michelle and Leif had a lovely baby boy early this morning. He was nearly a Caesarean but beat the doctor to the theatre.' A soft smile crossed her face. 'He's gorgeous.'

She blinked and refocused on her mother. 'And poor Mr Beamish broke his hip on his cattle-grid and I'm dreading the new regional CEO will step into his job until they get someone else.' She glared at the tablecloth. 'I hope it's soon,' slipped out.

'Poor Mr Beamish. I went to school with his wife.' Leanore tilted her head. 'A new regional CEO? What's he like?'

Cate stirred her coffee vigorously and the coffee spun dangerously around in her cup. 'Taller than Dad, looks like he works out, but he's a human logarithm and very much the city boy.' She glared at her coffee. 'He's domineering and annoyingly sure of himself.'

Cate's mother took the spoon from her daughter and set it in the saucer with a clink. 'Interesting.' She smiled to herself. 'He seems to have made a big impression on you. But the last part is a harsh indictment. I imagine the man would have responsibilities that call for most of those qualities. Does he have a name?'

'Noah Masters.' Cate shrugged and took a few sips of her drink before she set it down. 'I don't want to talk about that man. Thanks for the coffee, Mum. I have to fix the gate in the top paddock and move the cattle.'

'Do you want me to come?' Leanore started to untie her apron, still with a small smile on her face.

'No. Thanks.' Cate thought she may as well do this last job before Ben came home. 'I need to get out and I'll call if I need help.' She slipped the family mobile phone onto her belt. It was her father's decree that anyone in the paddocks carry it in case they needed help. Three years ago he'd lain all day with a broken back when the branch of a tree had fallen and crushed his vertebrae. With the farm work falling to Cate and Leanore now that Ben had gone, he could keep in contact with them from the house. Cate would have carried anything to get out of the house and burn off some energy.

Wednesday 7 March

When Cate arrived at work that afternoon, she'd packed a case with enough clothes for a week. Her father had predicted she wouldn't get home for a while.

'Noah Masters had better watch out!' Cate dropped the report of the regional hospitals' meeting, which she'd taken home to study, down on the desk. It hit with a clap similar to the thunder outside.

She impaled her drover's oilskin on the old-fashioned hatstand as if she were hanging Noah Masters out to dry on it.

'And happy Wednesday to you, too, Cate.' Diminutive Amber Wright stood up to flick the door shut behind her friend for some privacy. The nursing supervisor of the previous shift at Riverbank Hospital shook her head. 'You're like a whirlwind some days, Cate. You make me dizzy.'

Cate dried her hands on the damp scarf she pulled from around her neck and hung that up, too. 'Maybe the weather makes me mad.'

'Yeah, right.' Amber had her head in her hands.

Cate tucked her handbag away. 'That good, is it?' said Cate as Amber lifted her head. Her friend nodded.

'Ten staff called in flood-bound and we're still five down without replacements, but it could have been worse. Most are flooded in while some are banking on staying home so they don't get flooded out of their own homes.' Amber sighed.

'Plus, I have to be at preschool in twenty minutes and barely have time to fill you in on what's happening on the wards.'

Cate looked up quickly. 'That's a bit early. Cindy's not sick or anything, is she?'

'No. I have a meeting with the teacher.' Amber looked at her watch and Cate interpreted her frown. Amber really couldn't afford to upset the teacher at the preschool Cindy attended most days while her single mother worked.

Cate picked up her pen. 'Heaven forbid that you keep the teacher waiting. Come on. Fire away and we'll get you out of here on time.'

Amber shuffled the papers and pushed her glasses back up her nose. 'I've had orders to encourage the doctors to discharge as many as they can to lighten the load, but most of the people who could go don't have the support at home, and home care is a bit iffy should the highway be cut off.'

Cate leaned forward but her voice was soft. 'So whose orders were they?' As if she didn't have an inkling.

'Noah Masters.'

'I'm just about sick of his directives. I found out he's a doctor of medicine, and has only been involved in the corporate side for two years. Apparently he's shooting up the administrative totem pole at a great rate of knots.' She screwed up her nose. 'How could a doctor leave medicine and become a number-cruncher?'

'Excuse me?' Amber pulled a face. 'You only work half your time as a midwife and the other half in administration.'

Cate sniffed. 'Totally different. I need the quick shifts. An afternoon shift followed by a morning shift lets me work on the farm. If there weren't enough midwives I'd go back to full-time midwifery like a shot.'

Cate watched as Amber punched the last of the entries for staff changes into the computer. 'The office part of this job is a pain but as for shift coordination…' Cate shrugged '… I believe I can make a difference if I ensure that everything runs smoothly.'

'It's true. The place runs like a watch when you're on shift.' Amber shot her an urchin grin. 'But you also like being boss. Hell, I was on your tennis team and we had to win or else. One day you're going to meet a man that won't let you boss him around. Maybe it's Noah Masters.'

Cate's laugh sounded more like a snort. 'Somehow I don't see that as prophetic.' She folded her arms and glared at her friend. 'And as for tennis, what's wrong with being champions three years running?'

Amber laughed out loud. 'I rest my case,' she said. Cate acknowledged the hit with a wry smile.

Amber went on. 'Our regional CEO is officially filling in for Mr Beamish.' She looked at Cate. 'He said to call him Noah, which made me laugh a bit as we've probably got a flood on, but he doesn't seem too bad.'

'The man's a walking calculator!' Cate stood up and paced the room.

Amber looked up with interest. 'Then he's a well-packaged calculator.' She shrugged. 'I'd almost welcome his slippers under my bed if I wasn't off men.' She raised a quizzical eyebrow at Cate. 'Struck a few sparks yesterday, did you?'

That was the last thing Cate wanted Amber to think. 'No.' The word came out louder than she'd intended and Cate fought not to blush. 'It's not a matter of liking or disliking. The guy is a threat to Riverbank—and if he had his way our hospital would be downgraded to cottage hospital status.'

Amber blew a raspberry. 'You don't know that.'

Cate didn't meet Amber's eyes. 'Well, I don't want to find out the hard way. Can we leave Noah Masters, please?' Cate sat down. 'What else is happening here today?'

Cate couldn't mind Amber's teasing. She couldn't remember a time when Amber hadn't been in her life. They'd shared rag dolls and horse blankets since kindergarten. Experience told Cate that something else was bothering her friend.

Amber smiled but Cate still felt she was stalling, which wasn't like her. 'Let's get you home. Is something wrong, Amber?'

All amusement left Amber's face and she sighed. 'I'll start with the bad news.' She put her hand out to cover Cate's. 'Iris Dwyer is our critical patient and her friends are with her in the palliative care room, but her son hasn't arrived yet.'

Iris... Cate fought back the sudden dread and managed a professional nod to Amber. But her mind whirled. Iris, not Iris! There was only one reason a patient would be admitted to the hospital's soothing palliative care suite with its very comfortable bed, and Cate didn't want to think about it.

Iris was the sort of woman every girl would have loved having as a mother-in-law. She was certainly everything Cate wanted to be—independent, with a home and farm and a loving son to care for. Mr Dwyer had died some two decades earlier and, far from withering, Iris just seemed even more determined and in control.

And now that would change. Cate acknowledged the sympathetic look from Amber. Iris and Brett had been a big part of her life before the break up of their engagement.

'Brett's mother has terminal cancer?' Cate shook her head in disbelief. 'Why didn't I know she was sick? Why wouldn't she tell me? Maybe I could have done something...'

Amber understood. 'Don't feel bad she didn't tell you. Iris has always been a self-sufficient woman. She must have preferred it that way. I don't think she told anyone before she came in here.' Amber shot a look at Cate to watch for her reaction to the next news. 'Brett will be here soon.'

Cate sniffed. 'Why isn't he here now? He'd better get here in time…' Cate was still reeling from the more devastating news.

Amber sighed. 'You take too much on yourself, Cate. Nobody knew about Iris's illness. She went to Theatre this morning for an abdominal mass and it was an open-and-shut case. Nothing they could do. She's been running the farm up until her admission and it looks like she's organising the way she dies just as efficiently.'

A cold lump settled in Cate's stomach and the back of her throat scratched as she fought to control the surge of emotion that welled. Brett had better make it. While her ex-fiancé was quite capable of behaving less than responsibly, she'd always enjoyed the company of his forthright and capable mother.

Cate sometimes wondered if her fondness for Iris had been half of her attraction when Brett had come back on the scene.

Amber touched her arm. 'How do you feel about seeing Brett again?'

Cate gave a tiny shrug—that was unimportant by comparison. 'Like a fool for ever agreeing to marry him. But apart from that, I feel sorry that he's going to lose his mother.' Cate blinked away the sting in her eyes.

'There's a hard time ahead for him,' Amber said with a catch in her voice, and Cate remembered that her friend had always had a soft spot for Brett. She could have him.

'Poor Iris.' Cate blinked the sting out of her eyes and met Amber's sympathetic gaze. 'You need to pick Cindy up from preschool. I'll find the rest out when I go up and see her later on the ward.'

Amber nodded and glanced at her clipboard. 'Iris is our most critical. The other patients in Medical are slowly improving, which means they're pretty much the same as they were when you went off yesterday. They have two spare beds.

'Theatres are running to time, and Theatre Sister asked, as you were doing a quick shift, if you could take Theatre call tonight as it's her husband's birthday.'

Cate shrugged at the chance of having her eight-hour break between shifts broken by an unexpected theatre case, as it had the last time she'd done the quick shift. 'No problem. Have you marked it down yet?'

'No. But I didn't look for anyone else. Marshmallow centre—that's you—

but at least a lot of people owe you favours!' Amber grinned and wrote down Cate's name for the call.

'Surgical?' Cate took the theatre list Amber handed across and scanned the list of operations that had been that morning.

'No spare beds so any emergency admissions or accidents will cause a reshuffle of beds or early discharge.

'Children's Ward has three in with gastroenteritis so don't play with them if you want to spend time helping in Maternity,' she teased.

'And how is Maternity?' Cate settled in the chair.

Amber flicked her reading glasses back up her nose. 'Just how you like it. They have babies coming out of their ears and two more in early labour.'

Cate nodded. 'I love it when it's like that.'

Amber rolled her eyes. 'Intensive Care has three in, all day-two myocardial infarcts, who are progressing well. And last, but not least, Emergency is surprisingly quiet for the moment, but we all know how that can change in the blink of an eye.' Amber put her reading glasses in her case and handed over the clipboard and the large bunch of keys. 'Have fun with Noah Masters. I'll look forward to the next instalment of Cate versus Goliath.'

Amber stretched up and hugged Cate. 'I'm sorry about Iris.'

Cate returned the pressure. 'She's a wonderful woman and deserves more—but thanks.' She pushed Amber towards the door.

Cate shivered in sympathy as she watched her friend cross the car park from the office window. The rain was pelting down and Amber's umbrella turned inside out from the wind as she struggled to get the keys into her car lock.

Cate envied Amber her beautiful daughter but not Amber's marriage to the domineering man she'd divorced.

Cate dreamed of a home and family more than anything, and she'd thought she'd found the answer with Brett. But her great love affair hadn't worked out either. Cate didn't waste any sympathy on herself—she should have known better. Brett had ruled by emotional blackmail and she'd been lucky they hadn't married. She thought of Brett's mother and sighed. Poor Iris.

She painfully rolled her shoulder. She'd pulled a muscle yesterday trying to straighten the top paddock gate. Served her right for being too stubborn to call her mother for help.

And now it looked like Noah Masters had moved into Mr Beamish's office indefinitely. Life was suddenly too much.

She didn't feel like being cooped up in the office. She needed to be busy and if they were short-staffed, there would be plenty of work to do.

By late afternoon, Cate had secured relief for extra-busy wards from the less frantic ones, helped with the birth of a baby in Maternity, arranged casual staff who lived in town to replace those flooded in for the next shift, and updated the computer with the latest staffing statistics. She'd briefly spoken to every patient and a host of their relatives, and everything was under control. This was what she loved—having her finger on the pulse of the hospital.

By five o'clock she'd made several visits to Mrs Dwyer in her darkened room, and she decided to pop in for a moment before tea. When Cate entered the room the old lady lay so still and quiet that for a moment Cate thought Brett had left it too late. Then she noticed the gentle rise and fall of the sheet covering the frail body and she bit her lip. Iris had only been deeply asleep. The old lady stirred and opened her eyes.

Brett's mother looked frail and it was as if the light had been turned out in her usually sparkling blue eyes. Cate could see that time was short and she felt useless as she stared down at the woman she'd grown to love. 'Can I get you anything, Iris?'

Iris smiled. 'No, darling.' The skin on the older woman's hand was callused from hard work and yellow-tinged with jaundice. But her grip was still strong. 'I'm quite comfortable. Even the dawn chorus of coughing and urinals is different to the birds at home but quite amusing.'

Cate couldn't help smiling, which was what Iris wanted. 'Would you like some music to drown out the ward clatter? I could bring my CD player in.'

Iris shook her head. 'You do too much as it is and I don't need to add to your load. There'll be plenty of time for music in heaven.' Cate winced and Iris frowned. 'Stop it. I've had a good life and at the moment I'm enjoying the sound of humanity. It's like a radio show and guess-the-secret-sound as I try to recognise a noise. Don't worry about me.'

Iris closed her eyes but she was still smiling and Cate wondered if she'd fallen asleep again. Cate could see from whom Brett had inherited his eyebrows and nose. A shame he hadn't inherited his mother's determined chin. Almost as if she'd caught Cate's thoughts, Iris opened her eyes.

'I'm sorry it didn't work out for you and Brett, for his sake.' Her eyes twinkled briefly. 'As much as I love him, I know he probably would have driven you mad. I've come to think he needs someone to lean on him to bring out his best. But I would have known he was OK with you.' The frail hand tightened in Cate's. 'Look after yourself, Cate. You need to find a strong man to depend on. Sharing the load brings its own strength so if the chance comes, don't fight it too much.'

Cate dropped a kiss on the wrinkled cheek. 'How like you to try and tie up my loose ends as well. Think about yourself for a change. I'd better get on with my work. You rest and mind you tell Sister if the pain gets worse.' Iris shut her eyes and she was asleep before Cate turned away.

Cate tried to regain her composure. Sometimes life was very unfair. She couldn't believe Brett hadn't arrived yet. She'd kill him if he didn't get here in time. She pushed herself off the wall she'd leant her head on and hurried out of the room with her emotions a jumble, and pushed her sore shoulder straight into a solid wall of muscle. Two strong hands steadied her until she regained her physical balance and her traitorous body relaxed for a moment against the man. Her emotional equilibrium was harder to recapture.

'Sister Forrest. We meet again.' Noah's hands loosened as she stepped away a pace but he could still feel the aftershock of her surprisingly luscious body against him.

Noah redirected his gaze from the vulnerable line of Cate's neck to her face as she straightened herself to look at him.

'I'm sorry. I wasn't looking.' The slight catch in her voice sounded strange, coming from the tough cookie of yesterday. In fact, she looked like she was in some pain.

'Did I hurt you?' Noah tilted his head and then reached out to touch her shoulder. She winced and his brows drew together.

She brushed his hand away. 'It's an old bruise and I've just given it a reminder. I'm fine. Was there something I can do for you?'

She didn't look as together today, but she certainly wasn't any friendlier. It had been amazing how many little things he'd remembered about her. Like the way her blue eyes narrowed and then seemed to glow like flashing blue sirens when she was annoyed with him. And how the expressions on her face seemed to shift and change like the sea.

Enough. Noah compressed his lips. He'd spent too much time thinking about her last night and he wasn't going to get bogged down today. But she was a challenge. He refocused on her question.

'I've come up to see how the medical resident went with discharging non-critical patients. I assumed there would have been more clients able to go than we've managed to discharge.'

He watched her close her eyes for a minute to marshal her thoughts.

When she opened them he was staring quite openly at her and she glared at him. He'd bet she couldn't help herself. She'd be a dreadful poker player, he thought as he watched more emotions flash across her face when she spoke. 'Those that are still here would be at risk if they were discharged. Until the rain stops we can't guarantee that the community nurses will be able to take them on or that relatives will be able to get to them if they're needed.'

There was that fire and passion for the patients again. He had to harden his heart. 'So what you're saying is that if it wasn't raining you'd be happy to send them home?' She would fight him all the way, but that wasn't a problem. He felt more alive than he had for years—perhaps it was the country air he hadn't looked forward to.

She did look determined, though. 'What I'm saying, Dr Masters, is that an early discharge for these *clients* would most probably result in readmissions—which cost more money by the way—so nothing would be gained by putting them at risk.' She folded her arms across her chest.

'What about the risk here if you have an influx of sick patients and minimum staff to care for everybody? I'll have a list of other possibles anyway, please, Sister Forrest.'

He watched her shrug and realised she probably thought he hadn't heard a word she'd said.

Cate tilted her chin. 'Then it's on your head.'

'That's what my head is here for.' His attempt at humour failed to draw a smile and she stared stonily back at him. He shrugged. He had other things to worry about. 'I assume you're aware that I've taken over from Mr Beamish in the interim as this hospital's CEO?'

'The news had made it to my desk, yes.' She glanced at her watch.

Noah could feel his temper rise. So he was holding her up, was he? 'I hope I can rely on your support during this unsettled time, then.'

'Of course,' she said. So why did he feel that her fingers must be crossed behind her back?

Then she said, 'I always have the hospital's best interests at heart.' This time her voice wasn't so meek. Her pager sounded and she tilted her chin before moving away.

Noah shook his head. Right. He'd have her support as long as she totally agreed with his plans, and he watched her turn the corner towards Intensive Care without looking back. But she didn't know whom she was up against. He narrowed his eyes thoughtfully at the spot where she'd disappeared from view.

Cate couldn't get away fast enough. Bumping into Noah Masters straight after seeing Iris had left her in turmoil. She'd actually felt comforted by his strong grip on her arms and her step back had been a defence against the inexplicable desire to stay and lean on him for a moment.

Of all the people to feel like leaning on! She needed to get a grip on things. Why hadn't Brett come so she could stop worrying about it hanging over her head? She hoped it wasn't going to be awkward to see Brett but it was the first time face to face since they'd broken their engagement.

Luckily she was busy. The rain continued and the calls from marooned staff members also flooded in. Cate glanced out of the corridor window as she made another trip to Maternity and realised that if the rain kept up she'd be one more person blocked by rising waters from going home. Though after her phone call to her parents earlier, she knew her brother was at home now. They said they'd manage fine without her. She wasn't sure how she felt about that.

Cate pulled open the door to Maternity. Michelle and Leif were going home a day early with baby Lachlan and they were waiting to say goodbye. Early on Tuesday morning, Cate's sleep in the nurses' quarters had been interrupted to set up for an emergency Caesarean section when baby Lachlan's descent through his mother's pelvis had apparently stopped.

To everyone's relief, he'd made his precipitous arrival in the normal way in the operating theatres before the surgeon had scrubbed his hands.

'Lachlan looks much better this morning, Michelle. And so do you.' The new parents looked up and smiled, and Cate's day brightened to see the baby feed contentedly at his mother's breast.

Michelle was small-boned and blonde, and she stroked her son's thick crop of black hair. 'Thanks, Cate. It's amazing how much they change in just two days. He was so blue and his head was such a strange shape when he was born.'

Cate grinned as she remembered the marked moulding of Lachlan's head caused by his squeeze through his mother's pelvis. 'I remember. Thank goodness babies' skull bones are designed to do it. If he'd just tucked his chin in he would have made it much easier on both of you.'

Leif laughed. 'And your sleep. He was such a cone head. When I asked if his head would change shape, the doctor said if newborn heads didn't there'd be a lot of funny looking people walking around town. That's when I knew he was going to be all right.' They all laughed at the mental picture of a town full of people with misshapen heads. 'Everyone has taken such good care of us.'

'And so we should.' Cate had gone to school with Michelle's older sister. The beauty of working in a small town hospital was that she knew most of the patients or at least one of their relatives.

The new parents wanted to make sure they could make it home before their road was cut off.

'Now, you're sure you have enough supplies?' Cate stroked Lachlan's tiny hand as he lay in his mother's arms.

Michelle reached up and kissed Cate's cheek. 'Leif's picked up everything on the list this morning and we have enough stuff to last us a couple of weeks. Hopefully the flood won't linger, but luckily our house is on a hill. At worst we'll be on an island, but I want to be home if that happens.'

'Of course you do. Good luck and hopefully the roads won't be shut long. Remember to ring the ward if you're unsure about anything to do with you, breastfeeding or Lachlan.'

Cate left them to pack the car in dashes through the rain, and got on with her own work, but she couldn't help comparing her life to that of Michelle.

Michelle was five years younger than Cate's thirty years. She already had a husband who adored her and a new son and her own tiny farmhouse on the outskirts of town. It sounded idyllic and Cate sighed.

Something was missing in her life and she could almost see herself ending up alone, with nothing but patients and cows to look after, when all she had ever wanted had been a home and family. Even Iris had had a child and Cate was beginning to wonder if she'd ever have a baby of her own.

Perhaps that fear had been a factor in allowing her relationship with Brett to grow. She'd grown up with the local boys as friends. As casual boyfriends they hadn't seemed to mind the fact that she was better at most things than they had been, but Cate had never found any reason to become heavily involved with someone she'd known.

Until Brett had returned from medical school to complete his residency in Emergency at Riverbank. He'd stormed her citadel with flowers and pretty words and hadn't been intimidated by Cate being in charge—quite the opposite. Their pairing had seemed to suit all round.

Early on he hadn't seemed so self-centred and perhaps she'd encouraged him to expect her to look after him. Iris's comment that Brett needed someone to lean on him to bring out his best could be very true. She'd thought that together they could have made a good life, although to be honest she'd seen herself as the stronger of the two. To achieve a love affair like her parents' might have been stretching the fantasy, but her dream of a caring husband and a home and family had seemed within her grasp.

And Cate had always admired Iris. Over the course of her twelve-month engagement with Brett, she'd stifled the doubts that had crept in occasionally because of that. She wasn't proud of almost marrying a man she hadn't loved. She should really thank her brother Ben for making it impossible for her to follow Brett to Sydney like he'd wanted. With the choice between leaving her parents to manage on their own and her loyalties to Brett, who had wanted Cate to himself, Brett had come a poor second.

But now her future alone seemed to stretch ahead of her. It would be better once Brett was here and she could stop worrying that he might expect to take up where he'd left off—or that she might be tempted…

Speaking of temptation, there had been that feeling of Noah Masters's hands not so long ago, resting gentle but strong on her shoulders. Cate shrugged her shoulders and stormed to her office. Of course the phone was ringing and Cate reminded herself that there was no time for temptation when there was work to be done.

She reached across the desk to lift the phone to her ear just as a shadow darkened her doorway. Noah Masters blew into the room like a hail-filled cloud and seemed to shrink her office to half its size.

CHAPTER THREE

THE PERTLY ROUNDED rear and long, long legs of Cate Forrest as she leant across a desk was a sight to gladden any hot-blooded male's day. Noah just wasn't used to it happening to him. He'd barely noticed any woman's femininity for the last two years and here he was stifling a wolf-whistle like some callow youth. He must be going potty with the rain.

He dragged his eyes away and took a turn around the room to divert his libido from more of those fantasies of tall, leggy women he'd resurrected since yesterday. He glared out of the window and stoked up the embers of annoyance that had sent him to search her out. The wretched rain still teemed down and the idea of a flood was becoming more believable every day. A brief scenario entered his head of Cate and himself marooned together on an island for a couple of days with nothing to do…

Cate concentrated on the phone call and tried to pretend her heart rate hadn't accelerated at Noah's presence. She had to admit he had a presence—but it was just the *unexpectedness* of his entrance that had startled her. She spoke into the phone and her voice was even. 'Sister Forrest. Nursing Supervisor.' She straightened to perch on the edge of the desk and the phone cord pulled tight as she turned her body to watch Noah prowl around the office impatiently.

Annoyed with how much he distracted her, she tried not to tense as she ignored him to listen to Stella Moore. The emergency sister had called to warn she might be late for work.

Cate's attention returned to the phone call. 'Take care. We'll manage until you both get here. I think it's a great idea to come in together. But if it looks too dangerous, don't even attempt it, Stella. Let me know as soon as you both arrive. We'll probably have to catch up on some shifts if the casuals have to cover for too long so I appreciate you coming. Thanks for the warning and make sure your husband looks after that new carpet. Bye.'

Well, that saved her having to find another experienced emergency sister to work the night shift. Stella had arranged to share a lift with the night resident doctor in his heavy-duty four-wheel-drive vehicle.

She put the phone down gently and glanced up at Noah, who was glaring out of the window again at the weather. 'Yes, Dr Masters?' Cate searched in her memory for something recent she might have done to annoy him, but couldn't come up with anything.

His eyes were more like frozen chocolate this time and his usually beautiful lips were a straight line. 'Sister Forrest, would it be too much to assume that you could have kept at least one free room in the staff quarters for me to sleep in during this crisis? I've just been to the nurse manager for a key and Miss Glover tells me all rooms are taken.'

Cate's brow wrinkled. 'I'm sorry. I've given them to the nursing staff who live out of town and are willing to stay and be available for at least one shift or more a day.'

He glared down at her. She still wasn't used to looking up at men and he was almost intimidating when he was annoyed. Almost. But she didn't like even a fraction of that feeling. Cate walked around her desk and sat down where she felt more in control. For some reason she liked the desk between them. 'Take a seat.'

He was still glaring at her. 'So I'm to sleep in my office? Is that correct?' He almost growled as he perched on the edge of her desk exactly where she'd been sitting. She wondered if the desk was still warm and the thought caused an uncomfortable tension in her stomach. This was ridiculous. He was here to complain.

Cate tilted her head. 'That's right. As the nurse manager will be in hers. And goodness knows where I'll sleep.' The man was behaving like a spoiled baby, and impatience tinged her voice. 'As someone who, I assume, spent some time as an intern during your medical training, surely you've roughed it before between shifts.'

His expression hardened for a moment then cleared. 'Oh, I've done my time in Emergency and roughed it to get some sleep. But I'm older and wiser now and would have preferred not to have had the choice made for me.' His eyes lightened. She couldn't see what she'd said to restore his good humour but maybe he didn't hold grudges. Good. She hated grudge-holders.

He picked up a pen from her desk and started to doodle on her notepad. Without his jacket, the overhead light gave a sheen to the swell of muscles in his arms. Quite impressive they were, too. Amber had said he was a nicely packaged calculator.

When he spoke she jumped. 'So. You're not going home either?'

She glanced away as she realised she'd been staring and tried to marshal her thoughts. Going home. Right. 'I doubt I'd get through, and if I did I wouldn't get back. Most of the bridges upriver are flooded so some roads downriver will close about twelve hours later. Hopefully the rain up at Point Lookout, that's our main catchment area, will stop and all this will be over in a day or so.' Since when did she babble? Cate snapped her mouth shut.

Noah swung his leg and his thigh muscles bulged and relaxed under the fine material of his trousers. Bulged and relaxed, bulged and relaxed, and hypnotised her. She restrained the urge to shift her chair further back, as if he were invading her space. There was some sort of aversion-attraction thing going on here and it needed to stop right now.

Then, when he smiled at her, she couldn't help but smile back until she realised what she was doing. What was she doing? She was not going to become obsessed with this man.

This was a man who worshipped the dollar more than his Hippocratic oath. He would return to the city after the downgrade of Riverbank Hospital. She needed to remember she had loyal staff like Stella Moore willing to be cut off from her family to ensure the hospital was covered during the crisis. Cate looked away from him.

He looked at her quizzically. 'Now what's made you frown?'

'You don't want to know,' she said, and looked back at him with her lips compressed. 'Is there anything else I can do for you, Dr Masters? I have to get on with my work.'

'Damn. The ice maiden is back.' He dropped the pen on the desk and stood up. 'Let's call a truce, at least until after the rain stops. If you call me Noah, I'll go off and leave you alone quite happily.'

Cate considered the first part of his request and was surprised how much she wanted to stop fighting with him. It looked like this flood drama was going to continue for a few days and it would be more sensible if the two of them worked harmoniously. Or at least tried to keep every discussion away from being based on who was going to win.

She didn't quite meet his eyes. 'As for the truce, I'll give it a go, but if I disagree you'll know about it.'

He laughed. 'I never dreamed of anything less. And calling me Noah?'

She shook her head. 'I'd prefer to keep things professional, if it's all the same to you.' His face became more serious as he stood up, and this time his tone contained no laughter. 'Then I'll settle for Mr Masters. I prefer not to be called "Doctor".'

When he left the office she stared at the empty space where he'd been and considered his parting comment. Why did he dislike being called a doctor? Why had he given up practising medicine? There was a story here. Maybe he had a good reason. Then the phone rang. She glanced at the clock. It was almost teatime. She did have work to do and thinking about Noah Masters wasn't getting it done.

When Stella Moore and the resident failed to turn up for the night shift, Cate chewed her bottom lip. She'd tried the resident's mobile phone but there was no answer. Evening staff had agreed to stay back until further notice but most of them had already been rostered for the next morning and they needed their rest.

An hour after they were due, an ambulance pulled up outside Emergency with the missing pair inside. Stella's cheek was cut and Dr James was scratched, bruised and had suffered minor head injuries. Thankfully, with rest, they'd be fine. But the tree they'd hit had blown Cate's night shift staffing out of the water.

Relieved that neither was hurt badly, Cate left the evening staff to treat their injuries while she assessed her options.

Noah Masters could sort the medical part. Militantly she knocked at his office door but her battle plan hadn't included Noah opening the door half-dressed.

'Yes?' He wore his lack of clothing like a night at the opera. Cate stared and suddenly the oxygen content in the room fell below the usual twenty-one per cent.

Noah's voice was impatient. 'You knocked, Sister Forrest?'

Cate blinked and tried to stay focused on Noah's expression and the warmth of a blush embarrassed her even further. This was ridiculous. She must be more tired than she'd thought. Her eyes travelled down and she wrenched her gaze away from what seemed like acres of firmly muscled chest and a sprinkling of dark springy hair—hair that curled out of sight into his unbuckled trousers—and she bit her lip. Compared to her previews of what she now saw as Brett's pigeon chest, she was impressed.

Just when she thought she had her brain back in gear he confused her again.

'Why aren't you off duty? Don't you know how to delegate?' His voice was clipped and the exasperation in it jolted her out of her sensual haze quicker than anything else could have.

'I don't have the luxury,' she snapped back. 'Delegation is more your angle.'

His eyes narrowed at her response. I've annoyed him now, she thought. Good. The problem needed a fix. She glanced at her watch. The evening staff needed to get to bed.

'Well, come in.' He stood back to allow her past him into the office and the momentum of the moment carried her through the door and dumped her in the middle of the room. His trundle bed was pushed up against the wall and the door shut behind her with a click. Cate turned to face him and realised it was a very crowded room and most of it seemed to be filled with Noah Masters.

Exasperated and half-naked, Noah glowered at her and Cate moistened suddenly dry lips and tried to remember why she was here. Thankfully, her thought processes came sluggishly to life. Staffing.

Cate cleared her throat. 'The night emergency team have been involved in an accident and we need to find replacement staff for this shift…' Noah walked across the room to lift his shirt from the chair back and Cate's voice trailed off.

He looked up and caught and held her gaze. Noah shrugged his way into the sleeves slowly as if staring at her had slowed his fingers. Cate couldn't help but stare back. There was something disturbingly intimate in the way he was so steadily arranging his clothes in front of her. The muscles in his shoulders and chest rippled as he lifted his arm to slide it through the sleeve, and Cate's breath lodged somewhere deep in her chest. This man affected her *way* more than he should, especially when she knew he was in Riverbank for such a short time. She shook her head in denial of the attraction, and tried to concentrate on the problem she'd come with, and not the way his fingers fastened the buttons on his shirt.

She looked away with a jerk. 'I need to replace the evening staff so they can still work the morning shift. I don't have any more emergency sisters to pull from anywhere, at least until daylight, because I'm not putting more people at risk to drive in this weather.' She glanced back just as Noah tucked his shirt in and tightened his belt. Her gaze flicked away again but then his voice drew it back.

'And you want me to do what?' The words were very soft as he leaned his long fingers on the desk and of all the things she wanted, she wished he'd left the door open the most.

Cate shrugged with a forced nonchalance. 'Find me a doctor to work with and I'll do the nursing part of night shift in Emergency.'

Noah scanned the options in his mind. 'We don't have any spare doctors.' He rubbed the back of his head and Cate only just heard the oath he muttered. He looked up. 'It would take too long to drive another resident in from one of the other hospitals. I suppose I could ask the rescue helicopter to fly in a locum.' He shook his head as he finished the thought. 'But you're right about the risk. The rain is still too heavy for safe flying.'

Cate raised her chin and forced herself to meet his eyes. 'There is still one doctor left who could work.' He didn't react to her suggestion and she wondered how he'd take it when he realised what she meant. She shrugged again and hammered the option home. 'You do still have your registration, don't you?'

Any subtle awareness of his attraction to Cate, awareness he'd been trying to ignore in the closeness of the room, evaporated at her words. Rumbling lust was driven clear away by the knee-jerk denial of her suggestion.

Him in Emergency? He'd sworn he'd never go into front-line medicine again after Donna had died. And Cate Forrest had no right to push him towards it!

To be fair to the woman, she had no idea how disturbing the idea was to him, that the chance of someone else dying because he couldn't save them scared the life out of him. He just hoped she couldn't see it.

'No.' His voice was firmer than he'd intended but he couldn't help that. The word hung in the air and there was no room for argument. 'Get the evening resident to stay on and I'll arrange a replacement for him in the morning.'

Cate put her hands on her hips. 'He's already done a sixteen-hour shift.'

'I'm the CEO and it's my call—not yours. Thank you, Sister Forrest.' He crossed the room and opened the door for Cate. She glared as she went past but by the time she was halfway up the corridor she couldn't help trying to figure out why he was so adamant. His harsh denial only confirmed her suspicion that there must be a reason he was so determined not to work as doctor.

Noah watched her stride away. He'd thought he'd been safe in administration. Then this had to happen. Of course he still had his registration.

Noah kicked the door shut behind him as he went back into his office. As an administrator, was he willing to run the risk that the overtired resident would be up to handling the night's emergencies as they came in the door? He swore softly under his breath. If anything happened, he'd be morally to blame anyway. He'd have to do the shift himself. Damn the woman.

Noah strapped on his watch and checked his pocket for a pen. He'd be interested to see just how good Sister Forrest was at the clinical stuff.

An hour later Noah had to admit she was good. Very good.

Emergency wasn't overrun with patients. The rain had kept the usual minor illnesses at home but the range of complaints was challenging.

After her initial pleased surprise at his presence, Cate had all the cubicles prioritised and waiting, so that Noah almost felt like a production line worker as he moved between them. It suited him. Emotional involvement was the last thing he needed when doing something he'd sworn never to do again.

Unfortunately, the man in cubicle five was a challenge to ignore. Mr Ellis had been washed into a tree while herding his cattle across a small creek which had turned into a raging torrent. Noah tried to remain impervious to the friendly man who peered intently around the forceps to see the sutures go into his own leg.

'That's not a bad job, you're doin' there, Doc.'

'I'm glad you think so, Mr Ellis,' Noah said dryly, and continued to pull the edges of the deep ragged wound together. 'What time did you say you did this?'

'After lunch. I taped it together but the bandage kept soaking through and the missus said I better get it fixed 'cause I had a lot of work to do in the next couple of days.'

Noah grunted but the silence stretched. He sighed inwardly as he felt compelled to chat with this nice old bloke in spite of his better judgement. 'Did your wife come with you?'

'Nah. She hates boats and our creek's flooded the road. Lucky I parked the car on the other side yesterday. She's at home, putting most of the stuff from the house up into the roof in case the river comes over the verandah.'

Noah tied off the final suture. 'Don't you think it would be more sensible for you both to stay in town until the rain stops?'

The grin died in the weathered face. 'No. We'll ride it out.' The man looked down at the neat line of stitches running across his calf. 'Thanks for that, Doc. Better get going, then.'

'Sister has to dress that first.' Noah turned just as Cate entered with a roll of bandage and a bottle of friar's balsam. He raised his eyebrows.

'Friar's balsam to help keep it waterproof. Mr Ellis will try to keep it dry, won't you, Mr Ellis?' She smiled at the farmer and he grinned back.

'Now, Cate, you know I gotta move them cattle up on high land.'

'Take the bottle with you and mind you put it on a couple of times a day. It will help keep the germs out. You get that leg infected and June will have to do all the work on her own.'

Noah stood up abruptly. 'Which cubicle next, Sister?'

Cate gave him a questioning look. Her answer was even shorter. 'Four.'

As he stepped out of the cubicle he heard her give instructions on when to return for the removal of sutures. Hell! He should have done that, but he was out of practice. He was whistling down the tunnel of medicine and mayhem again and all the old demons were laughing at him. The lack of staffing was bringing it all back, the disbelief and anguish when he'd found out there hadn't been enough doctors to save his own wife. And the guilt. The only thing he'd been thankful for had been that Donna had never known that her own husband was the doctor who hadn't been able to save her. Would she ever have forgiven him?

Noah shook his head and briefly he resented Cate. How had that woman managed to get him here? If he could just get through this one night, he'd make damn sure that Riverbank had more doctors than they could possibly need. And he'd keep his distance from the patients.

In cubicle four an old lady sat stoically on the chair with her hands in her lap. Her face was the map of an interesting life and, white-haired and tiny, she reminded Noah of his grandmother. He could tell she was in pain but nothing obvious stood out. Until she lifted her hand from her lap. Her thumb was red from the base to the swollen tip that stuck out at a bizarre angle.

'Ouch!' Noah pulled a chair gently up beside hers and cradled her wrist in his hand to see the thumb up close. 'I'm Noah Masters, the doctor, and I can see you've dislocated your thumb. It must be very painful.'

When she didn't reply Noah wondered if she was deaf, but then she looked down at the offending digit and shook her head. 'It bloody well hurts.'

Noah bit back a smile. Maybe not so similar to his grandmother. 'We'll take an X-ray, but I'm fairly sure it's not broken, then I'll have to put some local anaesthetic into the base of your thumb and block the nerves. The good news is that all the pain will go away for a while and when I put it back in alignment, most of the pain will fade even when the anaesthetic wears off.' He heard Cate enter the cubicle and she held an X-ray up for him to see. Mrs Gorse's!

Cate was too efficient and perversely he felt the prickle of his resentment again. 'Don't doctors have to order these before you can get them done?' He knew he was being testy but she was making him feel threatened with her capability.

'Mrs Gorse came in just as the evening staff were leaving. I had the resident sign the X-ray request before he left.' She didn't poke her tongue out but he had the feeling she'd have liked to. Instead, she handed him a silver kidney dish with two strengths of local anaesthetic and a syringe—and left.

The old lady cackled at him and suddenly he smiled.

'That's better,' she said, and her eyes nearly disappeared into the creases in her face. 'Thought you had a poker up your bum. You've met your match in Cate.'

Noah nearly dropped the dish. He looked at her from under his brows and gestured to her thumb. 'How did you do this?'

She snorted in disgust at herself. 'I was moving the bull and caught my thumb in his nose ring.'

'I should have known.' Noah waited for the local anaesthetic to take effect and then manipulated the joint back into place with a soft click. He glanced at his watch. 'You moved the bull in the dark?'

She shrugged her unaffected shoulder. 'The river won't wait for the morning.'

She still looked a little like his grandmother even if she didn't sound like her, and again he felt like chatting. 'So where are you going when we get it fixed for you?'

Mrs Gorse looked at Noah as if he were mad. 'I'm goin' home. There's a flood on, you know.'

Cate breezed in. 'You two seem to be getting on well.' She smiled at Noah and then bandaged the old lady's thumb to give some protection. Noah assumed she realised that Mrs Gorse would be back at work as soon as she got home. He stood up and looked down at the two formidable women before he left the room.

So Mrs Gorse reckoned he'd met his match, did she? Now, that sounded more like his grandmother. He stifled the brief moment of loss he always felt when he acknowledged that the woman who had cared for him most of his childhood was gone. Nina Masters had been a strong woman and hadn't hesitated to tell him he was a fool for marrying Donna. She probably would have appreciated Cate. Most likely because she wouldn't have bored her to death like Donna had. He hadn't thought of Nina for ages and now just wasn't the time. He moved to the next cubicle.

A young girl had just been brought in with a raging chest infection and her hacking cough made Noah wince as he shook hands with her worried parents. Cate appeared beside him and handed over the chart with Sylvia's vital signs. Her temperature was elevated and her oxygen saturation was way down from what it should be.

Cate smiled reassuringly at the mother. 'This is Dr Masters, Gladys. Tell him what you told me.'

Gladys squeezed her daughter's hand and looked up with tired eyes. 'She's just not getting better, Doctor. Sylvia's been sick since she had the flu a week ago and tonight I noticed her fingernails were blue. Now she's got pains in her chest when she breathes.'

Noah nodded. 'She's certainly not well. I'd like to listen to your chest, Sylvia.' He looked at Cate who lifted the little girl's jumper up so he could place the stethoscope against her chest. 'How old are you, Sylvia?' Noah asked, and his voice seemed to soothe the frightened child. Cate was glad to see he wasn't trying to freeze the child out, as she'd noticed he'd tried to with the adults.

'I'm six.' The little girl looked at her mother as if to check she was right, and then sat quietly as Noah tapped with his fingers on her chest wall and listened.

'Can you make big breaths in and out? Big as you can, without hurting yourself, please, Sylvia.' Noah leaned forward with his stethoscope and listened to the child's air entry at the front and back of her chest, before standing back.

He spoke to her mother. 'We need to take an X-ray in the morning, but I think Sylvia has developed early pneumonia on both sides of her lungs. She'll need to stay in hospital for a couple of days, maybe more. Are you able to stay with her?'

Gladys turned to her husband and when he nodded she looked relieved. 'Yes. I can stay tonight at least and then we'll see how the flood goes. Normally it wouldn't be a problem but if the river comes up too far I'll have to help out with the cattle.' She looked pleadingly at Cate. 'But Sylvia has Cate and if I have to leave she'll make sure she's right, won't you, Cate?'

'You know I will, Gladys.' Cate nodded, and ruffled Sylvia's hair. 'Let's hope the rain stops, though.'

Noah frowned but he didn't say anything against more work for Cate. Instead, he spoke to Gladys and her husband. 'Sylvia is a sick little girl. It was a good choice not to leave her any longer. She'll be right in a few days.'

And so the night wore on. He heard tales of past floods from the older people, most of whom seemed to have had a relative almost washed away in the 1949 flood. Apparently the hospital had saved many lives. From the younger folk he heard of the sandbagging operations that were going on through the night. Never having been involved in this sort of crisis before, Noah couldn't help being caught up a little in the air of urgency. The one thing he didn't hear were complaints.

At five a.m., Cate came in with two mugs of coffee and sighed as she sat down beside him at the nurses' station. She looked more tired than he felt and Noah stifled the wave of tenderness she stirred in him. Suddenly, care was needed, or she could easily slip under his guard. He had been through enough with Donna, and the tragic consequences of their marriage, and he just wasn't ready to get involved with another woman. He was beginning to wonder whether the only way to avoid that was to leave town as soon as possible.

Cate sipped her coffee and stifled a yawn. 'Well, that was the last from the backlog. If you want to put your head down, I'll phone your room if anyone comes in who can't wait for the morning staff.'

Typical of her, he thought. She needed the sleep more than he did but already he knew better than to mention it. Noah shook his head and stirred his coffee thoughtfully as he settled back in the chair. What did make this woman tick? 'You seemed to know most of the people that came through. I gather your family have lived here a long time?'

Cate smiled and there was contentment in her voice. 'My great-grandfather settled at Riverbank just after the turn of the last century and we have a lot of relations in the valley. My parents and I work the original farm.'

Her eyes crinkled as she thought of her home, and Noah wondered what it would feel like to have such a network of family and friends surrounding you. He realised he envied her. 'So you're a real country girl.'

She met his eyes. 'You could say that—yes. Though most of us have it easier here on the coast than those further inland. I really admire the women out west who teach the kids and run the house and the shearing sheds, plus the admin side of farming as a business.'

He realised he was doing what he'd just told himself not to do. He shouldn't be so interested. His voice became more flippant. 'Well, I'm a city boy and mean to stay that way. It would feel strange to know the people you treat all the time. I'm afraid I like a bit of distance from the patients.'

Cate gave him a level look. 'I noticed.' Her voice was dry. 'Is that why you chose to go into administration? Because you don't want to get involved with patients? I heard you used to be a surgeon. You have special skills, Noah, and what you do now seems to me a waste of your training.'

His face closed. 'I've chosen not to work as a practising doctor any more. I can do more good where I am at the present and I believe that. And there are other reasons.'

'Which you're not going to share?' Cate didn't have high hopes but wasn't afraid of asking.

His eyes hardened. 'That's correct. So don't expect me to work in Emergency again.' He smiled but she could tell he meant it as he stood up. 'I think I will go to my office. You can ring me there.'

'Certainly, Doctor.' Cate nodded and watched him leave. Whatever his reasons, they seemed to be very heavy baggage—and she had a strange urge to try and comfort him.

CHAPTER FOUR

Thursday 8 March

THE NIGHT FINALLY ENDED. Cate headed for bed after handing over to the morning casualty staff. She could sleep at least until after lunch, but there was still her afternoon shift as supervisor to cover, which she'd swapped with Amber.

The supervisor's office was in full use through the day but Cate had been offered an empty patient room in Maternity until they needed it. She didn't stir until lunchtime and when she woke to the sound of a baby crying, she turned on the patient's radio beside her bed. The river and bridge level updates were on and her eyes snapped open. All but the last of the upriver bridges were closed. A minor flood on the Macleay, at least, was a reality.

She tossed and punched her pillow but couldn't recapture the dream she'd been enjoying. She was too wide awake. Cate climbed out of bed. If she hurried, she could make sure those who wanted to go home before the last bridge closed made it out in time.

Cate showered the mist from her brain in the private bathroom and smiled to herself as she wondered where Noah was showering. Then she frowned with unease as she remembered her reaction to a half-dressed Noah. And tried not to imagine how devastating he'd be entirely naked…

An hour later, she ran into a bleary-eyed but immaculate Noah in the cafeteria as he made himself a coffee. She couldn't help the small smile about her private thoughts and suddenly all her senses felt amazingly alert.

Cate bounced over to him. 'I've sent the rest of the upriver staff home that wanted to go. The last bridge to cross upriver will be closed in an hour. If it keeps raining they mightn't get home for a week.'

'You should have kept them in case you needed them.' He was obviously not happy about his lack of sleep. He glared at her. 'What are you doing? You don't start until three.'

She grinned. 'I've had five hours. It's enough.'

He grunted but didn't disagree. 'So the flood is closer?'

Cate nodded. 'We've had two hundred and sixty-six millimetres of rainfall up at Point Lookout today. It looks that way.'

He gestured with his hand to ask if she wanted a cup of coffee, but she shook her head. 'No, thanks. By the way, we've had a few calls from women at the outlying villages who are due to have their babies. They're worried they'll be unable to get in when they go into labour. How do you feel about the really overdue women coming in?'

Noah shook his head. 'Don't weaken. We don't have the staff for extra patients but if they want to come into town they can stay with friends or relatives.'

Cate didn't like the coldness of the answer and she frowned. 'What about the ones that don't have either of those in town?' Cate thought of Michelle and Leif and how their timing had worked for them. Others wouldn't be so fortunate and some could panic. 'I don't want people taking risks either if they feel they have to stay home until the last moment.'

His face hardened. 'Not our problem.' Cate frowned harder but he ignored her. 'If they're that worried they could stay at a motel.' He headed for the table. 'If the worst comes to the worst, I'm sure the state emergency services will get them in here.'

Cate could feel her temper rise as she followed him. Didn't he know these were real people he was talking about? 'That's a big ask for the state emergency services. What about women with fast labours or first babies who don't know how long they have in labour?'

He waited for her to sit down and then did so himself. He shook his head. 'It's not your job to take the worries of the world on your shoulders. If a labouring woman needs to come in and can't, that's when *I'll* worry about her. We are not having pregnant women taking up beds "in case" they go into labour. We might need the beds. Do you understand?'

Cate couldn't believe this guy. How dared he speak to her like that? She stood up again, aware that she'd better leave before she got herself into real trouble. 'Right' was all she allowed herself and marched away. All the things she should have said ran through her brain as she stomped up the corridor but it had still been a good idea to leave then. She liked her job.

Cate screwed up her nose. Amber would probably wax lyrical about Noah at shift handover. Lately, she seemed to bring Noah Masters into every conversation she could, dwelling on his good points, as if he had any, and today Cate wasn't in the mood. Maybe she could divert Amber with Brett, the only other person Amber seemed to want to talk about.

Noah watched her stomp away and ran his hand through his hair. The first thing he had to do was get a few more doctors to help with staffing. He'd have to check supplies were adequate in the kitchen if the highway shut, and he had an appointment with the SES controller in half an hour. Now, there was another strong woman, he thought with a grin.

He just didn't have time to think about the look of contempt Cate had flung at him before she'd left or why it bothered him. But it did.

Much later in the evening when he caught up with her, he wondered if she'd cooled down. It might be politic to mend fences. It might even be fun. Fun was something he hadn't had much of the last two years, and for some reason Cate seemed to amuse him.

'So how many disasters have you dealt with so far, Sister Forrest?' She was at her desk when he dropped in, ostensibly to look for the nurse manager who hadn't been in her own office.

She looked up but she didn't smile. 'We don't have disasters here, *Mr* Masters. We have moments of unusual interest.'

'Ah.' Noah nodded sagely. He saw that she was alone and decided to put off his search for the nurse manager for a few minutes. He rested his hip on the corner of her desk and looked down on the top of her head. All he could see was blonde-to-the-roots thick hair that sprouted up at him and made him want to brush it to see if it was as silky as it looked. She continued to be absorbed in her paperwork. Or pretended to, he'd wager. He cleared his throat. 'Cate, truce.'

The pen in her hand was thrown down on the desk and she tipped her head back to look at him. It was a nice angle.

'How can I help you, Mr Masters?' Her blue eyes were doing their police siren thing again. At least he didn't bore her.

How could he explain what he was trying to say when he really didn't know himself? 'Cate, I know we can both do our jobs while running a cold war between nursing and administration, but it's much more pleasant to be in sync. As far as our discussion from this afternoon goes, I don't believe we've reached the stage where we need to encourage people to be admitted before they are genuinely required to be here. I need your support on this. We can't let the public abuse our resources at this early stage.'

She pushed her chair back. 'What you don't seem to realise is that the *public* around here don't abuse resources like you seem to expect them to.'

Noah smiled—at least she was talking to him. 'I admit you have more experience with these people but, believe me, if someone needs to come in urgently, we'll get them here.' He put out his hand. 'Truce?'

At least he was listening to her. Cate looked at his hand and thought of the last time she'd touched him. She rolled her fingers in hesitation but then forced herself to shake. His hand was warm and firm and there it was again, a frisson of awareness zapping from his fingers to hers, and Cate pulled her hand away. She glanced at her watch and stood up. 'I'm going for tea.'

'Then I'll come with you.' He was laughing at her. She could either get angry or laugh back. She chose the latter.

The tension eased in the room and they were still smiling when Janet Glover, the nurse manager, came in.

She gave each of them a knowing look. 'Hello, Cate, Mr Masters.' Looking at Noah, she said, 'I want to speak to you.' She glanced around Cate's office. 'Here will do.'

'And, believe it or not, I've been looking for you, Janet.' Noah turned to Cate. 'Sorry. Rain check.'

Cate nodded. 'I'll leave you to it, then.' She was glad he hadn't been able to come, she told herself as she walked towards the cafeteria.

So how did she feel, knowing that Noah had sought her out to pacify her after their words this morning? And, more importantly, why should it matter to him what she thought? She had to admit she was coming to enjoy his company and it certainly couldn't hurt her cause if she could influence him to see the needs of a rural community. Not just in crisis either. With her help, maybe he could grasp the importance of a well-funded and well-staffed community hospital. She could be pipe-dreaming but she'd give it a shot. Of course, that would be the only reason to get to know the man.

Strangely, after a lonely tea, the rest of the shift started to drag and Cate went over to see Sylvia before the little girl went to sleep for the night. The child's mother had had to go home and Cate had promised to come over and say goodnight to Sylvia.

'Hello, darling.' Cate sat on the edge of the bed and Sylvia's little hand crept into hers. 'So poor old Mummy had to leave you to help with the farm?' Cate stroked Sylvia's hair with her other hand as Sylvia nodded.

'Well, the secret is you have to push the buzzer on this cord if you need one of the other nurses to come and sit with you. OK?' The little girl nodded again. 'If you get really sad you can get them to wake me up. I'm sleeping over with the babies at the moment because I can't get home to my mummy either.'

Sylvia's eyes widened. 'Are you going to have a baby, Auntie Cate?'

Ouch. Cate blinked and squeezed Sylvia's hand. 'I hope so. One day. Not for a while, but when I do, I hope I get a lovely little girl like you. Now, I'll tuck you in and we'll both have a good sleep. I'll come and see you when I get up in the morning. OK?'

She dropped a kiss on Sylvia's cheek and the little girl kissed her back. 'Goodnight, Auntie Cate.'

'Goodnight, darling.' Cate hugged her close and felt the warmth of her tiny body snuggled against her. Cate swallowed the lump in her throat as she disentangled Sylvia and tucked her in.

The rest of the shift passed slowly and Cate didn't see Noah again that evening. Odd that she felt like she missed him. She shook herself. Last night's extra shift must be catching up with her! Cate was glad to see the night supervisor come in to relieve her of the keys so she could head to bed. At least she didn't have to get up for the early shift…

Friday 9 March

Cate woke early with nine hours to go until she started work. She lay on her back and stared at the ceiling as she listened to the local FM station give out the flood warnings.

Despite the easing of local rainfall, the minor flood warning was official. Even the garbage men couldn't do their jobs and residents were requested to bag and keep refuse out of any sunshine until collection could be resumed.

It was the little things you didn't think about when a town became floodbound, Cate thought. The next item grabbed her attention when it was announced that the lower Riverbank floodgates were to be opened at eleven a.m.

That news gave her a jolt. She'd have to ring her parents if the phones were still working. As downriver farmers, the land in Cate's family was mostly river flat and alluvial soil. It would nearly all go under when the open floodgates took some pressure off the minor streams. She chewed her lip as she thought of her frustrated father in his wheelchair and her mother and Ben having to cope. Maybe she should have stayed home to help? But it was too late now.

Any chance of a sleep-in was lost. Even though she had another quick shift tomorrow, it just wasn't going to happen.

Before she went over to see Sylvia, she dialled her parents' number and the phone seemed to ring for a long time. Finally her brother answered and Cate heaved a sigh of relief. She would have spent the whole day worrying if there had been no answer. 'It's me, Cate. How's it going?'

'Cate! Good to hear your voice!' Ben's voice was deeper than she remembered.

A lump lodged in her throat as she realised how much she'd missed him. But she never would understand how he could have left the farm with just Mum and her to run it. What was it with men? Brett had taken a hike when she'd said she wouldn't move to Sydney with him and leave her family in crisis, and Ben had left when they'd most needed him.

Her brother was talking and Cate brought herself back to the present to concentrate on the news.

'The bottom flat's gone and they haven't even opened the floodgates yet. But the cattle are safe. You should see them all around the house! Mum's put a rope up to keep them off the verandah.' Ben's voice was quietly confident that he had it all under control. Her little brother? Ten years younger didn't count once he got to twenty, she supposed. It seemed like she'd always been there to tell him what to do.

She tried to picture him two years older than when she'd last seen him. 'So all the supplies are fine and Dad's OK?'

'Everyone is fine. The house has never been touched in previous floods, so we're hoping we're safe. The water line is still a fair way away at the moment. How's the hospital?'

A picture of Noah filled Cate's mind. 'We'll manage.'

'If they have you in charge they won't have any choice.' They both laughed but Cate was uncomfortably reminded of Amber saying something similar about her need to run things. Was she that bossy? She'd always been a leader but maybe people got sick of being led. She sent her love to her parents and hung up.

After showering, Cate's feeling of disquiet lingered. She visited Sylvia but the little girl had a new admission to talk to now, another girl her own age, also with pneumonia. Cate left them to it and headed for breakfast. Maybe she was hungry. When she entered the cafeteria, Noah was already there. It would be churlish to sit at another table, she told herself, and took her cereal over to stand beside his chair.

'Feel like company?' Her voice was more forlorn than she'd intended.

He glanced up, saw who it was and smiled. 'Feel free.'

He stood up until she'd sat down and this time it gave her a warm feeling in the pit of her stomach that he'd do that for her. Cate couldn't help but smile at him and her uneasiness lifted a little.

'That's better,' he said. 'You looked worried a minute ago. And you shouldn't be worrying until your shift starts at three. Tell Uncle Noah.'

She stirred her muesli and looked across at him, amused. 'You're no relative of mine.'

He shook his head and laughter lines she'd never noticed before creased his eyes. It made him even more attractive, if that were possible. 'I thought you were related to everyone in the valley?'

'Only locals.' She pointed her spoon at him. 'And you're not a local.'

His nod was judicious. 'How do you get to be a local, then?'

She laughed. It was a joke for all newcomers. 'At least twenty years and a few kids born here would help. But even then it usually takes a couple of generations before you're *really* a local.'

'Well, I'm only on the coast for a couple of months. I'll have to live without local status.' He shrugged and Cate felt a little pang of emotion at his words. This was getting ridiculous, she thought. Did she *want* him to stay or something?

'So, tell me what's upset you.' Noah's voice made her turn back.

'How do you know I'm upset?' She stared at him.

He shrugged again. 'I've had more practice with that emotion than seeing you euphoric.'

Cate sniffed. 'So I'm not only bossy, I'm cranky as well.'

It was his turn to frown. 'Someone said you're bossy? You sound tired.' His voice gentled. 'Go back to bed, Cate. I've watched you the last couple of days. You do a great job, you give everything, but you're going to wear yourself out.' He laid his hand over hers for a moment. 'Sure, you're bossy.' He smiled to take the sting out of it. 'But you have to be. That's what bosses do.'

She must be getting soft in the head because she felt like crying when he'd praised her. Which was ridiculous. She spooned a mouthful of muesli in to distract herself and help push the lump away from her throat. But she could feel his gaze on her and when she looked up he was smiling at her.

His voice was deep and lazy and something inside her responded to it. 'You need to get out and away from here. Want to come for a ride with me down to SES before you start work? I've another appointment with the controller to check out the sandbagging site this morning.'

He was only being kind, but Cate had to admit she liked the fact that he'd asked her. A tad too much, if she was honest. Then there was the thought of getting away for a couple of hours before another tense nine-hour shift. The idea had merit. To hell with it. 'Sounds good. I'd like to.'

'I'll see you in half an hour out the front, then.' He stood up and they both glanced at the time. Noah laughed. 'Do you want to synchronise our watches, Agent 99?' His impersonation was dreadful, but she laughed anyway.

When she met Noah at his car, his eyebrows nearly disappeared into his hair. Cate was dressed in gumboots, cut-off jeans, an oilskin rain jacket and black Akubra hat. The clothes were different but her long brown legs were gorgeous and he tore his eyes away with reluctance. A pair of gardening gloves poked out of her pocket.

'I don't think I've ever seen you look so relaxed,' he said as he opened the door of his car for her.

Cate hesitated before she slid into the plush seat. 'Is that a polite way to say I look like a hobo?' She didn't wait for an answer. 'Nice car. Should I take my gumboots off? Or I could even walk down.' She frowned and gestured to the SES centre, which was plainly visible from the hospital. 'I don't know why you're taking the car anyway.'

'In case it rains and I'm needed back here urgently.' Noah caught her look. 'I'm not lazy—just sensible. Cate Forrest, you are the most forceful woman I have ever met.'

He looked her over and she wasn't sure if it was her imagination that his gaze seemed to linger on her bare legs. 'Why are you dressed like that?'

She threw up her hands in a pose. 'This is what all the best-dressed sand-bag-fillers wear!'

He chuckled before turning the key to start the car. 'I suggested an outing—not a second job! Are you really going to fill bags?'

She grinned at his expression. 'The bags need filling and I need the exercise. I've been inside for three shifts, and a couple of hours of physical labour will be good for me.'

Noah could think of a more pleasant way to burn off energy. He shook his head and stamped down his baser instincts. 'You're mad! But I had an idea of that anyway.' He pulled out into River Street. 'So, what do you do on this farm of your parents?'

'Fencing, manage the cattle and horses, maintain the vehicles. All the usual farm stuff.' She shrugged it off.

Noah was intrigued. He'd bet she was good at all that physical labour, too. 'My impression has always been that farming was done by the farmer, not the farmer's daughter.'

Cate shot him a look. 'Don't be sexist. My mum helps as well. Dad manages the business side of the farm now. He was an Australian horseman of the year before his accident landed him in a wheelchair.'

Noah winced in sympathy. 'A horse-riding accident?"

Cate's eyes clouded briefly. 'No. A branch fell on him.' She didn't say any more and Noah didn't want to push it.

The silence stretched and then Noah spoke up. 'Do you have any brothers or sisters or farm helpers?'

Cate stared straight ahead so that he couldn't see her expression. 'One younger brother, who left home a couple of years ago. But he's home for the flood and seems to be doing everything I did. They're managing well.'

He shot a look at her profile. 'You sound surprised. Shouldn't you be happy about that?' He was pulling up at the SES centre and suddenly Cate wanted to get out without answering. She *should* be happy that Ben was coping perfectly without her. She just had to get used to it.

Noah seemed to be able to read her too well for the short time they'd known each other. It might be wise to maintain some distance from him. And remind herself he was here to downgrade her hospital, before leaving again for Sydney.

But she'd decided to worry about that part of his portfolio after the flood. She had to admit the minor crises she'd laid at his door had been sorted quickly and efficiently. He was very good at his job, even if it wasn't the one she thought he should be doing. She lifted the doorhandle and slid out of the car—to safety.

CHAPTER FIVE

THE SES CONTROL centre was manned by a dedicated band of volunteers who didn't complain when they were pulled from their beds to attend to some emergency. The sandbaggers were even more eclectic. Each mound of sand had its own work party of bag-fillers and another group retrieved and loaded the bags onto a truck to transport to one of the levee banks.

Cate pulled on her gloves and joined one of the smaller gangs, eager for something to divert her mind from Noah. The others in the gang, most of whom she knew, looked up with tired smiles but didn't pause in their shovelling.

An hour later, Noah walked over to where Cate toiled happily. She didn't see him approach and he stood for a moment and watched her easily shovel the sand into the bag held by one of the other women. To Noah, there was something carelessly sensual in the way she dug and lifted and emptied the sand in a rhythmic sequence. A sheen of perspiration on her well-shaped arms testified to her efforts. The stacks of filled bags proved the collection of people were a team.

He couldn't think of any of the women he knew in Sydney who would consider doing this to help out. But the controller had told him that between the different sandbag operations there were nearly a hundred women and two hundred men, not usual volunteers to the SES but all helping during the flood for the common good.

It was becoming a worry that he admired Cate more every time he saw another facet of her personality. She looked up and saw him and her smile drew him to her side.

He cleared his throat. 'I have to go back. Janet Glover has an emergency.'

Cate leaned on her shovel for a moment and wiped her forehead. Tiny grains of sand trailed across her face. 'I'll walk up later.'

'Close your eyes.' Noah leaned forward and brushed the streak of sand off her face and immediately regretted it as he felt the smooth softness of her skin. Now he would feel her under his fingers for the rest of the day. What was it about this woman that penetrated the shell he'd thought impervious?

He looked hard into her face as he said, 'I'll see you this afternoon, then.'

Cate watched Noah stride back to his car. What had he been looking at? She really hoped he hadn't heard her small gasp as his fingers had brushed her face. She flushed as she imagined those fingers sending electricity through her whole body… What was wrong with her?

Cate glanced around at the other volunteers in her gang, hoping they hadn't noticed her distraction. Luckily, the two grandmothers, four teenage boys and half-dozen men were too absorbed in their work. Soon they'd need another mound of sand. Apparently there were bagging gangs on both sides of the traffic bridge and along the levees as well.

By lunchtime, Cate was feeling much better and, having helped a bit, was ready to go back to the hospital. Out of the corner of her eye, she noticed that one of the grandmothers, Ida Matthews, had paused in her shovelling to rub her foot. 'Mongrel thing,' Ida muttered, and shifted her body weight to get comfortable.

Cate handed her shovel to another young lad who had just arrived. 'Have mine. I have to go.' She moved across to the elderly woman. 'Sore foot, Ida?'

Ida put her foot down gingerly. 'I stood on a nail in the garden a couple of days ago and it's giving me trouble today.'

'How are you for tetanus coverage?' Cate bent down and slid the gumboot off Ida's foot. The sole where the nail had gone in was hot and red. 'I'll hitch us a ride back to the hospital and you'd better see a doctor in Emergency about that foot. I don't like the look of it.' She smiled at Ida, who was a known chatterbox. 'It would be terrible if your jaw locked up from tetanus.'

Ida smiled back tiredly and shrugged. 'If you think I should. I didn't like to take their time if they're busy.'

Noah should hear this, Cate thought wryly. 'That's what they're there for. Let's go.'

Cate left Ida with the emergency staff and took herself off for a much-needed shower and some lunch. There was still an hour before work—time to phone her parents to see how they were faring as the water rose.

Her father answered the phone. 'Hi, Dad. It's me. How are you going down there?'

'Hello, Cate, love. We're fine but I'm glad we got out of dairy cattle and into beef. At least we don't have to milk cows in a dairy a foot under water. The road is cut off and the milk trucks can't get in next door. Poor devil will have to throw his milk out until they can pick it up. But it could be worse.'

Cate smiled at the expression. Even in hospital when her parents had found out about his paraplegia, they'd both said, 'It could be worse.' 'How's Mum?'

'Your mother is wonderful, as always. She's enjoying having Ben home and she's taking photos to show you. She's not happy about the influx of snakes, though. They're heading for high ground and I guess the house paddock is it. Ben had a black snake try to climb into the saddle with him yesterday. It was the funniest thing.'

Cate joined her father's laughter as she imagined it. 'Rather him than me.'

William Forrest's voice became more serious. 'How are they going in town? What have you been doing?'

'I'm fine. I went to SES this morning to help fill sandbags before work. The town is gearing up for the water to top the levees.'

'Well, let's hope it doesn't. That will be hardship for a lot of people.' His voice held the memories of previous floods.

She could hear the sound of a calf lowing in the background and tried to imagine the cattle all around the house. Cate wished she could transport herself home just to see that they were all OK. To use her parents' expression, it could be worse. At least she had the phone. She glanced at her watch. 'I'd better go. Love to all. Bye, Dad.'

'One thing before you go, love. I've forgotten his name. The CEO at the hospital. How're things going with him?'

Cate felt the heat flood up her cheeks. What had her mother said? Her brain froze and she said the first thing that came into her head. 'His name's Noah Masters and he's a bit infuriating at times. But we're getting on fine, Dad.'

'That's not the name. Fellow by the name of Beamish. That's who I meant. How's his leg?'

Cate cringed and felt like an idiot. 'Oh. He's comfortable, Dad. Mr Beamish will be in for a few more weeks yet but he's on the mend.'

'Right. That's good. Bye, love,' he said, and hung up.

Cate put the receiver down slowly. She was fixated on Noah Masters and it had to stop. Cate stared out of the window and wished she were home. Surrounded by water, it would be even safer. She tried to picture how the farm must look to drive the image of Noah out of her brain. The sun was shining outside the hospital today, maybe that was what was making it all the harder to imagine her home.

When Cate entered the supervisor's office, Amber and Noah were standing beside the radio for the two o'clock news. For some weird reason, she didn't like seeing the two of them so close together. She closed her eyes for a moment and promised to beat herself up about that later. She moved over to stand beside them to listen.

A moderate flood warning had now been issued for Riverbank township with a peak at four p.m. Schools and preschools were being evacuated and the water would soon creep over the highway between Seven Oaks and Frederickton.

After switching the radio off, Cate and Noah listened as Amber gave an abbreviated report of the status of the hospital.

'I won't be able to come into work on Monday if the schools are still closed,' Amber said.

Cate shrugged. She couldn't get home anyway, she thought and handed Amber her umbrella. 'Try for childcare on Tuesday, maybe.' Unconsciously she copied Noah's dictum. 'We'll worry about it if it happens.'

Amber turned for the door. 'By the way, Brett arrived to be with his mother. I had lunch with him and he's very upset.'

Cate looked up with a questioning look but Amber was halfway out of the door to pick up her daughter.

Noah allowed himself to enjoy just seeing Cate again. The frown that she'd worn earlier had gone and she seemed renewed by the exercise of the morning. Most people would be still in their beds—but not Cate. 'You look better' was all he said.

'Clothes maketh the woman,' she quipped as she moved around the desk to answer the phone.

'I didn't mean the clothes.' He waved and left the room. Cate stared after him. So what had he meant? She picked up the receiver—the call was from Emergency. It was Stella Moore.

'What are you doing back at work already, Stella?'

'Well, I can't get home so I may as well do what I came to do.'

Cate could hear a baby crying in the background. 'How's the head?'

'Fine. You brought in Ida this morning, is that right?'

'Yes. I was wondering what happened with her. How is she?'

'Starting to show signs of tetanus poisoning,' she answered bluntly. 'She's on antibiotics but we need to send her to Sydney for possible hyperbariac oxygen treatment at North Shore. We're up to our eyes with patients out here. Could you do me a favour and arrange it all and let Ida's family know? She'll have to go by helicopter.'

'No problem. Look after yourself and ring me if you need a break.' Cate finished writing down the information and pulled out the phone book.

'Thanks,' Stella said, and hung up.

It took Cate an hour to sort out the transfer of Ida Matthews, photocopy her admission notes and get her family in with some belongings for Ida to take with her.

A further hour later, Cate hugged the woman as she was transferred to the helicopter that waited at the hospital helipad.

'We'll be thinking of you, Ida. See you when you get back.' Cate helped the wardsman pull the stretcher away from the helicopter door.

Ida nodded forlornly, too sick to speak, and then the door was shut.

Cate and the wardsman stood for a moment with their hands over their ears as they watched the rotors start. At least the rain had stayed away but the cloud cover was thick and seemingly impenetrable. Cate was glad she wasn't the one flying. After her father's accident her mother had gone with him in the helicopter and Cate had spent the next few hours positive the helicopter would crash. She hated flying.

Back inside the hospital, Cate made her way to Iris Dwyer's room. A once-familiar figure stood beside her bed and Cate hesitated in the doorway. But it was too late—he'd seen her.

Brett came swiftly towards her and enveloped her in a smothering hug. 'Hello, Catie-pie.' For a moment it was hauntingly familiar but then it irked her.

How had she ever thought that pet name was sweet? 'Hello, Brett.' Cate untangled his arms from around her neck and, as he leaned forward to kiss her, she turned her cheek in the nick of time. Cate studied his angular features and couldn't help but compare him to Noah. It was no contest. Poor Brett.

She stepped to the side and around him into the room. Thank goodness she wasn't as flustered as she'd thought she'd be. Time eased a lot of awkwardness.

'When did you get here, Brett? How's your mother?' Cate's voice was almost a whisper as she moved to stroke Iris's hand.

Brett frowned at Cate's avoidance of him and followed her to the bed. Iris appeared to be sleeping. 'I had a rough trip up in the car. The highway's almost covered in water, and I just managed to get through.' He looked at his mother and sadness welled in his eyes as he answered the second half of Cate's question. 'How do you think she is? She's dying!'

Cate winced at his lack of tact at his mother's bedside. She didn't say that hearing was the last sense to go because they both knew it. She sighed. 'Have you been to the farm yet?'

He looked aghast. 'Why would I go to the farm?'

Cate shook her head. 'The animals? To see how it's faring with the rain? To reassure your mother that everything is all right maybe?'

He shrugged. 'Mum will have arranged for people to do that. I want to stay with her.'

Cate did believe that. He loved his mother and was a kind man at heart. He didn't see that he could be incredibly selfish because his mother had always arranged everything for him. 'So how have you been? I know they've had a problem trying to contact you about your mother's illness.'

'That wasn't my fault.' He sounded petulant and Cate sighed again. How had she ever considered marrying this man?

But he'd been different when he'd first come back from Sydney. Perhaps being several years older than her had helped. She'd never had time for men before Brett and it had been head-turning stuff to be treated like a precious woman for once. She'd never actually figured out what it had been he'd wanted from her, unless it had been to have something that no one else in town had had—herself. But he hadn't even got that.

She'd had this vision of herself and Iris on the farm, caring for Brett and hopefully their children. For a while there it had looked like working. Brett had been loving and had seemed happy for Cate to organise their wedding. Then, out of the blue, he'd mentioned he'd applied for a position at a Sydney practice and what a good doctor's wife Cate would make. What he'd really wanted had been Cate's undivided attention in a role she hadn't been interested in. Cate's world had come crashing down and she'd realised that she'd fallen in love with the dream more than the man.

After Cate's brother had left home and she'd said she'd stay to help on her parents' farm, Brett had realised that she wasn't going to totally devote herself to him. So he'd broken off the engagement and had gone to Sydney without her.

Cate had been left with a guilty relief. She should never have agreed to marry him when she hadn't truly loved him. And here he was back, at his mother's deathbed, treating Cate as if he'd never been away. How typical.

Cate needed some space from Brett and her own guilt. She looked down at Iris as she slept. 'I have to get back to work, Brett. Give my love to Iris when she wakes.'

He nodded. 'I'll come and find you after six o'clock. We'll have tea together in the cafeteria. Just like old times.'

Cate closed her eyes for a second. 'Not quite like old times, Brett,' she said dryly, 'but if I'm not busy I'll have tea with you.' She straightened the cover on Iris's bed and stroked her arm. 'Bye, Iris,' she said softly, and nodded at Brett as she left.

'Later,' she heard him say as she walked away. Cate rubbed her temples and glanced at her watch. She needed to check that everyone had tea relief organised and she wondered where Noah was.

Now, there was a totally different scenario. Imagine being married to Noah! That would be a different marriage to one with Brett. The woman who married Noah would have to submit to him being the boss. There was no way Cate would tolerate submission to any man. A sudden vision of a home with Noah and a tribe of strong-willed little children curved her lips before she realised what she was thinking.

Blimey. What *was* she thinking? Cate started to walk even faster than her usual pace as if to get away from the startling picture she'd painted.

Her pager beeped and she headed for Emergency. Diversion was at hand. Hopefully the place would be wall to wall with people.

When Cate entered the department, Stella looked calm as usual amidst the chaos. 'I need to clear some of these patients. A heavy vehicle was swept off the causeway. We've got the three passengers, who clung to trees in the middle of the river for an hour. Two have broken bones and all of them have hypothermia. Which ward can we put them in? I can't see any free beds on my admission sheet.'

Cate picked up the phone. 'I'll try to send them to Maternity. Two more mothers were discharged today from there. We have a three-bed room over there that's empty and we'll just have to hope the storms don't bring on the babies.'

She spoke quickly to the maternity staff and hung up. 'That's fine. They'll come over and transfer them to save you the work. What else have you got?'

'I've a resident with a migraine who's trying to work, two men with chest pain and a waiting room full of cuts and bruises, plus the first few cases of gastro.'

Cate picked up the phone again. 'Noah?' She didn't realise it was the first time she'd called him Noah without thinking. 'It's Cate here. We need another resident. One of the ones in Emergency has a migraine and the place is snowed under. OK. Ring me back, I'm in Emergency.'

Stella raised her eyebrows. 'Good luck,' she mouthed, and moved away to attend to a small child who had lost his mother in the mêlée.

Cate turned back to the desk while she waited, and checked the notes of the new admissions. They could go straight to Maternity when the staff arrived to take them.

She chewed her lip. The gastroenteritis was a worry. If the water kept coming up, the risk of an outbreak would increase. She shrugged. That was Noah's worry.

When she turned around, the subject of her thoughts was standing there with a stethoscope around his neck.

CHAPTER SIX

NOAH LOOKED SO solid and reassuring, but Cate was surprised to see him. 'I thought you weren't going to work in Emergency ever again?'

Noah didn't smile. 'One last time and not for long. I've already arranged for two medical residents to arrive from Newcastle. They'll be here in an hour and I'll work out here until they arrive.' His eyes pierced her. 'Do you want me to get extra nursing staff from another hospital before the highway is cut off?'

'No.' She couldn't provide doctors but the nurses all knew their responsibilities. 'Our own staff are capable of managing a local problem, thank you. I've had calls from staff making themselves available if I need them.'

He looked around at the ordered chaos. 'Well, use them. Get extra staff when you need them.'

Cate's eyes widened in surprise. 'Hallelujah. What about the budget?' She shot a startled look at him. 'Who *are* you? What have you done with Dr Masters?'

'Very funny.' He bared his teeth and Cate smiled.

'I thought it was.' She watched his eyes darken. Then she realised it offended him that she thought so little of him. What a joke. She thought too damn much of him. That was the problem. Still, it was safer for her own peace of mind if he didn't see she was fighting a burning attraction.

Cate held up her hands. 'Fine. Thank you. Stella will be pleased to have extra staff.'

'Since when have you waited for permission?'

She became serious. 'To my distress, sometimes I do. The happy medium is hard to find. But I don't have to worry about that today. I'll just say I did what I was told.'

As she turned towards her office, she heard him mutter, 'I wish.'

It was six o'clock before Cate had the staffing as she wanted it. When she looked up, Brett was lounging at the door to her office.

'Ready for tea?' he queried, and she could tell he expected her to come right away.

He struck a pose and handed her a rose, probably stolen from the hospital garden, she thought. She closed her eyes as she sniffed it. The scent reminded her of other times that he'd brought her flowers.

She dropped the rose on the desk and stood up. 'OK. Let's go. But my pager will probably ring half a dozen times so there's no use getting cranky with it.'

'I never get cranky,' he said. Brett slipped his arm through hers and clamped it to his side before she could pull away.

Petulant, not cranky, she corrected herself, and he could be very sweet. But she still thanked her stars she hadn't tied herself to this man-child for the rest of her life.

When they entered the cafeteria, Noah was there. Not sure why she should feel so relieved to have already disentangled her arm before they'd gone in, she still felt strange, with Brett by her side and Noah looking on. Which was ridiculous. Especially when Noah didn't appear at all interested.

Cate chose a table by themselves and deliberately she directed Brett into a chair so that she had her back to Noah. Unfortunately her neck itched the whole time she sat there.

Brett talked enthusiastically about his junior partnership in the Sydney practice but half of Cate's concentration wondered if Noah had left.

When Noah appeared at her shoulder she jumped, and Brett looked surprised at the intrusion. Reluctantly Cate introduced them.

'Brett, this is Mr Masters. He's the area CEO. Mr Masters, Dr Brett Dwyer.'

Brett held out his hand. 'Mr Masters.' They shook hands and Brett winced at the pressure. He flexed his fingers and then looked fondly at Cate. 'What Cate didn't say is that I'm her fiancé.'

Someone dropped a tray of crockery at the same time as Cate said, 'Was. Past tense, Brett.' Hell. Cate doubted if Noah heard her as he was looking at Brett, but she couldn't justify repeating it. She didn't know why it bothered her what Noah thought, but she felt better when she kicked Brett under the table. Cate directed her voice at Noah. 'Brett's mother is terminally ill in Medical.'

Noah nodded. 'I remember. Mrs Dwyer. I'm sorry about your mother's illness, Dr Dwyer.' He nodded at them both. 'I'll leave you to your conversation. Good evening.'

Brett stared after him. 'Seems OK for a CEO. Not a bad job, that. Maybe I should look into it.'

Cate couldn't help but laugh and that was the sound Noah heard as he left the cafeteria.

Noah needed to breathe the outside air. Urgently. It had been a long day and he was tired. He'd been hoping to catch Cate at teatime but the last thing he'd expected had been for her to be with another man, let alone her fiancé.

Though she had said, 'Past tense.'

Still, she must like the guy if she was eating with him. And Dwyer must want her back if he was willing to say they were still engaged. Noah pushed open the door to the garden.

Funny, she'd never mentioned a fiancé before. She'd always struck Noah as brutally honest. Obviously he hadn't asked the right questions.

So what was that news to him? Noah ducked under a tree branch and slapped the trunk as he walked past.

At the very least it was disconcerting to find himself upset by it. She *had* crept under his skin. What Noah had seen in Cate had amazed him. A woman as smart and determined as he was and someone who understood that sometimes hard decisions had to be made. As long as it wasn't to do with her hospital, of course!

True, she was totally different to the type of woman he'd usually been attracted to, but much more exciting. He'd been enjoying the challenge. The more he came to know her, the more he liked what he saw, and appreciated that she could be the perfect partner for him.

Which was probably what Dwyer thought, too!

Later that evening, before she went to bed, Cate listened to the latest radio bulletin. The meteorological bureau had issued a projected peak height for Riverbank at six-point-five metres at noon on Saturday. Which meant the highway would be cut off on both sides of town and there would be a flood of water in the main street and through the business district some time during the next morning.

Noah had told her that the army and navy were sending helicopters to pick up stranded families and those needing assistance. Food drops were being organised and extra ambulance personnel were on their way from Newcastle. Cate shook her head as the announcer confirmed that the town had been officially declared a disaster zone.

All these years of hearing about the floods and now she was here for one. She prayed that no lives would be lost. That was the most important thing.

But only two things were certain in this weather—the hospital was built on a hill so it couldn't get flooded, and tomorrow would be another busy day.

Saturday 10 March

Cate woke to the sound of rain on the roof. A few minutes later, the thump of helicopter rotors vibrated through the air and she lay and listened like a bemused child. She swung her legs out of bed and stood up to stretch the kinks out of her back.

When Cate went in for breakfast at seven, Noah looked in fine form. He sat opposite a very crumpled Brett and she struggled to keep a straight face. Considering the similarities of their profession, she couldn't think of two more different men.

When she went over to the table Noah stood up. Brett must have thought he was leaving because he looked confused when Noah sat down again when she did.

She swallowed a hiccup of laughter and pretended not to notice. 'Good morning, Noah.' She turned to her ex-fiancé. 'Good morning, Brett. How's your mother?'

Brett was obviously pleased to have Cate's attention and he edged closer to her. 'She woke a couple of times during the night but her condition is much the same as yesterday. I slept in the chair beside her bed.'

'I was just saying he looked like it,' Noah commented.

'That was kind of you, Noah.' Cate kept her shoulder turned towards Brett. 'Iris must have been pleased to have you there. But I'm sure she'd think you should go to her house for a sleep today.' Her voice softened. 'I can phone you if she needs you.'

Brett visibly drooped. 'I am tired. Maybe you could come out to the farm this afternoon after work? We could have tea there before coming back here.'

Noah shook his head at Cate. 'Sorry, Dwyer, but I've booked Cate to come for a ride in the SES boat this afternoon. The controller especially asked for her. And then we have to discuss what we find in relation to health factors.'

Cate nearly choked on a mouthful of muesli. When Noah offered to pat her back she declined with a glare. Brett just looked more confused.

What was Noah playing at? Cate glanced at her watch. It was later than she'd thought. She'd have to go soon. 'You look exhausted, Brett. I have to go to work and you should be in bed. Drive carefully. At least the farm is on the flood-free route.'

He nodded. 'You will wake me if there's any change or even just to say hello.' Brett looked so forlorn Cate dropped a sisterly kiss on his head before he got up to leave.

'I'll let you know, don't worry.'

As Brett sauntered out of earshot Cate narrowed her eyes at Noah. 'I've never heard so much rubbish in my life. Why would anyone from the SES ask for me?'

'Angela likes you. Actually, she asked me and I asked for you. I thought it would be a good chance for you to get out for an hour or so. Then you can fill sandbags or whatever afterwards.'

'So why do you want me…' she tapped her chest '…to come?'

Noah shrugged and pretended to whine. Unfortunately he sounded very much like Brett. 'You're my only friend here?'

Cate's head lifted. 'That's cruel. His mother is dying.'

Noah looked disgusted. 'I have sympathy for his mother, but her son is a dweeb. How could you be engaged to that?' He shook his head in disbelief.

Cate glared at him. 'He treated me with respect.' She tilted her head defiantly. Noah stared implacably back.

'You deserve respect.' His voice was clipped. 'Give me another reason.' His face said he couldn't think of one good enough.

Cate couldn't meet his eyes. 'I thought I could love him.'

Noah snorted. 'Came to your senses, eh?'

How dared he? 'This is none of your business.' Cate tapped her fork. 'And I have work to do.'

Noah held her gaze for a long moment before saying firmly, 'Fine. Remember you have an appointment at four o'clock.' He strolled out of the cafeteria before she could say anything further.

* * *

At four o'clock, Noah opened the door of his car for Cate. This time she wore three-quarter-length black jeans and a red-checked shirt knotted at the waist. She had red sandshoes on and no socks, and he loved her in that black cowboy hat.

'Do you always have footwear appropriate to the occasion?' he said.

'I try.' She glanced down at his leather shoes and bit her lip. She couldn't wait to see him wade to the flood boat in them.

He caught her eye and smiled sardonically back. 'My gumboots are in the back so you can stop gloating.'

She inclined her head in appreciation of his forethought. 'So how does a city boy have gumboots in the back?'

Noah stared ahead at the road. 'Is that a riddle or a question?'

A smile tugged at the side of her mouth. She knew what he was doing. 'You're stalling for time while you think about something else, aren't you?'

He glanced across at her and his face was serious. 'Doesn't it amaze you that we can be so in sync?' His eyes returned to the road. 'We understand each other too well sometimes.'

Cate frowned and tried to make sense of his comment. Then the sight ahead diverted her. The car had to backtrack to the highest cross streets to get to where the SES boat waited at the flooded road. Cate's eyes widened. She hadn't been born in 1963 for the last big flood and it was bizarre to see the main road to the centre of town disappear under the water.

The flood boat was waiting, pulled up on the bitumen. Noah parked his car back on a slight rise opposite the ambulance station.

They pulled on lifejackets and one of the other men shoved their boat off so that they were propelled slowly down the main road in a metre of water. Angela Norton, the controller, an enthusiastic thirty-year-old, looked more tired than she usually did. She pointed out the waterfall over the levee, with water streaming across a lake that used to be playing fields.

'The Kemp Street levee overtopped at midday and the water came through the center of town pretty fast after that. A metre of water in less than an hour caught a few out. Most emptied what they could from the shops overnight,' Angela said.

The boat turned into Stuart Street for an eerie float through silent streets. Some shopfronts were filled halfway up the window height with water. Lounges bobbed up and down and everywhere strange objects floated out of context past their bow. People waved from the top stories of buildings and everywhere, despite the brown water covering familiar landmarks, the people they saw were cheerful enough.

Noah shook his head. 'It would turn me off, having a shop in a flood zone,' he said.

Angela nodded. 'There's a lot of work to fix it. But the water will go down.' She steered the boat around a submerged car. 'One of the oldtimers used to say, "You can always come back with your livestock after the water has gone, but always go early and shift in daylight hours, not in the dark." Luckily, we had a fair idea she'd go over today.'

A television news helicopter thumped noisily overhead, no doubt taking their photos for the nightly news. When it had moved on, Noah asked about the other helicopters they'd heard were coming.

Angela nodded. 'We've got a few. There's a Chinook that landed at South West Rocks in bad weather and decided to stay. Plus the three Seahawks from the navy, six from the army and an Iroquois aircraft. The Chinook's gone to Bellbrook as there are a hundred stranded people to move from there.'

Noah winced at the numbers. 'So those people go to the local high school refuge centre? Do you have enough food and bedding?'

'We'll have over two hundred refugees there tonight. The church ladies are buttering up a storm of sandwiches at the showground and others are packing food drops. A lot of bedding and clothes have been donated from the families in town and hopefully it will only be for a few days. There's a queue of trucks both sides of town that were on their way between Sydney and Brisbane. They can't get through but at least the hospital and people on the west side of town have the train line to deliver food supplies.'

Cate could see Noah was impressed. She was conscious of a lump of pride in her chest at the smiling faces around her. Most were willing to bide their time and get on with life when mother nature had finished with them. The rest of the boat ride passed mostly in silence.

Noah was still quiet as they drove back towards the hospital and Cate pondered where she could be the most help for the next couple of hours.

Those victims cut off from home struck the closest chord with Cate. 'Drop me at the high school and I'll have a scout around to see how they're coping.'

Noah turned to look at her. 'Don't you ever stop?'

'Why? I might find a health risk. Besides, I can't sit on my hands until tomorrow's shift.'

Noah shrugged and turned the car. 'Fine. I'll come with you. The hospital can page me if they want me.'

By the time they'd spent two hours at the high school, finding necessities for people and arranging for others to contact relatives, Noah and Cate had heard more hair-raising stories than they could possibly remember. They'd listened to plenty of praise for the volunteers who had saved what they could from the water and some of the stories were harrowing. Times present and past when the access to the hospital had been a deciding factor in saving someone's life seemed to strike Noah the most. Cate planned to take full advantage of it. Hopefully, Noah would see more 'town need' than dollar signs when he returned to being an administrator.

Noah agreed to drop two of the stranded women off at the showground on his way back to the hospital to help with the food preparation. Cate suggested they go in to say hello.

Inside the old weatherboard building she knew every face, because whenever there was a crisis—be it flood, fire or man-made disaster—these were the people who always turned up. There were a lot of elderly men and women—arthritis and stiff legs didn't bar these people from buttering enough to feed the multitude—Noah smiled, shook hands and congratulated people on their effort. Cate felt a warm glow spread through her as she watched him.

Back in the car, again Noah didn't say much and Cate stared out of the window, praying he was receptive to the needs of the community.

It was close to eight o'clock when they pulled up at the hospital and Noah turned off the engine. Cate had leaned to open her door before she'd realised he hadn't moved. She sat back in the dark and waited for him to speak.

'That was pretty incredible,' he said, and the emotion in his voice was testimony to his reaction. He turned to face her and a beam from a streetlight illuminated the strong planes of his face. 'It's the human spirit thing, isn't it? I think I lost it two years ago when my wife died and now this flood has given me a touch of it back. Thanks for sharing it with me, Cate.' He leaned across and kissed her cheek before reaching to open her door.

'Goodnight, Noah.'

Cate climbed out and leaned on the door to look back in.

Suddenly, it seemed neither of them were ready to end the evening and Noah heard himself say, 'I'll park the car but it's still early. Are you up for a game of pool in the nurses' home?'

Cate hesitated. She'd probably spent too much time in Noah's company than was good for her. But the competitive demon inside her couldn't resist the challenge. Maybe this was a chance for her to win at least one round against him. 'One game. Then I'm going to bed. We country people go to bed early, you know.' She shut the door and stood back.

Cate watched him start up the car again. She stroked her cheek where he'd kissed her. So Noah was a widower? More clues as to the nature of his baggage and more intriguing questions she didn't know the answers to. Cate kicked a stone as she turned away and it skidded ahead of her and disappeared into a shadow. A bit like the pieces of Noah's life that she wondered about.

Cate entered through Emergency and for a change it seemed quite civilised. Stella was on the evening shift again and lifted her hand in greeting as Cate walked through. They should compare hours worked at the end of this, Cate thought with a wry smile.

The hospital corridors were quiet as she continued until she came to the children's ward. She dropped in to see Sylvia but the little girl was sound asleep. Cate wrote a quick note and folded it like a card for Sylvia to find when she woke up. She propped it on top of her black hat so Sylvia would see it and know Cate had been by if she woke in the night. Then she slipped out of the back door.

Cate followed the path beside the nurses' quarters to the old laundry which had been converted into a games room. Most of the equipment had been donated and two junior nurses were having a rowdy game of pool when she pushed open the door. They were just finishing up, with only the black ball left on the table. Cate grinned at them and plonked a coin onto the edge of the coin-operated pool table to claim the next use, then wandered over to battle the pinball machine until Noah arrived.

A few minutes later, Noah nodded to the nurses playing pool. Their girlish voices made him feel like Methuselah and he wondered when he'd become so old. He stepped over to stand behind Cate as she gyrated at the end of a prehistoric pinball machine and suddenly, ridiculously, he felt sixteen again.

Her thigh pressed against the metal as she bumped it with her pelvis every now and then to direct the ball, and he watched, fascinated, as she threw her whole concentration into the game. For the first time in his life he wished he'd been born as an arcade machine. The thought made him smile.

The fact that Cate had barely noticed his arrival didn't escape Noah. She was immersed in the game. The silver ball flew around the course and her long fingers tapped madly at the flippers to block the ball from sinking.

He hadn't seen one of these machines for a long time but obviously Cate was no stranger to it. She was good, a lot better than he'd be, and he grinned at her intense concentration as she gripped her bottom lip with her teeth in determination.

The digital counter flew into the hundred thousands in response to her unerring aim at the targets and she muttered to herself as the last ball eluded her and disappeared down the centre hole. She'd just missed out on a free game.

'Pretty good score, Sister Forrest.' When she turned and grinned up at him he felt like dropping a kiss on those pink lips of hers but he hesitated a moment too long. She turned back to the machine to calculate her score. This wasn't the place, anyway, he consoled himself. Maybe coming here hadn't been a good idea.

Across the room, the young nurses finished up their game and waved goodbye. Now that Cate's machine had stopped ringing and beeping, when the door shut behind the girls with a whoosh, it was silent in the room.

Cate flexed her fingers and patted the machine then she turned to the pool table. Her eyes sparkled blue and challenging and he couldn't help the answering smile that tugged at his lips. She vibrated with energy and he felt the tension zapping between them. He wondered if she did.

Lately he hadn't found her so easy to read. Sometimes he wondered if she felt anything at all when he was around. It was very disconcerting.

Cate hopped from foot to foot like a champion tennis player. 'Let's see how good you are at pool, then, Mr Masters.' She lifted her favourite cue from the wall-mounted rack. 'One game. Choose your weapon.'

Noah perused the rack of cues and decided on a nicely weighted mid-length. So, she thought she could beat him, did she? He hid his smile. 'Set 'em up.' He reached for the triangular rack and placed it on the table as Cate inserted the money and collected up the balls from the drop-tray. 'Would you like to make a small wager on the outcome?' His voice was nonchalant.

Cate was chalking her cue and she looked up equally innocently. 'Sure. Whoever loses…pays for the game.' She threw him the chalk. 'You break.'

Their eyes met across the table as he dusted the cue tip with the chalk, and his fingers slowed. Suddenly there was a lot of heat in that look and he was intrigued that it was Cate who looked away first. Maybe she wasn't as oblivious to him as he'd thought. He stared down at the more than adequately chalked cue tip and dragged his mind back to the game. The woman was addling his brains!

Cate was quiet as he broke the stack, and with more fluke than skill the number ten spun off into the side pocket. 'Looks like I'm after the big ones, which is only fair seeing as I'm taller.'

Cate nodded but her smile didn't reach her eyes. He saw that she was actually planning her next move and he grinned at her competitiveness. He shot again but the ball missed the pocket and she brushed past him as she moved around the table to line up her target so that she was opposite him.

When she bent over the table he had to avert his eyes from the straining buttons on her shirt and the soft swell of her breasts as her neckline opened. He'd thought a game of pool would be fun before turning in for the night but he was afraid this could be more in the way of torture. Clunk went the ball.

She slid past him to lean in front of him and he stepped back out of her way to admire the view as she bent low over the table and the short jeans tightened across her bottom. A bit like his jeans were tightening. At this rate he'd be spending the night in a cold shower. He gritted his teeth. Clunk.

Noah averted his eyes again as Cate leaned even further down on the table, then came back to the present with the sound of another ball thudding home into a pocket. Startled, he saw that she'd sunk all her balls and only the black eight ball and his four coloured ones were left on the table. Thankfully, the black ball bounced harmlessly off the cushion away from the pocket.

He moistened his lips and loosened the tension in his shoulders. 'Nice of you to give me a shot.' His voice sounded incredibly normal, and Noah narrowed his eyes to concentrate.

She smiled up at him. 'You'll only get the one chance.'

She thought she had him and Noah felt like playing dangerously. 'Then let's up the ante.' Noah lined up his shot. 'Loser pays for another day's game as well.' He paused, then added, 'And the winner gets a kiss.'

Cate sent a startled glance across at him, but didn't meet his eyes. She was in no mood to lose. 'You can bet what you like because I'm going to win and I don't want a kiss.'

Noah just smiled and proceeded to coldly sink his four balls and then the black.

Cate winced ruefully. 'Damn. Well done, smart alec. Obviously I shouldn't have let you off the hook.' Cate shook his hand. 'Enjoy your win. You can live without the kiss.'

Noah inclined his head. 'Gracious Cate. I'll look forward to another game when your shifts allow it.'

He gestured at the clock. 'Are you sure you don't want another game now?'

Cate was backing away and shook her head. It wasn't the thought of the game that unsettled her, rather the atmosphere that was thick between them. She was very aware that the sounds everywhere else had quietened for the night. Then there was the fact that the hairs on her arms rose whenever he brushed past.

It had been building all day and there was that kiss he'd dropped on her cheek in the car that she hadn't wanted to dwell on, as well as the startling news he'd dropped just prior to that.

For the last twenty minutes she'd worked hard to block out his presence while she played, but it was as if someone had thrown the switch of her immunity and now she could feel every glance like a caress. It was time to get out of there. Quickly. 'I'm for bed. I'm on an early shift in the morning.'

'Goodnight, sweet Cate.' He walked towards her and her heart thumped as he drew closer. She wondered if he was going to ask for his kiss and couldn't help but wonder what it would feel like to be kissed—properly—by Noah.

He paused in front of her and in the end he just reached out to take her cue. She looked at the floor in case he saw the disappointment in her eyes and told herself she was glad that he hadn't demanded his prize. She was safe.

He replaced their cues in the rack and strolled over to the pinball machine. 'I think I'll stay for a while. I need to practise on this thing if I don't want to get beaten.'

Cate forced a smile and turned for the door. Just before she went through, he stopped her.

'One minute, Cate.' She didn't turn, couldn't turn, and she heard his footsteps come towards her across the room. It felt like someone had superglued her feet to the floor and her heart thumped so loudly she felt it vibrate through her skin. The air seemed to have been sucked from the room and her respiration rate increased to accommodate that and the fluttering discomfort in her belly. Brett had never had her in this state. Brett had never had her in any state.

Noah stopped behind her, and she still didn't turn. But she could feel his breath on the back of her neck and then his hand on her shoulder. The warmth seeped through her shirt and into her skin as he turned her to face him. She didn't even think of resisting.

'It's only fair I get one kiss.' His eyes darkened to black Sambucca, and his finger lifted to stroke her cheek. Cate's heart thumped even faster at that single touch and then he cradled her chin firmly until his lips lowered to hers.

His lips were warm and firm as they brushed against hers, then his mouth took possession. Cate closed her eyes and let him have his way. Because she couldn't lie to herself any more. She wanted to be kissed by Noah. Needed to find out what it was like to be kissed by this man. To be held against him, to breathe him in and be thoroughly kissed. Just once before he left.

And it was nothing like she'd expected. Her few previous kisses disappeared in a purple haze of pressure and taste and heat between Noah's mouth and hers. She floated and soared and whimpered with delight as Noah stamped his mark on her mouth and her heart, and her body flattened against him. She finally realised why she'd never lost her head with Brett. Because it hadn't been like this.

And then he stopped. His hand loosened on her chin until, stroking gently, his fingers released her. His mouth drew back with a few last nibbles and he stepped back. Cate almost stumbled and he caught her shoulder briefly to steady her before he turned her back to face towards the door.

'Goodnight, Cate.' His voice seemed to come from a long way away and Cate flicked a glance over her shoulder at the closed expression on his face. She drew a deep breath, not caring if he heard it, and closed her eyes for a moment. Then she turned and looked him straight in the face. 'Goodnight, Noah.'

The door slammed behind her as she left and she winced. Outside, the night air washed over her face and she gulped in the night scents and the coolness. Her skin tingled in the cold air and the fact that every nerve ending seemed to be more alive than ever before amazed her. She tried to work out what had just happened, but couldn't.

She felt like jumping in her car and speeding down the road to escape for a while and sort out her feelings. But the only open road led to Brett and she wasn't going there.

Which led to another awkward question. Why hadn't she been lost to all reason with Brett like she had with Noah? Scary stuff. She'd almost married Brett.

A few minutes later Cate was back in her room. She showered and crawled into bed and stared at the ceiling. Her mind swung towards Noah. She shied away from the kiss in the games room and focused on his comment in the car. The comment he hadn't explained. The one about losing his wife.

How had she died? Two years wasn't very long to get over grief like that. And why was she, Cate, so upset by the news that Noah had been married before? It took her a long time to get to sleep.

CHAPTER SEVEN

Sunday 11 March

IRIS DWYER DIED at five o'clock on Sunday morning—without fuss and with a smile on her face. Early morning was a time a lot of souls slipped away and strangely enough when a lot of babies came into the world, too.

Brett had asked the night supervisor to wake Cate and she had been there when his mother had breathed her last. He'd clung to Cate and she'd comforted him as best she could until finally Brett wiped his eyes. 'What am I going to do without her?'

Cate stroked his hair. 'She looked very peaceful, Brett, and her faith was strong. And you'll be fine. Have a few days at the farm to say goodbye and go back to your practice in Sydney. It's where you belong.'

'Come with me, Cate. We could be happy.' His mother's blue eyes implored her.

Cate squeezed his hand. 'You're upset, Brett. You know I'm not leaving here.'

'What about if *he* asks you? Noah Masters. Will you go then?' He pulled his hand away.

Where had that come from and why would Brett ask such a question? Was it that obvious that she admired Noah? Cate bit her lip. She hoped not.

There was no future in it and she didn't need to be a further object of pity by the people she knew.

Cate shook her head. 'You're out of line, Brett. But, no, I've no wish to leave Riverbank.' She pushed him gently towards the door. 'Go home to your mother's house, *your* house, and have a rest. I'll see you later today.' She hugged him once. 'Your mother was a wonderful woman. I loved Iris, too. Goodnight.'

Cate went back to bed but she couldn't sleep. Iris's death brought the mortality of human life close to home and it really made Cate think about the choices she'd made in life and love. Was the threat of Noah taking over her life, that loss of control, worth denying herself the pleasure she knew she could find in Noah's arms?

Cate resigned herself to her sleepless state and rose again. Maybe a walk would help. By the time she was dressed, the east was lit with a pre-dawn glow, and she felt calmer.

She ambled down to the Euroka lookout where the river rushed past like an angry brown anaconda, tumbling logs and branches in its wake. When the sun came up, she saw a cow float past on its side and she hoped it was alive.

There was a chance it could be. Yesterday she'd heard about a cow that had been washed through the floodgates, floated on its side for seven miles parallel to the beach and then turned up at Crescent Head where it had climbed out over the footbridge and ambled away. The newspaper had christened it Bubbles.

Life was strange like that.

Maybe that was what she liked about hospitals, and Maternity in particular—the strange ups and downs but always the continuity of life. Would she have to leave it all behind to follow Noah?

She glanced at her watch. It was nearly time to go to work. It had been a long week and she was due for a couple of days off tomorrow. But if Amber couldn't come in, Cate guessed she might as well stay on for another shift and have extra days off after the flood crisis was over. But she was tired. And confused. Before Noah had come along she hadn't been like that.

Just prior to going on duty, Cate rang her parents. She sighed with relief when Leanore answered the phone. 'Hi, Mum. It's me.' Cate felt her throat close over and swallowed a couple of times before she could talk.

'What's wrong, love?' Her mother's voice was warm and comforting as only a mother's could be.

Cate sniffed. 'Iris Dwyer died this morning. And I needed to tell you that I love you.'

'I love you, too, darling. I'm sorry about Iris. Was Brett there?'

'Yes. He'll go back to Sydney in a few days.' Cate brushed the tears away from her eyes.

There was silence at the other end of the phone for a moment as her mother thought about the news. 'You must be tired. It's been a long week for you, too.'

'I'm OK. How's the farm and everyone?' Normality at home seemed so far away.

'We're fine. The water is still about ten metres from the house but we took turns at keeping watch last night in case it sneaked up quickly. The cows have ruined my garden but we haven't lost any stock yet, which is wonderful. The only nuisance is that the electricity failed yesterday and we're eating the perishables like mad before they go off. When you see us we'll probably be all ten kilos heavier.'

They both laughed and Cate silently thanked her mother for being there. The hospital's power had been fine so it was probably only the outlying farms that had been affected. Another thing to be grateful for.

'I'd better go. I'll probably give you a ring tomorrow. Love to everyone. Bye, Mum.'

'Bye, darling.'

Cate replaced the receiver and let her shoulders droop. Everything was OK. She'd just plod on for another couple of days and then she could go home.

Her thoughts turned to Noah. Would he be in the cafeteria this morning? How would she feel when she saw him? Did he think last night's kiss had been a token for the winner of a game of pool or had it meant more to him, too? Now he'd managed to land her in unfamiliar territory again.

The lift in her spirits, when she saw him, was proof of how much his company was beginning to mean. Was it still less than a week since he'd come? The shock of that awareness made her tone more abrupt than she'd intended.

Her plate hit the table with a tiny thump. 'Every time I come here you seem to be here. You spend a lot of time in the cafeteria.'

He raised his eyebrows at her. 'Good morning to you, Cate Forrest. That statement is very similar to one you made the first day I met you.' His brown eyes captured hers. 'You really do think I'm a lightweight, don't you?'

Cate sat down opposite him. His broad shoulders strained against his shirt as he leaned back in the chair and his relaxed demeanour belied his ability to know what was going on at any given moment.

Her heart ached as she realised how much this man could come to mean to her. She had to stop this. He'd leave soon. 'No. I don't think you're a lightweight. As much as I hate to admit it, I think you're very good at your job. I don't know anyone who could have done it better. I just wish you were on my side.'

He leaned across and squeezed her hand. 'Did you ever consider that I might be?'

If only she could believe that, because there was another matter that had come up just before she'd come in to breakfast. 'Good. Because Susie Ryan, a first-time mum from Gladstone, rang me just now and I want to bring her in before she goes into labour.'

He pulled his hand back as if it had been snapped by a mousetrap. His voice was deadly quiet. 'You don't give up, do you? I said, no pre-labours and no unnecessary admissions. This hospital is not a motel. Surely you can see we have to keep as many free beds as possible?'

Cate tried to reason with him. 'My instinct tells me this woman needs to come in.'

Noah was adamant. 'When you get an order from a doctor she can come.' They glared at each other and all conversation was halted as they entered into some kind of staring match.

'Right.' Cate pushed her cereal plate away and stood up. 'My fault for mentioning it. Hopefully you won't still be sitting here at lunchtime.'

She should have just arranged for Susie to come in. That was what you got for trusting the enemy. She walked quickly away before she said something she'd really regret and his voice drifted after her.

'Pleasure working with you.'

You have no idea, buster.

Adrenaline carried Cate through most of the morning and she ignored her growing headache.

Noah came into her office before lunch with Janet Glover, the nurse manager.

His voice was clipped, and he spoke to a spot just over Cate's head. 'We need you to make a list of possible extra staff to call in an emergency. There's a chance we could have a severe outbreak of gastroenteritis in one of the outlying towns. The sewerage system has flooded and we have the chance of raw sewage in the flooded streets.'

Two could play at this game, she thought as she spoke to the plant behind him. 'Why not evacuate the town until the danger is past?'

'Because most of them won't leave.' Noah saved a hard look for Cate. 'Country people are stubborn.'

Janet looked amused at the tension between Noah and Cate. She drew them back to the matter at hand when she added her opinion. 'We're setting up public information leaflets to explain the risks and outline the precautions for the townspeople to take, so hopefully the situation won't arise. But Mr Masters seems to think that you may not have the staff resources if you need them. Should we have other hospitals on standby?'

Cate ignored Noah and spoke to the nurse manager. 'I've been inundated with calls from off-duty staff willing to come if we can pick them up. The SES have no problem with that, as long as there aren't any other crises at the time, so I'd say we're well covered.'

'Thank you, Sister.' Janet looked smugly at Noah. 'Does that satisfy you, Mr Masters?'

Noah nodded at Cate and they both left. Cate crossed her fingers that they wouldn't need the staff. Gastro was a horrible illness and the numbers could swell before you knew it.

The rest of the shift was routine until just before shift handover to the evening staff. Her pregnant friend, Susie Ryan, rang again.

'Cate?'

'Yes, Susie? You all right?' Cate saved what she'd been doing on the computer and listened.

'I think so but I hope I'm not getting paranoid. I thought I'd run it by you.'

Cate frowned. Susie sounded agitated. 'Great idea. Go ahead.' Cate sat back in the chair.

'I've got pressure down below but no pains.' Susie spoke fast, as if she wanted to get it out without sounding too much like a fool. 'I haven't had any pains like they said I'd get, but everything feels different down there. What should I do?'

Cate's mind ran through the possibilities, the most likely being early labour. 'Listen, Suse. Because it's your first baby it's probably OK. But I'm off duty in less than an hour. I'll see if I can get a lift with one of the flood boats up to your house and come for a visit. Would that be OK?'

'That would be great. Pete's away, trying to save the oysters.'

Cate winced. 'Floods and oysters don't mix, do they?'

'No. It looks like we'll lose ninety per cent of them but Pete told me to worry about the baby, not the oysters.'

Cate had to smile. 'He's a good man. I won't be long.'

Susie didn't seem to want to hang up. 'It's funny. I'm getting nervous. The last hour I've been feeling really strange.'

'I understand. I'll see you soon. Ring me if you need me earlier and we'll get a helicopter to pick you up.'

Thankfully, the evening supervisor was early and as soon as possible Cate dashed over to Maternity to grab an emergency delivery pack. She slipped the tiny packet into the big pocket of her windcheater. She was sure she wouldn't need it but felt slightly better with its presence.

Cate drove her utility to the spot where she and Noah had embarked from yesterday. As she'd arranged earlier, a yellow SES boat was waiting with a burly teenager at the engine.

The two of them took off in a wave of brown water. 'I'm Paul,' the young fellow said. 'Normally we have two boats if we're going into the main river, but the other boat got called away. You OK with that, Sister?'

Paul seemed quite confident and Cate nodded. They drove past the semi-submerged town and into the main river, keeping towards the less turbulent side. The sun shone off the brown water and the sky was filled with fluffy white clouds. It was really quite beautiful as they steered with the current down the river. Cate could see it would be much more exciting coming back against the flow as she watched Paul avoid the floating debris. The sun was shining off the water and flocks of water egrets circled overhead as they watched hungrily for fish.

It took about half an hour to get to Susie's farm and, amazingly, the water came to about a hundred feet of the house. The grass looked strange to Cate, and Paul handed her a can of insect repellent. She looked at him and he pointed to the ground. The grass and trees near her were a mass of spiders of all different sizes as they scrambled for dry ground. She shuddered and sprayed her legs with the repellent before stepping out.

Susie had come out to the verandah and Cate hurried up the steps to hug her.

Cate took one look at the fear in her friend's face and made her decision. She'd worry about Noah later. Susie was dressed in a skirt and blouse and her rounded belly poked out in front like a beach ball. The fabric tightened over the bulge every time she moved.

'You're coming back with me. You should be happy at this time, not scared witless. Can you get a message to Pete to let him know you're going in?'

Susie's relief shone in her eyes. 'I said I might go back if you said it was all right. Pete was happy about that. He'll ring as soon as he saves any oysters he can. My bag's packed.'

'Good girl.' Cate stepped into the house and lifted the bulging bag beside the door. 'Let's go. I'm not impressed with your watchdog spiders.'

Susie shivered. 'The snakes are worse. We must have five varieties hiding under the house.'

Both women were glad to get to the boat. Cate helped Susie with her lifejacket and then they sat together in the middle of the boat. There was a slight breeze and the first part of the ride was peaceful as they crossed over submerged fences and paddocks towards the river. Paul radioed Control to say they were heading back with precious cargo.

Noah was there and he couldn't believe he'd heard right. Cate hadn't told him she'd planned this and if he hadn't been down here at the control centre he wouldn't have known. He flexed his fingers. He visualised the river they'd only briefly skirted yesterday and he could almost feel the force of the water in his imagination. Wasn't that woman afraid of anything? Well, he bloody well was. He'd strangle her. As long as she didn't kill herself.

Back on the river, Cate had found something to fear. The boat had just made it into the main stream when the engine spluttered twice and died. Even though it had been in the background all the time, the sudden silence from the motor accentuated the grumbling roar of the rushing river.

Cate's hold on Susie's hand tightened as they listened to Paul abuse the boat as he pulled the cord to restart the engine. Strangely, Cate had a sudden vivid image of Noah and the thought steadied her. Susie clutched her stomach.

Paul fiddled with the fuel line and swore again as the nose of the boat swung back the way they'd come. As their forward speed dropped off, Susie moaned. The boat rocked and was swept away with the river and out towards the middle of the flow. The hull thunked as floating logs jostled with it in the wash.

When Noah heard the distress call come through on the radio, his stomach dropped. He met the eyes of Angela and the worry in her face was enough to chill his blood.

'Get me on the helicopter that's going after them.'

Angela was calm in the crisis and contacted the nearest army helicopter. She glanced up at Noah. 'There's one at the hospital helipad now. I'll ask them to wait for you.'

Noah strode to his car and the engine roared as he accelerated up the hill to the hospital. He drove the wrong way up the one-way lane and parked beside the helipad just as the rotors started up.

'What's happening?' he shouted as he ducked his head to climb in.

The pilot ignored him as they took off and the navigator gestured for him to come closer. 'We've got them on radio and are talking Paul through re-priming the engine. It's their best shot.'

Noah couldn't believe it. 'Why doesn't he know how to do that without help?'

'He does. But it's better to talk it through in moments of crisis.' The navigator pressed his earphone closer to his ear. 'He's got it going and the boat is turning.'

Noah sagged back on the bench seat until he saw the navigator press the earphone to his ear again. 'Copy that,' he said, and wiped his face. 'Hell. At least we have a doctor on the chopper.'

'What?' Noah almost shouted.

'The patient's water's broken and it looks like the baby's coming.' The soldiers in the cabin exchanged looks.

A baby Noah could deal with. Cate's boat without power on the river was more of a problem. 'Get them to the edge of the river. And get us down there.'

The next few minutes passed in a blur for Noah as he stared out the window and willed Cate's boat to find somewhere safe to land. The river flashed below him and the flotsam and debris all looked like Cate to Noah.

Finally their quarry stopped and the helicopter settled a little further back from the edge of the fast-flowing water.

Noah was the first out, his face like a thundercloud. He pulled Cate from the boat, hugged her once and then thrust her aside to gather up the pregnant woman in his arms.

'Let's go,' he shouted at Cate as she stood, stunned, and stared at him.

Cate couldn't believe it was Noah. She'd never been so glad to see anyone in her life. She had to admit she'd been scared. Birth was natural but boats and cold winds were not normal for newborn babies and a dead motor in flood waters was just too much.

Now she had to get into the helicopter and she hated flying. Her hand started to shake and she nearly dropped Susie's bag. She couldn't get in, but Noah was already inside with the mother-to-be—and Susie needed her.

Cate felt like throwing up as she was pulled inside and with the thump of rotors above them it all swam in front of her eyes. They were finally in the air. Cate had hold of Susie's hand again but she wasn't sure for whose comfort it was.

Susie moaned and closed her eyes. The baby's birth was very close and Cate blocked out the thought that they were hundreds of feet up in the air skimming across a river that would love to gobble them up.

'It's OK now, Susie.' She poured as much reassurance into her smile as possible.

Susie's eyes sprang open. 'That was pretty wild, Cate.'

Cate squeezed her hand. 'Guess whose baby is going to be a real rural survivor?'

'It's coming now.' Susie's eyes widened and her breath shortened. 'How can that be when I haven't had any pains?'

'Your baby is doing this his or her way.' Cate smiled. 'Every now and then that's how it works. But you've known all day it's coming so that's like labour.'

Susie's hand tightened and she spoke through gritted teeth. 'I have to push.'

'Well, push, Suse.' Cate knew that nothing would stop the birth of Susie's baby and all she could do was make it seem as natural as possible in a noisy helicopter surrounded by five men, four dressed in camouflage. She smiled at Noah with the knowledge that he was there to help. Susie and her baby would be fine.

'Let's get organised.' She reassured Susie before reaching down under the blankets to remove her underwear.

She heard Noah ask for a medical kit and some towels and she remembered the kit in her pocket. She pulled the plastic bag off it and spread the wrapping open to make a tiny clean area. Inside were a plastic kidney dish, a pair of scissors, two plastic cord clamps and a pair of gloves. You really didn't need much to have a baby, she thought whimsically.

Susie moaned and Cate soothed her as she settled the blanket back against itself to reveal Susie's legs and the tiny sliver of baby's head as it peeped through his mother's perineum. Cate donned her gloves and waited for Susie's baby to arrive.

Slowly more head appeared as Susie opened like a flower, her labia spreading as the dark-haired child unflexed its head and then rotated it into the world. Cate rested her hands gently on each side of the baby's head and checked carefully for cord around the neck. When she didn't find any, they waited for the next contraction. Suddenly, with a gentle rush, the baby slid into Cate's hands. Damp and slippery, the little girl mewled at the faces around her.

'Look, Susie. What have you got?' Noah's voice was deep and soft.

Susie opened her eyes and gazed in awe at her daughter. 'It's a girl.' Cate wiped the baby with a towel and clamped and cut the shiny purple lifeline as Susie unbuttoned her shirt so her daughter could lie inside next to her skin and keep warm.

Ten minutes later they made a strange procession as they came through the doors of Maternity, a soldier pushing one end of the trolley and Noah the other. Susie and her baby were buried under a mound of army blankets. The baby didn't cry at all.

Noah left them at the door to Maternity when his pager beeped, and Cate took over his end of the trolley. His eyes pierced Cate's and his voice was implacable. 'Ring me when you're finished.'

She found herself simply nodding.

Surprisingly quickly, Susie was settled into bed with baby Chloe in a cot beside her. Cate wrote up Chloe's birth information in her mother's medical records and the birth register. When that was done, Cate laid down her borrowed pen, rested her head in her hands for a moment and thanked God it had all turned out well.

She massaged her forehead. Could she have done anything differently? Had her association with Noah affected her ability to trust her own instincts? Could she have known without hindsight that it would have been safer to fly Susie out of there? Or had it been a chain of circumstances that had just happened? She'd never know.

The other disturbing fact was that her thoughts had gone to Noah in her neediest hour, and he was a man on a mission who was just passing through. How was she going to feel when he went back to Sydney?

Noah pushed open the maternity door. He hadn't been able to wait. His fear while the boat carrying Cate had tossed at the mercy of the swollen river had ripped his heart out. A picture of Cate, lifeless on some muddy bank, sat in his brain like a spectre.

He was furious. With Cate for putting herself at risk. With himself for not listening when she'd wanted the woman to come in. With SES for having a boat with an engine that had died and even with baby Chloe for deciding to be born at such a dangerous time. And all of that anger was ridiculous and he knew it. Just couldn't help it.

Because he'd nearly lost someone who matched him in every way. Someone who filled him with the knowledge that he was alive and living life to the full. And the more he learnt about her, the more he cared. And the really scary thing was that he knew he'd be happy to keep learning for the rest of his life.

But she should never have gone out on that boat alone, and he was going to tear a piece off her so that she would never do anything so dangerous again.

Then he saw her, her head in her hands as she sat at the desk in the office. She looked forlorn and was probably beating herself up for everything not turning out perfectly. Suddenly all the anger seeped out of him—he just needed to hold her.

Noah shut the door and then stepped up behind her and rested his hand on her shoulder until she turned.

'Stand up,' he said, and for once she did what he asked without questioning. He turned her to face him and gently pulled her into his arms to hold her close.

She resisted and he shushed her and then she was soft and pliant against him. He cradled her head against his cheek and reassured himself that she was solid and warm and safe in his arms. His Cate. That subtle perfume she wore wove a tighter spell around his heart and he closed his eyes for a moment.

'We have to talk.' His voice was low and deep and it sent shivers across Cate's neck.

His arms felt strong and comforting around her and she'd never felt so warm and safe and feminine. She'd always thought her femininity would make her weak but she felt stronger with his strength around her.

When his lips met hers she understood that kisses could be many things. This was different and wholesome and awesome and Noah. Cate felt welded to him with heat and homecoming. He crushed her against him and she gloried in his strength. Her fingers spread up and over his shoulders and she held him against her as if to confirm this was where she belonged. It all felt so right.

Insistently, the phone rang beside them on the desk and reluctantly they broke apart. Cate felt renewed and smiled softly and intimately at Noah as she picked up the phone.

CHAPTER EIGHT

IT WAS BRETT and the mood shattered into a million jagged pieces. 'I thought I'd find you there. I'm in the cafeteria. Come and have tea with me.'

It was the last thing Cate wanted to do but she'd promised she'd see him today. It seemed days since Iris had passed away and yet it had only been this morning. She hesitated and Noah raised his eyebrows in question. The warmth in his eyes scattered her wits and she turned away from him to answer. 'Give me five minutes,' she said into the phone. 'I'll meet you there. Bye.'

'Who was that?' His brows had snapped together.

It was his tone that did it. He expected to be obeyed. Cate frowned. 'Have you designated yourself as my keeper now?'

'I said we need to talk.' His voice was low but inflexible.

'Perhaps,' she said more cautiously as she realised he'd planned to railroad her and she'd nearly crumbled. 'Perhaps not.' Her decision was made. 'I have to go.'

He caught her hand as she brushed past him and she stopped. Cate looked down at where he held her until his fingers loosened and he dropped her wrist. 'Very sensible' was all she said, and she walked away.

Noah took a deep breath as he watched her disappear up the corridor. She was stubborn and he'd been a fool. He couldn't force her to listen to him and he certainly couldn't expect her to feel the same as he did.

All he was sure of was that today, terrified he would lose her, he'd realised without a doubt that he loved Cate. Why had he tried to steamroller her just now? He'd make up for it next time, unless she did something to make him forget.

Brett stood up when Cate appeared at the table beside him. She admitted wryly to herself that he'd always been a fast learner. 'How are you, Brett?' They sat down together and he leaned across and rested his forehead against hers.

'Sad. And lonely.' His voice was mournful and she sighed. She was beginning to wonder if she'd spent the whole year engaged to him exhaling in frustration.

Cate concentrated on consoling him but the weariness inside her was hard to hide. 'You'll always be sad your mum isn't here to talk to. She loved you so much, and she'll watch over you. That's not my job, Brett. Go back to Sydney. Some wonderful woman one day will capture your heart and you'll settle down and have a family and be someone's dad. You'll recapture the essence of your parents when that time comes.'

He squeezed her hand. 'Are you sure it can't be you?'

Cate shook her head. 'I've changed, Brett. I'll never be that woman. But you will always be special to me.' Cate didn't have the strength or the inclination for this. Iris had been her friend, too, and the day had been too much. And then there was Noah. She could feel exhausted tears hovering very close. 'Look after yourself.' She stood up. 'I have to go.'

Brett gestured to a salad he'd ordered for her. 'What about your tea?'

'You have it. I'm not hungry.' She was sure she'd choke if she ate anything.

He stood up as well. 'Someone else can have it. Walk me to my car, then. Amber's invited me to tea if you were too busy.' Cate nodded. He wasn't going to make a scene, and in relief she even let him take her arm as they went.

In his office, Noah turned away from the window as they walked across the car park. He didn't need to see this. After a few minutes, when he thought he'd be safe, he turned back in time to see Cate give Brett a brief kiss. He swore softly under his breath and turned away again. That had been stupid. Served him right. They said that curiosity killed the cat but he'd have preferred to kill Dwyer.

Cate was exhausted. There had been a cold moment on the river when she'd thought all of them in the boat could lose their lives. And then the helicopter ride had terrified her. She should be thankful to Susie for taking her mind off the flight while she'd had her baby.

Life was funny like that. Things that you'd considered important didn't mean as much if something more momentous was taking place. Soon Cate would walk past Noah's office on the way to her room in Maternity. That kiss they'd shared had only confused her more. Why couldn't she have felt like that with Brett and not Noah? She felt hollow inside and wondered if the ward had any medicinal brandy. She needed a drink and a shower. Or maybe she just needed Noah?

Her feet paused of their own accord and she considered going in to face him. But what would she say when she didn't know what she wanted? Cate resumed walking. She felt emotionally bankrupt and her feelings for Noah were too big a problem to be faced tonight. Tomorrow would be soon enough.

'We still need to talk, Cate.' Noah's voice came from behind her and Cate's heart thumped, a strange feeling, similar to the one she'd felt before getting into the helicopter. She turned slowly and faced him.

His face was all harsh planes and angles. She couldn't do this now. 'I did consider it, Noah, but I'm tired—'

He stepped up beside her and cut off her words. 'I know you are. We're both tired, but I would appreciate it if you would step into my office for a moment.'

His eyes held hers and she tried to look away but couldn't. She remembered the relief she'd felt when he'd appeared on the riverbank and even the thought of him while she'd been in the boat. She walked past him into the office.

The sound of the door as he shut it behind her made her heart thump again.

Noah walked to the window, stared out for a moment and then turned to face her. His eyes bored into hers. 'Are you considering going back to Dwyer?'

Cate had had enough. 'The man's mother died this morning. I don't think this is a good time to discuss my relationship with him.' What was Noah's problem now? When it all boiled down, she'd kissed Noah twice and he thought he owned her. She stamped down the thought of what kisses they'd been… Her chin came up. 'What makes you think it's any of your business, anyway?'

'I'm sorry about Mrs Dwyer. I know she was your friend.' He stepped towards her until there was only a hand's breadth between them. Despite her body screaming for escape, she refused to step back.

He ran his hand through his hair and his eyes softened. 'But I decided you are my business when I thought I'd lost you in the river today.' He stepped closer until her vision was blocked by his body and she felt the barest touch of his chest against her breasts. A shudder ran through her body and his voice was barely above a whisper. 'And it became my business after I held you and kissed you today.'

Cate tipped her head back to look at him and typically, when she was too close to Noah, her mind worked sluggishly. It was hard to think when all she wanted to do was lose herself in his arms and recapture the taste of him. Then her mind cleared.

Lose herself! Her half-closed eyes snapped open. This was getting out of her control. She needed to remind herself there was little hope of a future in this relationship. He was going back to Sydney soon. She tried for flippancy. 'I thought the kissing was mutual. I'd hate you to take all the credit.'

His teeth snapped together. 'If that's the case, why were you kissing Dwyer?'

So that's what all this was about. Men! Her own temper surfaced as the implications set in. Cate stepped back and looked meaningfully towards the window that faced the car park. 'Doing a spot of peeping Tommery, Noah? Is that what all this is about? Dog in a manger?'

His eyes glittered and she stepped back a fraction. 'I think we have more than that between us.' He bit the words out and spun away from her. Cate drew a deep breath at the sudden space around her. She saw him roll his shoulders to ease the tension in his neck and she remembered he'd been in the helicopter, too. She imagined it might almost have been harder to watch than experience—especially if he was beginning to care for her. How did she feel about that? She realised she'd never really thought about how he might be affected by all this.

He turned back to face her and he smiled ruefully at her. Slowly, but with purpose, he leant down and very softly brushed her lips with his.

'I'm sorry. It's been a big day for both of us. And I'm rushing you.'

He kissed her again.

Not fair, Cate thought as another shudder ran through her body. She tried to stay rigid and unmoved beneath his insidious onslaught. If he used force she could push him away, slap his face and get out of there. But this was a dare—a challenge to stay unmoved as with the barest whisper his lips paid homage to her mouth and her brow and jaw, and it was the most difficult thing in the world for Cate to fight against.

And Noah knew it.

She could feel his breath against her face and the beginnings of his abrasive bristles rasped across her cheek. His thick, curling lashes rested on his cheeks—lashes that any woman would have given her eye teeth for. They didn't match his businesslike veneer and gave him a vulnerability that was at odds with what she knew of him. Vulnerability that she found achingly attractive, and it didn't help to keep her immune from his power. She needed more time.

She could feel herself softening against him and the moment had come to either bail out or admit to him that he could move her more than she wanted him to.

She stepped back.

He opened his eyes and she almost lost herself in their sleepy passion. He stroked her cheek. 'I never took you to be a coward, Cate.' The warmth in his eyes caressed her. 'Admit we have something special going on here.'

Cate panicked. 'Why? So you can slum it with the country bumpkin?' She was backed into a corner and she knew it. But she wasn't going to admit to anything when she wasn't even sure how she felt. She'd done that with Brett. She wouldn't let herself be seduced into a relationship that should never be.

Noah gripped her arms as if he wanted to shake her. 'Dammit, Cate, can't you see this is no game? When this is all over we need to talk about the rest of our lives.' He took a shaky breath. 'I want you to come back to Sydney with me. We should be together.'

That completely floored her. After all she'd gone through with Brett, here she was, receiving another offer to be a Sydney doctor's wife. Assuming Noah *was* talking marriage. How did she get herself into these situations? He'd expect her to leave everything she loved and held dear, desert her friends and colleagues at her hospital and play happy housewife to Noah in Sydney. After knowing him for less than a week! 'I can't' was all she could manage, but a tiny part inside her was tired of fighting the strength of her feelings for Noah and urged her to listen.

'That's not the answer I wanted,' he said as his arms dropped to his sides. Weak tears hovered behind Cate's eyes. Confusion and indecision wasn't like her and she hated the feeling. Disgusted with herself, Cate needed to get away. She turned on her heel, flung open the door and almost ran down the corridor.

She'd never run from anyone in her life and she hated the thought that Noah had seen her run from him.

Monday 12 March

After a restless night's sleep, Cate woke to bright sunlight. Even Point Lookout had had barely three millilitres of rain. The highway was still cut off and would be for days, but the water was going down in the town centre. Emergency vehicles could even drive through some of the streets.

The schools were still closed and, as expected, Amber was unable to come in. Cate worked the morning shift and tried to vary her routine to avoid seeing Noah. She wanted to sort out her feelings, and she reminded herself how short the time was that they'd known each other. She didn't need to rush. She didn't go down to breakfast and spent more time on the wards than in her office.

Now that the rain had ceased and the upriver levels were falling, the SES had the chance to offer to ferry hospital staff across the river. This allowed those who had worked to have a break and new volunteers to take extra shifts. The rooms in the nurses' home were vacated as staff moved more freely between home and work.

Wryly, Cate slipped a room key into an envelope and wrote Noah's name on it. At least he might get a better night's sleep in a proper bed.

All in all, the hospital appeared less of an outpost in the middle of a huge inland sea. The water covered the land in every direction and houses popped above the mirror-like surface like islands. Incredibly, morale was good.

Except in Cate's office. She wanted to go home, where she couldn't be rushed into something she wasn't sure of. She'd come perilously close to falling in love with Noah Masters, a city-bred, budget-conscious despot who agreed with the downgrading of her hospital—and expected to dominate her personally. She couldn't do it. So why did she still want to give him another chance?

The phone rang and Cate snatched it up with relief. It was Stella Moore. 'Big problems, Cate.' Cate switched modes as Stella went on. 'I've got young Barry Kelso, Jim Kelso's ten-year-old boy, with severe abdominal pain and a white cell count of twenty-six thousand. The resident thinks he's about to rupture his appendix. He needs to go to Theatre pronto and they don't think an airlift would get him to another hospital quick enough.'

Cate frowned. 'But we've already got one theatre going and I don't have more theatre staff on duty—or a surgeon, for that matter. So we're better to fly him out.'

Stella wasn't having it. 'You can be the scrub nurse, and what about Masters? You told me he trained as a surgeon in Sydney. It's not a big operation but if that appendix blows we're going to have one sick kid. He needs attention now.'

Cate thought quickly and weighed up the chances of arranging a second theatre team. If Stella thought time was that critical then it was. 'Get the resident to ring Dr Masters and I'll see if I can find a scout nurse at least. Ring me back with his answer.' She ran her finger down the list of staff on duty and located one of the nurses who usually worked in the theatres doing a shift in the medical ward. She called Stella back and confirmed that surgery would take place.

Cate looked at her watch. 'Prep Barry and send him around to Theatre. I've sent a nurse inside to start a set-up in Theatre two and hopefully Dr Masters will have organised an anaesthetist.' Cate grabbed her pager and pulled the office door shut behind her. She was too tired for this. She hadn't worked in Theatres for twelve months and she wasn't looking forward to working with Noah.

But she needn't have worried. Noah only spoke to her when absolutely necessary. He looked pale and tense and she felt a prick of concern and that niggly feeling again.

The resident was an able assistant, which made Cate's job easier. But she hated the loss of rapport that she'd been used to with Noah.

As she handed the special appendix forceps to Noah they could all see how careful he would have to be. The bloated offender hovered on the brink of exploding as it was tied off and severed from its anchor. A chain reaction of sighs reverberated around the room when the inflamed tube of tissue lay harmlessly in the kidney dish.

Noah, internally at least, allowed himself to relax. It had been even harder than he'd imagined to force himself to operate. When he'd entered the room fully scrubbed, they'd all been waiting for him, and the fact that it had been two years since he'd picked up a scalpel had crashed in on him.

The ghost of Donna had seemed to hover in front of the table until the moment he'd seen Cate's eyes above her mask and then, strangely, his wife had disappeared. But not the nerves.

His surgical skills had returned with gradually increasing ease and he remembered he'd always enjoyed Theatre work until that last time—but he'd still damned Cate for placing him in this position.

In fact, damn Cate for forcing him into a lot of things he hadn't planned on, like falling in love with a woman who didn't love him. And damn himself for being so irrational!

Now that the surgical danger was past he just wanted to get out of there. He couldn't stand the bleakness he saw in Cate's eyes above her mask. He'd only glanced at her once during the operation and that had been his only fumble.

Closure was fast and neat, and before Cate knew it Noah was leaving the theatres. He didn't even look her way as he pushed open the door, and she was surprised how much that hurt.

There was a sudden lessening of tension in the room with his departure and the scout nurse cracked a joke, which the anaesthetist appreciated anyway. Cate just smiled tiredly.

Noah was an accomplished surgeon as well as an excellent diagnostician. And he didn't want to use either skill. She wished she knew why. Still, they were all grateful he'd been there today. Cate tidied the theatres on autopilot. There was so much she didn't know about Noah and some things she'd been wrong about. How far-fetched was the idea that they could make a life together?

When she left the theatres, she turned towards the gardens. She needed fresh air and a moment to gather herself. Apparently, so had Noah.

Cate hesitated, but then he looked up from the bench he was sitting on and stood up.

'Have a seat for a moment, Cate. Please.' The dappled sunlight cast shadows on his face and she thought he looked tired and, strangely, almost defeated.

She didn't say anything, just perched on the end of the bench, and he sat down beside her. She waited for him to speak and the leaves rustled with the light breeze to fill the silence. He didn't look at her when he asked the question so it took her by surprise.

'Tell me about your engagement to Dwyer.' It was the last thing she'd expected him to say.

Cate looked at the backs of her hands and her ringless fingers. There was no reason he shouldn't know. 'My engagement was a mistake. I entered into it for all the wrong reasons and thankfully Brett broke it off when I refused to go to Sydney with him.' She turned her head towards Noah. 'I thought what we had would be enough, along with a family, for me to be happy. But it wouldn't have been.'

She met Noah's eyes. 'Was your marriage what you expected?'

He sighed. 'My wife died two years ago. It was the worst day of my life.' Cate winced at the pain in her heart that statement caused. Of course he'd loved his wife.

Noah went on in a curious flat tone that showed he preferred not to think about these memories. 'The day started normally enough. We had another argument, another nail in the coffin of our two-year marriage. She wanted extensions to the house, and I felt like we'd just got rid of the last lot of builders living in the place.' He grimaced wryly. 'Stupid reasons to fight but our married life seemed to end up like that.'

He sighed. 'We didn't have enough in common and should never have drifted into that marriage. I regret we wasted so much of the time we should have enjoyed before she died.'

He rubbed the palms of his hands on his trousers. 'That day I left for work with arguments unresolved, and I remember feeling as guilty as hell, but I still left. That was the last time I saw her alive.' Cate lay her hand over his and he went on.

'When I got to work, I buried myself in the chaos.' He shook his head. 'Work shouldn't shield you from the responsibilities of your family. I had a responsibility to put my wife first.' Cate could see he'd almost forgotten she was there.

'Donna and our hassles were soon swallowed by the influx of emergencies. When the moment came it was like so many others that I didn't even have a premonition. There were two motor vehicle accident victims—emergency tracheostomy for a child, followed by the resuscitation of a woman in her twenties. We worked on the child first and by the time we started on the woman she was almost dead. That's when I found out it was Donna. She'd driven her car into another one and I have to believe her carelessness was because of the way I left her.'

'You can't know that.' Cate closed her eyes briefly at the pain in his voice and she couldn't help shifting closer to him to offer what comfort she could.

'Donna died and I was the one who lost her.'

Cate opened her mouth to speak but he must have sensed her intention because his eyes implored her to let him finish.

'It all happened so fast. Obviously, if there had been the resources and the time, I would have arranged for another doctor to take over her care, rather than be responsible myself. But there wasn't time. We rushed her to Theatre and we tried frantically to stop the bleeding, but it wasn't good enough.' He shook his head and his voice was flat. 'I wasn't good enough. I still don't know, if she'd been someone I hadn't been emotionally involved with, whether I would have been able to save her, or if it had always been hopeless.'

He looked around at the garden and then back at Cate. 'I've been living in a vacuum for the last two years. The guilt changed me. It wasn't my fault or that of any of the staff on that day. It was the fault of inadequate funds for staffing at major hospitals. But I couldn't allow myself to be placed in that situation again. Someone more influential than a director of casualty needed to address those issues. I decided I would see that it was done—for Donna and others like her.'

He shrugged. 'For the next eighteen months I shut myself off from social contact and concentrated on the fight to ensure that adequate staffing and funding would be directed towards hospitals with greater workloads.'

He shrugged again. 'In administration, I did make progress. When I was seconded to oversee the amalgamation of New South Wales regional hospitals, I felt I had a chance to ensure that funds were diverted to the areas that needed them most.'

He looked down at Cate and smiled at her. 'My crowning conceit was the short time I assumed I would need to sort out these tiny outposts of inefficiency.'

Cate gave a wry chuckle and he raised his brows ruefully.

'I knew it was only a temporary post, but if I managed to initiate the changes that my weak-kneed predecessors hadn't been able to achieve, with those credentials behind me I could make a difference where it really counted. Somewhere it affected a major city so that what had happened to Donna and others would never happen again.'

He smiled down at her. 'I thought I'd start with Riverbank. Thank God I did. I met this gorgeous, war-like creature who stood up for her hospital and showed me that Emergency facilities are needed everywhere—city and country.'

Cate closed her eyes as she felt a rush of understanding, and of relief. Then she ventured a comment. 'Do you still feel you can't practise medicine?'

'Tenacious as always.' Noah looked at her. 'I'm not ruling it out.' He stood up and he stared down at her as if imprinting her face on his memory. 'That's all I wanted to say, Cate. I hope now you can see why I've done what I've done, said what I've said, and that you don't hate me too much.' And then he left her.

She stared at the spot where he'd disappeared through the doors. *Now* what did she think?

She felt like she was on an out-of-control train rushing down a hill and she wasn't sure if she wanted to strap herself in or jump off before it was too late. She needed time out.

She went to see Sylvia and played dolls for half an hour until Gladys came for a brief visit to her daughter.

Cate returned to her office and, of course, the phone was ringing. Lately, she'd almost felt like throwing the thing against the wall. It was definitely time to have a few days off.

It was Amber. After the pleasantries to which Cate lied and said she was fine, Amber dropped her bombshell. 'Brett has offered to babysit Cindy so that I can work Tuesday.'

Cate's eyes widened. 'Do you think he's in a fit state of mind to do that?'

Amber was serious. 'He says it will keep him busy and he wants to.'

'He's always been good with kids,' Cate agreed, and wondered what else was going on. But it was none of her business. Amber knew Brett's failings and he did have good points. Cate just didn't appreciate them and obviously Amber did. It would take some getting used to but the idea wasn't crazy.

Amber rang off and Cate replaced the receiver. She could go home at the end of this shift. Tonight. If she could find someone with a boat to take her. Amber would work tomorrow's shift.

Susie's Pete was more than happy to drop Cate off on his way home after she'd finished work. It all became too easy. She didn't see Noah, although she hesitated outside his office again. She heard his deep voice on the phone and continued past. She wasn't rushing into anything. It was better this way.

When she stepped off Pete's boat not far from the doorstep of her parents' house, it felt strange to be home, almost as if she didn't belong there any more.

Water stretched in every direction and the fences had disappeared beneath the surface. The late afternoon sun had turned the expanse of water to burnished copper and for such destruction it held incredible beauty.

Then her mother came down the verandah steps and enveloped her in a hug. 'Welcome to Forrest Island, darling,' she said with a laugh, and Cate didn't feel so strange.

Cate hugged her back and they moved onto the verandah. Her father rolled out in his wheelchair with Ben behind him and they crowded around Cate. She realised that Ben had grown and there was no doubt he was now a man. She'd have to stop bossing him around, that was for sure. Maybe it was time for him to stay and her to go.

'So, did you organise the hospital the way you wanted to?' Ben teased.

Cate bit her lip. 'Actually, they had a new CEO who did a pretty good job, but tell me all the news from here.'

They pulled her inside to sit around the kitchen table and the Primus stove was on the bench with a billy of tea bubbling away. The power was still off. They discussed the work involved to get the farm back on its feet once the water receded. The farm had lost all the winter hay bales, most of the fences were damaged and the tractor would have to be stripped and rebuilt, but it was all doable.

William shrugged. 'Nature decides when we need a clean-out and we'll salvage what we can and be sorted out in a few months. I'm pleased for your mother that the water didn't come into the house. And it's good to have you both home.'

Later she and Ben had a heart to heart. When she asked why he'd left he met her eyes ruefully. 'Because you always seemed to be able to do everything better than I could. And I couldn't stand it.'

Cate squeezed his shoulder. 'I'm ten years older than you are. You're a man now, Ben, and we're equal. We don't have to compete and I don't even want to. Me not being here for the flood worked well for both of us.'

She gazed out the window at the water stretching into the distance. 'I had to be strong for Dad but I'm tired of being responsible. Who knows? If you stay I might have time for my own life.'

Ben looked at her with new understanding. 'I never thought of you as being tired, but I guess you have carried the farm with Mum for a long time.' He hugged her. 'I want to stay. I've missed the farm but I've learnt new skills that I can use here.'

So everything worked out in the end, Cate thought. Except she didn't know what she wanted any more. Perhaps she just needed her bed. Noah's flood had exhausted her. But it was the man and not the flood that filled her thoughts as she drifted into sleep.

Tuesday 13 March

The sun was rising when Cate woke and she stretched luxuriantly in her own comfortable bed. When she turned her head to look out of her window, the golden pink dawn sent shimmering rays of multicoloured light to reflect off the expanse of water. Great flocks of white and black ibises lined the edge of the water as they enjoyed their breakfast, and cattle jostled for position around the hay bales Ben had left.

Cate hadn't stirred all night and as she sat up she felt refreshed and ready to face the day. And Noah.

He'd been right. She had been a coward. How long was the right length of time if you've met your soul-mate? One week, one month, one year? It didn't matter if you couldn't imagine them leaving. Noah had said he wanted to talk and she should have listened. It wasn't too late to tell him how she felt.

She got up and padded down the hallway before lifting the upstairs phone and dialling his direct number. She could feel the smile on her face, and she wondered if he was still angry with her. A bubble of anticipation simmered away inside as she waited for him to answer. She listened to the phone in his office ringing and then she was cut off.

Disappointed, but not surprised he wasn't there, she dialled the main hospital number and asked the switchboard operator to page him for her.

The receptionist's voice was bored, as if she'd passed this message on several times already. 'Mr Masters is unavailable. A Mr Brown has taken over in the interim but it's Tuesday and he's not in. Would you like to leave a message?'

Cate bit her lip. 'No. Thank you. Goodbye.'

Unavailable? What did that mean? He'd gone? Without a word?

But so did you, she reminded herself, and she sat carefully on the hallway stool and thought about the consequences and what control she had over the situation.

She phoned Amber at work. She needed to tell Noah that she was ready to talk about their future together. Amber would know where he was.

CHAPTER NINE

'CATE, I'M SO glad you rang.' Amber sounded anything but glad and her voice shook. With a flutter of alarm, Cate remembered the last time Amber had been reluctant to pass on news.

Cate tightened her grip on the phone. It had to be something to do with Noah. 'I'm glad you're glad. Now, tell me what's made you sound odd before I start imagining things are even worse than they are.'

Amber's voice wavered. 'It's been terrible. We had a fire in the children's ward last night.' She paused as if to collect herself. 'It was a very close call. One of the patients' older brothers was playing with matches. When the curtains caught alight it took over faster than anyone could believe.'

Cold dread filled Cate's stomach as she imagined the horror of what could have happened, and icy fingers recalled Sylvia with oxygen beside her bed. 'Tell me none of the kids were injured?'

'Sylvia's been treated for smoke inhalation and if Noah hadn't been reading to her, she would have been in real danger of being burnt to death.' There was a catch in Amber's voice and she was still noticeably upset. 'He carried her through a wall of flame that should have killed them both. I know you don't like him, but he's a hero, Cate, and nobody will listen to anything bad about him from now on.'

Cate's face felt wooden. Was that really what people thought? That she didn't even *like* the man she loved? Was that what *Noah* thought? A cold panic settled in her stomach as she struggled to get the situation straight in her head. 'So is Sylvia all right?'

'Yes.' Amber's voice trailed off.

'And Noah? Is he all right?' Cate tasted the blood from her lip and realised how hard she'd bitten it as she waited. *Come on, Amber, stop stalling. I'm going insane here.*

'He will be. He has second-degree burns to his hands but they think there will be no lasting damage.'

Cate sagged against the wall. 'Thank God for that. And smoke inhalation?'

'No. His lungs are fine. It's—it's his eyes.'

Cate felt like screaming. 'What about his eyes, Amber? Where is he?'

'His eyes were damaged and they're not certain if his sight is going to be badly affected. They flew him out last night in one of the helicopters to St Vincent's in Sydney.'

Cate didn't say anything. Couldn't. Just leant against the wall and tried to imagine big, strong, in-control Noah blindfolded and with both hands bandaged.

'Are you there, Cate?' Amber's voice squeaked down the phone, and Cate pushed the pictures from her head and tried to work out a plan of action.

'Yes. I'm here.' She rubbed her brow. 'Listen, Amber. Has Noah's family been notified?' She shook her head at her own lack of knowledge. 'I don't even know if he has family or even a house in Sydney. He must have one or the other. Find out for me. I'll try and get a lift to the hospital and I'll catch up with you then.'

Cate hung up and when she turned around her mother was standing there.

Leanore put her arm around Cate. 'What's happened, darling?'

'A fire at the hospital. Noah is hurt. He's been taken to Sydney and I need to go to him.'

'Noah, the domineering, human logarithm who works out?' She smiled gently at her daughter. 'You're in love with him, aren't you?'

Cate gave a small hiccup of laughter at Leanore's infallible memory and her disorientation settled. Was she in love with Noah? She looked at her mother. 'I guess I must be. I can't bear the thought of him disabled and defenceless. I have to be there for him.'

'Then I'll phone Susie's Pete again while you pack.'

The boat ride was uneventful, and even though the highway was still cut off and the planes were grounded, the trains were still running. Cate was able to secure a seat on the train to Sydney for later that morning.

Amber had found Noah's address but no evidence of next of kin. She'd taken one look at Cate's face and put her hand over her mouth. 'You're in love with him.'

'Yes. And he asked me to go back to Sydney with him.' Cate swallowed the lump in her throat.

Amber was wide-eyed. 'And you said you'd go?'

Cate turned away. 'I'm still here, aren't I? But I was a fool. I'd follow that man anywhere.' She looked at Amber. 'I have to go. I love him and he needs me.'

When Cate stepped down from the train at Central Station in Sydney it was late in the afternoon, coming up to peak-hour traffic and raining. She carried her case easily, a tall, confident woman in jeans and oilskin, her black Squatter Akubra hat resting comfortably on her head.

Some Japanese tourists smiled and waved and took a photo and Cate supposed she had farmer written all over her. She waved back and anxiously strode over to a waiting taxi.

'St Vincent's Hospital, please,' she told the cabby, and sat back to stare out of the window. She tried to glimpse the sky above the buildings that stretched up out of sight. She'd been to Sydney several times as a child to watch her father compete at the Royal Easter Show, but the tall buildings and the multiculturalism, compared to Riverbank, never failed to amaze her.

When the taxi pulled up at the hospital, she paid the driver and alighted at the huge entrance. She supposed there must be bigger hospitals but, compared to Riverbank, it was a monster.

She hurriedly followed the signs to Reception to ask to speak to Noah's doctor. Noah was under the care of an eminent ophthalmologist and Cate was allowed to speak to the great man's registrar.

Half an hour later she was standing outside Noah's room and the determination that had seen her through the long journey suddenly dried up and disappeared.

What if he didn't want to see her? What if there was some other woman in the wings? She should have asked the doctor that, too. Noah's wife had been dead for two years—it was possible there was someone else. Cate lifted her hat and ran her fingers through her hair. Well, standing out here wasn't doing anyone any good. She opened the door, picked up her case and walked in softly.

The curtains over the window were pulled and no one had been in to turn the light on yet. Her first glance had gone to the bed but it was empty. Then she saw that he was sitting in the armchair beside the window. He'd turned his head towards the door when she'd entered. His eyes and both hands were heavily bandaged. Cate's throat closed and her voice choked on the greeting she'd been about to offer. She could have lost him before she'd even appreciated what she'd found. She hoped he still wanted her.

'I'm not really in the mood for an examination right now.' Noah's voice was resigned and more hoarse than usual. She supposed it was from the smoke. The thought of him being hurt was too much and she crossed the room and knelt beside the chair.

She swallowed and tried to moisten her dry mouth. 'Hello, Noah.'

'Cate?' He smelt the rain on her oilskin and the herbal scent that she liked. She'd come. Noah averted his face. He'd been wishing for and dreading the possibility of her arrival. She was the woman he wanted to spend the rest of his life with—but not if he was blind. The thought of vital Cate tied to him as an invalid horrified him.

He hated her to see him like this but it was too late now. Her presence reminded him that if he lost his sight he would lose more than that. 'What are you doing here?' His voice was harsh with the see-sawing scenarios in his mind.

Cate wanted to grab his hand and hold it to her cheek, but his body language repelled any advances. She rested her hand on her own thigh instead as she knelt in front of him. 'I came when I heard. I thought you'd like to know that Sylvia is fine and going home tomorrow. And everyone is calling you a hero.'

He cursed his inability to walk around the room so she couldn't read his face, though he supposed most of his features were bandaged. He grimaced at the memory of the last time he'd tried to pace. That would be all he needed to complete his ignominy—to trip over a stool and fall flat on his face in front of her. The worst thing she could give him would be pity.

Damn this contrary woman! She wouldn't come when he wanted or stay away when she should. 'You could have phoned to tell me all that. There's nothing wrong with my ears.' His voice was cold.

'So you *can* hold a phone, can you?' There was emotion in her voice but he couldn't tell if it was anger or distress. She seemed to be ignoring his bad humour, and perversely that made him more angry.

'Low blow, Cate. No, I can't hold anything.' Not even you, he thought bitterly. When she didn't retaliate he shrugged, settled back in the chair and turned his face towards her. 'So what really brought Country Cate to the big, bad city?'

He heard her shift beside him and thought it was one of the few times he'd managed to discomfit her. Then her beautiful voice came from beside him and he could imagine the way her lips moved and the expressions on her face, and suddenly the picture in his memory made him want to bury his face in her neck and hide. He loved her and that was why he hadn't wanted her to come.

'I came because I needed to know that you're all right.' Her voice was quiet. 'I see that you will live, despite the bandages, but your manners could do with improving.'

Noah couldn't stand much more of this. He had to drive her away before he weakened and begged her to stay. 'Well, I'm glad *one* of us can see. My apologies for not standing up when you came in, but I tend to fall over.' He gave a short, sharp laugh and he felt Cate flinch beside him.

It was better to hurt her now than later. 'Listen, Cate. Go home. I don't want you or need you here. This is my town. I want you to go back where you belong.' There, he'd said it. Now he wished she'd leave him to be miserable in private.

There was a long silence before she said, almost in a whisper, 'I don't believe you, Noah.' Her voice was expressionless and she stood up and walked around the room.

Her footsteps stopped in front of him. 'How about I tell you what I think you should do and you listen?'

Noah snorted. Already she thought she could decide what was best for him. The next thing she'd be wanting to mother him. He'd throw himself out the window first. His voice was soft but brooked no argument. 'Be careful, Cate. Even blind and without the use of my hands, nobody tells me what to do, not even you.'

Unfortunately she didn't sound impressed. 'Well, I don't think you have much choice here, Noah. I've spoken to your doctor. If you have a carer, me, you can be discharged in a couple of days. Of course, that depends if the result is good when the eyepads come off tomorrow. Or you can stay here. Alone. Bored silly. Morose as hell until your hands heal in a week or more.'

Her voice softened. 'Why don't you let me stay so that I can take you home when you're ready? We can spar for the next couple of weeks and I'm sure the time would go more quickly.' She crouched down beside him and laid her hand on his leg. The warmth from her fingers soaked into him and he almost lifted his own hand to lay it over the top of hers until he remembered the bandages. What if his sight was permanently damaged? A picture of her leading him around his own house burst into his brain, like a Technicolor horror movie.

'No way!' The passion in his voice shocked both of them, and Cate sat back unsteadily. He tacked on a belated 'No, thank you' but it didn't change his vehemence.

Cate had known Noah could prove difficult to convince but this was daunting. He was dependent and he'd hate that. She'd even be pleased if he started to boss her around again—as long as he didn't tell her to go. She now knew that Noah was loving, caring, passionate, that he didn't want to dominate her, as she had feared. Sure, he was strong-willed and determined to be master of his own life, but that was just another reason why she loved him. It felt good just saying that to herself. She loved him. It gave her strength.

She smiled to herself. Perhaps this wasn't a good time to tell Noah, though. She squared her shoulders. He should have remembered who he was up against.

She stood and looked around to see where she'd put her case. 'Well, that was a definite answer. I guess I'll just have to keep coming back until you agree.'

Exasperated, Noah clenched his hands, and then swore at the pain he'd caused when he'd squeezed his fingers together. 'For heaven's sake, Cate. Can't you see I don't want you here? I don't want you seeing me like this and I don't want to have you caring for me when I'm weaker than a child.'

Cate wished she could share his pain, but she stopped herself from softening. She was just as determined as he could be, and she had to be strong for him.

'It's *because* of a child you *are* here. Sylvia owes her life to you.'

He snorted. 'So that's why you're here? Because of Sylvia?'

Cate gently poked his leg. 'No. That's not why I'm here, you big oaf, but we'll talk about that later.' Then she stroked his thigh. 'And why the hell can't I look after you? You need daily dressings—I'm a nurse. I'm experienced and quite strong. I can't see a line-up of people waiting for the job,

Noah, so accept my help graciously and get us both out of here. Sooner rather than later.'

There was silence in the room. He didn't answer and she stared at the rain running down the window.

Finally, he leaned his head closer to where he could hear her voice and his weariness was clear. 'You don't get it. Do you? I don't care where I am and I want to be alone.'

Cate bit her lip but refused to be daunted. 'Alone isn't an option, Noah. I'm staying in Sydney for the next few days at least.'

He rose shakily to his feet but there was no waver in the bandaged fist that pointed to the door. 'Out. Please.'

Cate swallowed the lump in her throat as she watched him feel his way to the bed. He looked so helpless and she could only guess how much he must hate that. Her voice was thick with tears and she hoped he didn't notice. Maybe he hadn't because he continued to awkwardly climb onto the bed.

'I'm sorry if I upset you by coming, Noah,' she said. 'But I'm not going home until after you see the doctor tomorrow and we know the prognosis for your sight.' She picked up her hat and her case. 'I'll go and find the YWCA for the night but I'll be back tomorrow. And the next day if you need me. And the next. And we'll face what the doctor says together. Then, if you still want to send me away, I'll go. But I'm not leaving Sydney before I'm ready.'

He didn't answer and he heard the door shut behind her. To torture himself, he pictured her as she'd looked that night they'd played pool. Long legs and blonde hair and her smile. And the way she'd moved around the pool table and the way she'd made him feel. And he couldn't even punch anything because his hands still felt like someone was running a blowtorch over them.

He heard the door open and the click of the light switch. For a moment he thought Cate had come back and, despite himself, he felt his heart skip with excitement. Then the nurse swished in. He recognised her sound and then her voice as he felt an aching disappointment.

'It's Karen, the nurse. How's the pain, Mr Masters?' She was young, he guessed, but she was competent. And she'd put up with his growling. 'I'm just going to lift your hands to see if there's any seepage through the bandage.' She did what she'd said and he let her. She mumbled something he didn't hear.

She rested his hands carefully back on his chest. 'Here's two pain tablets the doctor wants you to have every four hours—but remember, if the pain breaks through, you can have something stronger.' She helped him sit up and popped the tablets into his mouth and then he felt the straw against his mouth. He submitted because last time he'd said he'd do it himself he'd lost the tablets in the bed and had managed to wet his bandaged hands. At least Cate hadn't seen that.

'Thank you,' Noah said. He had a sudden vision of Cate in the streets of unfamiliar Sydney and a great twist of fear speared his gut. What had he been thinking? 'Is it dark outside?'

'Yes, it is. It's still raining, too,' Karen said.

Maybe they could stop her. 'My friend. The one who was here. Has she gone yet?'

'The lady with the black hat…' The nurse stopped and Noah smiled grimly to himself. Of course, he hadn't seen the hat but that was Cate all right. 'I'm sorry,' she said.

'It's okay. She always wears it so I knew who you were talking about. She said she was going to the YWCA. I'd like her to come back if you can catch her, please.'

There was doubt in the nurse's voice. 'She went down in the lift before I came in. And there's a taxi rank outside the hospital. I'll ring Reception but I don't think they'll catch her, Mr Masters.' She hurried out.

Noah sat tense and waiting and more worried about missing Cate than what he was going to say if she came back.

But it was the nurse who came back. 'I'm sorry, Mr Masters. The receptionist did see her get into a taxi. She's a striking woman and hard to miss.'

'Thank you.' He heard the door close after the nurse and Noah slumped back against the pillows. Yes, Cate was a striking woman. And fair game for any creep on the streets. He'd been lying here, feeling sorry for himself, and now Cate was out in the night life of Sydney, alone and country green.

If anything happened to her, it would be a hundred times worse than the position he was in at the moment.

And it would be his fault. How could he have been so stupid not to have foreseen this when she'd said she was going? Pride. Stupid pride.

He disgusted himself. It was just like his reaction after Donna died. He was going to save the world. Sydney hospitals were going to benefit and the smaller, less important ones would be downgraded to pay for it. As long as major centres took acute cases, all needs would be met. But Cate had shown him that the needs and the heart of every hospital were equal.

Emergencies would come and go in every town, regardless of size, and there would never be enough funding to go around. But if his sight returned and he could work, he would protect Riverbank and places like it from people like himself who didn't understand. Maybe not him and Cate together, but he would do it because now he understood.

Tonight all he could do was ask them to ring the Y in an hour and check if Cate had booked in. He couldn't lie here and wonder if she was all right. He'd go insane.

Cate didn't even give the night life of Sydney a second thought. She wasn't stupid. She stepped from the taxi and crossed the footpath to enter the sliding doors of the large YWCA in the centre of Sydney. She'd stayed here with her mother while her dad had slept at the showground all those years ago. It looked pretty similar, though maybe a little more drab, but it was somewhere she felt at ease. Most of the guests were from the country.

She registered at the desk and ordered a take-away meal from the restaurant to eat in her room.

She had heard the way Noah had said her name when she'd first gone into his hospital room. There was no doubting he'd been pleased before he'd thought about it. Then his stupid pride had stood in the way. But who was she to talk? When she thought of the opportunities she'd wasted at the hospital she was no better.

She had to believe she could beat his reluctance to have her around.

CHAPTER TEN

Wednesday 14 March

THE NEXT MORNING, Noah didn't hear Cate open the door because he was swearing at a piece of toast that kept slipping out of his bandaged hands.

'That's no way to talk to your breakfast. Let me cut it for you.' Her voice floated across the room and the tension in his neck disappeared. He hadn't driven her away. He couldn't feel sorry. He needed her today when the doctor came.

He dropped the toast again and the crumbs went down his shirt. But he didn't care. Thank God she was safe.

Of course she was safe. She was probably capable of throwing a hog tie on any mugger that had the audacity to accost her. His Cate.

'I'm sure, if you'd waited, someone would have come in to help you.' She had her nursing supervisor voice on now and it brought back good memories of the last week. Anything to take his mind off the doctor's visit this morning.

'Well, don't just stand there—butter the thing, please! I hate dry toast.' He gave a little chuckle and Cate felt a wave of relief wash over her. She buttered and cut the toast and brushed his lip with a piece. 'Your toast, sir.'

Noah opened his mouth and she popped it in. While he chewed, he tried to picture what she was wearing. But it really didn't matter. She'd look wonderful no matter what. He heard her pour the tea and then smelt the tealeaves. Everything took time to happen when he couldn't do it himself. Blindness meant compulsory listening and he could even hear Cate breathe.

She was very good at feeding him. 'Thank you, slave,' he teased. 'I think you should be feeding me grapes.'

'You're welcome, Noah.' She squeezed his wrist above the bandages. 'Of course I couldn't stay away when I knew I could have you in my power for a change.'

He rested back against the pillows. 'Is that so?' Enjoy it, then, because it's not going to last long, no matter what happens today.'

'We'll see,' she said. She straightened his pillow and a drift of her scent stayed behind on the pillowcase.

Then Noah heard the doctor's voice outside the room and he felt his skin go cold. All amusement disappeared. The time had come to find out just how visually impaired he was going to be. Cate took the breakfast tray away and rested her hand briefly on his leg. He was glad of the warmth and her support now, and he tried not to think about having to send her away if the prognosis was poor.

The door opened and the doctor came in. Cate took her hand from Noah's leg and stepped back from the bed, out of the way.

The doctor nodded to her on his way to his patient. 'Morning, Mr Masters. Morning, young lady.'

Cate could see that Noah wasn't up to pleasantries. His comment showed everyone else. 'Morning. Get it over with, please,' he growled, but the doctor seemed to understand.

'Impatient?' The specialist unwrapped the bandage from around Noah's head. 'Well, I can't say I blame you.' He looked at the sunlight streaming in the window and motioned to the nurse to pull the blinds. The room darkened considerably. 'As I said yesterday, the tests came back as positive news so I'm expecting a lot more vision than we originally hoped for.'

Cate saw Noah tighten his bandaged fists against his chest and she knew it must be hurting his damaged fingers. She could understand why he did it. Anything to distract himself. They all held their breath as the pads were lifted away from Noah's eyes. Noah kept them closed and Cate thought the suspense was going to make her sick.

She noted the redness from a heat sear across the upper half of Noah's face and the skin was peeling around his eyes. To Cate, it looked like the facial burns were mostly first degree, but his beautiful eyelashes and straight black brows were nearly all gone. She mentally shrugged. They'd grow back.

The jolliness was gone from the specialist's voice. 'I'll dab some saline over your eyelids to unstick them now.' He wiped both Noah's eyes carefully with special wet pads. 'All right, Mr Masters. Open your eyes.'

Tentatively, with jerky little movements, Noah stretched open his eyelids. It was too bright initially after the total dark under the bandages, and everything was wavy. He opened and shut his eyes gingerly a few times and slowly figures came into focus in the dark room. He saw the doctor for the first time, nothing like Noah had imagined from his hearty Swedish voice, and then he saw the nurse.

He couldn't see Cate. He turned his head and there she was against the wall, as beautiful as ever. Thank God. He sagged back in the pillows and closed his eyes. He could see.

'Well?' The doctor was leaning closer and with machiavellian nastiness he shone a small torch that made Noah flinch away. 'So they work!' He wrote on a notepad. 'How's the focus?'

Noah swore he would improve his own bedside manner if he ever worked as a doctor again. 'It's slow but it works.'

The doctor stepped back with a satisfied smile. 'Wear dark glasses for two weeks, and instil drops four times a day—the sister will give you the regime and a script to take home when you go.' He glanced at Noah's bandaged hands. 'These aren't my department. The eyes can go home tomorrow and come back to see me in four days for final tests. Good morning, to everyone.' And he departed. The nurse followed soon after and Noah and Cate were left alone.

Noah sighed and closed his eyes. He'd been incredibly lucky. He felt the bed shift as she hitched her hip on the edge. He remembered that hip. The back of his bandaged hand went down of its own accord and checked she was there.

She laughed and he loved the sound. 'Not only are you demanding but you're groping this morning. Have you decided it's not a bad thing I'm here now that your sight is restored?'

'I've decided that if my sight is as good as they expect, it might not be so bad to have you around and be my personal nurse.' He elbowed her gently. 'But I'm still the boss.'

'Really, Dr Masters?' She tapped his cheek with her finger. 'Open.' She put another piece of toast into his mouth.

Noah chewed and couldn't believe how light-hearted he felt. He felt as high as a kite. The next couple of days would be a pain but he could plan for after that.

He wasn't going to be blind and he could dare to dream of Cate again. The strain had been enormous and suddenly he was overwhelmingly tired. His eyelids grew heavy. It would all take time, he thought as he drifted off to sleep.

When Noah woke it was quite dark in the room with the blinds pulled, and his stomach told him it was well after lunch. Cate must have gone but he didn't doubt that she'd be back. By the time he'd struggled with his jocks in the adjoining bathroom, cleaned his teeth with the toothbrush between his wrists and stared at his two-day growth and hairless eyes, he was feeling depressed.

How on earth had he decided it was a good thing for Cate to see him like this?

Where was Cate? Noah walked through to his room and there she was, asleep like a gorgeous lioness in the chair by the window. There had been a time he'd thought he would never see anyone's face again, and it was Cate's he would have missed the most.

So should he send her away until he was normal again or should he live life to the full from the first possible moment?

Noah sat on the edge of the bed and stared at her. He brushed the blonde hair back off her forehead with his wrist and it felt like silk on his skin. He'd wanted to do that since he'd met her. She stirred and stretched, like the jungle cat she was, as she sleepily opened her eyes. 'Hello, beautiful,' he said. He hoped she wasn't repulsed by the face he'd just seen in the mirror.

'Hello, Noah.' And she smiled up at him. He felt the weight lift from his shoulders. Cate stood up and came across to hug him. She couldn't believe how much she loved this man and she thanked God silently that Noah had survived the fire. She shivered and he looked down at her in concern.

'You OK?' He dropped a kiss on her forehead and she snuggled in tightly against him for a moment to gather herself. He smoothed her hair again.

'I'll be fine. I was so frightened when I heard you were hurt.'

He touched her lips with his bandaged hand to silence her when she went to speak again. He needed to do this now before something else went wrong. 'Shh. I need to say something.'

He leant across and kissed her gently on the lips. She stared up at him solemnly and it was all he could do not to kiss her again. But he knew he wouldn't stop if he started.

He drew a deep breath. It was time to be brave. 'Thank you for being here today. I need to tell you. I love you, Cate. I'll always love you. When I'm well again, will you marry me?'

Cate looked at Noah, her man, her soul-mate, and the love that shone from his eyes lifted any shadows of doubt from her mind. 'I'd follow you anywhere,' she said. 'I must have known instinctively that the respect and love I saw in my own home were missing from my relationship with Brett, but it's not like that with you. I love you, Noah. And I can't wait to be your wife.' She kissed him this time. 'And we'll have a wonderful life.'

They sealed their plans in a deeper kiss and Cate found the home that was hers whenever she was with Noah.

Later, when the room had righted and she lay comfortably against his shoulder high up on the hospital bed, she had a question. 'Where will we live? Do you have a house in Sydney?'

He kissed her again. 'I do but we'll sell it. I didn't choose the house. We could go back to Riverbank. It seems a great place to bring children up.' He watched her eyes light up and he knew he'd been blessed to find her. 'But I'm not a farmer, Cate,' he warned.

She laughed with delight. 'A house in town will be fine. I love you, Noah.'

CHAPTER ELEVEN

THREE MONTHS LATER the wedding was the social event of the year in Riverbank. The bride arrived in a horse-drawn carriage, accompanied by Amber and two flower-girls, Cindy and Sylvia.

When Cate entered the church beside her father's wheelchair, Noah didn't see the full church or the glorious flowers or even hear the music. His whole being was focused on this woman who matched him in every way. She looked like a queen—his queen—as she swayed regally towards him in a plain white sheath and a tiny flower-encrusted veil. He could see her beautiful lips curve beneath the edge of the veil and his fingers flexed in anticipation for when he would hold her hand in his and never let her go.

When their vows were complete, the church bells pealed over the valley. In shops and streets and houses, people smiled at the sound because most of the townsfolk knew who was being married today.

When Noah left the church with his new bride on his arm he understood that he was part of a larger family than he had bargained for. The love and welcome from Cate's mother and father and brother warmed a place in his heart that had been cold for too long. Noah smiled and nodded at the people he knew, like old Mrs Gorse. Mr and Mrs Ellis were there and even Paul the SES boat driver. Noah could watch and almost smile as Cate kissed Brett and his wife, Amber. Everywhere people knew his Cate and welcomed him.

At the reception, the ladies from the church had catered for a picnic for two hundred people. Tables were laid under the shade sails in front of Noah's and Cate's big house on the river and the country band played into the night.

Later, down on the jetty, in a patch of silver moonlight, Noah and Cate were oblivious to the music that drifted from the house. Held in Noah's strong arms, Cate had found her dream, and the reality of Noah's love was more beautiful than she could have hoped for. Beneath their feet, the river flowed gently past into the night and would do so every night to come.

'Welcome to your new home, Cate.' Noah's breath drifted across her cheek and she smiled.

'I noticed that our house has two stories—is that in case of floods, Dr Masters?'

'No. That's to hold all our children.' And his lips lowered to hers with the promise of a wonderful love that they would share for the rest of their lives.

* * * * *

A Very Single Midwife

CHAPTER ONE

Friday

THE BIRTHING SUITE was quiet as Bella Wilson refilled the cup for Abbey to scoop ice chips as she needed.

Bella glanced across at her brother-in-law, Rohan, as he gently stroked his wife's back. Arched protectively around her on a low chair, his legs were either side of Abbey's thighs as she perched upright on the big blue ball. She rocked and moaned softly with the strength of the contractions and Rohan winced in sympathy with the sound.

Her sister's time was near. 'I'll ring Scott,' Bella whispered, and Rohan nodded. Nobody else seemed to notice the tremor in Bella's voice as she said it.

Although a very experienced midwife, Bella had chosen to be an onlooker at the time of birth rather than the person responsible for the safe arrival of the new Roberts baby. She wanted to see Abbey's face, and Rohan's, as her niece or nephew was born. She wanted to be a part of the whole experience and not just the mechanics of the birth. Scott should be the acchouchier.

Bella couldn't think of anyone she trusted more than Scott Rainford, Gladstone Hospital's Director of Obstetrics, to bring a baby into the world. Despite the fact there was still awkwardness between them, at least on Bella's side.

When she returned from the phone, Abbey's moans were a little louder and Bella went across to lay her hand on her sister's shoulder. 'It's OK, you're doing beautifully, nearly there.'

Abbey opened her eyes and stared at Bella as if to ground herself.

'I think I want to push.'

Bella nodded. 'Do what your body tells you to do.' Both women, as midwives, smiled at the litany and then Abbey's eyes widened as the feeling became stronger.

Rohan sat up straighter as he felt his wife tense with the change in sensation. 'You OK, sweetheart?'

Abbey nodded and Rohan rested his hands on her shoulders as if to transfer energy from his body into hers as she began second stage. 'I love you, Abbey,' he said, and kissed her shoulder.

Bella turned away. The strength of the bond between Abbey and Rohan brought tears to her eyes. She'd thought she had her chance at being a part of someone like that once, but now she believed that type of relationship wasn't for her. She could be strong on her own.

She heard the door open and there he was. The man who had once held her heart in his hands and let it go. Bella forced herself to meet Scott's eyes and their glances clashed before she turned back to Abbey.

The next contraction would be here soon and the birth was very close. She switched off all thoughts of Scott. 'Do you want the birth stool or are you going to move to the bed at the last minute, Abbey?' Bella hovered to help her sister when she'd made her choice.

'I'll sit on the bed, so I don't have to move afterwards.'

Bella nodded as she strained to hear Abbey's answer and lifted the beanbag onto the bed in readiness.

After the next pain, Abbey stood up and Bella and Rohan helped her onto the bed until she was sitting upright with her hands behind her knees. The next pain came swiftly and the baby's thatch of dark hair hovered at the entrance to the outside world before disappearing again.

'The baby took a look and went back,' Scott whispered, and they all smiled, though Abbey's smile was tired.

'I don't know how many times I've heard you say that over the years...' Her voice strengthened. 'Just didn't think I'd ever hear you say it to me.'

'One more push, Abbey.' Scott had always felt enormous admiration for the woman who had been midwife in charge until today, but during this labour Abbey had been inspiring with her belief in natural birth and her quiet acceptance of what her body required her to do.

'Here comes your baby,' Scott said quietly, and his heart constricted as the newborn eased into his hands as if the infant had finally decided it was time to arrive. Scott glanced at the clock as he gently lifted Abbey's baby up onto her stomach. 'Ten past three born. Wonderful, Abbey.'

A birth never failed to uplift him but when he looked at Bella and the joy in her face from this moment, it was as if the dam broke and his own loss overwhelmed him. He acknowledged the two things he'd most wished for in life would never be his. The woman he loved and the son he'd never met.

Scott heard Rohan let out a heartfelt sigh of relief that echoed around the room and it snapped him back into focus. As his medical partner and friend, Rohan had delivered hundreds of babies himself, but Scott could see that none had drained his friend like this.

'We have a son, Abbey.' Rohan's voice was thick with tears. His fingers stroked Abbey's cheek as if he still couldn't believe he'd been so blessed, and Abbey smiled up with a love and maternal joy that, despite its intimacy, shone to the darkest corners of the room.

Excluded, Scott had to look away as she decreed, 'We'll call him Lachlan.'

Bella smiled at the name Abbey had always fancied. There was something about that private glance shared between husband and wife that made Bella look at Scott, and for once the usually enigmatic Dr Rainford couldn't hide his bleakness.

Bella's heart squeezed at the look of raw pain in Scott's face, but then it was gone. He leaned forward to congratulate the parents and Bella was left with unanswered questions.

Questions for later, Bella thought as she kissed her sister, brother-in-law and precious dark-haired nephew, and returned to what she should be doing as the new midwife in charge. Euphoria at the safe arrival of Lachlan lightened her step as she bustled around and cleared the room of unneeded equipment. Abbey and Rohan deserved private time to share those precious early moments with their son and she would make sure it happened.

A fragment of her concentration tussled with possible reasons for Scott's depression as she pushed the green-draped trolley into the sluice room. Then she heard the sound of the doctor's footsteps as he followed her out of the delivery suite, and her fingers stilled.

'So you're the new unit manager now that Abbey has given birth earlier than anticipated?' Scott acknowledged the change in management but he didn't like it. He hadn't thought it through when he'd been told that Abbey's just-as-well-qualified sister would replace his midwife colleague during her maternity leave.

This last month he'd erected a wall between himself and Bella but now she was going to be in his face a lot more than he'd realised. Scott couldn't prevent the mocking note in his voice that he'd found was his only defence against this woman.

She turned to stare at him and shrugged delicately, and Scott could see the last glimmer of happy tears in her glorious lilac eyes. His heart contracted.

After yesterday's discovery of his full-grown son, today's birth was even more poignant. Perhaps if he hadn't pushed Bella away all those years ago he too would have had the opportunity to watch a son grow to a man. But having been proved a bad husband once, he'd chosen to let the young Bella go.

Bella had been eighteen and a virgin, to his thirty and divorced, and he'd felt a hundred. Freshly qualified in obstetrics, and new to town, he'd been so much under her spell he'd had to take drastic steps to protect her. He'd grown to love and respect Bella too much to risk her suffering the same pain he'd endured by marrying someone so much older than himself.

And today, to see Rohan and Abbey with everything that he desired, their happiness made the bleakness inside him crystallise into shards of pain that hardened on the outside. He felt old, which was the reason he'd never pursued the vibrant and beautiful Bella in the first place. Bella in his life, even a small amount, was a concept he needed to think about, something he couldn't do when faced with her.

She'd be hard to avoid now.

Bella's voice brought him back to the present and he'd missed the first part of her sentence.

'It was only a matter of days before Abbey was going on maternity leave anyway,' Bella said. 'Do you have a problem with me as Unit Manager, Scott?'

Her voice had always been gentle but lately he realised there was an underlying vein of inner strength that he'd never associated with Bella. He looked at her, slim and straight, and the top of her flame-red bun only came up to his throat—right where her presence caught him. He swallowed to clear away the tightness.

He'd no idea how he was going to cope seeing her every week day on the ward when all he wanted to do was carry her off to his house and lock her away from the big bad world that had tried to crush her.

Today's feelings, along with the hurt of realising his ex-wife had kept his son from him all these years, promised some painful hours of reflection in the coming weeks.

Too easily, he fell into his old defence mechanism of superiority until he could sort out this new relationship he'd have to deal with. 'I think you've taken on too much this time, Bella,' he said. 'Five days a week running the clinical and administrative side of the ward is different to working part time as the floating midwife.'

'Abbey managed it!' Bella sounded less confident than she should have but her older sister had always seemed to take responsibility in her stride.

'Abbey's an experienced manager,' he said, and made his escape before the emotion on her face and the emotions of the afternoon made him say something else he'd regret.

Bella stared after him and bit her lip. The man was insufferable, always had been, and she didn't know how Abbey had put up with him all these years.

Scott had been giving her, Bella, a difficult time since she'd started part-time orientation on the ward the previous month but it had never been as blatant as today. He'd almost vibrated with some inner rage and Bella hoped she was out of range when the eruption occurred.

He must be at least forty-two now, she supposed, though he looked much younger and as annoyingly handsome as he'd always been. Bella winced at the memory of the teenage infatuation she'd had for the gorgeous young doctor and, more painfully, his disclosure of her crush to Abbey after their mother had died. Even now, when she saw him, he flustered her just being there.

She really had been useless at love. There had been Scott, when she'd been eighteen. He'd seemed to return her feelings for an idyllic few months until she'd been mortified by his sudden change of heart.

Nursing had carried her through that rejection until she'd completed her midwifery.

Then she'd been pursued and won by the obstetrician she'd worked with in the birthing centre in Sydney. After three years of vague promises by Jason, he'd eventually admitted he'd been unfaithful from the start of their relationship and she'd run home. She certainly could pick them.

Finally, last year, she'd been drugged and the victim of a loathsome sexual attack by a vengeful old flame of Abbey's, which had almost destroyed the last vestiges of her self-worth. She'd wished the drug he'd slipped her had erased her memory of the attack and not just the strength to fight him off. That attack had been hard to come to terms with but out of the ashes of that experience had come her rebirth.

Somehow she'd conquered her fear and helped extricate them all when her attacker had returned to destroy Abbey. Dropping a plant pot on someone's head from upstairs didn't make Bella a heroine but it had had the desired effect! When the police had taken the man, Harrows, away, she'd felt the balance of power swing back her way.

She'd felt cleansed of the irrational but sapping guilt the attack had left her with. Instead of the usual scenario of big sister Abbey saving Bella—something Abbey had always done—Bella had saved Abbey! There was salvation in that thought and Bella had used it to drive herself to a new life.

She'd never be the champion her sister was, but she was learning to hold her own. And she would refuse to rely on a man for her happiness. So what Scott Rainford thought of her shouldn't matter.

Bella kicked a linen bag and the automatic kick-boxing hand posture that went with the kick made her laugh at herself. Her year of self-defence classes had turned out to be an absorbing challenge. She'd achieved many things in the last twelve months and Scott Rainford was not going to undermine her success with his bitterness.

She used that thought to insulate herself against the pricking pain she shouldn't be feeling from mere words. Furiously she cleaned the instruments and wiped the trolley down. He had no idea what she was capable of.

When Bella unlocked her front door it seemed a year since she'd left the house that morning. As she put down her bag, she realised that with all the excitement of Lachlan's arrival she'd forgotten she had to drive the youth bus tonight.

She stifled a sigh and hung her house keys on the hallstand. The chortling sound of a baby's laugh made her smile as she wandered into the kitchen.

'Your meal is on the stove, Bella.' Vivie, Bella's nineteen-year-old housekeeper, looked up from the last spoonful of vegetables she was trying to coax into her son's mouth. She grinned at Bella's appreciate sniff. 'I made your favourite. Pumpkin and macadamia soup. And congratulations on being an auntie.'

Bella ruffled the baby's hair and the little boy gurgled up at her. 'Thank you, Vivie. You're a treasure. I've just remembered I have two hours before my first bus trip. Do you want to slip up to see Abbey and baby Lachlan while I mind young Ro?'

Vivie's baby had been named after Abbey's husband, Rohan. They all shortened the baby's name to prevent confusion. Bella lifted the lid on the pot and closed her eyes as the soup's aroma filled the room. 'You should be a chef, Vivie. Your meals are fabulous.'

Vivie shook her head vehemently. 'I'm happy here, thank you. And I'd love to see Abbey and the baby for a few minutes if I could.' Vivie put the spoon down and wiped her son's mouth with his bib before she lifted him out and onto his play mat in the corner. 'We saw Rohan. He dropped in to see Aunt Sophie after he left the hospital. He looked pretty blown away by being a father.'

Bella smiled as she ladled soup into a bowl Vivie had left out for her. Rohan had a soft spot for Bella's elderly maiden aunt who resided in the front rooms of Bella's big house. An avid punter, Aunt Sophie's world revolved around her television set and penny-gambling on horse races via telephone.

'I'll take Aunt Sophie over to see them when they come home. She hates going out.' Bella smiled as she imagined her aunt's visit to Abbey and her baby in a few days. 'Who's home?'

Bella's family home had grown into a self-sufficient refuge for young women in crisis, something Abbey had unintentionally started before she'd moved next door with her new husband. Bella had expanded that aim when she'd taken over the house.

Vivie ticked off the people on her fingers. 'Melissa is still here, but she wants to go with you in the bus to the bowling club and needs to talk to you about a friend who wants to board.'

Bella looked up and mentally reviewed the rooms. There were three left. 'We'll see.'

Vivie nodded and went on. 'Lisa is still feeling unwell from morning sickness and is lying down, and Aunt Sophie said she's staying in her rooms until the last race. The twins have gone out but they did bring the washing in and put it away before they went.' She pushed the high chair back against the wall.

'Oh, and Dr Rainford rang and said he wanted to come on the bus with you tonight.'

The spoonful of soup on the way to Bella's mouth stopped in mid-air. 'Now, how the heck did he find out I was driving tonight?'

Vivie looked uncomfortable. 'He said he'd ring back when you got home and I mentioned you'd be in and out after seven. And it went on from there. Sorry.'

Bella put the untouched spoon back into the bowl and forced a smile. 'No problem. You go and see Abbey. Young Ro and I will stay here until you get back, then I'll get organised.'

Vivie smiled her thanks and dashed off to change. Bella lifted the spoon again. She did not understand how Scott Rainford thought he could barge into her private life uninvited. Why would he want to when he was obviously unhappy about her presence in his professional orbit?

It was five to seven and Bella had backed the cumbersome bus out of the garage into the driveway to allow her first passenger to board.

Melissa, at eighteen, was thirty-four weeks pregnant, and her yellow chenille trousers made Bella blink. Melissa's wrists jangled every time she moved her hands and her body piercing was nothing short of incredible. A sweet-natured girl, Melissa had been badly let down by the boyfriend she was still in love with.

'Vivie says you had something to ask me?' Bella smiled to convey that she was listening and waited for Melissa to explain. The girl drew a deep breath, as if preparing for the worst, and Bella looked back at her puzzled. 'Why so worried? I've never refused anyone in trouble, have I?'

'It's just that this is different. But not different! Well, it is different but shouldn't be.'

Bella blinked. 'Run that by me again.'

'My friend…' Melissa wrung her hands and the jewellery rattled and pinged with the movement '…is staying at the pub and it's expensive, and she's a really nice person. I guess, like me, the earrings and tattoos don't help people like them.'

'So you'd like your friend to stay at Chisholm Road until she finds somewhere to live. Is that right?'

Melissa twisted her hands again. 'Sort of. But different.'

Bella sighed. 'We're back to different. Different shouldn't be a problem.' She narrowed her eyes. 'Is she not pregnant, doesn't speak English, has two heads?'

'She's a he.' Melissa shot a glance at Bella and rushed on. 'His name's Blake, and he really is a sweetie.'

Bella stifled another sigh. She knew this had to come up some time. 'How old is your Blake?'

Melissa shook her head. 'He's not my Blake. I still love Thomas.' Her head drooped. 'Even though he doesn't love me.' After a few moments of wishful thinking Melissa straightened her neck. 'But Blake is twenty and my very best friend. He hasn't been in town long but he stood up for me when some people were giving me a hard time and we've spent heaps of time together since. And I said I'd ask if he could stay. Maybe he could work around the yard or something. He said he would.'

Bella smiled at the girl in the rear-view mirror and reached across to shut the door. 'We'll see. We'd need a house meeting. I'm not promising anything.' She started the engine and the radio came on with the ignition and gave her a respite from further discussion. She needed to think about this.

At least she didn't have to deal with Scott Rainford while she worked it out. Bella wasn't sure whether she was relieved that Scott hadn't come or annoyed that she'd wasted time deciding what to wear. Relief won.

Unfortunately, just as she pushed in the clutch, his car drew up at the end of the driveway. Bella sighed and opened the passenger door again.

Darn. She could have done without this. Her pulse skipped and she closed her eyes for a second to steady her nerves.

He was dressed casually in dark jeans and a yellow polo shirt that sat snugly across his broad shoulders and deep chest. To Bella, he looked disturbingly handsome and charged with a virility that she could more easily ignore at work—but not tonight. He seemed bigger and stronger as he loomed over her seat and he made her aware of how slight she was compared to him.

'Were you leaving without me, Bella?' Scott had climbed the two steps into the bus and chosen the front seat directly next to her so that every time she turned her head she could see him. Bella wrinkled her brow. A faint drift of his expensive aftershave floated towards her and she resisted the temptation to breathe in more deeply. She had more sense than to lean towards self-destruction.

An enigmatic smile sat on his chiselled lips and his face was inscrutable. Bella reminded herself it was a waste of time to wonder what went on behind those cool green eyes of his. She never had been able to tell.

Maintain composure. Be assertive. She raised her voice over the radio. 'I wasn't waiting, Dr Rainford. Luckily you weren't late.' Bella put the vehicle smoothly into gear and pulled out into the street.

'You handle the bus well.' There wasn't any condescension in his voice but his comment annoyed Bella anyway. She turned the radio up a little more.

'Did you think I wouldn't?' she enquired sweetly as she negotiated a roundabout without touching the central island. She glanced across at his face and he was smiling. Now what was funny?

The laughter was in his voice. 'So, where are we going first?'

Bella sighed and turned the radio down a little. There was no use gaining a headache just to annoy Scott.

'It's a set route and we start at the south side of town and visit the clubs and pubs until we end up back where we started. First stop is Southside Bowling Club. Melissa is getting out there.'

Bella shut her mouth with a snap. Until someone got on, she would be alone with Scott as they drove around. And this was the quietest time of the night. Great.

'Why are you here anyway?' She listened to her own voice and the belligerence in it made her bite her lip. There was no excuse for bad manners. 'I'm sorry. That came out poorly.'

'Please, don't apologise. That's one of the reasons I'm here.' His words surprised Bella so much she reached over and turned off the radio.

Scott's smile was wry at the sudden silence in the vehicle and from the corner of her eye she saw him rub the back of his neck. So the great Dr Rainford was uncomfortable. Bella wasn't sure how that made her feel but it was good to know he wasn't one hundred per cent comfortable all the time.

Scott held his silence as they drew up to the bowling club and Bella flicked on the indicator and steered the minibus under the entrance portico. The door hissed open at the first stop and Melissa swayed belly-first down the aisle to carefully descend the steps. She turned back at the bottom step.

'You will think about it, won't you, Bella?' Bella nodded and the girl went on her way. The expression on Scott's face as he watched her leave made Bella smile.

When Melissa was out of earshot, he looked at Bella. 'Melissa makes me think of that Adam Harvey song about the girl who fell face first into the fishing-tackle box.'

'You're showing your age,' she said, and she saw him wince.

'That's because I'm old.'

The humour of the reply didn't quite come off and Bella shot him a look and changed the subject. 'So what was this about you apologising?'

His expression softened and Bella was surprised how good that made her feel. Danger lights flashed. She should not feel anything. Scott's hang-ups were no concern of hers.

He turned to face her fully. 'I'm not good at apologies so bear with me.' He took a deep melodramatic breath and his face was solemn.

'Bella Wilson, I…' he placed his hand over his heart with exaggerated sincerity '...Scott Rainford, apologise for any slur or aspersions I may have cast on your ability to run Gladstone Maternity Ward. It was uncalled for and inexcusable and not a true indication of my faith in your ability. Please, forgive me.'

Then he smiled. Bella looked into his eyes and it happened again. The world shifted and she knew he understood everything about her—just like that day twelve years ago when she'd fallen in love with him.

But she wasn't going there. She didn't need this. Bella fumbled with the gearstick until she found a gear and jerkily pulled away from the club as if to drive away would leave the words behind. She'd thought she'd sigh with relief when Scott stopped baiting her but now that he seemed so warmly approving she felt more off balance.

Even while she battled with the cumbersome bus in traffic, the awareness of Scott beside her didn't go away. The air in the bus seemed charged and no matter how much Bella berated herself for the resurgence of all those emotions she'd fought against as a teenager, she couldn't deny it—Scott's presence excited her.

Excited her in a way the three years with the permanently unfaithful Jason had never done. But excitement passed, she reminded herself, and she wasn't stupid enough to fall for that story again.

'Apology accepted,' she said quietly, and avoided his eyes.

Thankfully, the next stop saw two young women and a pimply youth board the bus and their friendly chatter helped distance the sensation that Bella was being drawn, inexorably, towards a fatal attraction she'd later regret. Because it wasn't going to happen!

Scott had also been quiet since that unmistakable awareness had passed between them. Bella had no idea of his thoughts. Perhaps he regretted he'd come tonight. Maybe now he'd apologised he'd go home after the run. She could only hope.

Bella dropped the three passengers at a noisy pub and the bus was empty again. 'After the next stop, I head home for nearly an hour before I do it all again.' She glanced at Scott and his eyes seemed to warm her from across the aisle. Her imagination was running away with her. Scott wouldn't look at her like that.

'It gets busier later in the evening.' Her voice cracked as she strove for normality and she wished he'd say something. Anything to break this mounting awareness that had come from nowhere and seemed to drain the strength from her body. She pulled into the last stop and two young blonde women, obviously twins, waved gaily as they clambered up the steps.

'Hi, Bella.' They looked at Scott curiously. 'Hello, Dr Rainford,' they chorused as they took their seats. Trish and Trina were just seventeen and Bella was pleased to see them heading home. Their mother was in hospital for a major operation and the girls had come to stay with Bella while she was away rather than with their stepfather whom they didn't get on with.

Bella glanced into the rear vision mirror. 'You ladies home for the night now?' The girls nodded.

Scott observed the interplay between Bella and the girls. She treated them with respect and yet he could see that she had a natural authority that came across despite the gentleness of her voice.

Authority was something he hadn't associated with Bella. This afternoon, after rational thought, he'd realised how badly he'd behaved to belittle Bella's ability to run the ward. If she'd been an unknown replacement for Abbey's job he would never have dreamed of undermining the new NUM's confidence. Just because he had a problem looking at Bella dispassionately he had no right to take it out on her. He'd always believed in fair play and in retrospect he'd been dismayed at his behaviour. They needed to let go of their past and establish a good professional friendship.

Then he'd found out Bella was driving the youth bus and the idea of her safety weighed on him as well. And a little aching curiosity about how Bella coped with young adults—people the same age as his son—something he didn't associate with beautiful but fragile Bella. Something he didn't associate with himself. He shelved those thoughts for later. It was enough trying to remain rational around her.

Tonight had seemed a good opportunity to apologise for his lack of support at her promotion and see her in action. The trouble was, when he let his barriers down, the depth of his attraction to her swamped him like it had now and his plan of just being friends became difficult to stick to.

The bus pulled up at Bella's house more sharply than expected and everyone jerked in their seats. 'Sorry,' Bella murmured as she opened the door. The twins giggled as they waved goodbye.

Bella glanced at Scott. 'Are you on call for the ward?' Scott nodded and patted his pager and Bella raised her eyebrows. 'What were you going to do if your pager went off and they needed you in Maternity?'

'I was hoping the bus driver would drop me off. It's a small town.'

Bella smiled and his own lips curved. Hell, she was beautiful. She was still talking and he tried to concentrate.

'Are you going home now or were you planning to wait for the next run in an hour?'

Waiting with Bella would be exquisite torture but, now he realised there was a chance she'd be alone in the bus to pick up strange young people, he'd never settle at home. 'I'll wait.'

Bella glanced at him and he couldn't tell her thoughts from her noncommittal voice. 'Were you planning on coming on all the trips tonight?'

He avoided her eyes. 'I don't like the idea of you being here on your own.' He stood and watched her squeeze out from behind the wheel and waited for her to go past him before following her out. Her no-nonsense jeans hugged her tiny waist and stretched over the subtle curve of her buttocks and down her long legs like a second skin as she descended the steps. Scott closed his eyes.

At work he could control the direction of his thoughts. But tonight, after the decision he'd made today to get used to Bella being in his life again, it was much harder to stay detached.

In the old boarding-house-cum-family home it was quieter than he'd expected for just after eight o'clock in the evening. The bustling family atmosphere he'd vaguely assumed would distract him from lusting after Bella wasn't there. Now he was in trouble.

'Drop in and say hello to Aunt Sophie. She'd love to see you,' Bella said over her shoulder as she headed for the kitchen.

Scott glanced at the closed door in the foyer and accepted that the light streaming from under it meant that Sophie was awake. He knocked and a querulous voice called for him to enter.

The white-haired old lady was hunched in front of the television, watching the horse races as he'd expected, and she cackled softly when she saw him. Her bird-like face widened into a grin and he wondered not for the first time how she managed to eat with so few teeth.

'Bit late for a house call, Dr Rainford,' Sophie said.

Scott walked across the room to stand beside her chair. 'I'm doing the bus run with Bella tonight. How are you, Sophie? Keeping the house under control as usual?'

'Bella runs it. I just watch. And soon I'll see my new great-nephew.'

Scott smiled at the old lady's delight. 'He's a fine young fellow and Abbey looked wonderful when I saw her before tea.'

'They deserve their happiness. And so do you. You might think of doing something about it before you get too old.'

Scott raised his eyebrows but, in fact, nothing Bella's aunt said could surprise him after all these years of being her doctor. Sophie's eyes had strayed from his, back to the screen, as a new race started. He'd ceased to exist.

'Funny you should say that,' he murmured. More loudly, he said, 'I'll go, then. Good luck with your punting.'

She flicked him a sly glance. 'Good luck with yours.' And turned back to the television.

Scott bit back a sigh as he left the room. One thing about old age seemed to be that you could say what you wanted, when you wanted!

CHAPTER TWO

BACK IN THE FOYER, the twins had disappeared up the stairs and then a barely audible thumping beat vibrated through the house. He looked down where the noise seemed to be seeping through the floorboards under his feet. Thump, thump, thump. He wondered if his son liked that kind of music and even if Bella did. He was definitely too old for Bella. He thought wistfully of his own quiet house until Bella returned from the kitchen and then age was forgotten.

She was munching an apple and he couldn't help the sudden connection in his head to Adam and Eve and the malicious serpent of desire. Even in jeans she embodied the essence of womanhood and he could feel the too-familiar surge of frustration at the unfairness of fate.

'It seems Vivie's gone to bed.' Bella said as she rubbed the uneaten side of her apple against her breast to shine it. Scott almost groaned at the undulation of tissue under the fruit. Oblivious, she went on, 'Her baby was unsettled last night and she's probably trying to catch up on some sleep.' Bella tilted her head and he could see she was unsure what to do with him. 'Do you want to listen to music in the study until the next trip?'

Scott tore his eyes away from the tightness of her shirt and dragged his thoughts back under control as he followed her into the book-lined room.

He remembered the room they used as a study from when Abbey had lived here, but the aura was different.

Bella had painted the walls a soft lilac and replaced the old curtains with white linen. She gestured to an under-stuffed chair as she moved across to turn on the CD player. 'Please, sit down.'

Before he knew it Carol King had started to sing softly in the background about a life and a tapestry and he relaxed a little at the pleasant music. Bella crossed the room back to him as he sank into the chair. And sank comprehensively until his knees almost came up to his chin. He pretended to be comfortable though he felt like he'd been swallowed whole. At least it took his mind off Bella's breasts.

Bella perched on the arm of a sister chair and Scott could see why. Bella would disappear if she sank as far as he had.

Her eyes twinkled. 'Sorry about the chairs. There used to be a chaise longue in here but Rohan asked if Abbey could take it with her when they got married. Something to do with happy memories or something and I couldn't say no.' She grinned. 'He's so romantic and Abbey is so matter-of-fact. Love is grand if it works out.' She shrugged and patted the chair.

'I found these really cheap at a garage sale.' Her smile faded and she glanced out of the window at the house next door where her sister and brother-in-law lived. 'Poor old Rohan looked strained today while Abbey was in labour.'

She turned back to stare thoughtfully at Scott. 'And so did you after the baby was born. What happened to a show of relief and joy at the birth of the new Roberts baby?'

She was different in her own home, more decisive and assertive, and it knocked Scott off balance. So much so that he answered by speaking about something he'd least intended. Something he hadn't told anyone since he'd found out yesterday.

'I was thinking about my own son.'

Bella blinked. 'You have a son? Since when?'

She looked so incredulous that Scott winced. 'It is possible, you know. I am a man.'

Bella snorted, not unlike her maiden aunt, and raised her eyebrows. 'I've been aware of that for a while.' And suddenly it was back—that aura between them that had shimmered in the bus. She blushed and looked away but not before he saw her moisten her lips with her tongue. That brief glimpse of pink softness almost undid all the hard work he'd expended on controlling his lust.

He rose, not without difficulty, from the softness of the upholstery, and walked over to the window. He had to move away or he'd pull her into his arms and do something he should have done many years ago.

He clung grimly to a topic that could divert him. 'As to "since when", a letter arrived from him yesterday. My son, Michael…' he shook his head as if still unable to believe he was a father '…apparently was adopted by his maternal grandparents not long after his birth, when his mother was killed in an accident. Until they died, and he came across his birth certificate, he didn't even know he had other parents. He only mentioned that he'd discovered his real mother was long dead and the letter was to let me know my ex-wife had died. "In case I wondered", he added, and he might come to visit me in a month or two. He doesn't seem very keen to meet me.'

Scott turned back to Bella and the sympathy he saw in her face made him fiercely regret telling her. 'Considering I've done nothing for him, I'm not surprised, of course.'

Bella shook her head. 'If you didn't know about Michael then someone made it hard for both of you. Why didn't his mother tell you?'

'That's not something I'm ever likely to find out. We were totally different and never really understood each other. She probably thought I'd be as useless as a father as I was as a husband.' He saw her flinch at the bitterness in his voice. What did she expect? All those extra years he had on her were filled with mistakes.

Bella's voice was reasonable. 'As you're not useless at anything else you attempt, I find that hard to believe.'

'That's a compliment, considering I've been less than pleasant to you since you came back.'

Bella patted the chair and encouraged him to sit down again. 'We'll talk about that another time.' When he walked past her to his chair she touched his arm fleetingly and this time there was healing in her sympathy. To his relief she didn't pursue the subject.

Bella outlined a few changes she was looking at for the ward and the time passed swiftly. Before he knew it, she'd glanced at her watch and stood up. 'Let's go drive a bus.'

This time, as they circumnavigated the town, surprisingly there was little strain—on Bella's side anyway. More young people got on and off than the last trip and they all knew Bella.

Scott tried to concentrate on where they were driving and not the driver. He'd been aware of the bus campaign but was amazed at how much the service was used. No wonder the number of teen car accidents was down if this many kids weren't driving the streets.

When they returned to Bella's house the lights were out in Sophie's rooms. They were the only ones awake in a sleeping house and there was one more run to go. He felt his inner tension increase another knot and his steps slowed.

'Do you want to go back into the study and have some coffee?' Bella didn't appear to notice as she stifled a yawn.

Scott pictured another episode of trying to extricate himself from the carnivorous chair and, despite its diversional properties, he couldn't face it. 'Can we sit in the kitchen?'

Bella stared at him for a moment and the laughter in her eyes told him she'd guessed about the chair.

'Certainly.' She led the way into the old-fashioned kitchen and indicated a huge boiled fruit cake under a glass cover in the middle of the scrubbed oak table. 'I'll make coffee and you can cut us some of Vivie's cake. Then you can tell me about your marriage.'

She looked so innocent as she assumed he'd just do as he was told and bare his soul. For some reason her assumption chipped a little more at his composure and he couldn't help his need to try and regain some control.

Bella wondered if she would get away with it. Hopefully Scott wouldn't take offence at her question. It would be nice to know more about the man she'd once thought she loved. Someone, she realised now, who'd always treated her like a child.

Without warning, he caught her arm as she moved towards the sink to halt her progress away from him. Apparently, Scott wasn't ready to discuss his marriage any further. It was the first time he'd touched her in twelve years and he wasn't touching her as if she were a child. Bella's pulse jumped with the unexpectedness of it.

'Who says I want to talk about my marriage?' His voice was deeper than usual with a touch of danger that accelerated her heart rate even more. 'You're being very bossy all of a sudden. When did this shift in power happen?' he asked with gentle sarcasm.

This was a startling side of Scott she'd never seen. Bella looked down at her own pale wrist captured by his much larger hand and then up at his face.

Her mouth was dry and she moistened her lips with her tongue, lost for words. Suddenly he was staring down at her like a dying man in a desert without water. The air crackled with tension and she could almost taste the scent of the storm to come.

She said quietly, 'Maybe I've changed and you've never noticed.' This time when she ran her tongue over her lips she did it to deliberately provoke him, but his response exceeded her expectations.

Bella felt his fingers tighten on her wrist even more and her eyes widened as he pulled her all the way towards him until she was hard against the rock of his chest with her head tilted up at him.

His voice lowered and the conversational tone he used belied the hungry look in his storm-green eyes. 'It drives me insane when you lick your lips. If you do it again I won't be responsible for the consequences.' Scott's fingers loosened and he dropped her wrist to sit down.

Bella blinked and pressed her lips together, rubbed her wrist and turned away. Her mouth was dry, and a heaving, almost sickening excitement she didn't want to feel coursed through her stomach as she filled the kettle. At least she'd found out the tiger's tail could be pulled, she thought shakily.

When she returned to the table with the mugs of steaming coffee, Scott had cut two pieces of cake.

A tiny green flame simmered in his eyes and Bella threw up her chin at the challenge—something the Bella of a year ago would never have done—and she gloried in it. 'So, does this mean you don't want to talk about your first wife?'

Scott's hand froze as he reached for his cup.

Ha. Good, she'd surprised him, she thought with sudden satisfaction, and for once she could read his mind. 'You really haven't seen how much I've changed since the court case, have you?'

Scott paled and clenched his teeth as he fought back the impotent fury that invaded his mind whenever he thought of Bella at the drugged mercy of her attacker. He took a deep breath. 'We seem to have successfully avoided each other for most of the last year since you've been home. I didn't get the impression it helped you when I was around.'

She shrugged delicately and her fragility belied the strength in her voice. 'They say good comes out of even the worst scenarios. That experience taught me to rely on myself and not other people. And not to expect my big sister to always save me. I've worked on that over the last year.'

Scott frowned. 'To say good came out of a brutal attack seems a tad forgiving of a creep who drugged and abused you.'

Bella winced with distaste and her voice shook a little. 'He can rot in gaol, but surviving his attack has forced me to grow and learn. You weren't here straight after the attack, but for a while I was ready to crawl away and die.'

Scott had shut off a lot of the memories of Bella's attack because he'd felt so useless in her hour of need. He'd been away and had come back to find a shattered shell of the woman he'd known. She'd refused to see him when he'd come to offer comfort so he'd gone away again and gained what reassurance he could from information gleaned from Rohan. Scott felt he'd already hurt her enough all those years ago to feel he had the right to push his presence on her when she was vulnerable.

'But I don't want to talk about me, I want to hear about you…' She trailed off and managed a small smile of encouragement.

He smiled grimly. 'So it's my turn, is it?' He could see that she'd sat far enough along the table away from him to be out of reach. At least he'd made her wary but it hadn't stopped her impudence.

'How old were you when you were married?' The question drifted towards him and he would have liked to know why it was so damned important for her to hear this. He considered refusing to answer but he never had been able to deny Bella anything if she wanted it badly enough.

His voice was expressionless. 'Married at twenty, but she left less than a year later. Pretty well most of med school was spent trying to forget my marriage. We fell in and out of love very quickly. Or at least she did.'

Scott could see the brevity of his answer irritated Bella and it gave him a little satisfaction that she could be frustrated for once.

'Then why get married?'

'I was young and stupid and she was older and no wiser. It blew incredibly hot and then, before I knew why, our relationship was as cold as ice. She left me for another man, a man her senior who could support her, and filed for divorce.' A distant echo of a crushing hurt was in his voice and Bella felt more mature than Scott for the first time in her life. It was an interesting concept.

Luckily he wasn't looking at her. His voice was flat when he went on, 'Apparently my wife was pregnant when she left me. I just wish I'd known I had a child and could have been involved in some part of his life. The last two days I've agonised over why she shut me out so completely. I rang and checked. I am Michael's true father.'

He shrugged. The image of the pain in Scott's face in the birthing suite that morning came back to her. 'And you've learnt nothing else about your son?'

'What's there to learn? He's a man now. I imagine from his side I'm the father who's done nothing to help him. It must be more of a shock to him than it was to me.'

Bella drained her coffee and set the cup down. She glanced at the clock on the kitchen wall. 'It's almost time for the bus run again.'

Scott gave her a wry smile and stood to pull out her chair. 'Well, that will end our session of truth and dare for the night. Thank goodness.'

'It's not healthy to keep all this stuff bottled up, Scott.' Bella was stern in her new role. 'When the shock wears off, you'll be glad you told me.'

'Right,' Scott said cynically, and waited for her to precede him out of the room.

When they'd settled in the bus and Scott saw Bella stifle another yawn his original misgivings came back to him. 'This is ridiculous. You shouldn't be driving this bus. Can't you find someone else to do it?'

Bella shook her head. 'The government has promised funding for next year. That includes the employment of a salaried driver. I can survive until then.'

'But why is it your problem?'

Bella shrugged. 'Because if I didn't do it, no one else would. I agree with my sister in the basic goodness of the younger generation. The advantages of the service are worth the effort.'

The conversation came to a halt because the bus had reached the first stop. A large group of young men and women clambered on and the noise level in the bus made conversation between Bella and Scott impossible, which was OK because he had enough to think about. Not the least was how soft Bella had felt in his arms and how hard it had been to let her go. Her support for his dilemma with his son was also surprisingly comforting.

At each stop the bus became more crowded until finally people started to get off and head home. By the time Bella had arrived back at Chisholm Road there were only Melissa and a young man left.

Bella had glanced in the rear-view mirror a few times. Blake—Bella assumed it was the Blake Melissa had befriended—had a sweet smile and laughter-filled eyes. In fact, Bella had liked him on sight.

When they moved to the front of the bus to alight, Melissa's pleading eyes left Bella in no doubt of the young man's identity.

'This is Blake, Bella.'

Bella swivelled in her seat and held out her hand. Blake's long brown hair looked clean and his goatee was interesting, though she wasn't sure if she was thrilled with the small scorpion tattooed on his wrist or the skull and crossbones piercing his eyebrow. Scott's going to love this, she thought.

She met the young man's green eyes and nodded. 'Hello, Blake.' Blake shook Bella's hand. 'This is Dr Rainford.' The two men nodded at each other but neither held out their hand. Bella smiled wryly to herself. 'Perhaps you could come and see me tomorrow and we can discuss Melissa's idea.'

Blake nodded. 'Thank you. I will.' He glanced at Scott once more and then followed Melissa out of the bus, where they went into a huddle for a minute before he headed off down the street.

Bella realised she'd been swayed to coolness by the fact that Scott was there, and the thought irritated her.

'What was all that about?' Scott's timing was way out.

'Nothing important.' She put the bus into gear and reversed it carefully down the driveway. 'Let's get this bus parked. I'm tired. It's been a long day.'

He waited until she switched off the engine in the garage before pushing his luck. 'For nothing important, there was a lot of eye contact going on all round. What does he want?'

Bella stifled a sigh and measured her answer. 'Blake has offered to do odd jobs around the house in exchange for lodging. I'm thinking about it.'

Scott frowned and shook his head. 'I can do odd jobs around the house. I don't think introducing a young man as a boarder is a good idea.'

Bella held back the comment that it was none of his business. Her voice was sweet. 'And here I was thinking that having a large country medical practice and most nights on call would be enough to keep you busy. I must start a list of repairs for you.'

She stood up and eased herself from her seat. 'Goodnight, Scott.'

He followed her out and towered over her beside the bus. 'I enjoyed your company, Bella. We must do it again.'

'Any Friday and Saturday night,' Bella said dryly, and walked away.

Scott's firm voice drifted across. 'Then I'll see you at seven tomorrow night.'

Bella thought of those moments in the kitchen and how much she had cared about Scott's distress over his son. She closed her eyes and didn't look back. 'I don't think that's a good idea,' she whispered to herself.

CHAPTER THREE

Saturday

'BELLA, BLAKE'S HERE.' Melissa's voice drifted from the front door. Bella put down the morning newspaper and stood up from the kitchen table. She met Vivie's eyes and Vivie shrugged.

At breakfast, Bella had spoken to Aunt Sophie about the possibility of a male boarder and her aunt had sent the ball back into Bella's court with a noncommittal shrug. 'If he's likeable and honest, it's not a bad thing to have a man about the house,' she'd said.

All the other girls except Vivie had met Blake previously and thought it 'cool' that he might move in with them. Bella had had to bite back a smile as they'd unanimously agreed to hand the mowing and the garbage-bin duties over to him if he joined the household.

Bella walked into the hallway and smiled at Blake. 'Come through into the kitchen, Blake, and we'll have a coffee and see if we can work something out.'

Blake shot a glance at Melissa who nodded encouragingly and hung back to watch them go.

Vivie brought the coffee-pot over and when they were all seated at the kitchen table, Bella looked across at the young man. Tall and good-looking under the ponytail and eyebrow stud, there was something about the square chin under his goatee that invited a smile.

She couldn't help but like him. 'You haven't met Vivie, have you, Blake?'

Blake smiled at the young woman. 'Hello, Vivie.'

Vivie nodded but didn't say anything.

'Vivie runs the house. She shops and is a fabulous cook and we're very lucky to have her. That's why she's in on this discussion.' Vivie blushed and looked down at the tablecloth.

Bella moved on. 'If we were to think about inviting you to move in, Blake, it's only fair that we'd run through the expectations we have for everyone in the household.'

Blake nodded that he understood.

Bella continued, 'Melissa said you might be willing to do some odd jobs around the house.'

Blake shrugged. 'I don't have employment at the moment, and I get bored if I'm not busy. I'd enjoy the chance to do some work around here. In Sydney I worked for the Salvation Army Depot and restored furniture, so I can fix most things.'

Bella nodded and considered his answer. 'Why did you move to Gladstone?'

He grimaced. 'When my parents died I went off the rails a bit. The guys I was with started to get into some heavy stuff and I didn't want to go there.' He looked embarrassed. 'I thought it might be a good idea to leave town while I could still drive away. I ended up here.'

Blake smiled sheepishly. 'I thought if I went to a country town there was more chance of a fresh start. I like the idea of moving into the house.' He couldn't keep the anxiety out of his face.

Bella held out her hand. 'We'll go for a week's trial and we've room for another car in the garage besides the bus. My car's just died a decrepit death and it can be relegated to the back shed.'

Blake smiled a huge smile and he didn't notice that Vivie looked ready to pass out with the brilliance of it. 'You could drive mine. Maybe I could fix yours, too. I like mucking around with cars.'

'Don't give yourself too much to do or we'll miss you if you decide to move out.' Bella smiled. 'Welcome to the house, Blake.'

She looked at Vivie. 'Would you like to show Blake his room? He can have the end room at the back of the house. That one has its own bathroom, even though it's pretty rough.' She looked at Blake with a challenging stare. 'You clean your own bathroom every week. We don't do men's rooms.'

'I'll show you how.' Vivie managed to enter the conversation finally. 'When you get your stuff I'll make the room up for you—then it's up to you. You get clean sheets on a Friday.' Vivie had moved into housekeeper mode and Blake followed her out of the room.

Bella could hear Vivie explaining about mealtimes and how he had to tell her if he wasn't planning on being there for a meal. It would do Vivie good to have some male company other than her year-old son, Bella thought with a smile. Vivie had been on the receiving end of a bad experience, like Bella herself, and she needed to practise her feminine wiles. Bella had decided she didn't need her wiles.

Later Bella was stepping out of her front door for the first bus run of the evening when Scott fell into step beside her.

'Good evening, Bella. Here we are again,' he said.

'So I gather. Hello, Scott.' She looked up at him. 'This really isn't necessary you know.'

'Humour me,' he said as they walked together towards the garage.

Bella sighed and waited for the fireworks. She stepped past a fire-engine red, low-slung, two-door SLR Torana with silver mag wheels and BITE ME splashed across the front windscreen. Scott's eyes widened as he followed Bella onto the bus.

'Where on earth did that car come from?' Scott twisted his neck and screwed up his face in disgust.

Bella settled herself into the seat before she answered and didn't look across at her passenger. 'It's Blake's car. He moved in today.' She started the bus's engine and revved it. It was a diesel engine and she shouldn't do that before it warmed up, but the motor's noise successfully drowned out Scott's reply.

Scott glared across at her. When the engine was back at an idle he tried again. 'Does Abbey know you now have a male boarder?'

Bella could feel the elevation in her blood pressure. At least she assumed that was what the red mist in front of her eyes meant. 'Excuse me?' She turned to Scott and spoke softly but the edge was unmistakable. 'Perhaps you'd like to trot up to the hospital and tell my sister while she's breastfeeding. I can't wait for her to tell you it's none of her business.' To reinforce her point she opened the door again and waited.

Scott met her eyes and raised his eyebrows at her reaction. 'That's not what I meant, but I'm sorry if I upset you.'

Bella said nothing. The door closed again and she put the bus into gear and drove out of the garage.

Scott held his peace as they drove the circuit but mentally he gnashed his teeth. He couldn't believe she'd been so reckless and invited some unknown youth into her house. And judging by his car, the boy was loud and a hothead as well. Scott remembered the boy's pierced eyebrow and tattoo and clenched his fists. If anything happened to Bella he'd grind the pipsqueak into a pulp.

They didn't talk much during the first trip. There were a few more young adults than last night's early trip and Bella was kept busy stopping and starting the bus.

By the time they were back at Bella's house she had calmed down enough to accept she might have overreacted and Scott was being careful.

They almost made it to the next bus run as they talked of ordinary things and then suddenly, as they stood up to leave, it was as if he couldn't restrain himself. Scott threw in a contentious question.

'So where does Blake sleep?' The words hung in the air between them.

Bella blinked and raised her eyebrows. How dared he? 'That's funny.' She tilted her head. 'I was under the impression that the guests in my house had nothing to do with you.'

She glared but this time Scott stared back without expression and wouldn't be silenced. 'It's not unreasonable for your friends to be concerned if we consider you've made an ill-judged decision.'

'Ah,' said Bella. The red mist was coming back. 'Patronising! That's the Scott we all know and love.'

Scott glared back. 'Don't avoid the issue. You're just asking for trouble. You can't know anything about this person. What if he tries to break into your room in the night? He could have a criminal record as long as your arm. I'm concerned for you, Bella.'

'I like him and I trust my instinct.'

'Abbey trusted her instinct with Clayton Harrows and look where that led both of you.'

'How dare you?' Bella couldn't believe he'd brought her sister's ex-fiancé into the conversation. She'd just managed to get those memories of her attack back in their box after last night, and he was opening the lid again. She couldn't believe it. Where did this man get off?

Scott wasn't repentant. 'I dare because I care.'

'So what changed you to care?' The bitterness in her voice made Scott wince. He couldn't help the step he took towards her and before he knew it he had her pulled against him.

He looked into her eyes and his voice was barely audible. 'I've always cared!'

She smelt of some herbal shampoo and flowery perfume that triggered the response he'd been fighting against all night, and his body quickened with desire and a stupid jealousy that she believed some twenty-year-old over him.

Oblivious to the tightening of his fingers, Bella tossed her hair and glared back at him. This was a Bella he'd never seen. 'Big effort, Scott. Be careful, or someone will hear you,' she taunted. 'I have to watch what I say in case you run to Abbey with it, like you did when I was eighteen.'

The bitterness in her reply shocked them both. Scott lowered his voice. 'I "ran to Abbey" to protect you. Don't you realise? I was *twelve years* older and you were only eighteen. I couldn't trust myself.'

'So what's changed now?' This was crazy and needed to stop. Bella could hear the scorn in her own voice and she consciously relaxed her shoulders and attempted to step back.

But it was too late.

Scott pulled her against him and lowered his face. His eyes burned into hers as he captured her chin firmly in his hand so she couldn't step away again.

When his lips touched hers they seared then softened and he sighed into her. Bella tasted a mixture of anger and regret and a glimpse of incredibly sweet homecoming that seemed to settle over her like a fine warm fog, and it was tantalisingly delicious. The room swam before her eyes as she leaned into him. To be in Scott's arms was everything she'd been afraid it would be.

This feeling was too dangerous after all she'd been through. Bella didn't want to go there—not without thought. She turned her face to break the spell, shrugged out of his hold with a practised move she'd gleaned from her self-defence classes and backed away so that he stepped back too.

'I'm sorry,' he said. 'I shouldn't have come tonight.' The words were clipped, as if he was still striving for control. 'I'd better go.'

This was like a nightmare. Here she was, wanting Scott to kiss her so she could open herself up to pain a fourth time. 'Please, do,' was all she said.

Bella stood ramrod straight in front of him and full of purpose. She'd grown up and he hadn't seen it until now. She didn't need protecting by anyone. Not even by him.

Bella glanced at her watch. 'I'm quite capable of doing the trips on my own.'

He nodded. 'I can see that. Goodnight, Bella.'

'Goodnight, Scott.' Bella watched him go and now she was more confused than ever. She wasn't quite sure where all that emotion had come from but it had better get back where it came from because she was finally self-sufficient and happy. The last thing she needed to do was get tangled up in some angst-filled relationship with Scott Rainford so that he could get cold feet again and break her heart a second time.

Later that evening, Bella had just crawled into bed when someone knocked quietly on her door. Her heart jumped and for a moment her chest felt heavy with panic. Scott's dire warnings about Blake still rung in her ears until common sense told her it was probably one of the girls.

'Yes?' It was more of a squeak than an enquiry. She sat up and cleared her throat to try again. 'Who is it?'

'It's Blake.'

Bella couldn't help the hand that flew to her chest. It was as if Scott was at her shoulder saying, *See*. The feelings she'd conquered a year ago echoed in her memory. She steadied herself. She mustn't jump to conclusions.

Bella drew a deep breath to steady her nerves and deliberately padded across to the door and opened it slightly.

'What do you want, Blake?' She couldn't help the snap in her voice but then she saw the concern in his face and realised he posed no threat to her. Damn Scott Rainford for putting those suspicions in her head.

'It's Melissa. She thinks she's in labour.'

Bella nodded and opened the door wider. 'I'll just get my dressing-gown.'

When they'd moved down the hallway to the girl's room they found Melissa sitting wide-eyed and trembling on the edge of the bed.

Bella sat down beside her. 'What's wrong, Melissa?'

Melissa grabbed Bella's hand for comfort. 'It's the backache, and it keeps coming and going. It wasn't too bad earlier but in the last half an hour it's coming much quicker and now I'm getting these bad cramps in the front, too.' She looked up at Bella with frightened eyes. 'Do you think it might be labour?'

Bella smiled wryly. 'It certainly sounds like it. Why didn't you come and see me earlier?'

'I didn't think you were home and it wasn't so bad before…' The girl stopped and her face contorted with pain. Bella laid her hand on Melissa's abdomen and the hardness of the uterus under her fingers confirmed the contraction. She shut her eyes for a second while she thought of what they had to do.

'The contractions are strong. We need to get you up to the hospital to see if we can stop your labour.'

'What if my baby is born today?' There was real fear in Melissa's voice.

Abbey hugged the girl. 'We'll have to see how big he or she is. Some thirty-four-weekers have few problems but most need special care for several weeks. It's mainly the poor feeding that will keep your baby from coming home as quickly as a full-term baby. Now, let's get you organised.'

She looked up at Blake. 'Thanks for getting me, Blake.' She glanced around the room. 'At least we packed Melissa's hospital bag last week.'

The young man looked less worried now that Bella was there to take command, but his anxiety wasn't over as Melissa grabbed his hand.

'Come with me, Blake. Thomas won't come, and I'm scared.'

Blake backed away and he looked at Melissa with reluctance. 'Are you sure you want me? Bella will be with you. You'll be fine.'

Melissa's eyes implored him. 'I want you, too. Please.' Bella watched the interplay. Whatever was best for Melissa was fine by her.

Blake swallowed the lump in his throat and nodded. 'OK. If you think it will help you, Melissa.'

He looked at Bella. 'What do you think?'

'You can stay up at the head end of the bed, Blake,' Bella reassured him with a smile. 'Just hold her hand and tell she's doing a great job. That's all you have to do.'

Bella left a note for Vivie in the kitchen on their way out to say where they'd gone.

'We'll have to take the bus,' she said as she remembered her car was out of action.

'Take mine. I'll drive.' At least Blake felt confident about getting them there.

Bella nodded and helped Melissa into the front. She stifled a grin at what Blake would do if Melissa's waters broke all over his luxurious lambswool seat covers. In fact, she would have preferred to have her first drive in a hot rod in a less stressful situation and without Blake's lead foot, she thought as the houses flashed past.

The upside was it only took them five minutes to get to the hospital, though they'd probably wakened the neighbourhood.

When they arrived at Maternity, the ward was busy with a woman in labour in the other birthing unit. Rather than short-staff the night girls, Bella admitted Melissa to the ward and settled her into bed. Blake sat on the chair beside Melissa and held the young girl's hand.

With the night staff so busy it fell to Bella to ring Scott. Bella sighed as she dialled his number and listened to it ring. So much for avoiding Scott.

'Hello?' Considering it was after midnight, he sounded wide awake.

Sunday

Bella's mouth was suddenly dry and her voice came out huskily. 'Scott, it's Bella.' Before he could think she'd rung him for personal reasons, Bella hurried on. 'I'm at Maternity with Melissa. She's in labour at thirty-four weeks and I'd say she's well established.'

There was a couple of seconds' silence as he processed the information and then he said, 'I'm on my way,' and put the phone down.

Bella replaced her own receiver gently and turned to Melissa. 'He's coming in now.'

'That's good.' Melissa's voice was faint. 'Because I think my waters just broke and these contractions are getting pretty bad.' She met Bella's eyes and tears welled up and overflowed. 'Will my baby be OK?'

Bella hugged the girl. 'Your baby will be fine.'

'I don't think I can do this any more.' Melissa's eyes were wild as she glanced at Blake, then at Bella, and then around the room as if to find a place to hide from the strength of the contractions.

Bella nodded and soothed her. 'I know. The contractions are very strong and it is hard. You're doing wonderfully.'

'You are, too,' Blake said loudly, as if he'd just remembered his lines.

Bella hid her smile as she turned on the foetal monitor and they all listened to Melissa's baby's heart sounds gallop along merrily. 'How about Blake goes outside for a moment and I'll check to see how dilated you are? If there's absolutely no chance that your labour will stop, you can jump in the shower. To stay lying down in bed makes the pain harder to bear.'

Despite the abdominal palpation she'd done, Bella wanted to confirm that the baby's head was coming first as well as check there was no cord prolapse after the waters had broken, though that scenario seemed unlikely with the strong foetal heartbeat they'd just heard.

'The shower sounds like heaven,' Melissa agreed.

Scott pulled up outside Maternity and the lecture he'd given himself, about maintaining composure around Bella, flew out the window as he saw *that* car parked outside. He glared at it and stalked up the stairs. The boy had already ruined one young girl's life with a pregnancy, and now he'd latched onto Bella. Well, *he* was watching him.

Sharon, one of the night midwives, met him at the door and took one look at his grim expression.

'You OK, Scott?'

'Fine.' He eased the scowl from his face and loosened his shoulders. 'I was thinking about something else.' He gestured to the two birthing suites. 'Which way first?'

'See Bella and then we're ready to have this baby in number one,' Sharon said as she peeled off to answer the buzzer from her own unit.

Scott nodded, plastered a neutral expression on his face, and went in to see Melissa.

'So, it's all happening, Melissa.' They all looked up with relief when Scott walked in. He could tell things were progressing fast and when Bella handed him the chart he glanced at her findings and nodded. He looked at Blake under his brows but didn't say anything. Bella had confirmed that Melissa's cervix was nine centimetres dilated and it was only a matter of time before her baby would be born.

Bella placed the ultrasound Doppler over Melissa's stomach. The strong beat echoed around the room and everyone smiled. 'He or she sounds happy about arriving early,' Scott reassured his patient, and Melissa smiled weakly back until the next pain arrived.

'I'd like to get Melissa into the shower until she's ready to push, if that's OK with you, Doctor?'

Scott grimaced. 'All you Wilson girls are the same. Nobody likes to look after people on the bed any more.' He waved them on. 'Try to be back here before we have a head on view. Sharon has the nursery ready if we need a crib. I'll go next door and see how they're doing.' He nodded at Melissa and Bella, ignored Blake and left.

Blake hung back as Bella encouraged the girl out of bed but Melissa was having none of it. 'You come, too.'

Bella bit her lip at Blake's discomfort but then she saw him accept that it was boots-and-all commitment if he was going to help Melissa. He went up another notch in Bella's estimation.

'OK.' His voice firmed. 'If I can help, just ask.' He followed them into the bathroom.

Bella helped Melissa to sit on the big blue ball in the bathroom and as soon as the hot water hit her lower stomach she sighed with relief. Bella could see the tension drain from her shoulders and made Blake sit behind her to gently rub the girl's lower back in a circular motion.

After an initial awkwardness, Blake settled into a soothing rhythm and Bella could see it helped Melissa. 'You're both doing wonderfully. Stay loose and it will all happen.'

The lights were dim and the sound of the running water was peaceful between contractions as they waited for Melissa's baby to start its descent through the birth canal.

Within half an hour Melissa stood up and the change in her breathing was clearly audible to Bella. 'I need to push,' Melissa panted, and Bella nodded.

'Listen to what your body is telling you to do. Don't be frightened. It's OK.'

Melissa couldn't help the involuntary downward pressure she was exerting and she squeezed Blake's hand as she pushed. 'I can feel it move,' she whispered. Blake paled and stepped back to let Bella closer.

'It's OK. Have a rest when the pain is gone.' Bella placed the tiny waterproof Doppler low down on Melissa's stomach and the clop-clop of baby's heartbeat echoed clearly in the bathroom.

'Your baby's still happy.'

'I'm not,' said Melissa.

Bella smiled and squeezed her hand. 'You are magnificent!'

Blake nodded in total agreement.

'Here comes another one…' Melissa gritted her teeth and Bella stroked the girl's jaw.

'Loose jaw, loose perineum, Melissa. Remember that all the power is travelling down and not to waste it in your face or arms.'

Melissa consciously relaxed her face and then her eyes widened. 'I think it's coming.'

Bella ran her gloved hands between Melissa's legs and sure enough a tiny bulge of baby's head had descended enough for her to feel. 'Well done, Melissa. It would have taken heaps more pushes than that if you'd stayed on the bed.' Bella glanced at the door.

'OK. We'd better shuffle back to the bed and keep the doctor happy.' As soon as the pain was gone, Bella cajoled Melissa into movement and Blake and Bella supported her to the bed. Bella pressed the call button and Scott and the night sister appeared within seconds.

When Melissa had climbed onto the bed everyone could see how close the baby was to arriving and Scott met Bella's eyes with a shake of the head as if to say, Too close.

Bella smiled sweetly in return and settled Blake back into the chair because he looked like he was ready to faint.

She could hear Scott washing his hands as she gave Blake a drink of water and the whistle of the oxygen as Sharon checked the infant resuscitation trolley. It was all happening very quickly.

'Gently now,' Scott murmured as his gloved hand rested lightly on the baby's head and Melissa whimpered. The sound made Blake squeeze Melissa's hand and put his cheek next to hers. 'You're nearly there. You're so clever and you get to see your baby soon.'

She nodded that she understood. Bella left them to it and watched the birth.

With aching slowness, Melissa's pelvic floor guided her baby's body through the twists and turns required to reach the outside world. The mechanisms of birth never failed to awe Bella. Her years in Sydney at the birthing centre had reinforced her belief that in the great majority of cases, a woman's body would achieve what it had to if the mother believed in herself.

The back of the baby's head extended to allow the forehead, nose and chin to be born in one sweep of the perineum and, with little delay, its head restituted to allow the shoulders under the pubic arch, followed by the rest of its body, and the infant came into the world in a slithery rush.

Scott lifted the baby up to show Melissa. 'Brilliant job, Melissa. Well done. So, what have you got?' he asked.

Melissa opened her eyes and stared up at the diminutive baby. 'Oh, it's a girl and she's so tiny. I want to call her Tina.'

Blake's eyes were shining with unshed tears as Scott laid Melissa's daughter on her mother's breasts.

'Hello, Tina,' Bella said as she tucked a bunny rug around them both while Scott clamped the cord.

'Do you want to cut the cord?' Scott asked Blake in a noncommittal voice.

Blake shook his head. 'I'm not the father.'

Scott blinked in surprise.

'Do it anyway,' Melissa whispered, and Bella could see Blake steel himself for a task he didn't relish. He took the scissors Scott handed him in shaky fingers and sawed his way through the sinewy tissue. When Tina was finally separated from her mother, Blake put the scissors down. Any remaining colour drained from his face, his eyes rolled and he flopped bonelessly back into the chair.

Bella stifled a smile and gently directed his head down to his knees and held him there until he groaned. 'What happened?' he mumbled.

'You were a bit faint. Stay there for a minute. You'll be fine.' She caught Scott's contempt when he raised his eyebrows as if to say, What do you expect? Bella glared back at him and his face crinkled with amusement at her predictable reaction.

Bella blinked. He was teasing her. It wasn't something she was used to from Scott and a small unwilling smile tugged at her mouth.

Sharon leant over to listen to the baby's heart and breathing and pronounced her fine. Because of Tina's early arrival they would still keep her in the crib overnight.

It took another hour for Melissa to be showered, see Tina settled into her humidicrib and then be tucked into her own bed. Finally she was settled enough to let Bella and Blake go.

Back at Bella's house, Vivie was up despite the fact that it was barely four a.m.

Blake was still blown away by the experience of childbirth and couldn't wait to share his excitement about the night's events. 'I think what Bella does for a job is amazing. Imagine being responsible for the safety of a baby so small.' He rolled his eyes. 'You all looked so calm!'

Bella smiled. 'Being a midwife is the best job in the world. We get to look after all the things that happen naturally. If you want pressure, you take the doctor's side of it and it's their job to come in when things start to go wrong. It gets a bit tense then.'

'I suppose so,' Blake didn't look like he was ready to go to sleep yet and Bella hid her yawn. Thank goodness it was Sunday today and she could sleep in. This week was going to be a big one at work and she wanted to be refreshed for it. Blake would probably buzz for hours. Vivie didn't seem in a hurry so she could keep Blake company. Bella stood up.

'I'm sorry, Blake. I have to go to bed. I'll see you later on.' Bella carried her cup to the sink and yawned again.

Blake jumped up. 'I'll wash them. Vivie said if I use anything in the kitchen, I have to wash it up. So I'd better do it.'

Bella met Vivie's eyes and they both grinned. 'I think that's a good idea,' said Bella, tongue in cheek, and took herself off to bed.

But she couldn't sleep. How could so much have happened in so short a time? Apart from tonight's birth, she had a new nephew, was in charge of a ward, in charge of a bus, in charge of a house with their first male boarder and now Scott was intruding in her life when she didn't need the distraction.

The kiss between them earlier had stolen some of her hard-won calm. The feel of his lips against hers, the weight of his hand holding her against the hardness of his chest, his breath mingling with her own. It had been heady stuff and something she'd refused to speculate on in the year since she'd moved back to Gladstone. She really didn't think she would survive another emotional disaster. She'd just have to refuse to let him distract her.

CHAPTER FOUR

Monday

WHEN BELLA PULLED up for work on Monday morning in Blake's car, she had a silly grin on her face from the rumbling and roaring sound the car made as it drove along.

Heads had turned even at six-thirty in the morning and it was a strange but exhilarating feeling and so out of Bella's experience that she finally understood why people drove hotted-up cars.

She noticed Scott's new Volvo was already parked outside. 'Boring car,' she muttered, and then laughed at herself. Before she'd locked the car behind her Scott had arrived, with a scowl on his face.

Bella refused to be cowed by his grumpy look and concentrated on why she was here. They must have had another birth so the day would be a busy one.

He met her on the kerb. 'Why are you driving his car?'

Bella raised her chin. She had finished with being browbeaten by anyone. 'Need a bit more sleep do you, Scott?' Bella asked sweetly.

Scott stopped and tilted his head. An unwilling smile touched his lips and he rubbed the bristles on his chin. 'Maybe.'

Bella could feel the shift in their relationship and his acceptance of her mild criticism. Actually, it was pleasant to have a bit of fun with Scott.

'Light' was a good way to keep their relationship 'distant'. Fun was something she hadn't ever associated with their past—intensity, awareness, frustration and embarrassment had all been there in spades, but never fun. Maybe her outburst yesterday had cleared the air a little.

She mentally shrugged. 'I'd better go in. Night staff will be glad to go home if they've had another busy night.'

Scott nodded and the smile was still in his voice. 'I'll do the ward round later. Maybe I'll be more civil.'

'Sounds good.' Bella carried on towards the steps and Scott watched her walk away.

Scott decided Bella had taken his initial shock at seeing her in that boy's car and flipped it back on him, and he'd deserved it.

The new Bella would take some getting used to but he had a feeling the journey could be worth the bumps in the road. Maybe he had been insufferable over the last month. He wasn't usually a moody person but the last week had played havoc with his mind.

Self-analysis hadn't really been his forte but Bella's home truths just kept coming. He sighed and headed for his car but he couldn't help the curl of his lip as he looked at that boy's vehicle. '"Bite Me",' he huffed as he climbed into the Volvo. He still wanted to know why she was driving that car.

When Scott came back for the ward round, Bella was buried in her office with a mountain of paperwork and he stood at the door for a few heartbeats and watched her. Her head was down and a tiny frown creased her forehead.

How could he not have seen she'd changed? Probably grown more than he had. Mentally he sighed. He coughed and she looked up. She smiled at him but the smile was distracted.

'You're back.' She stated the obvious and he raised his eyebrows.

'Funny, that.'

Bella ignored his comment and stood up. 'Abbey's ready to go this morning, and Melissa's Tina has had three bradycardias since I've been here. She's self-stimulating but we're keeping her on the monitor for the rest of the day.'

He nodded. It wasn't uncommon for premature babies to have runs of slower heartbeats every now and then, especially after feeds. 'Sounds sensible. As long as she's reverting back to normal rate on her own then I'm sure Tina will be fine. She'll grow out of it,' Scott reinforced Bella's thoughts as he followed her down the corridor.

They entered the first room and Rohan was cooing at his son while Abbey put the last of her pyjamas in a suitcase on the bed.

'Finally get to take your family home with you, Rohan.' Scott smiled at his partner and winked at Abbey. 'He's been like a cat on a hot tin roof, waiting for today, and cancelled a whole morning's appointments to take you home.' He concentrated on Abbey. 'How are you and Lachlan?'

Abbey smiled serenely down at her baby. 'I'm well and young Lachlan has moments of unusual interest—but I'm getting the hang of him. It's certainly easier showing others what to do than mastering it myself.'

They all laughed and Bella handed Scott the infant stethoscope to perform Lachlan's discharge check. Rohan laid his son carefully down in the cot and Scott undid the baby's little jacket to listen to his heart and check his hips. When he'd finished the examination he straightened and ticked off the sections in the newborn health record.

'What do you think of Bella's new car, Scott?' Rohan's intention of teasing Bella fell flat when Scott stunned them all with his vehemence.

'I think she's irresponsible for driving it and it's probably a death trap.'

Jaws dropped around the room and Bella could have kicked both men for ruining the happy going-home mood for Abbey. She brushed past the awkwardness in her quiet voice.

'Don't take any notice of Scott, he needs another few hours' sleep and a reality check.' She smiled at her brother-in-law. 'The car's great to drive and if Blake leaves I may have to buy it off him.'

'Like hell,' Scott muttered, and Bella met her sister's startled eyes across the bed.

What's with him? Abbey seemed to be asking.

Bella mouthed, 'Later,' and everyone pretended that Scott hadn't said anything unusual.

Rohan's eyebrows had nearly disappeared into his hairline. He seemed determined to keep putting his foot in it. 'I met young Blake over the fence this morning. He's a bit of a card.' Scott glanced without expression at Rohan who raised his eyebrows. 'I've always wanted a scorpion tattoo.'

Abbey laughed and said, 'I can just see it.'

The general amusement that followed lightened the tension. The rest of Scott's visit scraped through as customary.

Bella practically dragged him into the next room where he seemed to have regained his equanimity for his next patient. By the end of the round things appeared normal on the surface and Bella was glad to push him out of the door.

When he'd left, Bella headed back to Abbey's room to see if her sister needed anything before her discharge. She paused at the door and the thought hit her that it was a strange thing to see Abbey as a baby's mother.

Even more strange to see her big sister a little unsure of herself when her years of experience should have given her more knowledge and confidence than any other new mother.

But Bella could see it didn't work that way and it was a light-bulb moment. Maybe Abbey wasn't as infallible as Bella had always assumed she was?

Abbey looked up and smiled and Bella moved into the room. Her brother-in-law left to carry his wife's suitcase to the car and as soon as he was out of earshot Abbey said, 'So, what's going on between you and Scott?'

'Apart from the fact that he's tired and irritable today?' Bella shrugged. 'He came around on Friday and Saturday nights for the bus run and he's been different ever since.'

'How do you feel about that?' Abbey looked at her sister with some concern, last year's attack on both their minds.

'Better than I would have a year ago, but probably because I've got my confidence back. It will be a relief not to tread so lightly around him. Maybe we can get along better now.'

Abbey bit her lip and nodded but her silence spoke volumes. Bella met her eyes. 'I'm not interested in a relationship with Scott so don't look at me that way.'

'He's hurt you once,' was all Abbey had time to say before Rohan came back into the room and the conversation stopped.

'Scott's got a bee in his bonnet today,' Rohan said. 'When I heard you had a young man move into the house I thought it was a good thing. I don't think my partner agrees.'

'Scott has old-fashioned ideas.' Bella shrugged.

'What's Scott's problem with this young bloke? The guy's got good taste in cars.' Rohan was more interested in Blake's car if truth be told. 'I used to lust after an SLR when I was a teenager.' He glanced at his wife. 'When I was young and single.'

'Ha!' Abbey threw a look over her shoulder while she dressed Lachlan in his going-home clothes. 'You were single but never lived until you came to an exciting town like Gladstone.'

'It's the scenery I like around here.' Rohan nodded judiciously. 'And the beautiful women.' He swooped and kissed his wife.

Abbey laughed and rested back in his arms. 'I think you need to go home with your son.'

'And my wife.' He kissed her again and they both laughed as Bella slipped from the room. They were like newly-weds, Bella thought. For some people, marriage was the answer, but she liked her new-found self-sufficiency and the fact that she only had to please herself. That way she couldn't get hurt.

When Bella arrived home that night, Blake was peeling potatoes in the kitchen for Vivie. Vivie was laughing and young Ro was cruising the furniture on wobbly legs, looking for something to put in his mouth. It was a very domestic picture and Bella had to smile.

'So, what have you guys been up to today?' Bella asked as she pilfered a carrot stick off the pile.

Vivie grinned and then swooped to pick up her son and drag Bella from the room. 'Come and see. Blake fixed one of the chairs in the study.' Bella followed Vivie into the study and Blake leant on the door and watched them.

Bella sat experimentally on the seat edge of the stuffed chair. Instead of sinking into it, the chair was surprisingly firm and very comfortable.

'That's great, Blake. How did you do that?' Bella bounced a couple of times to experiment.

'I just added a board underneath and repacked the wadding. I'll do the other one tomorrow.' Blake grinned. 'Hope you didn't mind but it was pretty crook.'

Bella laughed. 'I don't mind at all. And I had fun driving your car.'

Blake coughed. 'Driving to work isn't fun. You should take it for a real run—go out to South West Rocks or down to Port Macquarie. There's a one-hundred-and-ten zone just past Port. Get it on the highway and really wind it out.'

Bella couldn't quite see herself cramped by the speed limit. 'Thank you for the offer. I might just do that one day.' They all trooped back into the kitchen. 'Aunt Sophie and I are going next door to see Abbey in a minute so if you're looking for me that's where I'll be.'

Abbey's house already had a visitor. All day at work Scott had thought about Rohan and Abbey, happy with their new family, enjoying all the things he'd never had. Not as a dog in the manger, more as a need to see what it could have been like if his wife had included him in the news of his son's birth. But even in the early days of his marriage he'd never had that rapport with his ex-wife that flowed between his two closest friends.

Although Scott had only intended a brief drop-in, Rohan had pressed him to stay and they had just finished the late afternoon tea the proud father had prepared.

Abbey stood up to answer her baby's cry from the bedroom. 'I'll leave you boys. My new master is calling and I want to change him before Aunt Sophie comes across.'

Scott stood as well. 'If you're having visitors, I'll go, too.'

Rohan waved him back into his seat. 'Sit for a minute. I want to talk to you.'

Scott eyed his friend warily as he sank back into his chair. 'That sounds ominous.'

'Not ominous. Concerned.' Rohan shrugged. 'My life's changed a lot in the year since I met Abbey. I have you to thank for that when I agreed to locum for you. I'm returning the favour.'

'Don't mention it.' Scott tried to divert his friend but Rohan was determined to say his piece.

'I had no idea that marriage and a family could be like this.' Rohan spread his arms to encompass the whole house. 'Every day is a diamond.' He shrugged, slightly embarrassed by his eloquence. 'And I think you should take the time to smell the roses, too.'

'Oh, I can smell them—' Scott's cynicism was clear '—but it's a bit late for me. Besides, I don't have time.'

Rohan shook his head. 'There's more to life than being on call for the town. I remember in med school, after that woman you married left, you were good fun and drove a car not unlike the one next door you seem to hate so much. I haven't seen that side of you since I moved here. You need to raise expectations of your life goals to include family and marriage again. Start having fun. In the last year I can't remember you socialising with anyone except us,' Rohan said.

'Can I go now?' Scott stood up and his friend rose, too.

'Yes, you can go.' Rohan looked at his partner under his brows. 'And stop picking on Bella.'

At that, Scott laughed. 'Have you listened to Bella lately? I think she could chew me up and spit me out.' He smiled at Rohan and held out his hand. 'Sorry I was short. I appreciate your concern, you're a good friend and I hear what you're saying.'

Rohan clapped him on the back. 'Lecture endeth.'

'Glad to hear it. Now I'm out of here before Sophie comes and tells me I'm going bald or my ears need cleaning, or worse.'

Rohan grinned. 'She must really like you. She never says that to me.' He glanced out the door. 'Too late anyway.'

Rohan turned towards the window and, sure enough, Bella and her aunt had almost reached the back door.

'You'll pay if she hassles me,' Scott said in an undertone, but his eyes were really on Bella. He didn't see Rohan bite his lip to hide his smile as he strode to the back door to open it for his aunt-in-law.

'Welcome, Sophie. Abbey's gone to dress Lachlan for your arrival,' Rohan said.

'Well, I haven't dressed up for his arrival.' Sophie glanced down at her lounge dress, the like of which she wore most days. Then she looked at Scott. 'But Dr Rainford didn't iron his shirt so I feel better now.'

Scott met Rohan's laughing eyes and as if to say, What did I tell you? 'Hello, Sophie, it's always nice to see you,' Scott said as he offered her his chair.

Sophie snorted. 'I'll bet.' She waved him away. 'I'm not sitting. I'll go and find my great-nephew.' She glanced at her niece who'd been silent beside her. 'Are you coming or staying with them, Bella?'

'I'll follow in a minute.' Bella shook her head and Scott couldn't take his eyes off her hair as it floated in a crinkled cloud over her shoulders. It was so rare that he saw Bella's red hair loose that she'd caught him unprepared. Suddenly what Rohan had said was all the more relevant. He was letting his life go by.

Bella was not some eighteen-year-old girl who hadn't seen the world. She was a flesh-and-blood woman that he'd given up for her own good. Maybe it was time to start afresh and see where it led.

'So, what are you fellows doing?' Bella seemed oblivious to Scott's scrutiny and Rohan clapped her on the shoulder.

'I'm off to hear Sophie's verdict on Lachlan and Scott's been here to sample my cooking. I made pancakes for afternoon tea.' Rohan preened.

'What a model husband,' Bella teased, and Scott watched her gaze follow Rohan out of the room. When she turned back to look at him her eyes widened.

'What?' she said, and brushed her nose. 'Have I got a spot on my face or something?'

Scott shook his head. The idea he'd had last night didn't seem so crazy today. 'You look incredibly beautiful with your hair down. You should wear it like that more often.' He met her eyes. 'Do you have to stay here with your aunt or can you come and see something I'd like to show you?'

Bella tilted her head. 'I'm sure Rohan can get Aunt Sophie safely across the yard. I'll just let them know. Will it take long?'

'Does it matter?'

He could tell she was puzzled by his persistence and not sure how to read the situation. There was nothing threatening in his suggestion. It was a little odd perhaps, but he could tell she was intrigued.

'I suppose not. Won't be a minute, then.' She left the room to find her aunt, and Scott stared thoughtfully after her.

He'd had the idea last night but had shied away from offering Bella something so personal. He still couldn't imagine Bella being a big part of his life. What had he to offer her that was different to twelve years ago? A twenty-year-old son? The bitterness twisted his stomach. She was vibrant and beautiful and full of life. The trouble was, when she looked as amazing as she did today he couldn't help trying. Rohan was right. He needed to take a few chances with his life or he might just be left with more regrets.

When Bella came back, Scott was at his most inscrutable. Bella kept looking sideways at him as they crossed the lawn to his car. 'Do you want me to take Blake's car,' she said, 'so you don't have to run me home?'

Scott gave her one of his 'spare me' looks. 'I'd be happy if you never took Blake's car again. In fact…' He stopped. 'Why are you driving that boy's car?'

Bella shrugged. 'Because mine died.'

Scott's frown lightened. 'Why didn't you tell me? I could get my garage to pick it up for you. I'm sure they'll have it going in no time.'

'No, you won't.' Bella stopped and turned to face him. 'Did I miss something here? Why do you suddenly think you can run my life?'

Scott winced. He'd spoken without thinking. The fact was, he really hated the thought of Bella's easy relationship with her new boarder. He didn't even want to think about the fact that there was less of an age difference between Blake and Bella than there was between himself and Bella. The green-eyed monster was going to get him into big trouble if he wasn't careful. 'I meant, if you'd like, I could get them to come for your car.'

Bella narrowed her eyes, and he could see she was only slightly mollified. 'There's no need. Blake says he'll have it fixed by the day after tomorrow.'

Scott swallowed the acid in his mouth at that statement and wisely held his peace. 'Fine. I would still like to show you something, though, if you'll come.'

Reluctantly Bella started towards his car again. 'So, what is it that you want to show me and where is it?'

He opened her door for her and the conversation halted as he walked around and climbed into the driver's seat. Scott didn't answer as he started the engine and put the car into gear. He hoped she wouldn't tell him to stop when she found out.

'Just to my place,' he said casually. 'What I want to show you is on the side verandah.' He'd felt her stiffen beside him when he'd mentioned his house but, as he'd hoped, the mention of the verandah drew Bella's thoughts away from the fact that they'd be alone in his house for the first time in too many years.

He'd read her thoughts correctly because she looked out of the window to avoid his eyes and said, 'Your house didn't have a verandah, but it's been a long time since I've been there.'

He couldn't help the picture in his mind. All those years ago Bella had come and blushingly offered him her heart. He'd never forget the pain in her face when he'd said he didn't return her feelings and never would. Luckily, she hadn't seen the pain in his as she'd walked away that afternoon.

'The house has changed,' Scott said as he forced his thoughts back to the present. 'I've had the verandahs added and the landscapers in. I think you'll notice a difference.'

It wasn't so much a difference, Bella thought ten minutes later, as a complete transformation.

The older cottage had been expanded to include the huge four-sided verandahs and a spacious loft that took advantage of the rural views and those onto the river.

Downstairs, it was the individual pieces of woodwork that drew her attention. The television was housed in a lowboy-type cabinet with clubbed feet and different types of wood inlaid across the doors. She walked across and ran her hand down a panel.

'I've never seen this type of pattern before.' She glanced around and there were occasional tables and a desk in the same design. 'It's beautiful.' She stroked the arm of a rocking chair obviously made by the same carpenter and then curled up in it to try it out. 'I love the strength and adaptability of wood.'

'I'm glad,' was all he said, and he held his hand out to help her up. 'Come and see outside.' She didn't want to touch him, was afraid to, but was trapped into taking his hand briefly until she'd found her feet. She disengaged her fingers quickly and Scott smiled at her strangely and followed her out onto the verandah.

The back yard had been converted to a miniature rain-forest hideaway with a tiny rock-lined swimming pool and spa reached by a Japanese-style curved bridge that led off the verandah.

'Love the bridge.' Bella couldn't help herself as she ran her fingers along the wooden rail.

'I'm pleased how it turned out.' Scott stroked the curve in the wood. 'I'd never done anything like it before.'

Bella turned slowly towards him. 'Did you make the bridge? And the rest of the furniture?'

Scott nodded and shrugged. 'Yes, I've been doing it for about twelve years, but that's not what I wanted to show you.'

Bella couldn't believe it. It was like she hadn't known him at all. There was this secret side of him that nobody talked about—or at least nobody talked about to her. Bella shook her head and followed him along the verandah.

Scott led the way around the side of the house and then he stopped in front of the most beautiful piece of furniture Bella had ever seen.

It was polished rosewood, a magnificently carved chaise longue. 'This was one of the first things I made. Do you like it?' His voice lacked his usual assurance and Bella glanced at him and then back at his work.

The chaise stood on an ancient and slightly moth-eaten Persian carpet that glowed with colour and reflected the pinkish hue of the wood so that the seat seemed to float above the floor.

'Like it? It's one of the most glorious pieces of furniture I've ever seen. But why did you want me to see it now?'

'Because I want you to have it.' Bella shook her head instinctively and Scott stepped closer. 'Because you said that Rohan took the one in your study. I don't use it and I'd like you to have it. To tell the truth, it was actually inspired by Abbey's old chaise a long time ago.'

His words shifted the mood in the room and Bella took one step backwards to distance herself.

Scott could see she was uncomfortable and he strove to lighten the mood. 'Besides, I can't stand the thought of sitting on that uncomfortable chair you have.'

'Blake fixed it.' As soon as the words were out of her mouth she regretted them. Scott's face hardened and he turned away. 'Fine. It was just an idea.'

Bella felt terrible. 'It's not fine.' She stepped up to him and rested her hand gently on her shoulder. He flinched under the light pressure and she couldn't help the soothing stroke that followed. 'I'm sorry, Scott.' She was unaware that she stroked him again. 'It's just that you took me by surprise and it's a gift of such magnitude I'd feel in your debt. And I don't like that feeling. I don't ever want to be in anyone's power again.'

Finally she felt him loosen under her hand. He turned slowly to face her and his expression was, as usual, difficult to read.

'I don't want you in my power, Bella. I do care for you and it would give me pleasure for you to have the chaise, but I can understand your reluctance. Let's forget I ever offered it. Come and see the garden while you're here.' He held out his hand.

She couldn't turn down that offer, too, so tentatively Bella put her hand in his. His fingers held hers gently and the warmth from his touch made the swirling in her stomach start again.

Unconsciously, she paused in her stride at the implications of her reaction to him. If she didn't care about him, why was she affected by the feel of her hand in his? Scott pulled on her arm gently and she flicked a glance up at his face. He was smiling and there was nothing but friendship for her to see. She kick-started her legs and walked down the steps with him onto the lawn below.

'It looks like a magazine garden. You must have a green thumb to keep all this alive.' Bella strove to keep her voice normal despite the tumultuous feelings just holding his hand was doing to her stomach and, further along, her legs.

Scott laughed with genuine amusement and Bella felt some of her tension seep away with the pleasant sound. 'The gardener has a green thumb. Mine's wood-coloured, but I do enjoy the way he can make it all flourish.'

Bella smiled back as they wandered down a winding path to a small fountain. 'I know what you mean. Vivie has the most fabulous herb garden and every time I look after it something seems to die.'

They stopped at the fountain and Bella could see golden fish swimming through the underwater greenery. She turned back towards the house. 'It's magical here, Scott. You must be very proud.'

He shrugged. 'The magic is in the person I'm showing it to.' Bella shot him a look and he shrugged without explaining, but the awareness was there again between them. 'Come on, I'll take you home.'

That was what she wanted, Bella told herself as they turned back to the house but she was walking more slowly. Bella thought about all the hours Scott must have spent carving the design on the chaise longue and why he'd want to give such a labour-intensive piece to her. Then she wondered exactly how long ago he had made it if it was the first thing he'd made. 'Can I see where you do all your carpentry before I go?'

Bella didn't know where the words came from but they had the subconsciously desired effect.

CHAPTER FIVE

'IF YOU WISH,' Scott said, and Bella nodded her head.

This was not a good idea, Scott thought, but he couldn't resist the temptation to keep Bella with him for even a few minutes longer. Seeing her drift around his house, her fingers trailing across his possessions like he'd once dreamed about, was too powerful a drug.

He turned off the path underneath a huge leopard tree and towards a building set on the edge of the property and the tension built in his shoulders. There had been a lot of emotions in that shed. It was his sanctuary and no one had been in it for many years. He ran his hand along a high ledge and produced the key to open the door. Then stood back to allow Bella to enter. He watched her enter like a watchful gazelle, sniffing the air and eyes darting for hidden dangers but filled with curiosity now she'd decide to take the risk.

All Bella's senses were on full alert as she entered the room.

The room was cool, soundproof and very tidy, but the smell of wood shavings and the lingering tang of varnish hung enticingly in the air.

She glanced around. 'Do you work in here often?'

His face shuttered. 'Nearly every day this week. When I need tranquillity. A problem that needs a solution, a sad birth.' He shrugged. 'The wood helps my thought processes.'

A cane basket sat in the corner on the floor almost overflowing with wood sweepings, and Bella walked across and picked up one particularly long and curly shaving. She closed her eyes and breathed in the scent of freshly cut timber and then hung it in her hair above her eyes. '"There was a girl who had a little curl, right in the middle of her forehead."'

Scott leaned back against the door and completed the verse. '"And when she was good, she was very, very good, and when she was bad she was horrid."'

'So what am I, Scott?' Bella couldn't help the slip into danger. 'Good or horrid?'

'Definitely horrid.' Scott crossed the room and stopped in front of her. He plucked the shaving from her hair. Their eyes met and time stopped for several seconds as they both thought of the kiss the other night. Scott said, 'Horrid but infinitely kissable.'

Bella blinked but didn't have much time for evasive action as Scott closed the distance between them and captured her lips with his. His arms came around her and he gathered her close into his warmth. Yet she knew his hold was loose enough for her to escape if she wanted to.

Bella planned to step back but somehow it never happened. The taste of Scott's mouth against hers meshed with the smells and coolness of the workshop. When he pulled her more firmly against the hardness of his chest that feeling blended with the masculinity of the environment and filled her brain with wicked mind pictures of woodshavings and strong benches.

She couldn't do anything but kiss him back and it was addictively delicious. Her fingers reached up and sank into his hair and his hands slid down and cupped her buttocks until she was on tiptoe, straining to stay attached to the floor. The kiss went on and on and suddenly the fire they'd ignited threatened to consume them both and Scott groaned as he lifted his mouth slowly and lingeringly from hers and set her down.

They stared at each other and both tried to steady their breathing. 'I get very passionate about my woodwork,' he said, and Bella nodded.

'It's passionate stuff.' Her voice was higher-pitched than normal and she cleared her throat as they both stepped apart. 'I think I should go home now.'

Scott nodded and gestured for her to precede him from the room. She waited while he locked the door and then headed for the house. She could feel his eyes on her neck the whole way and her face flamed as she remembered the way she'd ground herself against him—and how that had made her feel. Once they were inside the house, Scott still didn't say anything as he picked his keys up from the hall table.

Bella didn't know whether it was a good thing they weren't talking about what just happened or a bad idea. At his continued silence she started to worry. Was he going to pretend it had never happened? Or was he going to assume that any time he wanted to kiss her she'd be happy with that? Bella squirmed. It had only been that wonderful smell of carpentry that had brought out the wanton in her.

Finally the silence got to her. Honestly, she thought, he was a doctor, you'd imagine he'd be skilled at putting people at ease. 'I don't think much of your bedside manner, Dr Rainford.'

Scott glanced across at Bella and almost pulled the car over to kiss her again. She was flushed and he could see she was embarrassed and she probably wanted to tear his eyes out. He hadn't spoken because he didn't know what to say. He'd almost pulled her down on the floor of the shed and lost himself in her and she'd have been helpless to stop him because they'd both been blind to reason. Didn't she realise that?

'There's nothing wrong with my bedside manner.' The sex maniac inside his head whispered, When I put a couch in the workshop I'll show you. He almost groaned at the picture that painted.

She folded her arms across her chest and stared out through the windscreen. She probably thought he was insufferable. Scott suppressed a smile. When the car pulled up outside her house, without looking at him, she said, 'Thank you for bringing me home.'

Before she could pull the handle he said, 'Stay there, I'll open your door.' He could tell she fumed as she waited. She probably wasn't sure whether she was more angry at him for telling her what to do or at herself for doing what she was told. He hid another smile and opened her door.

She climbed out as if the hordes were after her. Scott just stood there as Bella muttered, 'Thank you.' And marched up the front path. Scott wasn't sure if he'd advanced his suit or killed it.

Tuesday

The next morning Bella had decided to ignore the events of yesterday. The kiss had definitely been down to proximity, that and the ghosts of twelve years ago in Scott's house which had still been at the back of her mind. The fact that their kiss had transported her to a place she'd felt inclined to linger in she didn't want to think about.

Bella tugged the brush through her hair in punishing strokes. She wasn't the naïve girl from the past—the one awed by a handsome young doctor who'd seemed to understand everything about her.

The Scott of today didn't understand her at all and she didn't want him to.

When Bella went downstairs, Blake had Vivie's baby, Ro, on his lap and both Vivie and the baby were laughing. Blake looked up when Bella entered.

He grinned and bounced young Ro on his lap. 'Your car won't be ready till Monday because we're waiting for a part for the engine.'

Bella poured the cereal into her bowl and nodded. 'Monday's fine. I can take the bus if you need your car. I never thought mine would ever go again.'

Blake rolled his eyes. 'Take my car, please. That bus is embarrassing.'

Bella grinned and finished her breakfast. 'You're a vehicle snob, that's what you are.'

Fifteen minutes later she parked Blake's car outside Maternity and she smiled as the engine gurgled its way to silence. Her brother-in-law's car was here so he must have been on call.

Rohan was at the desk when she went in and he winked when he saw her. 'Hi, Bella. So, where did you get to yesterday with Scott?'

Bella looked around at the interested faces at the desk and raised her eyebrows. 'Is this start-a-rumour day, Rohan?'

Rohan didn't even have the grace to look a little guilty as he realised how his statement must have sounded.

'Oops,' he said with a wicked smile, and left.

Bella sighed as she sat down.

Sharon, despite her eagerness to get home after the night shift, leaned towards Bella and pretended to elbow her. 'And what was that all about, boss?'

Sharon and Bella had been in the same class at school and Bella knew she wasn't going to get away without replying.

'Scott showed me a piece of furniture he'd made, and the rest was Rohan's imagination.' She looked at Sharon. 'Did you know that Scott was a carpenter?'

Sharon nodded. 'He gave Abbey a beautiful round table to auction the year before last when we wanted to raise money for the ward.' She smiled at the memory. 'Half the women in the hospital bid for it but I think it went to some rich widow who fancied him. It didn't do her any good. The money bought a new Sonicaid.'

'Oh,' said Bella. 'Abbey didn't mention it.'

Sharon shrugged. 'It was before you came back from Sydney.'

Bella pushed away the thought that Abbey hadn't talked voluntarily about Scott to her for many years. She nodded and sat further back in her chair.

'So, what happened on the ward through the night?' Sharon shot a quick look at Bella and then shrugged as if to say, Was that it?

Bella raised her eyebrows and waited and Sharon grinned. She started the handover report.

An hour later, Bella had had time to speak to all the patients and was back at the desk. Scott strolled in and Bella tried to think cool thoughts to stop the blush that she could feel in her cheeks.

'It's warm this morning,' Scott said with a saintly smile, and Bella narrowed her eyes.

'So it seems,' she said with restraint. She didn't look at him again as she moved off down the hall with the patient files and Scott had to follow.

In the first room, Melissa's baby was in her mother's arms. 'Tina seems to have stopped her bradycardias,' Bella said.

Scott cupped the baby's foot in his big hand and the sight pulled strangely at Bella's stomach. She was noticing more and more about him every day and she couldn't seem to stop herself.

'That must make you feel better, Melissa.' Scott smiled at the girl.

Melissa smiled back. 'Yep. When I heard the machine noises slow down I could feel my own heart go faster. It was pretty scary. Are you sure she shouldn't have the machine when I go home?'

Scott nodded. 'Yes. I'm sure.' He sat on the edge of the bed. 'Tina's bradycardias don't change her skin colour so even though her heart rate and breathing slows down her breathing doesn't stop. She's still getting all the oxygen she needs. You'll find that any bradycardias that she has now will usually be after a feed and she will have fewer and fewer of them as she grows. I would be very surprised if she was still having any by the time she's ready to go home.' He smiled sympathetically. 'You need to get used to the idea there won't be a machine to listen to her all the time, but I know it's hard.'

Melissa nodded and glanced ruefully at Bella. 'That's pretty much what Bella said.'

Scott looked across at Bella and his face was deadpan. 'Sister Wilson and I agree on everything.'

Bella nodded, and refused to dispute anything that would undermine Melissa's belief in Scott's words.

When Scott looked a little disappointed by her lack of dissension, Bella had to suppress her smile. He looked back at Melissa. 'How's Tina with her feeds?'

Melissa shrugged. 'I can't get her to feed from me but she'll take my milk from a bottle every second feed. Bella says that's pretty good for her prematurity.'

'My word, it is.' Scott nodded and glanced at the feed chart. 'And how are you after the birth?'

The girl shrugged. 'I don't even feel like I had a baby. I can't wait to take her home but I know I have to be patient.'

'It's tough,' Scott agreed, 'but you're doing a great job.' He stood up. 'I'll see you tomorrow.'

They left Melissa and the rest of the round was accomplished swiftly.

Back at the desk, Scott couldn't resist commenting, 'I see you're still driving the hot rod.'

Bella nodded. 'Mine won't be ready till Monday and it's more fun than the bus.'

Scott's lip curled. 'It's a death trap.'

Bella shook her head. 'Now I'll have to disagree with the great Dr Rainford there, which is strange when we agree on everything.' Bella shrugged. 'In fact, I'm planning on taking it for a spin this afternoon down to Port Macquarie. Just to open it up on the highway.'

Bella had no intention of doing anything of the kind but Scott's persistent ridicule of Blake's car annoyed her.

Scott was silent for a minute and Bella waited to hear what disparaging comment he'd make now. 'Want a passenger?' Scott's question hung in the air between them and Bella froze. Her mind blanked and she had a horrible feeling her mouth was open.

'Well?' There was an underlying amusement in his persistence as he pressured her, almost as if he knew she'd never meant to do it.

'Sure! Why not?' Bella threw back at him recklessly, and they stared at each other, each daring the other to back down. In the end Scott nodded and headed for the exit.

'Better bring a spare pair of underpants,' Bella muttered.

Scott froze on his way to the door and looked back at Bella incredulously. '*What* did you say?'

Bella looked up innocently. 'I said I'd better check the spare on the off chance.' Scott didn't look convinced and Bella glanced with pretended nonchalance at the clock on the wall. 'I'll pick you up at six. That will give us almost two hours of light with daylight saving. Unless you want to change your mind?' She showed her teeth.

Scott bared his right back. 'I'll be ready.'

When Scott had gone across to the other side of the hospital to see his patients in Children's Ward, Bella sank into the chair and put her head in her hands. What had she done?

She had little time to worry about it. The day nurse, Michelle, had just made them coffee when Bella heard the front door open. She walked out to see who it was and her heart plummeted.

A terrified young mother rushed up to Bella and thrust her limp baby into her arms. The baby was blue and lifeless. 'She stopped breathing. She's sick. Get the doctor.'

'Michelle!' Bella's call had Michelle on her heels as she ran to the nursery with the baby in her arms. Bella hit her fist against the raised red cardiac-arrest button on her way to the infant resuscitation trolley, and the reassuring beep echoed through the corridors. Help would be here soon. Bella squeezed back the panic in her throat and concentrated. 'Airway. Cardiac output,' she said under her breath.

She placed the baby's head towards her on the trolley, in the 'sniffing' position, but couldn't see any reason for the baby not to be breathing. Quickly she tried to hear a heartbeat with the stethoscope but couldn't find one.

The baby's mother was crying and wringing her hands and Bella glanced briefly at her. 'Did you find her like this or did she stop breathing on the way here?'

'She wasn't breathing when I found her in her crib but she started again when I picked her up. Then she stopped again on the way here.'

'That's great. You did the right thing. Help is on the way,' Bella said as she twisted the knob to send oxygen surging through the mask of the resuscitation bag. She held it over the baby's face and gave three quick puffs of the clear bag, watching the infant's lungs inflate and deflate. So there was no obstruction.

Michelle came to a hurried stop beside her and Bella handed her the bag. 'Grab this and bag her, please. I can't find a pulse and we'll do ECM until help arrives.'

The next two minutes felt like a lifetime and although the baby didn't breathe, her colour improved and Bella thought she heard a tiny thready beat when she stopped after the second two minutes.

Scott skidded into the room and Bella had never been more pleased to see him. Two younger doctors from the emergency department followed him in, and if the situation hadn't been so grave Bella would have laughed at how out of breath they were compared to the older doctor.

She gave verbal handover to Scott. 'Mum found her limp in bed. Baby started to breathe when picked up and stopped again on the way to hospital. Limp and blue on arrival and I couldn't hear a heartbeat. Think there's one now, though.'

'Good stuff.' His face was intense as he examined the infant.

Bella continued with the ECM except when Scott listened to the baby's heartbeat.

'She's got a good heart rate now.' Bella changed places with Michelle when Scott indicated she could stop cardiac massage and Michelle drew the mother to a chair to sit down.

'Close. Very close.' They put a head box with oxygen around the baby's head and watched her. 'We'll put an IV in and get her hooked up to the monitors, then transfer her to Port Macquarie so the paediatricians can give her a thorough going over.'

He glanced at the mother and lowered his voice. 'I'd say this was a too-close-for-comfort, sudden-infant-death-syndrome scenario. They may never find out why her baby did this, the poor woman.'

Bella nodded and she could feel the sting of tears in her own eyes. She couldn't imagine anything more frightening than the thought of losing a child. She wanted to hug the young mother but Michelle was doing that so Bella smiled mistily at Scott instead.

Scott stayed while they waited for the ambulance to transport mother and baby to the larger base hospital. One of the emergency doctors was going with them just in case.

Scott reassured the mother before she left. 'Because she's been so stable since she's woken up, it does look better for her. The paediatricians will look after you both.'

Bella hugged the woman. 'Take care.'

'Thank you.' She brushed away her tears. 'I'll come and see you when we get out of hospital.'

'I'd like that,' Bella said, and she stood beside Scott as the ambulance drove away. Bella wanted to cry to relieve the tension but she fought it. As if he sensed how she was feeling, Scott rested his hand on her shoulder and leaned his forehead against hers. It felt so comforting Bella wanted to stay there all day.

'Good job, Bella,' he said, and she felt the tears prick her eyes again.

'I was very glad to see you,' she said in a shaky voice, and he smiled as she stepped away.

'That's what I like to hear.' He tilted his head at her. 'Make sure you're glad to see me at six o'clock. That's if you still want to get out this evening?'

Not surprisingly Bella had forgotten about their plans for Blake's car. The thought of wind in her hair and being right away from the hospital sounded good.

'I'm no piker,' she said bravely, and turned back into the nursery to help Michelle clean up.

At six o'clock Bella's misgivings had returned and multiplied ten times. Blake had thought it a great idea for Bella to go for a 'decent spin', as he called it, but he'd looked at her strangely when she'd mentioned she was taking Scott.

'I think it will be good company for Bella to take Dr Rainford,' Vivie said, and Bella smiled weakly back.

'Thanks, Vivie.' She glanced at the clock again. 'Could you leave my dinner in the fridge, please? I'll reheat it when I come home.'

'Sure.' Vivie tilted her head knowingly. 'If you've already eaten, I'm sure we can find another hungry person to feed it to.'

Blake looked up, not unlike a starving puppy, and both women laughed. Bella jingled the keys and waved on her way out.

Scott was standing on his front verandah with a small basket when she pulled up. Bella leaned across the seats and pushed opened his door.

He climbed in. 'Thank you,' he said.

'I wasn't being polite.' Bella grinned. 'That door doesn't open from the outside.'

'Great,' Scott said, and leaned over the back to rest the basket on the floor. 'I brought a picnic.' Then he tested that he could open the front door from the inside. 'So if we crash, the emergency services can't get in to me, is that right?'

'You're such a pessimist,' Bella said as she put the car into first gear and roared off down the street. Scott exaggerated the g-force slamback in his seat and Bella ignored him.

She'd driven with Scott before in the bus. There was no reason to feel intimidated by Scott sitting beside her now. She was a good driver and she did love the way the car cornered like it was glued to the road.

Bella double-shuffled back into second as she approached an intersection and then planted it as the lights changed to green.

Scott loosened his collar. 'Do you remember that Disney cartoon about the schizophrenic driver who changes when they get behind the wheel? Mr Walker becomes Mr Wheeler?' Scott's voice was conversational and Bella shot him a look.

'I've stayed within the speed limit.'

'Granted.' Scott's voice was dry. 'At least turn your headlights on so the other cars have more warning that you're coming.'

Bella looked over the top of her sunglasses at him as if to say, It's broad daylight. But she switched the lights on and then pushed her glasses back up her nose.

Scott ignored her sarcasm and tried some of his own. 'Can't wait for the highway.'

Bella had no intention of breaking any speed limits but he was being insufferable. She pushed in the tape deck and some high-voiced rap artist talked repetitiously with a mind-numbing bass beat in the background. She sneaked a glance at Scott's horrified face and relented, but couldn't help the giggle. 'Sorry. That time I was pulling your leg. It's not my taste either.'

'Thank God for small mercies.' Scott pretended to wipe his brow and Bella relaxed into her seat. This was fun. In fact, much of the last few days had been fun and not a little exciting. But she was too busy to worry about that now.

They left the outskirts of town and Bella sped along the highway with the windows open. The little car whipped around any slower vehicles in the overtaking lane and the roar of the wind drowned out any hope of conversation.

By the time they'd driven to the turn-off to Port Macquarie, Bella was bored with the highway. 'How about we head past Wauchope? At least I can play with the corners.'

Scott shook his head and grinned back at her. 'I have a cast-iron stomach. You won't make me carsick. Do your worst.'

Bella flicked on the indicator and they took the doughnut over the highway and sped down the tarmac towards Wauchope.

The Torana seemed to be enjoying the outing and Bella decided that she could become addicted to rally driving.

Half an hour later Scott pointed to a sign. 'I see they have a picnic area down by the river, and I brought a picnic. Let's have a break.'

Bella nodded and turned off the road. The tarmac soon disappeared and they bumped along the dirt for what seemed like miles before coming to the river. Bella pulled up in the huge deserted parking area. 'They must have been planning on a party for this place.'

Scott looked around and there was no sign of life. 'Must be an off week.' He leaned over the back and lifted the basket and waved it at her.

'Hungry?'

Bella nodded and climbed out. She found a tarpaulin in the boot to spread on the ground.

Scott planted the basket in the middle of the blue sheet and proceeded to stretch out on the ground and put his elbow over his eyes.

Bella glared at him. 'What's this?'

Scott didn't move his arm and his voice was muffled. 'Chauvinism.' Bella bit back a smile but, truth be told, she was dying of curiosity to see what was in the basket. 'Then you have to pack up afterwards.' That was all she said as she flipped off the lid.

Chicken, Camembert, avocado, what looked like shop-made potato salad, some crusty rolls and two bottles of non-alcoholic white wine. Plus a jar of sliced mango. Not a bad effort for a confirmed bachelor. 'What? No coffee?'

This time he did remove his arm but he put it back over his eyes when he saw she was joking. 'Got me,' he said.

'Well, come on, look alive. I'm starving and I want to get home not too much after dark.'

Scott sat up and edged along the tarpaulin to sit next to the basket.

While Bella made up the plates, he opened the wine and poured it out into two plastic goblets. 'To small cars and speed limits.'

Bella grinned and took a sip. It wasn't bad. She relaxed back on her elbows and breathed in the fresh air.

'This is actually quite a radical thing to do on a weeknight,' Bella mused.

'Very,' Scott agreed, and raised his glass again for another toast. 'To radical things on weeknights,' he toasted.

They clinked plastic and both of them laughed at the dull clunky sound.

Bella stared at the clouds that were turning pink in the sunset. 'What's the most radical thing you've ever done, Scott?' The question popped out without much thought.

CHAPTER SIX

'WHAT MAKES YOU think I've ever done anything radical?' Scott stared pensively into his wine and Bella glanced across at him with a frown.

'Everyone has done something mad at least once in their life.' She smiled encouragingly and then her smile faltered. 'Tell me you have.' There was a long pause and she stifled the disappointment that accompanied the worry Scott might never have done anything remotely mad.

'You mean, apart from running off with a woman fifteen years my senior and being left soon after?' Scott watched Bella blink and for the life of him he couldn't think of anything radical he'd done since alienating Bella all those years ago. Suddenly he remembered the family planning seminar he'd been to last week. The company reps had been giving out freebies and he'd stuck a couple of condoms in his wallet to give to Rohan, along with a crack about spacing babies. 'But I don't want to talk about that radical mistake. How about something radical I have with me?' Maybe he could make her laugh.

She relaxed her shoulders as he teased her. 'But I'm not sure I want to tell you and I don't want you to get any ideas.'

Bella bristled again and he suppressed his amusement. Here with Bella, tonight, offered a precious hour of joy from nowhere, and he was savouring it.

Bella glared at him. The man was laughing at her. 'You're just saying that to whet my appetite.' His slow smile warmed that fluttery feeling back into her stomach. She took a gulp of her drink and thanked her stars that the wine wasn't potent. 'So? Give!'

He smiled again and shifted along the tarp to be closer to her. He reached into his pocket and pulled out his wallet.

Bella frowned. 'What are you doing?'

'I'm showing you something mad that I've got.'

His hands flicked open his wallet with painful slowness and slid his fingers into the back section to pull out a small package. He placed the packet in the palm of his hand. 'That's it.'

Bella peered at his hand. 'What?'

'It's a glow-in-the-dark condom.'

There was something so bizarrely out of character about Scott and his possession of a glow-in-the-dark condom that it made Bella shut her eyes and bite her lip. Serious, conservative and dignified Dr Rainford, luminescent with lust. An ordinary, flesh-coloured, non-ribbed condom discreet in his wallet perhaps, but glow-in-the-dark?

A bubble of laughter slid its way up her throat and she tried to hold it back, but the amusement escaped in a deep-throated giggle. That chuckle was followed by several more hiccups of mirth, and before she knew it Bella was rolling around on the tarpaulin, holding her stomach. Scott watched her with pretended offence until she could control herself. She lay on her back and gasped for air, holding her aching diaphragm.

Finally she managed, 'What a Boy Scout.' And wiped the tears from her eyes.

'I can see you're impressed. In fact, I've got two. I'll give you one to keep. Now, tell me about something you've done.'

Bella shook her head. 'I can't top that one.'

Scott wasn't taking that. 'It's your turn—tell me.'

Bella leaned back and stared at the darkening sky. The silence lengthened. She'd always been a wimp. 'I went topless in the hospital pool one night after lights-out.' She sighed with disgust. 'I kept my panties on because I couldn't even do the full monty.'

'That idea has potential,' he said, and glanced suggestively towards the river.

She shook her head. 'I don't think so.' Bella finished the wine in her goblet and dropped the empty cup into the picnic basket.

That fluttery feeling was coming back in her stomach and Scott's glance seemed to be getting warmer. 'Well, my compliments to the chef. It's been very pleasant, but we should go.'

Scott nodded without apparent reluctance and Bella assured herself she was glad.

'Work tomorrow,' he said. 'You have a wander down to the river and I'll do my part of the bargain and pack this away.'

Bella stood up and brushed the last crumbs from her hands. 'Thank you, kind sir.' Superfluous, she wandered down towards the rocky bank of the shallow river and stood beside a huge weeping willow with all the leaves and branches eaten off to cow-neck height. She smiled at the exactness of the bovine pruning line and turned back to the car.

Scott had folded the tarpaulin and put the basket back in the car and looked to be waiting for her to return.

'Coming,' she called as she scrambled back up the stony slope to the car. 'Do you want to drive?' she offered, but Scott shook his head with a smile.

'I like to live dangerously—you drive.'

'Well, if those are the two most radical things we've ever done, driving with me probably constitutes dangerous.'

He opened her door and then walked around to the passenger side to climb in. Bella leaned forward and twisted the key in the ignition, but the only response was a thready clicking noise.

Scott swivelled his head to look at Bella and folded his arms. 'I hope that wasn't what I thought it was.'

Bella glared at him and tried again. The clicking noise returned but that was it.

Bella inhaled slowly and then deliberately exhaled. 'OK, Dr Mechanic Rainford, what is that noise?'

'That, Sister Wilson, is the sound of a flat battery. Did you turn off the headlights when we stopped?'

Bella's gaze flew to the light switch and, sure enough, it was on. She switched it off hurriedly as if to make up for her lapse but, of course, it was too late. Bella slapped the steering-wheel and chewed her lip. 'You told me to turn the lights on. Why didn't you tell me to turn them off?'

Scott smiled cynically. 'A woman's logic.'

Bella glared at him and then she brightened. 'I'm a member of NRMA Road Service.'

Scott gave a half-laugh. 'Not in this car, I suspect.'

Bella frowned at him. 'Won't they come to me because I'm a member?'

Scott pulled out his mobile phone and handed it to Bella. 'Try them. But I bet you ten dollars there's no reception down in this hollow.'

Bella almost snatched the phone and punched in the six-digit number for Road Service, but the phone was dead. She passed the phone back carefully to Scott and then succumbed to an insane flurry of slapping hands on the steering-wheel again.

Scott grinned and looked away before she could see his smile.

Bella stopped, blew a strand of red hair out of her face and consciously relaxed her shoulders. Then she glared at him. 'You planned this.' Bella's accusation made Scott's eyebrows lift.

'Now, that would be radical,' he murmured, and Bella hung her head.

'I'm sorry. That was stupid. What are we going to do?'

Bella's reaction to the breakdown was strangely different to his. Scott was feeling remarkably calm and not a little pleased with the thought of spending the evening with Bella in unusual circumstances. Which was strange, as he'd normally be obsessed with being at work on time tomorrow, and available should the remote possibility arise of Rohan needing him overnight. Not to mention the fear of scandalmongers.

Scott shrugged and gestured to the darkness that was quickly falling. 'At a guess, I'd say we're going to sleep here tonight and walk to a phone in the morning.'

Scott wound his window up. 'I'd recommend winding your window up until after dusk or we'll be fodder for the mosquitoes.'

Bella hastily agreed and then she sat back in her seat and tried to think of a solution. They hadn't passed a house on the way in off the highway so that made it a couple of miles' walk at least. Then there was the dark factor.

No car was going to stop in the dark to help them anyway. She couldn't find an answer that improved on Scott's suggestion. She doubted anyone would find them or even start looking until tomorrow. Even Vivie would think she'd stayed out to tea and no one would be any wiser until she didn't turn up for work next day. She winced. The rumours would be horrendous when they did go back.

'Let's run away to Perth,' she said half-jokingly.

Scott smiled. 'Thinking about the gossips, are you?'

Bella nodded and sighed. 'Is this a radical thing to do?'

'Right up there.' His hand came across and closed over her fingers. 'It's really not a tragedy. Tomorrow morning we'll try and push the car up the slope and maybe we can clutch-start it. But it's a bit dark to do that now.'

'But when I don't turn up for work, they'll ring Vivie and she'll ring Abbey and Rohan will ring you and you won't be home...'

'Shh.' Scott squeezed her hand and Bella could hear the thread of laughter in his voice.

'Look at it this way—we're safe, and being slightly embarrassed is nothing. As for work, I'd be a little more worried if Rohan wasn't in town, but he is. He can handle anything that needs to be handled and Sharon or whoever is on night duty will stay until you arrive.'

Bella sighed one last time and then straightened in her seat. 'You're right. I won't moan any more and I think you've been very good about this considering it was me that left the lights on.' She felt very self-righteous taking the blame and she looked across to see if Scott commended her for it.

No such luck. 'I think so, too,' he said, 'but, then, I was saving recriminations in case we got bored later.'

Bella shook her hand out of his and crossed her arms, but when she looked back he was smiling. She stared at him. Who was this man? 'You've changed so much from the grumpy shirt of last week that I barely recognise you.'

'Grumpy shirt?' he repeated wonderingly, and then became more serious. 'It's been a big week.'

They sat there for a while in surprisingly companionable silence. Then Scott leaned his head back, closed his eyes and started to talk. 'Since finding out about my son...' he grimaced '...and coming to terms with the fact that I didn't have the chance to watch a child of mine grow up, something I would love to have memories of, I've reassessed my life.'

She heard him sigh before he went on.

'Michael's existence and the fact that I've never seen him has changed my perspective. It's made me look at other areas of my life that I should have seen to years ago.' He smiled at a memory. 'And Rohan gave me a serve that had me thinking as well.'

Bella was intrigued. 'What did Rohan say?'

Scott opened his eyes. 'He was fairly succinct,' Scott said wryly. 'That I need to raise expectations of my life goals and that I can't just be there for the town. He also said I should take time for myself and start having fun.' He turned to look at Bella with a grin. 'Guess we've started on the last one.'

It was dark outside the car, and a cow bellowed not far away. Scott looked at his watch. 'It's eight-thirty. The mosquitoes should be gone now. Do you want to stretch your legs?' Bella nodded and Scott opened his door.

'At least there weren't any cowpats near the car,' Bella said brightly.

'And it's not raining, Pollyanna.' Scott was rummaging in the glovebox for anything else useful. 'Ta-da.' He brandished a box of matches. 'I shall build a campfire, and with a bit of luck someone will come to tell us to put it out.'

'I'll help gather wood.' The idea of a campfire shining benevolent light was very appealing and Bella tried to remember if she'd seen any broken branches on her short walk. It wasn't ink black yet and she could see outlines of obstacles in front of her.

After half an hour of hard work they had a reasonable-sized firewood pile in the middle of the parking area.

Bella had brought the tarpaulin from the boot again and spread it out on the ground. The first flickers of flame seemed to spread light in gradually increasing circles and by the time the fire was well established, the whole parking area appeared friendlier. They stood together and admired Scott's handiwork.

'Well done, fire king,' Bella said. 'Now what do we do?'

Scott took Bella's hand and pulled her sideways in front of him then gently back so he could encircle her with his arms as they faced the fire. 'Are you one of these people who have to be amused all the time?'

Bella could feel the hardness of his body against her back and buttocks, and the warmth of his arms felt right, and not something she wanted to fight against.

'No,' she said in a voice half the volume of what she'd intended. She felt his chin rest gently in her hair and then the movement of his lips as he dropped a kiss on the top of her head. Bella closed her eyes. This wasn't what she'd imagined when she'd started this trip today but it felt so good she couldn't help sighing. But she needed to be careful. There was a fine line between special moments and those she'd live to regret.

They stood there for a long time and the silence between them was tranquil as they soaked up the unexpected solitude.

For Scott it was wonderful. Bella in his arms, relaxed and happy with his prowess as the fire provider, they had food and water at the river and a long night ahead to establish the beginnings of what could be the relationship he'd never allowed himself to dream of. 'Well, this is better than reruns of *Bonanza* on television,' he said with a smile in his voice.

Bella tilted her head. 'What's *Bonanza*?'

Scott shut and opened his eyes. Apart from the fact that it was an asinine thing to have said to a young and beautiful woman in his arms, her response was not surprising. She was too young to have ever seen *Bonanza* and he'd grown up with the show. What was he thinking of? He was a fool to think this relationship was going to work. His arms dropped.

'Reality check,' he murmured. 'It's an old TV show that was on before you were born.' And he walked over to throw another stick on the fire.

Bella bunched her fists against her sides. 'Now, that response was more like the angst-ridden Dr Rainford of last week,' she snapped, and Scott threw his head up and glared at her.

The words hung in the air between them. Suddenly the little picnic area wasn't as friendly any more. He took several large strides and before she knew it he was right beside her again.

He wasn't the one who was going to lose out by being with someone old and crotchety. He was trying to protect her and didn't she realise it was killing him?

'And which Dr Rainford do you prefer?' His voice was soft but that dangerous quality was back, the one from the kitchen when she'd asked about his marriage. Bella could feel the acceleration in her heart rate but she wasn't going to back down.

'I like the one in the car from an hour ago and the one from five minutes ago.'

Scott caught a thick strand of her hair between his fingers and used it to turn her head until there was barely an inch between their faces. 'What about the one in my workshop? Because I'm damned if I can get *that* Bella out of my mind.'

His lips came down on hers and Bella knew this was not a good idea, alone in the bush in the dark, and the hunger in his voice matched the hunger deep inside herself and she wanted to lean into him but she just wasn't ready for this. The warning she'd given herself was too recent.

Bella pulled away and slid out from under his arms and walked out of the circle of light towards the river.

'Where are you going?' he asked, and she turned back to look at him. The light from the fire was behind him and his face was shadowed yet surrounded by a fiery halo. He was everything she wanted in a man. It wasn't Scott she was afraid of, it was herself and the fragility of her own self-esteem if she ended in his arms tonight. She wasn't ready to risk everything she'd worked for in the last year because it felt good at the time.

'I need some space.' Time away from him to think about the ramifications of wanting to give herself to Scott and what could happen to her if he let her down again.

'Be careful,' he called after her. It was the 'be careful' that did it.

The next second her foot disappeared down a rabbit hole and her ankle twisted with excruciating sharpness as her full weight came down on it. Her cry was muffled but Scott heard it. The grass and rocks were digging into her hands as she tried to keep the weight of her body off her leg, and the tears sprang to her eyes as the burning pain shot up behind her knee. Any attempt to remove her leg from the hole made her whimper with distress.

'It's OK, sweetheart.' Scott appeared on his knees beside her and his hand ran down her calf and into the hole. 'You've jammed it good and proper and your ankle is starting to swell already. We have to get it out before it gets any fatter.'

'I do not have fat ankles.' Her voice was weak and she was trying not to cry with pain.

He patted her shoulder. 'Ankles, no, ankle, yes.'

The next few minutes were ones that Bella would have preferred to forget. When her foot finally came free, her head was swimming from the pain. Scott gathered her up in his arms and hugged her to him for comfort then carried her back to the fire where he propped her up against the picnic basket.

His cool hands ran lightly over the rapidly swelling bulge above her foot. 'We have to bind that ankle. I don't think it's broken, but we'll get you X-rayed when we get back.

'You need an ice-pack, which we don't have, but I'll nip down to the river and get some cold water.' He left her and gathered up the empty wine bottle to fill with water.

When he returned from the river, he'd stripped off his shirt and had it bundled, sodden in his hand, ready to wrap around her ankle. As he crouched beside her, intent on supporting the swelling, Bella diverted herself by the sight in front of her.

She'd never seen Scott without his shirt before. Maybe that had been good for her peace of mind—because she wasn't going to forget the sight in a hurry. His chest was deep and broad with only a fine sprinkle of dark hair across the tanned expanse, and she remembered the solid feel of the muscles in his arms when he'd carried her across to lay her down. His skin glistened in the firelight and it bronzed his tan even more.

There wasn't an ounce of spare fat to be seen as he knelt over her and in her dazed state she found her hand straying to trace the ridges of muscles in his abdomen. His skin was warm and firm under her fingers. She imagined him shirtless, rhythmically shaving wood in his workshop, the muscles bunching and relaxing with the sweep of the plane. Her head swam.

'Did I hurt you?' He stopped at her touch and she drew her hand back and shook her head.

'No. I just felt a bit faint. I needed to hang onto something.' She was glad the light from the fire wasn't shining on her face.

He smiled at her and Bella felt faint again. 'Your bedside manner is better than it was before,' she murmured.

He touched her cheek and returned to his bandaging and Bella had to admit the cold cloth felt heavenly against the heat in her ankle.

When he'd secured it as well as he could, Scott sat back on his heels and looked at her. 'I'm guessing your ankle is throbbing like a drum full of knives. I think we need to change plans about staying until morning. How do you feel about me leaving you for a short while to try for some reception on my phone?'

Bella looked at the darkness at the edge of the circle of light they'd created. 'I'll be fine as long as a cow doesn't decide to walk all over me.'

'I could squeeze you into the back seat of the car with the windows down,' Scott offered, but she shook her head.

Despite the throbbing in her ankle, Bella smiled. 'Leave me a big stick and I'll be fine out here. It's too nice a night to be stuck in a car.'

He nodded and returned with two sticks, one magnificent wand-like branch and the other a shorter but sturdier one. 'One for playing with and one for business.' He put them beside her, as well as the wine bottle full of water and the jar of mango slices. He'd stripped the lambswool seat covers off the front seats of the car and made her a soft backrest and a fleecy mound to raise her leg on.

'I'll be as quick as I can. Call out if you need me. The sound should carry and I'll hotfoot it back to you.'

Bella looked up at him. He'd already come to her rescue once today. The image of Scott rushing to save her like a shirtless hero on a safari made her smile. 'I'd like to see that.'

Scott tapped her nose. 'Do not cry wolf,' he warned, but there was a smile behind his eyes. 'I'm looking for the rise we came over before the parking area. I shouldn't be long.'

Bella twisted her neck to watch him disappear with long strides and he was beyond the light within seconds. The moon was slowly rising and it wasn't as dark as it had been. She looked in the direction of the river and the sound of frogs and crickets seemed louder now that she was on her own. All this because she hadn't wanted Scott to kiss her. Actually, because she'd really wanted Scott to kiss her too much.

CHAPTER SEVEN

ON HIS RETURN, Bella heard Scott's footsteps crunching on the gravel before she saw him. He loomed tall above her and his face was very dear and welcome as he stepped into the light.

'How did you go?' They said it at the same time and both smiled.

'I was fine.' Bella went first. 'Did you manage to speak to Rohan?'

He nodded as he crouched down beside her to look at her ankle. 'I had to go a bit further than I'd hoped to find reception, but he should be here in about an hour.'

He studied her face. 'How's the pain?'

'As long as I don't move my ankle—bearable. Thank you for taking such good care of me, Scott.' She looked away from his searching gaze.

His voice was gentle. 'If I hadn't frightened you, you wouldn't be in this predicament.'

She felt the blush in her cheeks and kept her head down. 'I overreacted. And was clumsy.' She plastered a smile on her face and looked up at him. 'Let's not talk about it any more. What did Rohan say?'

'Lots of things I'm not going to tell you.' He shook his head with a grin and looked across at the fire. 'I'd better build this fire up a bit so they can find us, then start collecting water so we can put it out when we go.'

Later, when Rohan's Range Rover nosed next to the bonnet of the Torana, they could see there were two occupants in the car. Scott scowled when he recognised the young man from Bella's house.

'I've brought Blake to be the mechanic because it's his car.' Rohan raised an eyebrow at Scott. 'I would have brought a shirt for you if I'd known you'd lost yours.' Rohan's eyes twinkled in the glare of the headlights and he ignored the frown on Scott's face.

He smiled at Bella as she waved from her seat on the tarpaulin. 'Hi, there, Bella. I've brought you some painkillers.' Rohan came and sat down beside her and handed the tablets over. 'What was that you were saying today about starting a rumour?'

She ignored her brother-in-law's question as she swallowed the pills. She wasn't looking forward to the moving bit to come. 'Thanks for these and for coming, Rohan.' She smiled weakly across at Rohan's companion. 'You, too, Blake.'

Blake leaned through the driver's window of the Torana and popped the bonnet before turning back to her. 'Vivie was beside herself, thought you'd had a crash,' he said, and grinned as he raised the red bonnet.

Bella shook her head. 'Poor Vivie. No. I just left the headlights on when we stopped and flattened the battery, then I fell down a rabbit hole.'

'One of those day's, eh?' Blake said with another grin. 'I'll leave the medical stuff to these guys and jump-start the car.' Blake walked around and leaned into the front seat of Rohan's car and pulled out the jumper leads. Efficiently he connected the two cars and started Rohan's car then climbed into the Torana and turned the engine over. It roared into life and Blake hopped out and disconnected the cars.

Scott knelt down beside Bella. 'Rohan and I will carry you together but I'm afraid this is going to be a little uncomfortable.'

'Typical doctor's understatement,' Bella mumbled under her breath.

'Put your arms around my neck and we'll be as gentle as we can.' Bella reached up and Scott's hands went beneath her and suddenly she was up against his chest again. His warmth surrounded her and she'd never felt so safe.

Strangely her ankle hardly hurt at all but maybe that was because Rohan supported it in the sheepskin and they eased her into the car with as little jerking as possible.

Bella caught Rohan's eyes as he watched Scott arrange her on the seat and she rushed into speech. 'That was pretty good. You guys should have been paramedics, though I probably could have walked.' It was all bravado because she wouldn't have been able to put her foot to the ground, but she hoped it would divert the knowing looks she was receiving from both Rohan and Blake.

Scott ignored the other two. 'I don't think so,' he said as he eased the other sheepskin behind her leg to wedge it from moving. 'Stop making a fuss.'

Bella's eyes widened at the unfairness of the comment. 'I did not make a fuss.'

'I know. I was teasing you. You've been very brave and I'll be pleased when they've X-rayed that ankle. I'll just go and make sure the fire's out.' He backed out of the car and Bella watched him go. He was so tall and efficient and he'd cared for her with kindness and compassion. She didn't notice that she sighed as he walked away. Rohan did.

Scott had actually been very calm about the whole cascade of events, she thought. If she had to be marooned with someone again, not that she was planning to be, she wouldn't mind if it was Scott. Of course, there wasn't much chance of that happening. The day had been a fiasco from start to finish. She'd be lucky if Scott wanted to talk to her after this night was over.

The click of seat belts from the front meant they were on their way and Bella gazed wistfully out of the window as the headlights made one final sweep of the area before pointing back to the road. Blake honked his horn as he overtook them in his car and his taillights gradually disappeared.

'Young fool,' Scott growled.

'Just young,' Rohan disagreed. Bella's ankle was too painful for her to enter the conversation. Thankfully Scott didn't pursue his vendetta against Blake and the conversation died a natural death.

When they arrived at the hospital, Scott seemed oblivious to the fact that he was shirtless and Bella was in his arms. Bella held herself stiffly although she felt like burying her face in his chest. To bury her face in his bare chest would actually be even nicer than burying it in his shirt, but she restrained herself.

The last thing she wanted was that feeling of being the subject of the hastily terminated conversations she'd gone through last year. Hopefully any rumours would blow over before she came back to work.

After an hour's wait for X-ray results, the emergency doctor agreed with Scott and Rohan and pronounced her ankle bruised and strained but not broken.

When Scott carried her back to the car, most of the staff of Outpatients were there to wave them off. Bella could feel the heat of embarrassment all the way to the tops of her ears. Considering how seriously Scott had always taken public opinion, he seemed unfazed. It was another puzzling facet of his recent behaviour.

Rohan assured Scott that he could manage to get his sister-in-law to her room without Scott's help and dropped him at his house. Scott leaned through the window before they could drive away. 'I'll see you tomorrow morning before work, Bella. Keep that leg elevated.'

Rohan was remarkably restrained for the rest of the drive home and Bella sighed with relief. But she knew her sister would be given a full account of his suspicions. Bella didn't want to think about that upcoming conversation because she wasn't ready to examine her feelings for Scott Rainford on her own—let alone with anyone else.

Wednesday

The next morning, Bella's ankle was less swollen but just as painful. Vivie brought her breakfast in bed and even Aunt Sophie had made it up the stairs to see the invalid.

'The whole trip sounds like a disaster,' Sophie pronounced. 'It's hard to look attractive when you've sprained your ankle.'

'At least he took his shirt off to wrap around my ankle.' Bella couldn't resist the opportunity to shock Aunt Sophie, but she was dreaming.

A snort indicated that Sophie was unimpressed. 'If he took his trousers off, that would be something to write home about.'

'Aunt Sophie!' Typically her aunt had come out on top. 'Scott was a complete gentleman after I was injured.'

'And what about before?' Sophie shot back. Bella blushed and Sophie cackled. 'You've made my day. You wait till I see him.'

'Aunt Sophie, don't you dare say anything to Scott or I'll never talk to you again.'

'Eh?' Sophie said as she heaved herself to her feet and cupped a hand over her ear. 'What did you say? Can't hear you.'

Bella shook her head as she listened to her aunt chuckling and wheezing as she went down the stairs.

Ten minutes later there was another knock and Scott opened the door. 'Good morning, Bella. How's your leg this morning?'

He looked very handsome and Bella couldn't help the tide of colour that rose in her cheeks as she worried if Sophie had seen him come in.

'I'm fine. I think it's a little better,' she said.

Scott sat down on the edge of the bed. 'Sophie said it was still painful.' Bella's cheeks burned hotter. 'Can I check it or would you rather someone else looked after you?'

Bella frowned at his diffidence. 'Now, why would I want that?'

He shrugged and she pulled back the sheets to expose her legs. The bandages were still intact from the treatment in the emergency department and he nodded with approval at the pillow under her leg. He gently ran his fingers over the bandage. 'The swelling's gone down quicker than I thought it would.' He undid the bandage and his cool fingers ran gently over her swollen skin. 'It looks much better.'

Bella had been rehearsing what to say to Scott all night. She bit her lip. 'Scott?'

He looked up. 'Yes, Bella?' There was amusement behind his eyes as if he knew what she was going to say.

'I'm sorry for the inconvenience yesterday.'

His eyes twinkled and she realised again how different he looked when he wasn't being stern. 'Why? I invited myself and dared you to say no.'

Bella smiled. 'Yes, you did.' She decided on complete honesty. 'Well, truth be told, I wasn't really going until you invited yourself and then I couldn't get out of it.'

Scott laughed out loud and Bella thought how few times she'd seen him really laugh over the last month. He should do it more often—it made him look more like someone else she knew but she couldn't place the resemblance. It also made him even more gorgeous.

'I'd say we're equally to blame,' he said. 'Next time we'll take my car. The Volvo beeps when I leave the lights on.'

Bella bit her lip at the thought of more day trips with Scott. She didn't know how she felt about that idea. She left it at a noncommittal, 'We'll see.' Luckily Scott didn't pursue the conversation.

'Keep that foot elevated today. How's the pain, really?' he asked.

'A little easier and those pills Rohan gave me help, but they make me vague.'

'Keep taking them today. If you rest properly you might be able to get up tomorrow.' He glanced at his watch and stood up. 'By the way, I rang the local bus service and they'll donate a driver for your youth bus this week.'

She felt like bursting into tears that he'd thought to do that for her, which was ridiculous. It was probably those stupid pills that made her emotions so fragile. Bella bit her lip and looked up at him. 'Thank you.'

'Rest,' he said, and left. Bella stared at the spot where he'd disappeared and then glanced at the clock to see how many hours until he came back. When she realised what she'd done she closed her eyes and called herself all kinds of fool.

There was another knock on the door and she opened her eyes. She wouldn't be lonely, she thought, and straightened her blankets and called for whoever it was to come in. Blake poked his head around the door but didn't enter the room.

'Hi, Bella.' He smiled and Bella couldn't help the feeling of *déjà vu* that trickled down her spine. He'd taken the eyebrow stud out, shaved and cut his hair, and it made him look older and infinitely more wholesome. 'Who is this gorgeous young man at my door?' she teased.

'It was Vivie's idea,' Blake said, and he ran his hand through the short brown spikes on his head. 'What do you think?'

'You'll get a swollen head if I tell you what I think.'

Blake blushed. 'I just wanted to know if you needed anything in town today.' He shrugged. 'Books, magazines, fruit?'

Bella indicated the chair beside the bed. 'Thanks for the offer, Blake. How about a conversation instead?' Anything to get her mind away from her last visitor. 'Can you spare me ten minutes?'

Blake shrugged again and walked across the room. He spun the chair backwards to straddle it. 'Sure.'

Bella watched him sit and his boyish enthusiasm made her feel old. 'I'm always rushing about and I haven't had a chance to ask you how you're settling in. So, tell me, how do you find living in a house full of women?'

Blake laughed. 'Actually, it's fun. I always wanted a sister, and it's like having six of them.'

'I've two sisters,' Bella said. 'Abbey you know and a younger one, Kirsten. She's due back from Saudi Arabia soon. Do you have any brothers?'

'Nope. And both my parents were only children as well. They were in their fifties when I arrived but they always had time to sit and talk to me. I miss that the most.' He kept his head up but there was a suspicion of moisture in his eyes.

'You sound very proud of them,' Bella said gently.

'I was…am. They were wonderful people. Dad died last year and my mum died a few months later. I miss them both.' He looked away and then back at Bella. 'They didn't own their own home and by the time I paid all the bills there wasn't much left to stay in Sydney for. I decided to come up here.'

Bella nodded. 'My parents died when I was a couple of years younger than you. Losing them was horrible. But I wasn't alone like you were. I've always had Abbey and she looked after Kirsten and me. Later on Aunt Sophie moved in with us as well. I can't imagine not having any family.'

He shrugged and then stood up. 'I don't need anyone.' He glanced across at Bella. His statement hung in the air for a moment, then he said, 'Can I ask you a question?'

Bella smiled. 'If I don't like it I won't answer.'

'Fair enough.' Blake stared down at the carpet. 'Are you and Dr Rainford going out together?'

Bella shook her head and then realised he couldn't see her answer. 'No. We're not. Dr Rainford thinks he's too old for me.'

She glanced across at Blake's face and saw his brows draw together and the dark frown made his face so incredibly like Scott's that she drew in a sharp breath. It had to be coincidence but since Blake had lost his beard and long hair the similarities between both men screamed out at Bella. No wonder she'd felt Blake was familiar—he looked a lot like Scott had when she'd first met him.

Blake was oblivious to Bella's shock. 'What about you? Do you think he's too old for you?' he said.

Despite her racing brain, Bella had to smile. 'I've never thought he was too old.'

'So you've fancied him for a while?' Blake certainly wanted the ins and outs. Bella laughed. 'I think this is where I say I'm not answering.'

Blake glanced across and grinned. 'OK.'

'I've got a question.' Bella wondered if she was mad but the conviction was growing. Now every time Blake's face changed expression he looked like Scott.

'Do you have a middle name, Blake?' It was a long shot and she didn't really have the right to pry.

'Why do you want to know?' He was more guarded and Bella trod carefully.

'Just curious. You don't have to tell me if you don't want to.'

'Michael,' he said, and Bella nodded.

Her voice softened. 'And what did you find out in Sydney that made you want to come up here?'

Unconsciously, Blake glanced towards the door. 'What are you getting at?'

'I wondered if you were searching for something—or someone.' She saw his knuckles tighten on the back of the chair and she didn't know how it could be but she knew that what she suspected was true.

'I don't want to answer that.' Blake's mouth had hardened.

'No problem.' Bella watched the suspicion grow in his eyes and she backed off. 'I've been meaning to say how much I enjoyed driving your car.'

Blake followed her lead in the change of subject but the suspicion was still there. He nodded. 'I like it. Sorry it died on you.'

'I often wonder if things happen for a reason,' Bella mused, and Blake let go of the chair and jingled his keys. He couldn't hide his eagerness to escape.

'If you don't want anything from town then I'll be going,' he said.

'No. I don't need anything. Thanks for asking,' said Bella, and he left. Vivie met him at the door but he didn't stop. Blake edged past her to disappear down the stairs a little faster than normal.

Vivie looked after him wistfully and then came into Bella's room with another cup of tea. Bella would be floating by this afternoon if she didn't stop drinking the stuff. 'Thanks, Vivie.'

Bella had to consciously avoid asking questions about Blake but the temptation was there. Fifteen minutes later Vivie left and Bella took two pills for the pain in her ankle but she knew she wouldn't sleep for a while as she mulled over her suspicions. Should she tell Scott?

When Abbey and baby Lachlan came to visit, the sisters talked about babies and motherhood for a while. It was Abbey who broached the subject they'd both been avoiding.

'Do you need to talk about Scott?' she asked, and Bella shook her head.

She should have known Abbey would instinctively offer to listen but not pressure her to answer.

'No, I'd like to get it straight in my mind.'

Abbey nodded though she still looked concerned. 'I still believe he did the right thing twelve years ago but I can see you are both different people now. I'm here to listen if you need me.'

Bella nodded and Abbey didn't stay much longer.

When Scott called in again that evening after work Bella had had time to think. There hadn't been much else to do stuck in bed. Unless Blake decided to confirm her suspicions, nothing would be gained by Bella's interference. The most she could do was try to help Scott see the young man in a more positive light.

'Vivie tells me Blake has been to see Melissa and her baby every day. That's pretty good for a young guy who's not the father of the child.'

Scott wasn't receptive when she mentioned Blake's sterling qualities. 'I came to see how your ankle was, not discuss him.' He cocked an eyebrow. 'I thought your house guests were none of my business anyway.'

Bella could have stamped her foot in frustration except it would have hurt. Instead, she gave up. 'My leg is fine. How was the ward?'

Scott frowned at her. 'The ward will be fine. Will you stop worrying about everyone else and just relax? The world won't stop turning because you're not there to sacrifice yourself.'

Bella glared at him. 'I don't sacrifice myself. I chose my life. And you're the last person who should talk about sacrificing.'

Scott shook his head. 'Now you sound like Rohan. And I didn't come here to bicker with you.'

Bella paused then asked, 'Why did you come, then?'

'To see that you were improving. I was also going to offer a run in my car on Saturday if you wanted to get out after being inside for a few days. But if you're as cantankerous as you are now, I won't worry.' The new, teasing Scott smiled at her and she could feel the traitorous melting feeling she seemed to have been afflicted with over the last few days every time Scott entered her vicinity.

Bella stopped and stared at him. Did she want to spend more time alone with Scott?

Unfortunately, yes.

She couldn't help the flutter of excitement in her stomach that accelerated as she considered his invitation. Yes. She'd like that. But she wasn't going to do anything she might regret later. 'I think I'd enjoy that. Thank you for thinking of me.'

He stood up. 'I have to go to Port Macquarie for a conference tomorrow and Friday, so I'll catch you Saturday, then? Say about ten?'

Bella nodded and smiled to hide the realisation that she was actually going to miss not seeing him tomorrow. Maybe she'd be better to cancel now because this was more serious than she'd anticipated. All these emotions from a few hours in his company had become dangerous territory.

It was almost as if he had read her thoughts, he said, 'It's just a trip to get you out.'

Later that night, when all the lights in the house were out, Bella lay and stared at the ceiling.

She thought about her relationship with Scott when she'd been eighteen, from the perspective of an almost thirty-year-old woman, and saw it for what it was—young adoring love on her part. She wasn't sure, but probably it had been infatuation on Scott's part. She just couldn't figure out why he'd encouraged her in the first place if he'd been unwilling to trust his instinct.

Realistically, she was starting to fall under his spell again, and she didn't know if she could trust him not to hurt her again.

Was she going to choose to let Scott into her life with all the risks that entailed if he cooled off again like he had twelve years ago?

Bella closed her eyes determinedly and willed herself to go to sleep. She was the one responsible for her own happiness—not him. She'd just have to go with her instincts.

Saturday

Come Saturday morning, Bella stared out the window at the lack of rain-clouds. Not one to be seen in a blue, blue sky. She'd have to go. The simmering excited side of her smiled but the sensible, wary side shook in its sensible boots.

When Scott arrived, the sensible Bella was waiting, unsmiling, in light trousers and a T-shirt at the kitchen table. Her ankle was almost better, but she'd strapped it and wasn't planning to overstretch it today because she needed to be right by Monday for work. She had to admit, though, Scott had been close to the mark about her going stir-crazy from being house bound.

'How was the conference?' Bella asked, and gathered her handbag and sunglasses.

He smiled. 'Fine. Have you been so bored you missed me?'

'Just bored,' Bella said as she walked carefully through the door Scott held open for her.

She stepped out into the sunlight with a feeling of relief to escape from the house but couldn't help a little trepidation at the thought of what she was going to say today.

Bella planned to be careful, go for the ride and come home heart whole and with some answers. While Scott concentrated on the traffic she stared at him thoughtfully.

He seemed relaxed today and the curve of his lips made Bella's mouth twitch. What was it about him that reached out and pressed all the right buttons? In her eyes he really hadn't changed much since she'd first known him except for his assurance. Now he carried himself as if he was accustomed to the responsibilities that rested on his shoulders. Responsibilities that he took seriously, to the extent that he was the person always available when needed, the local doctor who attended the most house calls and did the most after-hours calls. He'd always said that the town was his family and Bella suddenly realised how much they'd all relied on him over the years.

Externally, she couldn't see the drain it must have been on him. His chin had always been ruggedly square and seriously dark brows hovered ready to exclaim or frown above his jungle-green eyes. Even his hair remained black-coffee brown with no sprinkling of the grey that should have been there and no clue to the passing of years. He had such broad shoulders. Her gaze lingered.

The sudden memory of after she'd turned her ankle, the breadth of his chest as he'd easily carried her, the strength in his arms and the gentleness in his hands, twisted in her stomach and made her look away from him. She stared out of the window to lecture herself on finding that aloofness she'd decided to hide behind today.

'Do I pass muster?' There was a teasing note in his voice.

Bella looked back at him and met his next glance and smiled. She needed to stop feeling like a silly teenager around this man. 'You've always been attractive to me, Scott.'

Startled, he flicked a glance back at her and she was glad she'd spoken out. Every time she'd said what she thought, things seemed to improve between them. Though she was going to test that theory to its limit today. 'I was just trying to work out why.'

'Tell me about it,' he joked, and she frowned. Scott's insecurities had never been a factor in her rationalisation of the heartbreak she'd suffered at his hands.

She took a quiet breath to steady her voice. 'Maybe today would be a good time to clear out the cobwebs and get rid of some of the things I've never understood.'

'About what?' He asked the question but Bella had the feeling he knew what she meant.

'About what happened between us twelve years ago.' Bella watched his face in profile and she couldn't tell how her suggestion had been received.

'Perhaps,' he said, and the silence lengthened between them as she let him ponder her statement. Bella was content to wait.

The scenery flashed past. A farmer on a motorbike rounded up his cattle and she smiled at a blue cattle dog nipping around the edges of another herd. Then they turned off the road towards South West Rocks and Scott broke the silence between them.

'I thought we might go up to the lighthouse first, check out the view and maybe have a coffee. Which I remembered to bring,' Scott said.

'Lucky, after last time.' Bella nodded and they both smiled at the memory of her mock complaint at their last picnic.

The car wound slowly through the dim rain-forest drive up to Smokey Cape Lighthouse and Bella couldn't resist opening her window to feel the cool moist air of the heavy vegetation. The sound of cicadas and birds drifted into the car. She thought she caught a glimpse of a lyre bird but it was gone before she could point it out to Scott.

They popped out into the sunlight beneath the lighthouse and the sea stretched away in three directions past the headlands.

Scott stopped the car for a minute while Bella soaked in the view with a smile on her face. 'I'm so glad I came. I'd forgotten how lush and beautiful it is along that road and then this.' She spread her hands and her gaze travelled along the horizon and back again.

'Me, too,' Scott said, but he was looking at Bella. 'It's easy to forget what you have in your own back yard.'

Scott manoeuvred his car into the highest spot in the car park and then came around to open her door.

'I thought we could sit at one of the tables and watch for whales.'

'Thank you,' Bella murmured as he shut the car door behind her. 'I've never seen a whale.'

He nodded. 'I don't really think they go past here at all.' She laughed because she knew that they did. He lifted the familiar basket onto the picnic table, and this time he produced a Thermos of steaming coffee. 'Percolated!'

She shook her head. 'You're having me on.'

Scott grinned. 'Ground this morning. Of course, it's never as good as the freshly made stuff but we'll see.'

Bella sniffed the contents of her mug and the aroma was strong and rich. The azure sea stretched away to meet the lighter colour of the sky and a white-capped sea eagle circled overhead.

She sighed with pleasure. 'I could get used to this.'

Scott gazed out to sea as well. 'When I think of all the weekends I haven't done something like this, it makes me feel I should count the ones that are left.'

Bella frowned. 'That's a little morbid, isn't it? I'd prefer to think of it as thank goodness I remembered to come here, and I'm definitely going to try and come more often. Even knowing this is all here enriches my soul.'

'Pollyanna strikes again.'

She shook her head. 'It's more than positive thinking. It's accepting that life is full of experiences, good and bad. We aren't victims of fate because we can choose how we deal with those experiences.'

'Some people don't deal as well with life experiences as others.' Scott looked away and then back at Bella again. 'Take love, for instance. What have you learnt from love?'

Bella raised her chin. 'From love?' Her voice lowered and he had to strain to hear her. 'All bad things,' she said. 'It's taken me a long time to rebuild my self-esteem and for the moment I choose to stand alone.'

Scott winced at the part he'd played in her disillusionment. 'So you're never going to get involved with a man again?'

She shook her head vehemently. 'I didn't say that. I'm just not going to lose myself in the process.' She tilted her chin. 'And if I find someone, he'll get a better bargain. Not some wimpy clinging vine.'

'I used to like vines,' he mused. 'A woman's arms hanging on. There's a halfway mark, you know. Some vines are so strong people can grow with them.'

She smiled. 'Nice analogy. I was getting a bit serious there. Sorry.'

He shook his head and captured her chin in his hand. 'You were telling me how you feel. And I'm privileged that you feel you can talk to me.' He let her go.

Their eyes met and there was silence for a moment as everything from the past seemed to shimmer between them. 'I've always felt I could talk to you,' she said.

He refilled her cup. 'In the car you said you wanted to clear out cobwebs and old misunderstandings. What sort of cobwebs?'

Bella looked at him thoughtfully. 'Big cobwebs. Huge cobwebs. Cobwebs like why you let me think I meant something to you twelve years ago then abandoned me. Then told Abbey to keep me away from you.'

'Oh,' he said. 'Those cobwebs.'

CHAPTER EIGHT

'IT'S A LONG story but I guess we have time,' Scott said, and cast his mind back to a time that had made a great impact on his life.

Twelve years ago, Bella and her two sisters had stood at their mother's grave like red-haired nuns dressed in black. Abbey, the oldest, had been slightly bowed but upright under the weight of responsibility. Kirsten, the youngest, had looked confused and angry and her eyes had searched for answers. But Bella, frighteningly beautiful like her mother, had been completely lost.

Scott looked at her now. That young girl was long gone.

He removed the coffee-cup from her hand and took her fingers in his. He held them lightly as if he needed to feel her hand in his to tell this story.

'I remember the first day I saw you. It was your mother's funeral. You stood totally crushed, like a bruised and bewildered flame-headed butterfly, impaled on a tragedy too great for you to grasp. When I looked into your eyes that day, something shifted—irrevocably—and it didn't matter how hard I tried to tell myself it wasn't so.'

Bella felt the tears film her eyes as she listened. It was as if they were both standing in that moment of time. She could almost feel the nip in the air and the moisture from the rain that had fallen just before the service. And she could remember that look. The compassion in his eyes had soothed her as nothing during those terrible days had been able to do.

He went on. 'I'd lost my mother years before and I understood how devastating it was for you. I went home that night and I couldn't sleep. I told myself that I'd just help you.' His mouth curved cynically.

'I was so much older than you.' He looked at her. 'I'm still so much older than you,' he said dryly, and they both laughed at the ridiculousness of the statement.

It lightened the mood for a moment and they smiled at each other before he squeezed her hand and continued. 'I'd made mistakes, big mistakes, and you were so young and pure and so deserving of the best that life could offer you. I've never thought of myself as the best.' He stared straight ahead.

'I was brought up by a rich uncle and aunt who did what was necessary and sent me to the best schools, and I'm grateful for that. But I'd never felt as if I belonged anywhere until I moved here and the town welcomed me with open arms.

'Everyone trusted me and here I was contemplating the seduction of a vulnerable teenager.' He put her hand back in her lap and sat up as if the next part was harder to talk about.

'I was weak in the beginning because you needed so much comfort and I told myself I could step back when you were less destroyed by your loss. But the more I saw you the more you offered me, and if I hadn't stepped back I would have lost my head and we would have been lovers. I would have demanded you marry me, and I have first-hand experience of how such age-disparate marriages can fail. I couldn't risk the pain I'd experienced falling to you if our marriage failed. I cared for you too much to see you wish you'd never married me.' The starkness in his voice told her that he meant every word he said, and Bella spared a dark thought for the woman who had made him doubt himself so badly.

'Why didn't you talk to me about it?' Bella's voice thickened with tears and memories.

'I knew if I explained that to you then, you'd have said we should be together. You deserved more.'

She shook her head in denial. 'What did you tell Abbey and why?'

'I told her we were too close and that I was too old for you. Telling Abbey was the only way to make the break permanent.' He snorted with self-derision. 'I knew she would agree. That time you came back to my house we were playing with fire and that's why I had to send you away.'

Scott shifted on the seat. 'Abbey was the only one I knew who was strong enough to help.'

A single tear slid down Bella's cheek unheeded by her. 'What if I'd said you were all I ever wanted?'

He stroked the drop from her cheek until it disappeared. 'I wouldn't have believed you. Still wouldn't believe you.'

She nodded and stared out to sea again. Then it was hopeless all over again. All she said was, 'That explains a lot.' And left it at that.

'You said there were a few things you wanted clarified today?'

She couldn't take any more of his reasons for not loving her. 'Maybe later.' She dropped her cup in the picnic basket and stood up, suddenly needing to leave this place and the things that had been said. In fact, a slow anger was building and she needed to distract herself. 'Where else are we going today, driver?'

Scott shook his head. She amazed him and frustrated him and he couldn't read the mixed signals he was getting. This day was becoming more painful than he had bargained for as he could sense the beginnings of a horrible feeling that maybe he had done the wrong thing all those years ago to turn Bella away. That concept had implications for the negative experiences Bella had been through, which he didn't want to think about, and he concentrated on manual tasks to divert his thoughts.

After he'd repacked the car, they drove down towards the town of South West Rocks along the back road at Arakoon, then past the new country club and into town.

'Do you want to eat at a restaurant or take-away on the headland?' Scott left it up to Bella because suddenly he didn't know what he had planned. This day was spinning out of control faster than he could have imagined.

Bella glanced up the side road that ran up to the lookout. 'I used to have fish and chips on the headland with my family when Mum and Dad were alive. Let's do that.'

Scott nodded and parked in the parking area above the beach.

Horseshoe Bay was small and had a bluff of rock pools at one end and tumbled boulders at the other. Between was a curve of white sand in the shape of a horseshoe. Tall pine trees overlooked the grassed areas that ran almost down to the beach, popular with young families and older couples.

Today it boasted a dozen families and the lifeguard in charge was busy keeping the swimmers within the flags.

Bella pointed to a spot in the middle of the bay. 'I was caught in a rip there once. But it was a weekday and there wasn't a lifeguard.'

Scott looked out where she indicated and there was nothing to make it look dangerous.

'I can remember it as plainly as if it were yesterday. I was only about nine. Dad was swimming with Abbey. Kirsten was stung by a bluebottle in the shallows at the same time as I must have paddled across the rip.' She pointed to a darker line in the water. 'There's a rip.' She looked back at him. 'Mum was trying to calm Kirsten and Dad went to help her. The rip pulled me out into the deeper water before I knew it and suddenly I couldn't make any headway towards the beach and everybody on the beach seemed further away. I was terrified and tired from trying to swim against the undercurrent.'

She shivered at the memory. 'All of a sudden Abbey appeared beside me and told me to stop fighting the pull and we'd slip out the side of the rip in a little while.'

She looked towards the tumbled boulders. 'We climbed out of the water over there and I was crying and Abbey was telling me how clever I was to hang on for so long. But I knew if it hadn't been for her I would have drowned.'

She shook her head at the memories and smiled. 'Dad made us join junior lifesavers that summer to learn about safety in the sea, but I never enjoyed it much.' She laughed. 'Abbey used to win the races all the time. It's funny, the things that affect your life.'

Scott steered her towards a park bench and they sat down overlooking the bay. 'I wish I could have been there for you.'

'Abbey was there.' Bella shrugged. 'She's always been there. I guess that was why it was so devastating when I was attacked last year. I was already hurting from discovering that the man I loved had lied to me for three years. I was on the way to Abbey and her safe haven and then something even worse happened. I thought nothing more horrible could happen than that, and I blamed Abbey for not saving me. Until Abbey was nearly shot by that madman. Ironically, in the process of saving Abbey and Rohan, I saved myself.

'From not being able to look myself in the mirror, suddenly I could hold my head high. I realised that I do have power and that was when I decided that I would choose how to let things affect me.'

He stared at her. 'You've come a long way. You deserve to be proud of the woman you are now.'

'I am proud. And I'm careful. So I won't be rushing into anything.' Her words hung in the air between them.

She brushed away an ant that had climbed along the seat. 'Enough about me.' She turned to face him and the sun was shining in her hair and the fierceness in her eyes had been replaced by compassion.

'Tell me about your marriage, Scott.'

He didn't want to but maybe it was time for him to leave the past behind as well. He rubbed his chin. 'My marriage was a poor choice in a long line of poor choices. I was looking for a family, and a sense of belonging that I never had with my aunt and uncle. Maybe even a mother like the one I lost.'

He laughed bitterly and Bella put her hand on his arm. 'I don't know why Madeline married me but, whatever the reason, the reason went away and she couldn't get out of the marriage fast enough.'

Bella tilted her head. 'Maybe the pregnancy scared her?'

Scott grimaced. 'It seems likely in hindsight. We really had nothing in common but I would have stood by her. She didn't have a termination so it wasn't that she didn't want our son either.'

'Maybe she was protecting you?'

Scott couldn't see the logic in that. 'From what?'

Bella frowned at his lack of insight. 'From throwing away your life on her and a new baby. Did you ever say anything about not wanting children?'

He stared into the distant past. 'Who knows? I could have. I was young and selfish and determined to finish uni. We were fighting. Maybe I said something about being glad we didn't have children to hear the shouting. I don't remember, but it's not outside the realms of possibility. Perhaps she decided she wanted the child and not the father. I'll never know. I know that she ended up hating me so much she kept the birth of my son from me. I just wish she'd given me the chance to find out if I could be a decent father.'

Bella heard the bitterness in his voice. 'So Michael would be around the same age you were when you married his mother.'

He looked at her. 'I guess you're right.' He turned to watch a toddler splashing at the water's edge. 'I see a child like that little fellow and think how I missed out on seeing Michael that age.' He shifted his gaze to a young boy throwing a ball. 'And that age.' And then to a young man and his girlfriend at the next bench. 'To now.'

Bella nodded. 'So how do you imagine him now?'

Scott stared at the people swimming between the flags. 'I admit that in the last fortnight, if I see a young man walk down the street I think that I could walk right by him and not recognise him as my son. It's not a nice feeling.'

'Do you think he'd recognise you?'

He smiled. 'Do you mean an older face in the mirror?' He thought about it. 'It's a nice idea.' He laughed. 'And pretty scary for him.'

'You really are age-obsessed, aren't you?' She said the words lightly but he took them to heart.

'I don't even want to go there.' This was too close to naming the reason for all the mistakes he'd made. He wasn't sure of the final tally and what that admission could cost. He stood up. 'Let's find fish and chips.' Scott brushed off the negatives. The pain of catharsis, he thought cynically.

Then she cast her spell over him again and he couldn't help thinking of all the years they'd missed out on.

They sat on a blanket on the grassy headland overlooking the main beach and ate out of the white paper wrapping. The long crescent of sand stretched away in the distance to Trial Bay where the ruins of the old penal settlement were stark above the convict-built break wall. They munched hot golden chips and crunchy pieces of freshly fried fish covered in salt and lemon juice, and when he was finished Scott watched Bella lick the salt from her fingers. The savage twist in his stomach ensured that he turned away.

He looked back when she'd finished. 'You are torturing me, you know that?' he said.

Bella cocked an eyebrow at him and there was nothing childlike in the glance she sent him. 'Good. You deserve it. When I think of the devastation I suffered at your hands, I'm glad.'

He laughed out loud at her sudden defiance and reached across to steal the longest of her chips.

'Hey, I was saving that one.' She glared at him and tried to snatch it back but his arms were longer than hers and she brushed against him delightfully.

'Good,' he said, and dangled it closer so she'd reach again for the chip. When she was off balance he slipped his arm around her and pulled her onto his lap so that she was looking into his face. He dropped a kiss on her salty lips, and her eyes widened in surprise. He flicked the clasp out of her hair and then rolled her back onto her side of the rug so that he was leaning over her with her hair spread out behind her.

She looked so beautiful and vibrant, but despite his position of power he had the feeling she was nowhere near intimidated by him. 'What are you going to do about that?' he dared her.

'I could be very nasty from this position,' she warned with a glint in her eye, and Scott laughed and rolled off her.

'Ah, the self-defence classes.' He sat up again and offered his hand. 'Women's lib is such a pain.'

She let him help her up and finger-combed her hair back into its clasp.

'But useful.' She stared at him thoughtfully. 'Where do you think this new rapport we seem to have found is going?'

He shrugged and wouldn't meet her eyes and Bella's self-protective instincts kicked in when he said, 'I'm not sure. Does it have to go somewhere or can we just start again as friends?'

'What sort of friends, Scott?' There was a snap in her voice. 'It's a great idea but what about the fact that I seem to end up in your arms when I least expect it? That's not friendly, that's chemistry.'

He met her eyes and the warmth in his look felt like a breeze from the equator across her skin. She had no control over the way he could sear her with a glance. 'See!' she said.

He smiled and captured her hand between his. 'We've always had that and I don't know why. But at least I'm looking for an answer.'

Bella bit her lip. 'Well, I'm not looking for heartache again, Scott.'

Scott looked at her. 'I hear you when you say you don't want to fall into heartache. But if you fall I will catch you. I won't ever drop you again.'

She frowned. 'Am I the only one who thinks this change in our relationship is too sudden? I'm not sure I can trust you.' Bella shook her head and screwed up the paper roll her chips had come in.

He spread his hands. 'So how do you think we should do this?'

She met his eyes and the wariness was still there on her side. 'We'll see how we go.' She took one more look at the horizon and stood up. 'Thank you for the day. I'd like to go home now, please.'

Sunday

Sunday was for thinking and weighing up and having space to consider what it would mean to trust Scott not to hurt her again. And to realise even those few times in the last week they'd spent together had been enough to fan the attraction she'd always felt towards him. She needed to accept that he was her weakness.

It wasn't fair and it wasn't sensible but she needed to admit that she would always love Scott Rainford—and that she was falling 'in love' again.

Unfortunately she still had the same problem she'd had twelve years ago—he wasn't ready to commit to anything or tell the world he was in love with a younger woman, and she'd grown up enough to realise she deserved more. It didn't look promising.

She could stay firm and avoid Scott out of work hours but realistically when he turned the heat on she was like ice cream in the sun. A sticky puddle of indecision.

When the phone rang that afternoon, Bella took it in the hallway, fully expecting it to be for one of the girls.

'Hello?' She absently picked up a pen to take a message.

'Bella?' Scott's voice jerked her out of her daydream and into confusion.

She was hopeless. The least she could do was not let him know that. 'Yes, who is this?'

'It's Scott!'

She could hear the frown in his voice when he answered and she suppressed her smile.

'Yes, Scott. What can I do with you?' She stopped and replayed what she'd said in her head and winced. 'I mean, *for* you.'

'We'd better not go with the first one,' he teased, his good humour restored, and she felt like stamping her foot. She was nearly thirty years old. She should be calm and collected on the end of the phone.

He went on, 'I wondered if you'd like to come around. I've a chilled Verdello, we could eat Chinese take-away and share the sunset before we dive into another hectic week on the ward.'

'I don't drink and drive.' It was true and convenient.

He wasn't fazed. 'Then I'll pick you up and send you home in a taxi.'

She was going to say no but he must have sensed that. 'It's a pretty radical thing to do, to catch a taxi home on a Sunday night.'

Bella weakened. All the memories of that wonderful afternoon by the river came back and teased her. But she needed more time to think things through before she did her moth impersonation and circled his light bulb again.

'I don't think so, Scott.' But she couldn't help the indecision in her voice.

'One drink and dinner then I'll send you home.'

She could go or she could stay home and wish she had gone. Hard decision. 'I hope the taxi charges you double for weekend rates.'

'Fine,' he said. 'I'll be there in half an hour to pick you up.' The phone went dead.

Bella stared at the handset as if it were responsible for the panic she was in now. Today was supposed to be for reflection.

By the time she'd changed, told Vivie she wouldn't be home for tea, changed again because she didn't want to look like she'd changed, and spent ten minutes talking to herself in the mirror and promising not to get into any close clinches with Scott, he was there. She couldn't believe she was dumb enough to do this when he'd blatantly told her he just wanted to be friends.

'Have you ordered dinner yet?' She clicked the car seat belt into the locking mechanism and turned to face him.

He looked at her sideways. 'It's home delivery. They'll bring it when I ring. Are you in a hurry?'

'I don't want it to be a late night.' Bella stared straight ahead.

He glanced at his watch. 'It's five-thirty. I could probably have you in bed by seven.'

Bella jerked her head to look at him in shock and he took his hands off the steering-wheel briefly to ask the question, 'What?' Then he realised what he'd said and bit his lip, but his eyes were laughing.

'I meant to bed in your house—not mine.'

Bella felt like an idiot but she took a deep breath and tried to calm down. She'd worked herself into such a state and she'd been so focussed yesterday. That's what was really getting to her. She'd lost the plot and yesterday she'd had it all under control.

Scott sensed her turmoil. 'Relax. We'll have a pleasant evening and I'll send you home in a taxi.' He should never have asked her to come, Scott thought. She wasn't ready and he was pressuring her. He was a fool and there was a real risk that they'd do something she or he could regret. He didn't want that. 'Would you like me to take you home now?'

Yes, she thought. 'No, I'm fine,' she said.

It was a little easier when they arrived at his house. They walked around the garden to see which shrubs were flowering at the moment, and by the time they were back on the verandah Bella was feeling more in control. A large glass of Verdello helped.

The conversation flowed and they slipped into the old rapport that had been such a big part of their relationship all those years ago. Bella only had to half explain things and Scott understood the nuances and why.

But there was more humour between them now and the longer they talked the more relaxed Bella became.

The sun slowly sank over the river and they leaned on the verandah rail to enjoy the cascade of changing colours against the mountains in the distance. When the sun had set she sighed.

'I think we should eat.' Bella stared into her empty glass and Scott nodded.

'I've really enjoyed this, Bella,' he said. 'Come through into the lounge while I phone the restaurant. You can choose some music while we wait.'

Bella found some ballads that suited her mood and she flitted around the furniture admiring Scott's carpentry, still awed by the fact that he had furnished his house with his own creations. She wandered across to the mantelpiece where there was one single photo of Scott as a young man, flanked by an older couple. The resemblance to Blake was striking.

He came back into the room and tucked his wallet back into his trousers. 'What shall we do while we wait?'

'Is this your aunt and uncle?'

He crossed the room to her and stared at the photo. 'Yes. I was about seventeen. I've changed a bit since then.'

Bella stared at the photo. 'Not that much. Your hair was lighter and, of course, your build was more slight. Your son probably looks like that now.'

She saw him frown as he stared at the photo with more attention. She wondered if he could see the resemblance between the photo and Blake as he was now. Would Scott comment on the similarities between Blake and himself, and should she tell him her own thoughts? Bella didn't know what to do. 'What are you thinking?' she asked instead.

He looked at her and then back at the photo. 'It's nothing. A crazy thought.' Her heart rate accelerated and then settled when he shook his head to shrug it off. Then he smiled at her and subtly the mood in the room changed.

'Where were we?' he said.

Bella turned her back to him before he saw the awareness in her eyes. 'Monopoly?' She offered.

'Maybe I should just take you home now and they can deliver your part of the Chinese food to your house.'

'That's always an option.' Bella talked to the safety of the mantelpiece in front of her.

His voice came from behind her shoulder and although he wasn't touching her she could feel the heat from his body next to hers and the vibration of energy between them.

'You should be wary but we won't do anything you don't want to do, Bella,' he said, but they both knew that wasn't the problem.

'It's not *your* control I'm worried about, Scott,' she said dryly, and turned to face him. Bad idea.

He was very close. They stared at each other and she shook her head. 'Why do I feel as if I'm going to regret this if I do and regret it if I don't?'

'What are you talking about?' he said, and moved back a pace.

'I think you should just kiss me and let the rest work itself out.' Bella watched his eyes widen and his hands went back behind his body in denial.

'I don't think that's a good idea.'

Her eyes burned into his. 'Please?'

He shut his eyes for a moment and then leaned forward and stroked her cheek. 'Ah, Bella. I need to take you home because we're not ready for this. You don't know all the disadvantages there are to being with me.'

Bella had made her choice. She captured his finger and kissed it, and he froze. Then, unable to help himself, he slid his hand around her neck and pulled her close against him.

'One kiss,' he said, and lowered his mouth to hers. And the next time she breathed he was there. But it was never going to be one kiss if Bella had her way.

Nibbles of desire flickered along her limbs with every taste of his mouth. Every whisper of breath between them lifted the stakes higher.

She had to choose now or lay the blame at his door like the weakling she'd always been. She chose to raise the stakes.

If she didn't hold him now, properly, then any chance she had of convincing him that they were right together would be gone for ever, Bella feared. There was liberation in that commitment and she felt as if a weight had gone from her shoulders. She would live with the consequences.

She returned his kiss fiercely and he froze for a second as his arms went around her and she sighed against him. This was what she wanted and needed and, judging by the firmness of Scott's hold, he was in no hurry to let her go.

The taste of him entwined with the pressure of his mouth and created an enthralling environment any promptings of Bella's sanity couldn't compete against.

This *was* what she wanted, and what she'd been afraid of. Her hands crept up to his neck and threaded in his hair. His long fingers splayed across her hips and she was crushed against him. It was like a homecoming and she pressed herself closer, revelling in the danger.

Scott's mouth seduced and enticed her like a duellist and Bella cherished the possessive way he held her against him. Possessive yet with such sweetness that she felt the tears sting her eyes.

The music from the stereo flickered through her consciousness to match the kindling flames that flashed and roared inside her in time to the now rhythmic plundering of her mouth by his. Scott claimed her in a way that erased every kiss any other man had given her. The magic he created opened up a range of sensations that had her dazzled.

She moaned and whispered his name. Her body swayed as she leaned into him. To be in Scott's arms was everything she'd dreamed it would be.

Scott was in deep trouble. Here was the woman he'd always loved, adored from afar, yielding in his arms and enthralled, and it would be so incredibly difficult to do anything but complete the longed-for journey and make her his.

After a mighty effort he tried to calm the storm they'd created. It was the last thing he wanted but once he'd had her he knew he'd never be able to resist again. He still wasn't sure he was the best person for Bella. At such a time in his life was he loving Bella or seeking comfort from the hurt of being excluded from his son's life? Amidst all his emotional confusion, could he really trust his feelings? He tried to concentrate on that thought but it receded in the heat of the moment.

Scott groaned and tried to break away as he recognised how close they were to total abandon. But Bella wouldn't let him. She held him with her hands on either side of his face, as if for them to break apart would terminate the world she'd finally found with him.

He could see the last of his control spinning out of reach, and he dug deeper to regain it. No matter what the cost, he had to know if she really wanted this.

'Are you sure, Bella?' He wrenched the words out against her mouth and she stilled for a moment as if she comprehended, but he didn't think she did. Then her tongue touched his with emboldened innocence and he felt the spear of intense pleasure shatter his gut into a million pieces. He had to kiss her back and the vortex swallowed him.

The next time he surfaced she was in his arms, soft and pliant against his chest as he strode to his bed. They were semi-naked and he leaned over her when he laid her across the quilt in front of him. Red hair fanned out behind her in a crinkled wave, and the tips of her creamy breasts spilled from the lace of her bra. She was everything he'd dreamed of and had never imagined holding. The briefest window of sanity opened and it was up to him to make the final effort.

'Bella?' He stared into her eyes until she focussed, and he saw the exact moment when she realised he had control back. 'We need to stop.'

'Don't even think about stopping!' she whispered, and pulled his head down. He groaned and accepted that he'd lost and won and lost until he realised there was one more responsibility.

He reached for his wallet in his discarded trousers. The condom really did glow in the dark.

CHAPTER NINE

WHEN SANITY RETURNED, Bella lay snuggled in his arms and Scott stared at the ceiling. He could feel her body warm and sweet against his and he couldn't comprehend how they had come to this stage. All the years he'd wanted her, and now she rested in his arms as if she belonged there. He couldn't fool himself it would be for ever but for the moment it was worth grabbing and holding to cherish in the empty years to come.

He squeezed her against him and she burrowed into his chest and he thought he could die a happy man. But he didn't say it because he didn't think he would.

A short time later Bella stirred and edged away from under his encircling arm until she could sit up. He felt her rise from the bed and he stretched out his hand to detain her but unconsciously she evaded him. Even now, when his wildest dream had come true, he didn't know what she was thinking.

She stretched to reach his shirt that was lying in a scrunched heap near her foot and held it against her chest. The crickets chirped in the back yard and he could hear the sound of occasional traffic. She stood with her back to the bed and looked out into the lounge room where the music had finished. Thank goodness they hadn't turned the lights on. Mentally, he felt better in the dark.

The moon was rising so before he had to look at everything under a spotlight, he needed to think the events of the day through.

Bella walked away and he stared at the purity of line in the curve of her back. Then she was gone from his sight and he couldn't think of anything except the feeling of emptiness without Bella against him. It was as if he'd lost her all over again. He rolled back and stared at the ceiling again.

The responsibility for the last half-hour rested with both of them. But where did their future lie? What did she expect from him? He loved her too much to short-change her. He'd failed as a husband before, and failed as a father. If they had children together he'd be sixty before they left home. The picture chilled him. Maybe he should find and make peace with his own son before he risked his parenting skills on any children Bella might want.

The memory of the photograph in the other room haunted him, along with that crazy, improbable thought that had crossed his mind—long hair and piercings aside, the resemblance between Blake and himself in his youth was remarkable.

He pushed the thought from his mind. Bella deserved his full commitment, not just the part of him that didn't belong to the son he had to find. He needed more time so he could give her everything she deserved.

'Bella?'

She heard Scott's voice from the bedroom and she cast one more glance at the photograph before crossing the hall to slip back into the room. He stretched out his hand to draw her back to bed and she slipped under the sheet to nestle under his arm.

He lifted her fingers to his mouth and she closed her eyes at the reverence of his salute. It was the tenderness of his love-making that had undone her. Every caress had said Scott loved her. She didn't doubt that fact because it had been in his every searching kiss, every touch and in his superhuman efforts to prevent the one thing that she'd needed to feel whole again.

With relief, she became aware that any lingering disgust from last year's attack had dissolved and been replaced with the tenderness of her true love's consummation.

And she loved Scott. She always had. What came next should be simple, but she knew it wouldn't be. There would be a struggle to overcome his entrenched ideas of what she deserved in a husband.

'If you loved me, why waste twelve years that we could have been together? Why has it taken so long to get here, Scott?'

Bella's voice drifted across to him and Scott breathed in the scent of her skin one last time before he let her go. Every word she spoke was like a knife. This was what he'd been afraid of. She needed his total commitment. The whole man he'd never revealed to her. He was afraid she wouldn't find him the hero she expected him to be. 'Where do you think we are, Bella?'

He felt her shift onto her side and he turned his head to see her face close to his. The first of the lunar rays came in through the bedroom window and bathed the purity of her features and she was the moon goddess he was afraid of failing.

'I know you love me.' Bella's voice was firm with conviction. 'You've shown me in more ways than you can ever say and I won't believe you if you say you don't.'

'Of course I love you,' he said, and she sighed with relief. Then his voice lowered because the lies wouldn't come out in a strong voice. 'But I'm not sure of marriage or children or setting up house together or tying you to visiting me in the nursing home when I'm decrepit.'

She flinched and he felt the pain being dragged through his guts like an oversized grappling hook. Here he was again, wounding Bella for her own good. He hated it. He hated the whole bloody fiasco. And he almost wished she hated him so that he would never have to do this again. He sat up on the edge of the bed with his back to her.

'None of those things frighten me, Scott,' she said. 'So before you erect a wall between us...' she laid her hand on his arm '...I would like to know, if you weren't thinking marriage and commitment and children, what you were thinking when we made love.'

He refused to look at her. 'There was so much heat I didn't think of much at all. You stun me. The scent of you drives me out of my mind. There wasn't much room for deep and meaningful.'

Her laugh held a trace of bitterness. 'Why do you think I do that to you and you do it to me? As for chemistry driving us to abandon—I seem to remember it was more on my mind than yours.' She shook her head. 'You're lying. If that was all our *little romp*—' she watched him flinch at the words '—was to you, why did you try to stop it happening?'

At that he swung his feet over the edge of the bed and stood up, and the moonlight turned him into a silver stranger, strong-chested and implacable.

'You're not a child any more, Bella. Fairy-tales don't happen.' He stared at her. 'What we did may not have been the most sensible course for this stage in our relationship. I'm sorry I didn't realise that sooner.'

Bella couldn't believe he'd said that. 'Well, just so you know for future reference, your apology is not needed. I decide when and with whom I make love—it's my responsibility. From your comments it looks as though I took advantage of you. I believe what we have is beautiful and pure and if you're too frightened to reach for it I can't force you.' She slid out of the bed and collected her clothes.

Scott was still going to fight against something that should have been sorted out years ago. He couldn't deny that they created magic when they were together and she felt like screaming with frustration when he'd said it was all just proximity.

He loved her and finally she was sure of that. That in itself was liberating. She glanced back at him at the side of the bed and allowed herself a small mental hug at the memories of their time together and then walked from the room to phone a taxi.

She dressed and while she waited she put her head in her hands. How was she going to convince Scott that it was him she'd always wanted? Surely he didn't believe she thought him too old. No fool could believe that. But what was she supposed to do? She wouldn't give up. That was for sure. Today had been a major step forward—as long as he didn't shut her out.

Monday

Monday on the ward was busy, which was lucky as there was little time for personal concerns once Bella arrived for work.

A woman with an undiagnosed breech presentation in labour had been booked for urgent Caesarean section for eight o'clock. Bella needed to ensure all was ready for the patient to be transferred.

Rene Jackson had been at school a couple of years ahead of Bella, and the two girls had played hockey together.

Bella was thrilled to see her friend. 'Rene, I didn't recognise your married name. It's great to see you.'

Rene, a petite blonde-haired woman, smiled at Bella with relief. 'I'm so pleased you're on. Sharon said you'll come with me to the theatre.' Her voice shook. 'It's all been such a shock.'

Bella hugged her. 'Caesareans always are. The scary thing is that between ten and twenty per cent of women seem to end up with one.' She helped Rene dissolve her nail polish with remover so that the anaesthetist could see the colour of her nailbeds if he needed to.

Rene chewed her lip. 'I'm worried about Jim, my husband. What if he faints when the operation starts?'

Bella smiled. 'Not many husbands faint in Theatre. We set you up so that neither of you can see the gory bits. He'll sit in a chair beside your head and when your baby is born it's all worth it to be awake for the actual birth and to have your man beside you.'

Rene twisted her ring on her finger so Bella could tape it in place so that it wouldn't get caught on anything in Theatre. 'We talked about it and Jim is keen to be there for me.' She glanced at the travel clock on the bedside table. 'He should be here soon.'

As she spoke there was a knock on the door and a tall surprisingly young-looking man hastened in with a worried frown on his face and a huge bunch of roses in his hand. When he saw that all was normal in the room he visibly relaxed and came across to hug his wife. 'Sorry I'm late, baby. I wanted to get you flowers before you went in.'

Rene smiled mistily up at her hero and Bella slipped out to give them some privacy. It must be nice to be so sure you could declare your love to the world, she thought.

When she returned to prepare Rene for transfer to Theatre, Bella could see that Rene was even more nervous and Jim was downright terrified.

'Remember, you guys, even though you haven't done this before, we have! Lots of times. And we're very good at it.' The couple smiled and Bella helped Rene onto the theatre trolley for transport to the operating theatre.

'You walk beside Rene's head, Jim, and I'll walk on the other side. Pete, our orderly, is the engine.' Pete waved at the couple and the mood lightened despite the movement towards Theatre.

Theatre Sister met them at the door and good-naturedly grilled Rene on who she was and what she was there for.

Rene looked up at the circle of faces above her. 'Dr Rainford is going to find out what this big bump in my stomach is.' She smiled bravely and Jim looked like he wanted to cry with pride.

Theatre Sister produced the consent form and went through it all again with Rene and then they were through. Bella slipped away to change into her theatre scrubs and Pete took Jim into the surgeons' room to do the same.

By the time they returned to Rene, she was draped and in a sitting position.

Dr Knowles, the elderly anaesthetist, smiled at Jim. 'Now you're all here we can get started. If you'd like to hold her hand, Dad, I'll explain as I go.' Jim stood in front of his wife and she leaned her face into his chest.

'Right, then, Rene. I'm going to give you a local anaesthetic in your back first, and then the area will be numb. You won't feel the bigger needle or the little catheter that I leave behind to inject the anaesthetic into but you will feel some pushing and prodding.'

Rene nodded and Jim squeezed her hand. The whole procedure was completed ten minutes later when a long thick strip of sticking-plaster was placed over the tubing to keep it in place in the epidural space where the anaesthetic would bathe the nerves at that level and deaden sensation. By leaving a catheter in place, Dr Knowles could top up Rene with more anaesthetic if she needed it.

'My legs feel funny,' Rene said, and Dr Knowles nodded.

'They'll feel heavy and later when I check with some ice, you won't be able to feel the sensation of cold either.'

After a short while, Rene was moved onto the operating table and sterile green sheets were draped until she and Jim couldn't see her stomach any more.

'How are you going, you two?' Bella joined their little space for a moment before she had to get scrubbed.

'It feels weird to know they're doing things I can't feel,' Rene said, and Bella squeezed her shoulder.

'I know. But your baby will be here soon. I'll be back in a while and we'll gag all the people up the other end so Jim can announce what you've had. OK?' The two nodded and Bella ensured the resuscitation trolley was functioning.

She switched on the infant overhead heater and light on the resuscitation trolley.

She really had no part of the operation except to stand beside the assisting surgeon—in this case, Rohan—and wait for the baby to be born, when she would be in charge of any resuscitation required.

Because Rene hadn't actually gone long into labour and was under epidural anaesthetic and not general anaesthetic, the baby would be very unlikely to need any sort of resuscitation. So today was about as much parental contact in those first few minutes as possible.

Gloved and gowned, Bella stepped up to the operating table and Scott looked up. There was an aura between them that brought a blush to Bella's cheeks and she was glad that no one could see her face. His eyes met hers and while she couldn't tell what he was thinking, indifference wasn't the emotion. She'd never felt this way across the table from him before and she looked down to where she'd clasped her hands together to still the sudden tremor his presence caused. When she looked up again he was back at work. She stared down at the operation in case someone saw the confusion in her eyes.

She saw Rohan glance at the two of them and Bella could tell he'd decided that she and Scott had something going on. For him, he was surprisingly quiet.

But maybe that was because those last few seconds before the baby was born were always tense. The incision was made, the waters were broken and Scott had his hand inside Rene's abdomen. The baby's head was high in Rene's chest and Bella watched as first one foot and then the other and then two round little buttocks were eased out of the abdominal cavity, followed by the baby's chest.

'Breech is the only time you get to see what it is before you see who it is,' said Scott, and his eyes smiled as he met Bella's warning look. 'But we're not going to say it.' He slid the forceps in beside the baby's head and gently eased the last of the baby out.

Rohan clamped and cut the cord and handed the infant to Bella, who lightly suctioned baby's mouth and then scooted around to Rene and Jim with their baby in her arms. 'Well, Jim, what have you got?'

'It's a girl,' Jim said as the tears rolled down his face. He kissed his wife. 'You've given me a daughter, and she's beautiful like her mother. I want to call her Georgia Rene.'

When Georgia Rene had been cuddled, and with some tenacious manoeuvring by Bella and long-suffering agreement by Scott, the baby was breastfed on the operating table as the operation went on. After the feed, Bella, Jim and Georgia went back to the ward to wait for Rene to return.

'Now I want you to sit in Rene's darkened room and cuddle your baby against your skin.' Jim obediently sat on the chair and held out his arms. 'Take your shirt off,' Bella said, and Jim stared at her.

Bella smiled at his confusion. 'If she'd been born normally she'd have been placed on her mother's skin. Because she was a Caesarean it doesn't mean she can't have that same feeling with her dad.'

Jim shrugged. 'I'm game. Compared to what Rene had to go through, I get the best part.' He took his naked daughter from Bella and cuddled her against his not inconsiderable chest, wrapped in a blanket. Bella left them and Jim explained to his daughter about the new world as they both waited for the most important woman in their lives to come back to them.

An hour later Scott came around to the ward to see Jim. Father and baby were dozing in the chair and Scott pulled the door shut after backing out of the room. He went in search of Bella.

'What on earth is going on in that room?' he asked. 'Jim's semi-naked and the baby is glued to his chest.'

Bella shook her head. 'Welcome to the new millennium, Dr Rainford. It's called father bonding. They tested babies and those warmed against either parent's skin warmed faster than those warmed in humidicribs.'

'I believe you but thousands wouldn't.'

Bella raised her eyebrows. 'I can produce the study, I'll get it off the internet tonight.'

To her surprise he said, 'I'll drop around.'

'Why?' she asked.

'We need to talk.' He didn't smile but she heaved a sigh of relief. He wasn't going to pretend last night had never happened.

'After seven, then,' she said, and he waved and left the ward.

Somehow the rest of the day was tinged with excitement and Bella flew through her work with single-minded precision. The day was busy as she spent time with Rene as the new mother settled back into the ward.

Bella bent the rules and suggested Jim stay the night in Rene's room as her personal nurse and nanny to his wife and their baby until Rene could move more easily. It was something Gladstone hadn't seen but was quite common in the birthing centre where Bella had worked in Sydney. There were advantages to being the boss, Bella thought with a wry grin.

Come five o'clock, she walked out to Blake's car with a light step and she couldn't believe she'd caught up on all the administrative work that had accumulated while she'd been away as well.

By seven o'clock she'd organised the household accounts and even the linen cupboard. Aunt Sophie came out of her room and stopped her in the hallway with a poke.

'Are you on speed or something?'

Bella stopped and looked at her aunt and then she burst out laughing. 'No. I'm just feeling very efficient today and I'm capitalising on the feeling while it's there.'

'Balderdash. Something's going on.' She snapped her sparse white eyebrows together and stared at her niece. The doorbell rang and Bella looked at the door and then back at her aunt.

Sophie's lip twitched. 'Expecting someone?' She cackled. 'I think I'll get the door.'

Bella narrowed her eyes at her aunt and Sophie cackled again. 'Or I might just go back into my room and watch the next race.' She ambled away but Bella could hear her chuckling. The doorbell rang again and Vivie came out of the kitchen to answer it and saw Bella. She looked from Bella to the door. 'Did you want me to get that?'

Bella felt like stamping her foot. Now it was a production. Sometimes she did wish she lived on her own. She plastered a smile on her face. 'No, thank you, Vivie. I'll get it.'

Vivie nodded, disconcerted, and then shrugged and walked back into the kitchen.

Bella walked across towards the door before the person on the other side hit the doorbell again, but she was too late.

It rang and Blake came bolting down the stairs to get it just as Bella opened the door and father and son were left staring at each other.

CHAPTER TEN

IT WAS THE first time Scott had seen the new Blake. Short-haired and shaven, it was as if the young man from the photo on Scott's mantelpiece had stepped down into real life. Bella saw the exact moment that Scott confirmed the resemblance between himself and Bella's boarder. He shot an accusing look at Bella as if she'd known all along.

The younger man stared from Scott to Bella and the sudden tension between the two sharpened his senses. His eyes widened as Scott took a step towards him.

'Michael?' At Scott's question he backed away from the door.

Blake looked shocked and angry and spun away through the kitchen. A few seconds later Bella heard the back door shut and then the sound of his car revving as he drove away.

She sighed. 'I'm sorry about that. It was a misunderstanding.'

Scott stood still in the doorway and didn't say anything, just looked at Bella as if it was all her fault she hadn't told him.

'Please, come in, Scott. I know what you're thinking, that Blake is your son. I agree it's a strong possibility but I don't know for sure. I just had suspicions.' Surely, especially after last night, he wasn't going to shut her out of this.

Scott stared at her for a moment and then nodded. 'Considering you are the first to say it out loud, I'd say it's pretty clear that Blake is my son.'

Bella led the way through to the study and Scott sat gingerly in the big chair until he realised his own son had fixed it and he could sit in it normally. His mouth hardened at the irony of it.

'Am I jumping to conclusions?' he said.

Bella shook her head. She tried to block out that he hadn't said, Are *we* jumping to conclusions? 'I don't think so. Apart from the fact that he looks just like you twenty years ago, Blake's middle name is Michael, he's twenty, the people he knew as his parents died in the last year and he's an only child from Sydney. It all fits.'

'So how did he end up here?'

She smiled gently. 'At a guess I'd say he came to see what sort of man his father was.'

'An arrogant sort.' He winced. 'I haven't been very complimentary about him.'

'There's time for that. He's a wonderful young man and a joy to have around. But he's confused. Let him meet you halfway.'

Scott ran his hands through his hair. 'As long as he doesn't kill himself in that car.'

'Welcome to parenthood.' Bella smiled. 'You really have it in for his car, don't you?'

'Actually, I have some good memories of that car.' He met her eyes and there was a brief moment of intimacy before he dashed her sudden hopes when his mind returned to his son. She could feel the wall he erected between them. She wasn't invited into this area and Bella tried to contain the hurt that was spreading through her. He confirmed it when he stood up. 'I'll go. I need to think about the events of the evening.'

'Maybe I could help.' She sounded pathetic but Bella couldn't help herself. She hated to see him in pain and she hated that he didn't think she could help. She stood as well and followed him to the door. 'Don't be too hard on yourself. You couldn't have known.'

'Thank you, Bella.' He made no move to kiss her. 'I'll see you tomorrow.'

She watched him walk down the path without looking back. Maybe this wasn't going to work out after all if he could shut her out so easily.

Later that evening she heard Blake's car pull into the garage but he didn't seek her out. Like his father. Bella sighed and went to bed. Reality bites.

Maybe she needed a BITE ME sticker on her forehead.

Tuesday

When Bella went down to breakfast, Blake was there.

'I owe you an apology, Bella. I shouldn't have left both of you like that.' He met her eyes. 'I suppose you guessed I was Michael the day after you hurt your ankle.' He shrugged. 'You had to do what you thought was right.'

'Thank you, Blake. I appreciate that.' She poured her cereal into the bowl. 'But I didn't tell him.'

Blake stared at her and she shook her head. 'He came to the conclusion after he saw you and you left. It will take time but you're both special people, I'm sure you'll work it out.'

Vivie looked from one to the other. Bella continued with her breakfast as she listened to Blake discuss his father with Vivie.

She was glad he had someone else he could talk it over with. 'There may be one extra for tea tonight, Vivie.' Vivie nodded and didn't ask who.

'Your car is ready.' Blake gestured to the refrigerator. 'Key's on the fridge.'

'Wonderful, thank you, Blake. Though I'm going to miss that Torana of yours.'

Blake laughed. 'I think you'll find yours goes a little better than you remember. I've given it a birthday and it doesn't seem to feel its age any more.'

Bella looked up. 'Will heads turn when I drive down the street, do you think?'

'Unlikely,' he said dryly, and he looked so like Scott that she felt like giving him a hug. But more because she needed one than he did.

Later that morning, Bella helped Rene into the shower while Jim went home to change his clothes. Rene's intravenous line had been removed and a waterproof dressing protected her suture line.

'You're standing so straight, Rene, considering your operation was only yesterday.'

Rene walked carefully to the bathroom. 'I don't have as much pain as I'd expected. I'm stiff from lying in bed more than actually sore from the cut.'

Bella nodded. 'I've noticed that the women who have their Caesareans performed under epidural block seem to bounce back sooner than those who have a general anaesthetic.'

'I don't want to compare them to find out,' Rene said.

Bella smiled. 'OK.'

Twenty minutes later, when Rene was back sitting in the chair, hair combed and freshly made up, she sighed as she gazed at her sleeping baby. 'I'm so happy.'

'You have a beautiful daughter,' Bella agreed as she repacked Rene's bathroom bag.

'Jim is wonderful. I can't believe I fought against marrying him for so long.'

Bella sat on the edge of the bed to listen. 'So how much age difference is there between you two?'

'Ten years.' Rene shrugged and Bella blinked. She'd realised Jim was younger than Rene but ten years was close to the difference between Scott and herself.

'He just wore me down.'

Then her face sobered. 'One day I lost one of my girlfriends to cancer. She was my age. Life is too short not to grab happiness when you can.' She smiled the smile of a contented woman. 'I was a fool. Wasted time.'

Bella nodded but Rene's words played on her mind, and when Scott came for his round she couldn't help commenting about the couple.

'Rene and Jim are thrilled with their new baby.' Bella handed the chart to Scott and he glanced at his patient's observations on the graph.

'They're a lovely couple,' he said.

'Funny how the age difference doesn't seem to bother them.'

He glanced across quickly but Bella's face was expressionless. 'Was there a point to that comment?' He said.

Bella looked blandly back. 'Should there be?'

Bella picked up the charts and shuffled them. She chose one out of the stack and opened it on the way down the corridor. 'I'm happy with Melissa's Tina. She's nine days old and taking all her feeds at the breast now.'

They entered Melissa's room and the noise that was coming from such a tiny baby made Scott smile. 'She certainly sounds vigorous.' He looked at the feed chart at the end of the bed as Melissa changed her daughter's nappy. As soon as she finished the baby stopped crying and they all smiled.

'I hear that Tina is doing well, Melissa. Are you happy with her?'

'She's great.' Melissa rocked the cot. 'This morning she hasn't had any tube feeds. When do you think we could go home?'

Scott pulled the stethoscope from around his neck and listened to Tina's heartbeat. Then he watched the rise and fall of her chest. 'She looks and sounds great. We'll weigh her tomorrow and if she's still over five pounds, you can go home Thursday afternoon.'

'Woo-hoo.' Melissa's grin nearly split her face. 'Can't wait.'

Scott smiled and they moved into Rene's room where all was well. Rene nursed her baby confidently and Scott enthused over Georgia. He promised to come back the next day to check on their progress.

After Scott left, Bella went back to take Rene's temperature and her friend tapped Bella's arm.

'So how long have you and Dr Rainford had something going on?'

Bella looked away. 'We don't!'

'Yeah, right. I know that look in a man's eye and you're not immune to him either.' She looked at Bella measuringly. 'You'll have to chase him.'

Bella charted the observations. 'I tried that and it didn't work. I'm not much of a chaser. It's really not my style.'

Rene shook her head. 'Maybe when we were young it wasn't your style but I can see you've changed. You've suffered and you're stronger than you've ever been. Don't be afraid to push for something you want—even if it frightens you.'

She twisted the wedding ring on her finger. 'Jim didn't give up and I'm so glad he didn't.' She shrugged. 'I think it's easier for the younger one to push—because the older partner feels that they're getting the best of the bargain.'

She laughed. 'I know I thought everyone was going to say, "Look at that old hag with that young stud." And I'm still sensitive, but nothing on what I was, and I'm happier than I've ever been. If I'd kept being stubborn about what other people might think, I'd have missed out on the best years of my life and a love that I can't imagine not having.'

Bella felt the tears spring to her eyes and she hugged her friend. 'Thank you, Rene. I appreciate your honesty. And I will think about it.'

'You make sure you do.' There was a knock on the door and Bella excused herself as Jim came in to be with his wife and daughter.

She saw Rene wink and Bella smiled as she walked up the corridor. Maybe there was a ray of hope. Maybe she'd been selfish, not giving credence to Scott's fears. She tried to imagine how she would feel if Scott was Blake's age and she was in love with him. It was a thought-provoking concept.

Bella imagined falling in love with Blake, so young and naïve from where she stood at thirty. She imagined the raised eyebrows if she ran off with him. Maybe Scott hadn't been so out of line after all.

Even if she could remove the ten years of her own that had passed and be twenty and innocent again, she'd still want Scott. His maturity and confidence were exactly what she wanted. He had so much to offer her and she had so much to offer both Scott and his son.

All she had to do was make it happen.

At the end of the shift her car drove itself past Scott's gate and Bella hesitated over inviting him to tea. There hadn't been an appropriate time at work to float the notion to him but she could just suggest it and see what he said.

When he didn't answer the doorbell she followed the path around the side of the house, a bit like a lemming bent on nirvana. He wasn't on the verandah and she hesitated before turning onto the path to the workshop. The sound of rhythmic planing from the shed drifted among the trees and confirmed his presence.

When she took the fork under the leopard tree Bella could see him and she stopped and leaned against the trunk to watch him work through the open door. He planed smoothly and the sight was as she'd imagined once before.

Layer after layer, he worked like some old-fashioned craftsman from the past, no hurry, just sweeping strokes that pared the imperfections from the wood. A faint sheen of sweat glowed on his bare chest as he concentrated on the wood under his hands and carefully skimmed the roughness from the length of wood. Curls of shavings lay scattered around him like streamers at a monotone farewell party. She watched the bunching and relaxing of his muscles and her mouth dried as she remembered the feel and strength of him against her.

He laid the smooth piece down and picked up another. She must have made a sound because he looked up and unerringly focussed on where she stood.

The clatter of the wood as he tossed it onto the bench seemed discordant as their eyes held across the path and her head swam until she remembered to breathe.

'What do you want, Bella?' There was a caution in his voice that didn't correlate with what they'd shared. She wished she'd known what had gone wrong. But she wasn't here for herself.

'Nothing you don't want to give.' The words lay between them for a moment before she shrugged them off. 'I enjoy watching you work.' She paused but he didn't comment so she went on, 'I'm here to talk about Blake.'

He pulled his shirt on and came towards her and she couldn't help the leap in her pulse rate. 'Let's sit on the verandah,' he said, and waited for her to precede him up the path.

A cane table was set up beside the bridge and he gestured for her to sit. The sound of the water as it trickled over the stones was very peaceful but it didn't help the tension between them.

She sank into the chair and all she could think about was the last time they'd been here.

He said, 'How was Blake this morning?'

Bella ignored the flash of disappointment and refused to be intimidated by the fact that he towered over her. She crossed her ankles, and assumed a relaxed pose and told herself that he couldn't tell that was all it was. 'Fine,' she said. 'He regrets that he rushed away and confirmed he was your son. I explained that you had guessed yourself. Perhaps you should come for tea tonight?'

Scott turned away and gazed out over the garden. 'It will be awkward.'

'No more awkward than this,' she said. He looked at her from under his brows and a twisted smile acknowledged the hit.

'True, but I didn't ask you to come here.'

She forced herself to remain seated when she wanted to get up and shake him. She needed to take a grip on the truth that he didn't want her closeness at this time.

She raised her chin. 'It will be more awkward if you don't make a move. Blake may think you don't want to know him.'

'You're right.' Scott sighed. 'Thank you. What time?'

'Six-thirty, if you can make it. Aunt Sophie likes to eat early.'

Scott groaned. 'Can't wait for Sophie's comments.'

'You'll survive.' Bella stood and he gestured for her to go through the house and out the front door. Neither of them glanced into the lounge room and he was careful not to touch her.

When Scott arrived that evening, he maintained the wall between himself and Bella. Blake was in the yard, working on his car, and Bella showed Scott through the house and out the back door to talk to his son. After all, she told herself, that was the only reason he'd come.

Vivie and Bella hung back behind the curtain in the kitchen and watched from afar, but they couldn't hear what was said.

They watched Scott hold out his hand for his son to shake. Blake hesitated for a moment but then they briefly shook on their relationship.

For Scott it was a strange moment. This young man in front of him was of his own genes. Matured in some distant world that he knew nothing about and had contributed nothing to. How could Blake do anything but hate him?

'I don't hate you.' Scott felt the trickle of superstition down his neck at Blake's comment.

'Well, we must have some connection if you can read my thoughts. Unless I've got it tattooed on my forehead.' At the word tattoo they both looked at the scorpion on Blake's wrist and smiled at each other.

'So, am I what you expected?' Blake's own insecurities were there as well, and Scott shrugged.

'I didn't know what to expect.' He glanced up at the house. 'Bella seems to like you.'

'Bella is awesome. How come you two aren't together?'

'I let your mother down, and Bella deserves more.'

Blake screwed up his face in disbelief. 'That was twenty years ago. What's the real reason? She said you think you're too old for her.'

Scott winced. 'There's that.'

'More crap. But it's none of my business.'

Scott laughed. 'So is this what it means to have a son? They tell you when you're being a fool.'

Blake shrugged. 'Anyone could tell you that.'

Scott smiled again and suddenly it wasn't so frightening to meet his son. Blake's expectations were nowhere near as harsh as the ones Scott had for himself. Maybe that had been his problem all along. Maybe he should listen to Bella's expectations before he convinced himself he couldn't meet them. Maybe he *was* all kinds of fool. But that was for later.

Watching, Vivie and Bella sighed in relief. Both men looked under the bonnet of the car and once they heard Scott laugh. Thank God, Bella thought. 'Has Blake said much to you, Vivie?'

'I think Blake's getting used to the idea.' Vivie said. 'But he doesn't understand what happened between his real parents.'

Bella nodded. 'From what I can gather, I don't think Dr Rainford understands what happened to his marriage. He never knew about Blake until Blake wrote to him.'

Vivie shook her head. 'So Blake said. I hope it works out for them.'

'Me, too,' said Bella. The men didn't stay long down at the Torana and Bella and Vivie left their vantage point before they were caught spying.

When everyone had assembled for the meal, there was an uneasy silence. Sophie dived in. 'So? How does it feel to have dinner with your son, Dr Rainford?'

Thanks, Aunt Sophie, Bella thought with a groan, but Scott managed. He plastered a smile on his face and looked across at Blake. 'Pretty scary, if you want the truth.'

Unconsciously he'd picked the right thing to say, and Bella saw Blake shoot a glance at his father. Then he smiled and chipped in.

'I'm with you there.'

They all laughed. The conversation flowed more smoothly after that. Maybe Sophie had been right to bring it out in the open.

Scott and Blake didn't avoid each other in the discussions but they had a long way to go before rapport was established.

At least they had a chance of things working out in the end, Bella thought as Scott made no effort to single her out in the conversation.

When Scott had gone, again without making any moves to include Bella in his private life, she closed the door after him and leaned against it.

'So what's changed between you two?' Sophie's words came out of the doorway to her right, and Bella pushed herself off the door and went in to see her aunt.

She sat down beside Sophie and sighed. 'I thought we had a new understanding but he's become more distant…' since we made love, she thought '…since he found out about Blake,' she said.

'Give the man time. It must be a huge change to find you have family. He's not used to people caring what happens to him, and that includes you. He's been so busy looking after everyone else he probably feels it's wrong to be self-absorbed. It's a nuisance but men are pretty painful anyway.'

Bella considered her aunt's explanation. Maybe Scott *was* just having problems with change. He had been a little warmer before he'd left. The idea lifted her spirits. 'You're a very wise woman, Aunt Sophie.' Bella kissed her aunt's wrinkled cheek. 'Don't ever let me forget it.'

'I won't. Now, go to bed so you can knock his socks off with sex appeal tomorrow.'

'That didn't work,' Bella muttered as she left.

'Practice makes perfect,' her aunt called, and Bella had to laugh. For a spinster, Sophie delighted in the risqué.

CHAPTER ELEVEN

Wednesday

SEX APPEAL, EH? Bella had mused on her aunt's words overnight and a vague plan formed when she woke on Wednesday morning. It was time to stop hiding her femininity and bring out the big guns. Thanks to the other night, despite Scott's behaviour since then, she knew she was cherished, and it was time to use that power.

Bella gave herself an extra spray of perfume after her shower and donned her prettiest underwear for confidence. As she stood in front of the mirror she chose a soft red lipstick rather than her usual pink and left one more button undone on the front of her shirt. She clasped her hair back with combs instead of her usual bun, and it was amazing what a difference it made.

Blake whistled appreciatively when she walked into the kitchen, and she burst out laughing. 'Thank you. I'm not sure what I would have done if nobody had noticed.'

'What's the occasion?' Blake's question could have been awkward but Bella was feeling brave.

'I'm trying to seduce your father.' She listened to that sentence and shook her head. 'Actually, I'm going to seduce your father.'

'Watch out, old man.' Blake grinned and Vivie covered her mouth to giggle.

Bella pretended to frown. 'You're lucky you have good genes! He's not as old as you think.'

Blake shuddered as he sat down at the table. 'Too much information. I'm trying to get my head around him as it is.'

Bella hid her smile and patted his arm. 'I know. I think you're both doing as well as can be expected in the circumstances.' She poured her breakfast cereal and changed the subject.

'I heard there was a job going at the hospital in the maintenance department. Maybe you could ring and see if it's true.'

Blake shot his head up and grinned. 'What's the number? Doing what? What qualifications do I need?'

Bella passed across a slip of paper. 'I'd wait until eight-thirty but you should be able to get onto them and find out after that.'

Later on that morning, Scott arrived to do his round on the maternity ward. Bella had forced down the butterflies and met him at the desk with a sultry smile.

Scott frowned. Bella looked different this morning. His eyes strayed to the discreet gap in her blouse and stayed there until she covered her cleavage with the charts.

He heard her laugh and the gentle sound drew an absent smile from him. 'Are you coming on the round, Scott?' she said, and he blinked and refocussed on the rest of the world.

'Sorry. I don't seem to be plugged in this morning.'

'So I see.' She leaned over and flicked his collar straight and then moved serenely up the corridor. The scent of her perfume lingered around him and he had difficulty concentrating on work as he followed her. Even her skirt seemed tighter today.

She stood on the other side of Melissa's bed directly opposite him and when he glanced across she moistened her lips with her tongue and all his promises to himself that he'd stay immune to Bella flew out the window. Then he realised that she was teasing him deliberately, and a slow smile curved his lips. He shook his head at what it must have cost her to choose that path.

He'd been such a fool to worry about age when what they had transcended all barriers. Hell, she made him feel younger than the twelve years between them. He had to acknowledge that Bella had him going like a randy sixteen-year-old and it was very distracting.

He gave in to the dreams he'd never believed in and accepted that he had no defence if she was determined to seduce him. Thank God.

He returned her look with a molten look of his own that promised all manner of forbidden pleasures if she so desired. He watched her eyes widen and a pink flush stained her cheeks. He restrained his smile.

Melissa, absorbed in calming her baby, missed the byplay and when young Tina had stopped crying Scott forced himself to concentrate on the discharge plans for his tiniest patient.

When they left Melissa's room, they passed an empty two-bedded room and Bella steered him around the corner and into the vacant bathroom. 'I want to show you something,' she said, and flicked on the light and pulled the door shut behind them. It was a very small room.

Bella watched him look around and then back at her, and his slow, sexy smile warmed her soul. 'And what are you up to today, Bella?'

Bella could feel her heart thumping and the sound seemed to fill the tiny room. He was back with her. Whatever cold and lonely place he'd been hiding in, he'd managed to escape. She licked dry lips and then realised what she'd done. It worked anyway.

He slid his arms around her and lowered his mouth to hers. 'You are an incredibly sexy lady, do you know that?' he murmured as he kissed her.

She closed her eyes and leaned into him, briefly pulling away to mumble, 'I'm trying,' before she pressed herself back against him.

'I guess what you're saying is we didn't have a one-night stand the other night.'

'Mmm,' she said against his mouth.

'And that we should really spend more time together like this?'

'Mmm.' She twisted her fingers through his hair.

Scott groaned and deepened the kiss for several earth-shattering seconds and then pulled away.

'I've been a fool but this isn't the place to tell you how. Tonight. My place. I'll pick you up at six.' And he put her gently from him and opened the door to usher her out. It was difficult to hide the awareness between them, though they tried.

Rene winked at Bella as she left the room after Scott's round. The rest of the day passed in a dream for Bella.

Half an hour later in Scott's surgery, things had become even more bizarre. His first patient was someone he'd least expected to see.

Aunt Sophie hobbled in and sat in front of his desk like an avenging witch. She pointed her bony finger at his chest and stabbed the air. 'I want to see you.'

Scott looked at the old lady warily, still amazed that she'd ventured out of the house. 'How can I help you, Sophie?'

'It's me that's going to help you, sonny, though, goodness knows, you don't deserve it the way you fumble around the point.'

She shook her head and her neck made tiny cracking noises with the movement. Scott winced at her audible arthritis. Sophie ignored it. 'Will you stop this rot you two are going on with? She loves you. You love her. I know it. You know it. Everyone else knows it. For goodness sake, whip her away and do something about it.'

Scott bit his lip. Sophie was incredible and he admired her all the more for the effort it must have taken to get her here. But she expected an answer. 'I don't think kidnapping is really my style,' Scott said patiently.

Sophie pretended to spit and Scott laughed out loud.

'Look, Sophie, I can see I've been a fool and you're right. I do love Bella, have always loved Bella, and I'd already decided to do something about it. OK? I appreciate your effort and you've been outrageous enough for today. I will think long and hard about your suggestion.'

He helped her stand and she leaned on her stick more than she leaned on him. When he opened the door, Blake rose from one of the waiting-room chairs and came over to shake his father's hand. He met Blake's eyes and they both smiled over the top of Sophie's head. It was the first spontaneous acknowledgement between them and it felt good. Today was turning into an amazing day.

Blake lowered his voice. 'Then I'll see you at your wedding?'

Scott smiled. 'If she'll have me.'

His son rolled his eyes. 'As if not.' He helped Sophie as she began her journey across the room.

Taking Bella away wasn't feasible, but there was no reason they couldn't arrange something along the lines of a romantic surprise. Unfortunately it was only Wednesday and they had work tomorrow—although he was sure Rohan and Abbey would help him with that.

The thought made him smile. Maybe he was lightening up.

He wandered into his partner's room between patients, and it was surprisingly easy to rearrange his and Bella's schedule tomorrow. In fact, he ended up with the rest of the afternoon off to prepare his campaign. Rohan practically marched him off the premises and banned him from the practice until Friday morning.

When Bella walked into Scott's house that evening, it was filled with spring flowers and there was a huge banner hanging across the room. SCOTT LOVES BELLA!

She turned to look at Scott and her eyes filled with tears. He'd said he'd tell her tonight and she'd been too nervous to dream it might really happen.

The scent was heavenly and she moved from vase to vase. The table outside on the verandah was set with crystal and lace.

There was a small box with a red satin ribbon at her place at the table and Bella turned to face the man she loved. He drew her into his arms and she felt the rumble in his chest against her cheek as he spoke.

'I'm sorry, Bella. I've been a fool. I finally realised that my expectations of what I couldn't give you had blinded me to what I can. I was a fool twelve years ago and nearly a fool again.' She shook her head because, since her conversation with Rene, she could see his old dilemmas.

He went on because he had to make her understand what had looked like reluctance on his part. 'I love you. I was willing to sacrifice my happiness and dreams for you, but I have no right to sacrifice yours.'

He cradled her shoulders. 'That night we were together was the most amazing night of my life. I never told you that and I should have. But it brought home to me that I had so many things unresolved. You were so giving and I needed more time to ensure I could give you everything you deserved before I committed myself to you.'

He drew her against his chest and she could hear the thump of his heart. 'I see now I was crazy,' he said. 'I should have shared my fears with you. Trusted you to help me.'

Bella spoke into his shirt. 'What were you afraid of, Scott?'

'I've failed as a husband before, and didn't make it as a father. I thought you deserved my full commitment, not just the part of me that didn't belong to the son I had to find. I didn't even know if finding him would change me for the worse.'

He let her go and looked into her face. 'I should have known you would help me there, too.'

He drew her towards the table. 'I don't know what the future holds, but I do know I will always love you. I won't lock you out again. Will you marry me, Bella? Spend the rest of your life with me?' He took her hand and stroked her fingers as he waited for her response.

Bella stared up at him. This man she'd loved for so long was finally ready to celebrate their future together. It was unbelievable but she wasn't going to be the one who doubted now.

'Yes. Please. I love you, Scott. I've always loved you.'

He leaned forward and their lips met, and the tenderness and delight was there for both of them. A long while later he raised his head. 'That little show you put on in the ward was pretty enlightening.' He grinned wickedly and Bella blushed.

'I've bought us a present,' he said, and drew her along the verandah, down the stairs and along the path to his workshop. When she entered, Bella's eyes were drawn to the stylish sofa piled with pillows that had been placed against one wall of the shed. Beside it on a small table rested a beaded bottle of champagne, cooling in ice, and two glasses.

'I decided we needed somewhere soft in my workshop for you to sit when I work down here. You never know. The scent of freshly shaved wood might act as an aphrodisiac on my future wife.' He grinned as Bella curled up on the lounge to try it out.

Her smile was sultry. 'Do you think I'll disturb you?'

'Permanently,' he growled, and leaned down to nibble her ear. 'Don't ever stop.'

She laughed and then he kissed her and the champagne was forgotten as they found more enthralling things to do.

CHAPTER TWELVE

THE WEDDING WAS HUGE.

Abbey, magnificent as matron of honour, caught the best man's eye across the pulpit and blew her husband a kiss as they both remembered their own vows.

Kirsten, finally back from Saudi Arabia in time to be bridesmaid, grinned at such public displays of affection from her staid sister, but then a hush fell over the church.

Bella's entry stunned the congregation as she swayed like a radiant angel, complete with veil and floating dress, down the aisle to the man she loved. When she reached Scott's side, her husband-to-be clasped her hand as if he would never let her go.

The music swelled and then the words flowed around them and everyone heard their responses clear and true. All too soon it was over.

Scott's heart was full with the wonder of his blessings. Beautiful Bella, his new wife. His son, tall and proud beside him. His best friend and his new sisters-in-law. And a new beginning where he would make up for all the years he and Bella had missed. The tiredness he'd felt for years was gone and in its place was a thirst for love and life and all the dreams and joys of their lives to come.

'I love you, Bella Rainford,' he whispered in her ear.

Bella turned her face and kissed him. 'And I love you, my husband.'

They faced their friends and family and joyfully walked the rose-strewn carpet to a new life together.

* * * * *

Midwife In A Million

Dedicated to my husband, Ian, my caring and compassionate paramedic, and my own true hero.

CHAPTER ONE

Rory McIver stepped thankfully from the RFDS aircraft he'd hitched a ride with. It hadn't been one of the smoothest flights he'd ever been on. Maybe he should have driven from Perth but it had been such a hectic couple of weeks that the idea of driving three thousand kilometres on a whim didn't do it for him.

He bent to scoop a little of the red earth he'd watched pass below his window for hours, let it run through his fingers, then allowed the wind to blow the soil from his palm. He looked around. He never thought he'd return.

Even early in the morning on the airstrip the hot wind wrapped around him like an electric blanket on high, that all enveloping heat that only Western Australia's Kimberley could offer, a heat he hadn't felt for ten years and savoured now.

He touched his shirt pocket and gripped the bulkiness of his wallet in that habit he'd acquired since she'd sent the damn letter all that time ago. Enough!

As the plane bumped away on the dirt strip a cattle dog barked and the dog's lanky owner tipped his finger under his hat in greeting. 'G'day, Rory. Long time, no see.'

Here was a person who hadn't changed. 'Smiley.' Rory nodded to the cowboy leaning against the battered truck. 'Good of you to meet me.' They shook hands and Rory threw his swag in the back where a cloud of red soil smothered it as it landed. He smiled wryly and opened the passenger door against the wind. When the spinning top of a whirly wind tried to climb in with him he wondered about the implications of the strong breeze.

Smiley pushed himself off the truck and slid behind the wheel to start the engine. 'I wondered how long it would take you after Kate turned up,' Smiley drawled in that remembered way and drew a smile from Rory until the words sank in.

Rory grimaced. Well, apparently not long. 'I read in the newspaper that her father's sick. So she's been gone a long time, too?'

'Hmm. Left the same year as you. Went to school in Perth.' Smiley grunted and let off the handbrake. 'She's back to spend time with him but flies down to the station township a few days a week to relieve Sophie.'

Smiley glanced at a small four-wheel drive vehicle under a lean-to in the corner of the paddock and Rory gathered it was Kate's. 'She works at the clinic, and delivers the babies that drop in from the camps, as well as emergencies.' Smiley shook his head. 'I hear the old man isn't happy she's working here at all.'

Seems Lyle Onslow hadn't changed then. Malignant old sod.

'Her father was never happy.'

'He's dying.' Smiley turned to look at him and they both thought about that. Lyle was a hard man, and not always fair, but no doubt Saint Peter would sort that one out shortly.

Smiley shrugged the old man's problems away and slipped another matchstick into his mouth to chew. His lips barely moved but the matchstick danced at the edge of his lips in a skill passed down from Smiley's father. It brought back the good memories for Rory and there'd been many of those.

'So you told her you're coming?' Smiley said around the match.

No, Rory thought. He closed his eyes and the sleepless night he'd spent trying to work out how to do that hung heavily behind his lids. 'Try and keep a damper on that news, mate, until I get a chance.'

Smiley snorted, the closest he came to a laugh. 'Keep a damper on it? Here?' Smiley took the matchstick out and pointed it at Rory. 'The airwaves've been hummin' since your plane left Perth.'

Rory supposed he'd known that—just blocked it out—and he'd have to deal with the fact that he'd broken his promise when he saw her.

When he saw her. He didn't know how he felt about seeing the woman who'd dumped him after promising to wait. Had never answered his letters.

Had apparently been the cause of heartbreak and suffering for his parents, who had shown her nothing but kindness when her mother died.

He needed more time, or would there never be enough time between them? Now he'd almost achieved his life's goal he'd finally realised he couldn't move on until he'd settled the past.

'How's Sophie?'

Smiley's sister was the antithesis of her brother. Bubbly and extrovert, she bossed Smiley mercilessly and her dour brother just shrugged. There'd been a time the four of them had done everything together out on the sprawling million acres of Jabiru Station—another thing Kate's father hadn't liked, his daughter knocking about with the hired help.

'Nagging as usual,' Smiley said but there was pride in his voice and he elaborated, unusual for him, as if he sensed Rory's need for a change of subject. 'Now she's working at the clinic with…' He shot him a quick glance.

…with Kate, Rory completed in his mind.

'Anyway, having help means Sophie gets some time off for a change,' Smiley went on. 'So she's good. She's getting tips on baby-catching, she calls it, and thinkin' of doing her midwifery.' He looked back at the road. 'When do you go back?'

Kate the teacher for Sophie? Of course she'd changed. What did he expect? That she'd still think he, Rory, held the answers to the universe?

'I've a week off. I'll stay over at the Hilton until RFDS can pick me up in a couple of days.'

The Hilton was the town's tongue-in-cheek name for the extremely run down boarding house presided over by a tough ex-army nurse, Betty Shultz. Shultzie swore she'd never leave Jabiru Township, then again, Shultzie swore, loudly and often, all the time.

Her Hilton was nothing like the chain of exclusive hotels of the same name; her establishment was bare minimum and held together by pieces of wood nailed over the top of other pieces of wood.

'How was Charlie's retirement party?'

'Good food,' Smiley said. 'Don't suppose you'd want his job?'

After flogging himself to higher and higher levels until last month's appointment? Volunteer ambulance in the bush instead of Deputy Commissioner of the entire state? Actually, it held some attraction. Back on the road instead of budget meetings and troubleshooting.

'No. Afraid not.'

They didn't speak again until they drove past the huge cattle yards on the outskirts and pulled up opposite the rundown hotel in the main street of Jabiru Township, population a hundred and fifty through the week, three hundred—mostly ringers and cowboys—on the weekend. Town, sweet town.

He looked around. A big change from Perth city.

Another whirly wind scooted past Rory as he lifted his swag out of the back and he glanced at the pale sky for the first streaks of cloud. Not yet.

He thumped the roof and Smiley lifted his hand and drove away. Rory watched the truck until it disappeared in a ball of dust and wondered if he could change his mind and ride it back out to the airstrip.

He'd never run from a challenge before. Funny how attractive that thought was right now, but only for a moment.

Well, he'd arrived. He needed to stop making such a big deal of a visit home. It wasn't as if he had family here any more. He squashed that bitterness away too. The rest—meaning his reaction to Kate—would have to take care of itself.

He looked at the mostly boarded shops in the deserted street. It wasn't like Kate's father's homestead and the home station where he'd grown up, but in the years since he'd been to the commercial part of Jabiru not much had changed.

Except the collateral damage he'd caused to his family by his liaison with Kate.

Kate Onslow was born into the pilot's seat of an aeroplane; luckily, because it made the distance she needed to cover so ridiculously easy.

The two-hour drive between Jabiru Homestead and Jabiru Township was dust all the way and to fly cut the distance down to twenty minutes. Her great-grandfather had settled on the station a hundred years ago and when the township had grown exponentially her grandfather had built a new homestead away from the madding crowds. Though a hundred people didn't seem 'madding' to Kate, she could understand the improvement in position for the family headquarters.

The new Jabiru Homestead, many-gabled, encircled by verandas and sprawled over an acre, nestled below a range of ochre mountains that bordered the Timor Sea; the peaks gave water and provided glorious waterholes and a lush rainforest pocket, and all only a short distance from the sparseness around the house.

The old homestead at Jabiru Township that she could see in the distance now from the air, held the hospital clinic, the pharmacy, the one-roomed library of donated books and the garage for the town's only four-wheel drive ambulance truck.

As she closed in on her destination Kate saw the Royal Flying Doctor plane take off from the town strip and her heart rate dropped in a swoop as if she'd flown through a sudden wind shift, something her aircraft had been doing all flight, but this internal up-draught made her sick to the stomach.

She'd had three radio calls already to tell her Rory McIver was coming to town to see her.

Last month it had been hard enough to come back and face her belligerent father and the reality of his illness but that paled in comparison with Rory's unexpected visit.

She'd been able to face the idea of coming home because she'd known her father would never change her mind about anything again. But Rory? Once he'd been the world to her.

She would just have to survive this too. Her independence would help her survive it. The sudden sting of threatening tears she ignored—they never came to anything. She hadn't cried since all that had happened ten years ago and the lies. But the emotional turbulence had started and she hadn't even seen him. She was a big girl now and not some needy teenager with an adolescent crush on the manager's son.

Kate took a deep breath and straightened her shoulders. Too many years she'd spent telling herself she needed to stand on her own, rely on herself, be strong, and that determination would not be undermined by a man who had been out of her life for a long time. What did he want to see her for now, anyway?

Kate stripped Rory's intrusion from her mind and concentrated on her descent because that was her strength. Single-minded concentration on what needed to be done. But, as soon as the plane grounded, as soon as room for distraction arrived, the thoughts returned to stick like the plane's wheels to the ruts on the strip.

She gritted her teeth and secured her aircraft but the worry nagged at her all the way to town in her vehicle. Nagged her through the first half hour at work, right up until sixteen-year-old Lucy Bolton presented with the worst case of indigestion she'd had in her life.

Jabiru Township Clinic serviced the small town set in the baked earth at the edge of the station's southern mountain ranges, a place that hid lush waterholes and settlements, plus far-flung aboriginal communities and out camps for the station. If the situation was dire, the doctor might be able to fly in once a week—unfortunately he'd been in yesterday.

Kate took one look at Lucy and put her to bed in the four bed ward. 'Under those covers, young lady. No arguments. Where's your mother?'

Lucy was a big-boned, hardworking girl whose mother leased one of the four pubs in town from Kate's father. Usually happy-go-lucky and fun, Kate knew Lucy wasn't one to complain. They bred them tough out here—had to—it was a long way to twentieth century medicine.

'Mum's tired.' Lucy sat gingerly on the edge of the bed and kicked off her shoes. 'There was a big outfit in town yesterday and I didn't want to wake her.' Lucy sighed as she rested her head back on the pillow and closed her eyes. 'The queer thing is, Kate,' she whispered, 'I haven't eaten a thing 'cause I feel so rotten, so how can I have indigestion?'

'That's not good.' Kate stared down at the young girl and in a swirl of memories saw herself. 'Poor you.' She stroked her hair. She saw the slight puffiness around the eyes, the tiredness, that protective maternal hand that crept over her stomach. Her voice dropped. 'Any chance you're pregnant, Luce?'

Lucy's eyes flew open and the sudden fear in the young girl's face was enough confirmation. Kate sighed under her breath for the loss of youth coming Lucy's way and a smidgen for the prick of envy. She wished she'd had the sense to ask for help like Lucy had.

Though in Kate's day Mrs Schulz mightn't have been as easy to approach as Kate or Sophie would be, even if Kate had been able to get all the way to the township from the home station.

She stroked Lucy's shoulder. 'Everything will be fine. I'll just take your blood pressure, poppet. You don't look well to me either.'

By the time Kate had done a full physical assessment the window shutters were banging against the walls outside and the howl of the wind was clearly audible. Kate barely noticed it as her concern grew for the young woman in front of her.

The flying doctor would have to come back and pick her up because there was no way she could manage Lucy here. And there was no way she wanted to because she knew what it could cost.

The pregnancy test proved positive but Kate hadn't needed that; she could clearly hear the heartbeat from Lucy's little passenger inside and she was more worried about the dangerously high levels of protein she found in the specimen of Lucy's urine.

Lucy's uterus could be felt midway between her belly button and the bottom of her sternum, which meant she'd been hiding her secret for about seven months. Around eight weeks too early to birth, if the baby was growing well. Eight weeks to go!

Kate closed her eyes against the memories that wanted to surface. Right when the trouble had hit her all those years ago. She shook the unwanted thoughts away, not least because she didn't want to jinx Lucy.

Unless Kate was mistaken, Lucy's blood pressure would ensure labour happened soon anyway, and Kate knew how fragile premmie babies were. Not standard procedure around here, three thousand kilometres from Perth.

That was, of course, if Lucy wasn't in labour already and didn't know it. 'You're not having any tummy pains are you, Luce?'

Lucy shook her head carefully. 'Just this headache and rotten indigestion that's killing me.'

It isn't indigestion, Kate thought—it's your body telling you something is very wrong. At least Lucy had listened. Kate poured a small tumbler of antacid, more for comfort, and gave it to her. 'Sip on this, Luce. I need to talk to the doctor on the radio.'

Five minutes later Kate lifted the headphones from her ears and looked at them. No way could they do that. She settled the pads on her ears again and, strangely, the action had calmed her nerves. 'Say again,' she said, but there was little hope it would sound different this time.

'Medication and transfer. If I were you I'd transfer her today. The storm's a big one. The only way to transport is on the ground. If you decide to go you'll have to take her out by road before it rains again and we'll fly her from Derby. Or you could sit on her for another twenty-four hours with those symptoms and pray.'

Kate closed her eyes. 'It's six hundred kilometres of corrugations. What if she gets worse on the trip?' Kate had another, more practical thought and her eyes widened. 'What if she goes into labour?'

'You could hope she doesn't deliver.' Mac Dawson had been obstetric registrar when Kate had been a newly graduated midwife at Perth General. Now an obstetrician in Perth, Mac respected her knowledge and she knew he cared about her predicament. But he couldn't do anything about their options. There was nothing else he could suggest. 'You should have stayed with me in Perth.'

Kate rolled her eyes, glad he couldn't see her. He'd asked her out a couple of times and Kate knew he'd have liked to have pursued their relationship if she'd been interested. She should have been but wasn't. Mac's pursuit had been a factor in her choice to work at one of the smaller hospitals in the suburbs of Perth after graduation.

Mac went on. 'Her first baby, Kate. It's your call but I'm sure you'd prefer early labour to an eclampsia out there while you wait for the storm to pass. The weather could set in for days and your strip will wash out. It'll get tricky if she's as unstable as you think and the roads are cut.'

Mac was right. She'd just needed to hear it twice. Road it was then. 'Thanks for that, Mac. I'll get back to you when I talk to her parents.'

'Hear from you soon, then. Don't forget to give me a ring when you get in so I can be sure you made it.'

Kate pulled the earphones from her head slowly and walked back to her patient via the drug cupboard. She reached for what she needed, along with the tray of intravenous cannulas, and set it down on the table beside the bed.

Lucy had fallen into an uneasy doze and every now and then her arm twitched in her sleep. Kate rechecked her blood pressure and the figures made her wince.

'Lucy.' Kate held the girl's wrist as she counted her pulse. Lucy's eyes flickered open. 'I have to put a drip in your arm, poppet, and give you some drugs to bring your blood pressure down. Then I'll ring your mum. The doctor says you have to go to Derby at least. Probably Perth.'

Lucy's eyes opened wide and the apprehension in them made Kate squeeze her hand again. She looked so frightened. Kate had been frightened too.

'It's okay, I'll come with you most of the way but you'll have to stay there until after your baby is born.'

'Mum doesn't know I'm having a baby.' They both looked down at Lucy's difficult to distinguish stomach.

Kate remembered this all too well except she hadn't had a mother. Just a ranting, wild-eyed father who'd bundled her off to strangers before anyone else found out.

'We'll have to tell her, but no one else needs to know just yet. This is serious, Luce. You could get really sick and so could your baby. I'm worried about you so we have no choice.'

Lucy slumped back in the bed and closed her eyes and two big silver tears slid down her cheeks. 'I understand. Will you tell Mum?'

Kate looked down at Lucy's soft round cheeks and her hand lifted and smoothed the limp hair back off her forehead. Poor Lucy. 'If you want me to. Of course I will.'

The next half an hour made Kate wonder how some people could be so lucky. Lucy's mother sagged at the news but straightened with a determined glint in her eye. 'My poor baby. To think she'd been worrying about upsetting me when I'd be more worried about her. Here was me thinking all sorts of terrible things when now I can see why she's been so quiet lately. And you say she's sick?' Mary Bolton stared at Kate hard. 'How sick?'

'It used to be called toxemia of pregnancy. Her blood pressure's high and dangerous, for both her and her baby. I'm worried she could have a fit if it gets too high. They want her flown to Perth.'

Mary stared out of the window and then back at Kate. 'I had that 'clampsia thing. Scared the pants off the old man when he woke up and the bed was shaking, with me staring at him like a stunned rabbit unable to speak.' Mary shrugged. 'Or so he said—that was just before Lucy was born,' Mary said matter-of-factly and Kate's stomach dropped. Maternal history of eclampsia as well? So her mother had progressed to fitting. Kate closed her eyes. More risk for Lucy.

Mary glanced out of the window and frowned. 'But the Flying Doctor won't be able to fly in this weather.'

Kate looked out of the window to see what she already knew. The sky was heavy and purpling now. 'I know. We'll have to take her by road to Derby. Unless the weather clears further west and they can fly in and meet us at one of the stations along the way.'

Mary looked down at her daughter, then at Kate. 'You must be worried, Kate, if you can't wait here a day or two.'

'I am.'

Mary grimaced. 'We're lucky you're here. I'll have to arrange for someone to take over the pub and mind the other kids, then I'll follow. My sister lives in Derby. When does Lucy have to go?'

'Today. Now. As soon as I can arrange it.' And that was when Kate realised the implications. By ambulance. The usual driver, Charlie, had retired and just left on his lifetime dream holiday. There was no one else with any training to come with her, and she really needed some backup for this trip…

Sophie would be needed here and there was no one with any medical knowledge except—the second highest qualified paramedic in the state—she'd heard he'd got the Deputy job. The man from her past who'd flown in this morning to see her.

Rory was the last person she wanted to spend twenty-four hours locked in an ambulance truck with.

She turned away and looked into the room where Lucy lay. Maybe it wouldn't be too bad. Maybe what she'd felt for him when she'd been sweet sixteen and besotted enough to practically force him to make love to her would be different.

Of course it would. He was ten years older now—that made him twenty-eight. With his job the on-road experiences would age anyone, so he'd probably have changed, put on city weight, look a lot older. She'd be fine.

The call came in just as Rory finished unpacking. Betty knocked like a machine gun on his door and Rory flinched from too many sudden call situations in the city. Maybe he did need this break away from work.

Betty in a battledress shirt and viciously creased trousers was a scary thing as she stood ramrod-straight outside his door, and he wondered if he should salute her.

He opened the door wider, but gingerly, because the handle felt as if it was going to come off in his hand. The place was falling apart.

The fierce expression on Shultzie's face made him wonder if he was going to be put through an emergency fire drill. 'Yes, ma'am?'

'Kate Onslow's on the phone for you. Best take it in the hall quick smart.'

He moved fast enough even for Shultzie to be satisfied.

CHAPTER TWO

RORY PARKED THE ambulance outside the front door of the clinic and climbed the steps to the wooden veranda. His boots clunked across the dusty wood as the wind whipped his shirt against his body.

He could remember riding out to one of the station fences in weather like this to shift cattle with his father, a big man then that no horse could throw, with the gusty wind in their faces and the sky a cauldron above their heads. He could remember them eyeing the forks of lightning on the horizon with respect. And he remembered his father telling him to forget about any future with Kate Onslow. That it wasn't his place. She was out of his league.

His feeling of betrayal that his own father hadn't thought him good enough for Kate either had remained until his dad had been fired not long after Rory had left, after twenty years of hard work, and his dad's motive became clearer.

Lyle Onslow had a lot to answer for. The problem was Rory had always loved Kate. Not just because she'd hero-worshipped him since she'd started at the tiny station school but because he could see the flame inside her that her own father had wanted to stamp out.

He understood the insecurities she'd fought against and how she refused to be cold and callous like Lyle Onslow. She'd been a brave but lonely little girl with a real kindness for those less fortunate that never tipped into pity and her father had hated her for it.

It wasn't healthy or Christian, but Rory hoped Kate's father suffered a bit before the end. He shoved the bitter thoughts back into the dark place they belonged, along with the guilt that he'd caused his parents' misfortunes.

No wonder he'd never wanted to come back after Kate's letter. Kate, who hadn't needed him for what seemed a lifetime but needed him now.

The lightning flickered and a few drops of rain began to form circular puffs of dust in the road. 'Lovely weather for ducks,' he muttered out loud—his mother's favourite saying and one he hadn't said for years—to shake off the gloomy thoughts that sat like icy water on his soul.

He pushed open the door and walked down the hall to the clinic.

Rory's first sight of Kate winded him as if he'd run into one of those shutters banging in the street on the way.

He'd tried to picture this moment so many times on the way but she looked so different from what he'd imagined and a whole lot more distant.

She was dressed in fitted tan trousers that hugged her slim hips and thighs above soft-skinned riding boots. The white buttoned shirt just brushed her trim waist and an elusive curve of full breast peeped from the shifting vee of her neckline and then disappeared, a bit like his breath, as she turned to face him. He lifted his gaze.

Thick dark hair still pulled back in a ponytail, no sign yet of grey, but ten years had added a definition to her beauty—womanly beauty—yet the set of her chin was tougher and steadier and she'd probably reach his chin now so she didn't look as fragile as he'd remembered.

Lord, she was beautiful.

He'd have liked to have sat somewhere out of sight and just studied her to see the changes and nuances of this Kate he didn't know. Breathe in the truth that he was here, beside her, and acknowledge she still touched him on a level no other woman had reached. But his training kicked in. There'd be time for that later.

'Rory,' she said but she was talking to the wall behind his head, which was a shame because he ached with real hunger for her to look at him. 'Thank you for offering to help.' She barely paused for breath, as if to eliminate any possibility of other topics. 'I'm worried about Lucy and the sooner we leave the better.'

Her voice was calm, unhurried, unlike his heart as he struggled for an equal composure. 'I've fuelled the truck and packed emergency supplies,' he said. She nodded but still wouldn't meet his eyes again and suddenly it was impossible to continue until she did. 'Kate?'

'What?'

How could she keep talking to the wall?

'Look at me.'

Finally she did, chin up, her beautiful grey eyes staring straight into his with a guarded challenge that dared him to try and break through her barriers. There was no doubt he'd love to do that. But he knew he had no right to even try.

In that brief moment when she looked at him he saw something behind her eyes, something that hinted about places in her that were even more vulnerable than the delicate young princess he'd left behind, or maybe he was imagining it.

Either way, he wouldn't delve because he wanted to close doors on this trip, not open them. 'For the next twelve hours I'll drive, you care for your patient and I'll get you both to Derby safely.' Then he'd say his piece and leave. 'So we'll talk on the way back.'

She blinked and he could sense the loosening of the tension in the air around her. Sense it with what? How could he sense things like that about a woman he'd not seen since they were both teenagers and yet not be able to sense anything about others more recent? It wasn't logical.

'Of course.' Her glance collided with his for a long, slow moment before she looked at the clock. 'Thank you, Rory.'

When she turned away, Rory swore he could feel physical pain from that loss of eye contact like tape ripping off his face. There you go. He still had it bad and, to make it worse, he doubted she felt anything. But that was his problem, not hers. He looked through the door to the patient on the bed. They needed to go.

To Kate's relief, Rory had them ready to leave within minutes and she couldn't think of anything else she might need to take with her. Except maybe her brain.

The grey matter seemed to have slowed to about one tenth speed since Rory McIver had walked in and Kate found her eyes drawn repeatedly to his easy movements as he settled Lucy in the back with extra pillows. He didn't look at Kate again, which was good, because Lord knew what expression she had on her face.

Her friend Sophie had come in to man the clinic. 'Don't worry if you don't get back for a couple of days. We'll be fine.' Sophie hugged Kate.

A couple of days with Rory? Kate shuddered. She'd never survive.

Sophie was still talking. 'I'll ring the housekeeper about your dad while you're away and drive up to the home station after work if needed. Okay?' Sophie frowned and Kate knew she could see the worry on her face. 'Just go.'

Kate nodded again and cast one anguished look at Sophie. Kate was the only midwife. She had to go.

She focused on her patient. Lucy's blood pressure had settled marginally with the antihypertensives and Kate had packed as many emergency items as she could think of, including what she could for the birth. Kate just prayed she wouldn't need any of it.

Even better, Rory had spoken to Lucy and her mum and by the time he'd shut the rear door to the truck Lucy was looking more relaxed, which was a good thing. Kate doubted it was all to do with the drugs she'd been loaded with and a lot to do with the handsome man promising to get them through.

As much as Kate dreaded the trip with Rory, she could only be secretly thankful that he'd been here. Otherwise, with Charlie gone, she'd be embarking on this dash with the elderly mechanic due for his own retirement soon. Old Bob would have been little help in a real emergency, with his flaring arthritis and his hearing aid that never worked.

The driver's door opened and Rory climbed in behind the wheel—all six feet four of him—and Kate had to shake her head at her preposterous predictions this morning. So much for expecting Rory to be unfit from too many late night doughnuts and morose from his work; there was no doubt this guy was still seriously gorgeous, with a wicked twinkle a long way from surly.

Suddenly Kate was glad she had to stay in the back with Lucy because Rory's broad shoulders seemed to stretch halfway across the seat in the front and no doubt she would have been clinging to the passenger door to avoid brushing against him.

When he turned his head for one last check to see they were settled, his teeth showed white like a damn toothpaste commercial, Kate thought sourly, when he smiled at their patient. He didn't smile at Kate. 'You ready for your Kimberley Grand Tour, Lucy?'

The bronzed muscles in his neck tightened and his strong arms corded as he twisted, and Kate couldn't help the flare in her stomach or the illicit pleasure of just looking for a long slow heartbeat at this man from her past. No wonder she hadn't been able to forget him.

What she had forgotten was how aware she'd always been of Rory's presence and now, unfortunately, he'd hardened into a lean and lethal heartbreaker of a man who'd be even harder to forget. She wished he'd never come back.

She sank into her seat, glad of the dimness in the back to hide her momentary weakness, but even there she could pick up the faint teasing scent of some expensive aftershave, something the Rory she'd known would never have owned. The cologne slid insidiously past her defences and unconsciously she leaned forward again to try to identify the notes.

He looked at Kate. 'Did you get a chance—' he frowned at the startled look on her face and hesitated, then went on '—to let them know at the homestead you'd be away?'

The slow motion ballet of his mouth as he spoke ridiculously entranced her and, after another of those prolonged thumps from her chest, her hearing finally caught up. She blinked as his words registered. Stupid weakness.

'Yes.' That'd been a staccato answer so she softened the one word with a quick explanation in case he thought her unnecessarily terse. 'I said I'd be at least a day late coming back, if not two. They'll tell my father.'

She looked away from him and decided then and there that it would be best if she didn't look directly at the source of her weakness again. *Don't look at Rory.*

Her teeth nibbled at dry lips as she pondered her worst fear out loud. 'That would be as long as we don't get more rain and end up flooded somewhere along the track for a night.'

The road they were about to hit was known as the last great driving adventure in Australia. It was enough of an adventure just being on it with Rory, let alone if they got caught up in the middle of a flood.

He nodded. 'It's a possibility. Let me know if you want me to stop more often so you can check Lucy out. I don't expect to get much speed up or you'll both be thrown all over the truck.'

He turned back to face the front. 'We'll drive until after the first major crossing...' he paused as if he was going to say something but then went on as if he'd changed his mind '...and stretch our legs.' He started the engine.

'Sounds fine.' But all she could think of was how much she wanted to get going so this agonising exposure to Rory could be over with.

Kate checked Lucy's stretcher safety belt, forced a smile for her sleepy patient and buckled her own belt. She'd take it one hour at a time and not think about that talk she'd have to have on the way home. But it was hard when she had to decide what and how much to tell him.

Maybe she could leave him in Derby and drive the truck back herself.

The idea had merit but, unless Rory had changed more than she expected, he'd be unwilling to send her off on her own.

The wind whipped the scrubby grass and stunted gums at the side of the road as they drove towards the distant ochre ranges and lifted the red dust they stirred into the now grey-black sky behind them.

At least the wind would shift the dust cloud more quickly when the road trains drove past, Kate mused, and, as if conjured, Rory slowed their vehicle and pulled close to the edge of the road to widen the distance between them and an oncoming mammoth truck.

The unsealed road was an important transport access for the huge cattle stations that lay between the infrequent dots of civilisation.

Road trains were three and four trailer cattle trucks that thundered backward and forward across vast distances. These road monsters didn't have a chance of stopping if you pulled out in front of them.

Even overtaking a road train going in the same direction was difficult because the dust they stirred was so thick that visibility was never clear enough to ensure there wasn't other traffic heading your way, and the risk far outweighed the advantages.

Kate remembered pulling over and brewing a cuppa instead of following one heading towards Derby in the past. She was thankful this one was travelling in the opposite direction.

This truck sported a huge red bull bar that flashed past Kate's opposite window and three steel-sided pens filled with tawny cattle rattled after it. She sighed with relief when the dust was blown away by the ever-building wind and they could move on.

An hour and a half of corrugations later, they came to the first of the major rivers they'd have to cross, the Pentecost. There was barely any water over the road, a mere eighteen inches, but that would change as soon as the storm hit. Then they'd be stuck on the other side until it went down.

Kate caught a glimpse of a silver splash from the bank ten metres back from the road and shivered.

Thank goodness the height of water was easy to see because Kate had no desire to watch Rory walk the Pentecost to check the level.

Not that anyone walked across here. The Pentecost was populated with wildlife and a saltwater croc might just decide it fancied a roll with him. The name saltwater crocodile didn't mean these creatures needed to be near the sea. They were quite happy to eat you a couple of hundred kilometres inland in freshwater. Even with her dread of the 'talk', that wasn't how she wanted to avoid Rory's company.

Rory slowed the truck for the descent into the river bed, changed into low range and then chugged into washed gravel to crawl though the wide expanse of water. Once across, they steadily climbed out the other side until back on the road and trails of water followed them as the truck shed the water they'd collected.

She looked up front through the windshield to where they'd stop. Her stomach dropped. Not here!

Ten years ago, Rory and Kate had set up a picnic at sunset out here to enjoy the glory of the Pentecost River and the distant ranges. That night before Rory left he'd wanted a place that wasn't her father's land and this was where they'd come. A point on the triangle of vast distances people thought nothing of travelling.

The memory was etched indelibly and Kate felt the soft whoosh of time as she remembered. That sunset had been as deeply coloured as a ripe peach with the magnificent sandstone escarpment of the Cockburn Range in the distance. She blushed red-ripe herself at that memory because that evening she'd set out to seduce the diffident Rory and they'd both got more than they'd bargained for.

That was their round-bellied boab up ahead. She just hoped Rory would have more delicacy than to pull in there.

The truck slowed and turned off the road into the lay-by. She glanced around for an alternative. Trouble was, theirs was the only decent sized parking area clear of the road and their boab was part of it. She sighed.

Grow up, she admonished herself. She needed to check Lucy's blood pressure and her baby's heart rate but the memories of this place all those years ago crowded her mind as she waited for Rory to open the door.

Kate remembered the night before Rory left ten years ago and unfortunately it was as clear as yesterday.

'So you are leaving?' Kate couldn't believe it. Rory gone? What would she do without Rory? He stood tall and lean and somehow distant, as if he had to be aloof to say what he needed. This wasn't her Rory.

Safe in his arms was the one place she felt loved for herself. He was the one person who understood how lonely she'd been since her mother had died, the person who could make her laugh at life and made her complete.

'I'm leaving tomorrow morning. With the cattle on the road train,' he said and the words fell like stones against her ears. How would she bear it? How could he?

He went on, 'I can start my paramedic degree in two weeks. I have that. When I asked to marry you we both knew he'd fire me.'

He paused and looked away from her and she knew it was to hide his shame. He had nothing to be ashamed of. Kate wanted to hug the memories away from him. She knew what had happened. She'd overheard her father flay the pride from Rory as if he was a criminal.

She'd tried not to listen to the threats and abuse but if her father had thought she would think less of Rory from that exhibition then he was wrong. She was ashamed that she had Lyle Onslow's blood in her own veins.

'I'm sorry for my father, Rory.'

His eyes stared at the distant hills with a determination she'd never seen before. 'It doesn't matter.' He reached into his pocket. 'I have something for you.' He snapped open the box. 'Will you wear this until I come back?' he said, and pulled the ring free. She recognised it as a tiny pink diamond from the mines behind Jabiru—a token she had no idea how he'd managed to pay for—and slid it on her finger, where it sat, winking prettily at both of them. No matter that her father had refused permission.

She looked at the ring—Rory's ring—it could have been the largest diamond in the world and it wouldn't have been any more precious, but most of all she wanted to comfort Rory. Apologise for her father, show him how much she loved him. All she could do was pull Rory's face down to hers and kiss him. They were alone under the vastness that would soon turn to night. Their last night together.

'I want to marry you. I do,' she said. For the first time she dared to gently ease the tip of her tongue into his mouth, awkwardly but with all her heart and soul in that one timid adventure, and suddenly they had entered a whole new dimension that sent spears of heat flicking from her through to Rory.

He groaned and kissed her back, answering her challenge, each emboldened by the other, enticed by the danger until both were mindless with the desperation his leaving had ignited between them.

She needed to feel his skin, hear his heart and she fumbled open his shirt and slid her hands against his solid warmth, up and down, not really sure what she should do but needing to feel and mould the hard planes of his chest—a chest she wouldn't have near to lean on if he went.

She could feel the shudder in his body as he sucked in the air he needed for control, groaned with what she did to him, and she rested her hand over his heart and soaked in the pounding of his life force.

That was when she realised she had power. She could move him and make him lose a little of that tightly leashed control he'd always had. Push him to the edge and maybe he'd take her with him over to a place they'd always pulled back from.

He tried to put her away from him but she wouldn't let him, flung herself back against him, pulling his hands up to caress her in return. Then it changed; she wasn't the one in charge.

Suddenly she was in his arms, carried to the blanket she'd set up for their picnic, laid gently on the grass and he was beside her.

'Are you sure?' His whisper over her ear.

'Yes.' No second thought. 'Kiss me.'

Then they were unbuttoning, discovering the places they'd left secret, venturing with her murmurs of pleasure and encouragement to seal their pact once they'd fumbled with their inexpert attempt at protection.

Kate realised she had her hand on her throat and the pulse beneath her fingers rushed with memories. The truck had stopped and she dragged her thoughts back to the present with a shiver.

They'd be gone from here soon and so would the memories that clung to her in this place like entangling cobwebs. She'd only need a minute or two to check Lucy and hear what she couldn't as they rattled over the corrugations.

Still sleepy, Lucy stirred and opened her eyes. 'Where are we?'

Kate laid her hand on her arm. 'It's okay. Pentecost River. How're you feeling?'

Lucy blinked like an owl. 'I can hardly keep my eyes open.'

'It's the drugs for your blood pressure. Just doze as you can. I need to listen to your baby and check your observations while we're stopped.'

Lucy nodded sleepily and Kate slipped her stethoscope into her ears to listen for Lucy's blood pressure. All the while she was aware that Rory was walking around the truck towards the rear doors and any minute now she'd have to face him. That wasn't going to be as easy as it should be with those intimate memories so vivid in her mind.

Lucy slipped back under her sheet when Kate had finished.

Rory arrived, opened the back doors and waited to hear the verdict. 'Lucy okay?' His bulk blocked some of the light that spilled in with the open air and Kate was glad of the dimness because the heat had rushed into her cheeks and, uncomfortably, into other places too.

She licked dry lips. 'Better. Blood pressure's one forty on ninety. Much improved. I'm happy if it's still sitting at ninety diastolic.' Kate eased her cramped knee and sighed. She'd have to get out and stretch. It was crazy not to walk around the vehicle to move her legs for a minute before they set off again. She just hoped he'd move and she wouldn't have to squeeze past him.

As if he read her mind, he stepped away and, once out, it was hard to stifle the urge to catch a glimpse and see if their initials were still engraved on that tree.

She looked away to the river and realised Rory had moved up beside her, not touching but watching her. That was the worst thing. He didn't have to touch her—she could feel his aura and there was nothing she could do about the tide of heat that again ran up her neck. Or the aching desire to just lift her hand and rest it on his cheek. Where had everything gone so wrong between them?

'Our initials are still there, on the tree,' he said.

Kate's heart thumped at him reading her so easily. She was twenty-six, for goodness' sake, too old to be self-conscious about adolescent romanticisms. It would be horribly awkward if he saw how weak she was.

She stepped past and thankfully her breathing became easier. Away from him.

Rory didn't know what to say. The memories were there for him, bombarded him here, and he hated the way she threw an offhand glance at the tree. As if it meant nothing.

'We were vandals,' she said, and he winced at the unexpected pain her comment caused. 'You'd get fined for that nowadays.'

She was so cold, Rory thought, and more like her father than he'd ever thought.

She pointed to the river, no doubt to change the subject. 'I stitched up a traveller two weeks ago from down there.' They both looked. 'The croc only nicked his fingers when he bent down to fill his water bottle.'

Rory whistled through his teeth. 'Now that's one lucky man.'

Kate smiled grimly. 'Tell me about it.'

No. He wanted her to tell him about what had happened ten years ago. Why she'd changed so dramatically. Why she'd broken her promise and said she didn't love him. Sent the ring back.

Had her father made her? Had Rory's own parents had something to do with it? Now there was only Kate to ask.

Why had Lyle Onslow victimised Rory's father? Why fire him for no reason, stop his mother working anywhere on the station until they'd had to leave? Had the old man really been so afraid that Kate could love someone socially inferior like Rory?

Rory opened his mouth and then closed it. He sighed. 'I'll top up the diesel with the jerrycans while it's not raining.' He walked away.

It wasn't what he'd been going to say. Kate knew that. That was the problem. They'd always had an intuition about what the other was thinking and it seemed she hadn't lost hers either. She gazed out over the plains with the serpentine swathe of the river and the thick dark clouds almost obscuring the base of the ranges they'd watched that evening.

The day she'd become a woman. A day that would affect her for ever. And Rory didn't know. Would he understand? Would he hate her? Blame her? Feel sorry for her?

'You right to go?'

'Absolutely ready to go,' she said, and they both knew that was exactly what she was thinking.

Lucy had dropped into an uneasy doze and didn't wake when the truck started again. Kate watched her patient's flushed cheeks and a tiny niggle of fresh worry teased at her brain, pushing away thoughts of Rory.

'It was a beautiful sunset that day.' Rory's voice was quiet and she knew it wasn't only the sunset he was saying had been beautiful for them.

Not now. Not with the memories so fresh in her mind. She felt the tears sting and she waited for them to form but of course it didn't happen. She couldn't go there.

Thinking about that time of her life would open up all the wounds and grief and anger she'd bottled up for so long and she wasn't sure what would ensue if she let them out. She was used to being frozen now. It was safe.

Her glance rested on the young girl opposite her. With Lucy so sick, now was the time to be focused on her patient.

'I don't remember.' She met his eyes briefly in the mirror and shrugged before she busied herself with writing down Lucy's observations.

Rory didn't comment but, strangely, not once in the next hour did she feel his glance in the mirror as she had since Jabiru Township.

When Lucy moaned softly in her sleep Kate narrowed her gaze on the bulge of Lucy's stomach. She eased her hand down to gently rest on the top of Lucy's uterus through the sheet. As she'd suspected, Lucy's belly was firm and contracted beneath her fingers but, thankfully, after only seconds, the tightness loosened and her uterus relaxed.

It was probably a Braxton Hicks contraction and not the real thing, Kate reassured herself, but the fact that Lucy had felt it even when half asleep was a worry.

Kate glanced at her watch to note the exact time. She hoped Lucy didn't take up regular moaning because then she'd have to start thinking the unthinkable.

Please. She didn't want a premature baby born hours away from hospital in the back of an ambulance truck.

Closer to Derby might be okay. For about half an hour even the tiniest babies usually managed with warmth from the mum, and she could offer oxygen, but longer than that they had a tendency to crash. The risks increased dramatically for breathing difficulties, let alone all the other things that could go wrong.

She'd never enjoyed her stints in the special care nursery, no doubt because it had been too close to her own skeletons in the closet, and she knew premature babies became ill from lots of things. She knew that sometimes they didn't make it.

Like hers. Like the child she'd never even seen, for all those reasons she'd never been given, and the memories she didn't have that she'd blocked out successfully until now, until Rory had returned and allowed them to crowd her mind again.

Kate chewed her lip. 'How long do you think the trip's going to take?' She had a fair idea of the answer; she just needed to ask it out loud and to share the anxiety that was building as she jammed the untimely images from the past back into their hidden cave.

'Five hundred kilometres to go, at say fifty an hour is ten hours plus stops and moments of unusual interest. We've done two.' Rory looked up for the first time in a long time and caught her eye in the rear-vision mirror. 'I can shorten it by an hour but the ride will be rougher. Getting nervous, Kate?'

Understatement. Not about the labour—just the baby. 'Maybe we should have stayed at the clinic and had Lucy's baby there. At least we'd have electricity and more hands.'

'But they said ship her out.'

'I know. The problem is there's a real risk if Lucy's blood pressure continues to climb.'

Not to mention the haemorrhage risk, Kate thought, but didn't say it out loud in case Lucy woke up. Already placental vessels would be damaged and weakening from the constant high pressure of blood. If one of the vessels burst it would pour blood between the placenta and the uterus, then mother and baby would be in big trouble. Like Kate had been. She'd have to watch Lucy for pain that didn't come and go.

'I think she's starting to contract,' she said quietly to Rory. 'Still irregularly, but the Nifedipine doesn't seem to be holding her.'

Rory frowned. 'Are you saying nature wants that baby out and she might go into labour?'

'Most likely. I'm all for that.' Kate grimaced. 'Just not on the road.'

Rory looked up at her again through the mirror and, while his face remained serious, his sincerity shone through. 'That's why you're with her. I've got faith in you. And I bet Lucy does too. Everything will be fine.'

It was a platitude. An attempt to ease her strain. He was a very experienced paramedic and ambulance officer, a professional at calming people in stressful and extreme situations.

And it was the phrase he'd said to her many times over the years in her hours of need.

That first day at school... As the boss's daughter, she'd been left alone and lonely until big Rory McIver from Year Two took her hand and showed her where she could sit. 'Everything will be fine,' he said and something in his eyes and the caring tone of his voice allowed her to believe him.

That week her mother and stillborn baby brother died... When everyone else avoided her, not knowing what to say. When her father banned her from a final farewell at the funeral and Rory sought her out and held her and helped her make a special garden with a wooden cross where she would go to talk to her mother that no one else knew about. 'Every-thing will be fine,' he said.

Rory, listening the hundreds of times she was upset by her father's uncompromising stand on her behaviour and mixing with the hired help. He was always able to reassure her. Big things became manageable when she told Rory.

Now here he was, doing it again. The funny thing was, while she knew it was a platitude, his words and the memories of the past times he'd said it did make her feel better. He was right. Worrying would achieve nothing; she would do the right things and be prepared as best she could. Now he was doing it again and she wondered if he realised. She couldn't help the warmth of her smile because it was tied in with so many good memories she shared with him.

'Thanks, Rory.'

She saw his surprise, shock even, because she'd been sincere in her gratitude. Kate thought about that. For the first time she began to wonder how Rory felt about seeing her after all this time. She wasn't the only one who had memories. It put a whole new complexion on her behaviour towards him and didn't help her to keep her distance.

This wasn't good. She couldn't go there, begin impossible dreams or resurrect old emotions that could overwhelm her. She hastily shut the thoughts down.

'You're welcome,' he said, but this time he kept his eyes on the road and she was glad!

A short while later Lucy moaned again and Kate glanced at her watch before sliding her hand down to confirm the contraction. Fifteen minutes since the last one.

CHAPTER THREE

RORY SO WANTED to ease the lines of worry above Kate's eyes, smooth her brow and tell her again that everything would be fine, but she was the expert here and she wouldn't thank him for further interference.

Why he'd imagined he'd need to put himself through this torment when it was plain she didn't give a hoot about him, except to be vaguely irritated by his presence, he had no idea.

Had he needed to come back here and get it rubbed in his face in person? Hadn't the letter been enough? And the return of his ring? He must be a masochist. She'd told him ten years ago she didn't love him any more.

He just needed to get this trip over, Lucy to safety, and he'd never see Kate Onslow again. It wasn't as if Jabiru Station was anywhere near his normal world now.

He'd pulled himself up from nothing in his profession, had been promoted almost every year without pause until he was one step away from the top job. He had no need to feel like the hired hand he'd been ten years ago. It seemed he couldn't remove the stigma her father had left him with until he was an unqualified success. Until he had the one job that proved he was the best.

His appointment as Deputy Commissioner came into place in a week. After the closest battle between him and a more experienced officer, a family man who a lot of people said should have got the job, but the board had chosen wonder kid Rory because he'd promised them one hundred and ten per cent commitment.

Then, inexplicably, he'd wavered after reading an article saying that Kate's father was sick, and suddenly he'd needed to finish what lay between them. He'd promised the service he'd be back. He wished he'd never left Perth. Had turned back.

'I'm wondering if we should turn back.' Kate's voice intruded, almost as if she'd said out loud what he'd been thinking.

She was talking to herself and he didn't know whether to offer an opinion or not. Then she said something he hadn't expected. 'Rory? Have you ever seen a baby born?'

He dragged his mind away from his regrets and considered her question. 'Of course. And read the textbooks.'

She nodded but he could see she wanted more. 'When?' she asked.

'Last year. Just a couple of city babies in a hurry. All I had to do was catch and keep warm till hospital. But it's your area and your call, Kate.'

Rory remembered the cries of the woman, the fear in her face and the imploring way those eyes had begged him to relieve her pain. Apart from the methoxy' for her to breathe, there hadn't been a lot he could do except hold her hand. No, he wasn't comfortable with it but he'd cope.

Rory divided his concentration between negotiating the potholes and corrugations of the dirt track and Kate's face in the mirror. He had nothing helpful to add. She knew better than he the limitations distance imposed on keeping Lucy and her tiny baby safe.

She chewed those full lips of hers and he dragged his eyes back to the road. He remembered when he'd first noticed she did that. Always when she was worried. It had been when they'd started dating. And he'd kiss her to make her stop.

'It's hard to call it,' she said, and he concentrated on the red dust in front, anything to drag his eyes away from the damage she was causing. It seemed she needed to sound out her concerns and he was fine to listen.

'If we go back to Jabiru Township and Lucy doesn't go into proper labour until tomorrow or the next day, then I've placed her baby at a disadvantage.' She shook her head. 'This baby should be born at a level three nursery at least because, prem or starved, it will need watching.'

'No one said your job was easy, Kate.'

He heard her sigh. 'In an ideal world I'd like an ambulance with neonatal staff to meet us somewhere halfway if she goes into labour. I'm no expert on sick babies. I'm a birthing girl.'

He could hear the extra tension in her voice as she wondered out loud. 'Maybe they could fly in and meet us at one of the bigger stations, perhaps?'

He thought about it. 'Maybe.' But he knew she wasn't finished.

'This is Lucy's first baby—surely we'd have enough time for that?' She sounded more sure.

To Rory that seemed sensible. 'We could phone them.'

'How?' She shook her head and he saw again the depth of her concern. 'There's no phone coverage out here, unless you have a magic callbox in your pocket.'

He pulled his satellite phone from the glove compartment and waved it so she could see it. 'Boys toys. One of the perks of my job.'

She glared at him and it was queer how even that was endearing. 'How disgusting that you have a satellite phone in the city,' she said, 'and the clinic doesn't have one out here where the need is real.'

Technically, it wasn't a perk. He'd paid for it himself so he could be reached anywhere for his job. And she didn't need to know that he could easily afford it, but he made a mental note to anonymously donate one to Jabiru Township when he got back to Perth.

'Do you want me to connect you now and you can talk?'

She shook her head and he suspected she might even be a little ashamed of her outburst. 'I'll wait. Now that I know we can get advice I can sit until Lucy definitely goes into labour.'

'No problem.'

Her relief gave him an insight into the responsibilities of someone in her and Sophie's job at Jabiru. Like a road ambulance crew, they'd have to make the hard decisions too, without the backup of a nearby hospital, manage emergencies and manage the same horrific injuries he did, but on their own until help could arrive, sometimes many hours or even days later.

At other times they'd need to encourage people to leave their homes and families and travel huge distances for their own safety, at sometimes great expense as well, and occasionally the worst wouldn't happen. It made him realise his Kate was a big girl now.

Half an hour later Kate stared unseeingly as Lucy breathed in and out in her sleep and allowed her mind to drift until, unexpectedly, Rory slowed the truck and prepared to stop.

Kate peered through the windscreen to what lay ahead. At the side of the road a small but sprightly white-haired lady waved them down from behind her camper van. She wrung her hands together as she waited for them to pull up and Kate's stomach tightened. Not a mechanical breakdown, then?

The lady leaned in the front window as Rory pulled on the handbrake and Kate could see the glitter of tears on her wrinkled cheeks. Kate closed her eyes in dread.

'You're in an ambulance?' The little woman sighed and shook her head. 'Too late. How ironic.'

Kate was glad she wasn't driving without Rory because he was out of his seat and beside the woman before Kate realised his door was open. She blinked and tried to work out how he'd done it. She guessed that was what ambos did all the time. Quick on the scene, quick to prioritise and assess, she'd never really appreciated that before. Rory would be very good at it.

'How can I help you?' Kate could hear the gentleness in Rory's voice and, despite the woman's suggestion that there was little they could do, he didn't waste time until he confirmed it. He steered the woman back to her compact little van.

'My husband.' Kate could hear her careful enunciation, as if she spoke slowly the words would finally make sense. 'I was driving. John went to sleep the last time we stopped. He said he was tired. But I didn't know he'd never wake up again. He's cold now. I didn't even say goodbye.'

'Can you show me?' Rory said, still in that gentle, caring voice that brought tears to Kate's own cheeks, and she could just hear him murmuring sympathy as he went to confirm there was nothing they could do.

Kate glanced at Lucy, thankfully still asleep, and she hoped she wouldn't wake if Kate climbed through to the front and out of the passenger door in case Rory or the new widow needed support.

Kate glanced at the empty road around them and tried to imagine what the lady had been thinking before they'd pulled up.

It wasn't a common occurrence on the track but she'd heard of tragedies like this before and she wondered if her husband would have been happy to go like this. What type of sad courage would it take for his wife to drive all the way home to an empty house, wherever home was?

Kate chewed her lip and followed their stark footprints in the dust. She avoided looking at the van until the last moment and, when she did, she saw that it had a picture of a gaily painted wagon and the words 'John and Jessie's Jaunt' written on the back.

She winced as Rory and Jessie climbed back outside.

'There's nothing you could have done. He looks very peaceful,' Rory said, and he rested his arm around the woman's shoulder as he drew her towards Kate. 'This is Kate. She's from the Hospital Clinic up at Jabiru Township.'

Jessie glanced at Kate and bit her lip as she tried not to cry. 'Hello, Kate.'

'Hello. Jessie, is it?' Kate pointed to the painted names. 'I'm so sorry. We can phone the Kununurra police station and they'll meet you here as soon as they can.'

Jessie looked back at Rory. 'Thank you, both of you, for your kindness but I'll drive to the next town myself. They can meet me on the way. I've lived with this man all my life. I can drive now he's gone to the next.' She gave a watery smile. 'He'll be watching from above for the way I change the gears.'

Kate didn't know what to say. 'You do whatever feels right. Did you have any warning? Was your husband well?' She wanted to leave Jessie with an opening if she needed to talk.

'I thought he was.' Jessie choked back a sob. 'But he was in remission, and we've been having a wonderful time before the next set of treatment.'

'It must be very hard for you,' Kate said.

Jessie nodded and drew a deep breath. 'At least I don't have to watch him die slowly and painfully at home. When I get over the shock I'm sure his going will be a blessing.' Her eyes filled. 'But I will so miss him. Fifty years and he still made me laugh.'

Rory and Kate looked at each other over Jessie's head. Imagine a relationship like that! It seemed they were both thinking the same thing. As one they looked towards the van. How could they leave her alone with the body? 'We'll stay till the police get here,' Rory said.

Jessie thought about it. 'No. Thank you. I'll be fine.'

Kate moved closer and slid her arm around Jessie so the widow was supported by both of them. 'If we do go on, we'll wait until you feel ready to drive. Would you like me to make you a cup of tea before we leave? I've a Thermos in the back I filled this morning.'

Jessie sniffed. 'That would be nice.' She lifted her chin. 'And don't you worry about me. There's nothing for me to be afraid of. I'll just say my goodbyes as we drive and the children will organise the rest when I call them.'

Rory used his phone for the police at Kununurra and he and Kate stayed for another ten minutes until Jessie drove off on her final journey with her husband.

'She's very brave,' Rory said. 'He looked a kind old gentleman.'

'I'm glad. It's almost fitting to drive the last drive with just the two of them.'

Rory watched the van disappear. 'Would you do that?'

Kate looked away. 'I'll never be in that position.'

Kate sat in the back as the scenery flashed past. They passed another dust-swirling road train full of cattle and crossed two creeks but not much was said. No doubt Rory was as busy with his thoughts as she was with hers.

If she and Rory had still been together, they would be in their tenth year. So much time wasted wanting the impossible and she should have been looking for someone like John to share her life with. Before it was too late. But it was too late. She was too scarred for any man.

Jessie had children to help carry the load and Kate had a gaping void where hers should have been.

'What's wrong, Kate?' Rory's intrusion into her thoughts only made it worse.

'Nothing. Nothing you can help with.' Kate sighed. It wasn't Rory's fault. He'd been a brick to drive her to Derby and she hadn't really thanked him. In fact, she'd been hard on him and was lucky he was as even-tempered as he was.

She still didn't know what he'd come back for, except to see her. She didn't know how she felt about that, apart from terrified he'd break down the wall she'd hidden behind for so long. But he was right. There were things that needed to be said between them.

It was almost with relief that she heard Lucy moan because that put paid to worrying about either of them.

Lucy's eyes flickered open and she pushed her hand down onto her stomach. 'It hurts, Kate.'

Kate sat forward, even as her heart rate accelerated. A constant pain would be a dangerous sign. 'Where does it hurt, Lucy?'

'In here—' Lucy rubbed her stomach down low '—and in my back. It comes and goes.'

Kate was relieved. Labour was not optimum, but for a horrible moment she'd thought Kate was going to complain of severe headache or liver pain, or the signs of concealed haemorrhage—all ominous signs of internal damage from her hypertension.

Lucy screwed her face up and her eyes sought Kate's. 'What's happening?'

'I think you're going into labour, Luce.' She squeezed the young girl's hand and Lucy clung to Kate's fingers. 'Why don't you sit up straighter and get the weight off your back and side for a while?'

Lucy struggled into an upright position with Kate's help, which wasn't as tricky as it could have been because for the moment Rory had picked up speed and they flew along a freshly graded stretch of the road without the usual corrugations.

Lucy instinctively sighed a big breath out and her shoulders slumped; even her fingers loosened on Kate's. 'The pain's going now.' Her eyes sought Kate's and her voice wobbled. 'I'm starting to get scared. What if my baby is born out here on the road?'

Kate looked into Lucy's eyes and willed her to take in Kate's own faith in a woman's ability to give birth. Something her midwifery had thankfully reinstilled in her. Kate did believe that. Every woman's body had it—except Kate's, that was—but she wasn't going there.

She spoke slowly so Lucy could absorb the message. 'Your baby will be tough like his or her mother. Like you are. Have faith in your body, Lucy. Labour can take a long time and you'll know if you're getting closer to the pointy end. We can't do much about how your labour is going to work out here, just trust it, because everyone is different.'

Lucy nodded, so Kate went on. 'Go with it, ride the waves and relax, and think of your little baby waiting to meet you.'

Lucy searched Kate's face and must have seen the conviction there because she finally nodded. 'Okay. I can do that.'

Kate sat back and smiled, proud of her young patient's willingness to trust her own instincts—and Kate. 'I'm here and so is Rory. In a while we're going to ring the hospital in Derby and see if they can meet us somewhere if you get into strong labour. We'll look after you and your baby, no matter what.' Her eyes drifted to Rory's in the mirror. He was watching.

'Do you want me to stop so you can check her out?' he said.

Kate shook her head. 'How long to the next stop?'

He glanced at his watch. 'Half an hour to the general store. You could use the landline there too, talk to Derby; might be easier to hear if the satellite reception is playing up.'

Past the point of no return, then. At least Kate knew there was no turning back. 'We'll be fine till then, thanks. I'm just glad the real rain held off for this long.'

She smiled down at Lucy. 'You'll be able to get out, go to the Ladies and stretch your legs.'

Not long later a flash of lightning ahead and the almost immediate crack of thunder warned them they were heading into the thick of a storm.

Suddenly the heavens opened and the road ahead turned the previously smooth dirt into a sucking quagmire. As the heavy sheets of rain flooded the mud it made visibility and stability tough. Rory cursed silently under his breath and he glared skywards. If it had held off a little bit longer it would have been good.

His hands tightened on the wheel as he felt the truck slew sideways and he accelerated briefly until the off-road tyres caught and he had traction back. 'Might take a little longer,' he called over his shoulder and slowed down until the truck was barely making a brisk walking speed and they ground their way towards the hills through the middle of the storm.

'I'm glad I'm not flying in this,' he heard Kate say to Lucy.

'Me, too.' Lucy's voice wobbled and Rory looked out of the side window and winced as a flash of light illuminated the sparse scrub. He could agree with that but it wasn't much fun driving either. He was just glad that he was the one carrying such precious cargo because the retired Charlie had been night blind ten years ago and Bob was even worse.

A little over three-quarters of an hour later they pulled up at the rustic roadside store that marked the half-way point of their journey and Rory was able to pull up under cover to let them out.

They stayed just long enough to achieve what they had to. Kate rang Derby to update them and promised to phone at the next stop, if not before. Rory topped up the diesel and bought takeaway coffee for all of them to go with the sandwiches they'd brought, while Lucy slipped off to the Ladies.

He had a few minutes to quiz Kate, at least. She looked strained and he didn't doubt she was feeling the weight of her decision. 'So how do you think she'll go?'

Kate chewed her lip at him over the rim of her paper cup and for once there wasn't any of that reserve he'd felt between them since he'd come back. Somehow, that was even harder to bear.

She seemed to shake off her preoccupation while he waited and he wondered for a second if he was making this easier or harder for her by being the one to drive them to Derby. Then he mocked himself for even dreaming his presence made a difference.

Kate seemed to have come to peace with her decision. 'If Lucy labours and progresses to birth then we'll just do the best we can. I think she'll be fine. We'll be fine. If that's the way it goes, then we'll concentrate on the quickest way to get the baby to the special care nursery in Derby.'

So there was a chance they'd have the baby in the truck. Rory's brain froze for a second. Lord help them. That was definitely not what he'd expected her to say.

'Do you think that's going to happen?'

Babies. He knew next to nothing, really. Give him a ten car pile-up any day. He knew what to do with massive trauma and advanced life support. He knew how to coordinate disasters, reallocate staff, vehicles and modes of transport. But the idea of a premature baby—he remembered those pink and shiny, almost see-though miniature babes from air ambulance trips—relying even a little bit on him was more scary than he'd bargained for.

Kate looked serene now and Rory felt like shaking his head. She continued with, 'I'd say there's at least a fifty-fifty chance of her progressing to birth, especially now she's in early labour; it just depends.' He closed his eyes.

Oblivious, Kate went on, 'Of course, if she breaks her waters then I'll up it to eighty percent.'

He tried to keep his voice level. 'You seem pretty calm about it.'

'Not a lot we can do about it now.' Kate smiled at him. 'Who's the person who says everything's going to be fine? I can see you're not comfortable.'

Rory rubbed the back of his neck uneasily. 'Women should have babies in hospitals, where it's safe.' Not in the back of rough old ambulance trucks in tropical storms on a dirt road miles from civilisation.

'There's many that would disagree with you, including most of the Aboriginal women around here, but we'll save that argument for another day.' She obviously didn't think they were totally out of their depth so he'd just have to trust her.

He thought about her word choice. So she'd argue with him another day? Suddenly it wasn't so bad and he smiled at her. 'I'll hold you to that discussion at a later date.' And Kate would be there to do the baby stuff.

When Rory bundled them back into the truck for the next stage of the journey the rain had eased but still fell in soaking sheets.

'How do you feel after that walk around, Lucy?' Kate put away the BP machine. 'Your blood pressure's good.' Kate thought Lucy looked less sleepy, but she wasn't sure that was a good thing.

'Okay—' Lucy's voice dropped to a whisper '—but maybe I didn't go to the toilet enough 'cause I think I've just wet myself.'

O-oh. Ruptured membranes, Kate thought as she lowered her voice. 'Little wet or big wet?'

Lucy blushed and hung her head. 'Medium.'

Kate chewed her lip. Okay, then. 'You could have a little tear in your bag of waters around baby, Luce.' Kate dug into one of the emergency bags she'd brought. 'See if you can slide this feminine pad into your underwear. I know it looks like a big white surfboard but it'll make you feel more comfortable. As a bonus, we'll be able to tell if the dampness is from the water from around the baby and how much is coming away.'

When Lucy had accomplished that feat, not easy in a swaying vehicle, Kate pulled out the tiny Doppler to listen to Lucy's baby. The steady clop, clop, clop of Lucy's baby's heartbeat could be just heard over the rain on the roof.

So baby didn't mind someone pulling the plug out of the bath, she thought. They were all silent for a minute as they listened, that just discernible galloping heartbeat a reminder of why they were driving through the ridiculous weather to Derby.

'Should be about two hours to the next diesel stop,' Rory said when Kate put the Doppler away. 'Then, not long after that, the road will improve as we hit the main highway.'

'So we'll get through all right?' Lucy's voice was hard to distinguish over the rain and Kate repeated the question to Rory in case he hadn't heard.

'They said at the shop the next causeway hasn't risen too much with the downpour yet,' he said.

Kate hoped he was right but she wasn't so sure about the return trip for her and Rory. Not much they could do about that except worry later and see.

When they reached the next crossing the water had risen to a little over eighteen inches but the causeway was concreted and the vehicle high. The truck drove through smoothly without any water coming in the doors.

Kate was glad now they'd stayed only briefly at the last stop.

The rain eased more as they drove towards the next mountain range they couldn't see, she knew it was there, but today it was well and truly hidden in cloud. She mentally shrugged. If they kept going they'd find it eventually.

CHAPTER FOUR

'THE PAINS ARE getting stronger.' Lucy's forehead was wrinkled with the effort to breathe slowly and calmly and Kate smoothed out her own frown as she watched.

'I know, sweetheart.' Kate glanced up and caught Rory's eyes in the mirror again for a fleeting second, just for her own comfort, before she looked back at Lucy. 'Keep your breathing going, you're doing beautifully. It looks like this baby of yours is pretty keen on seeing what the world looks like on the outside of your tummy.'

Lucy grimaced. 'I think I just wet myself again. This time it's a flood.' She shuddered in disgust.

Kate smiled. 'Okay. We might get Rory to pull over for a minute while we sort out what's happening down there.' She looked to the front of the vehicle as they slowed. There was no doubt Rory was on antenna duty and could hear most of what they were saying, which saved her having to repeat everything.

There was nowhere sheltered to pull in so Rory edged to the side of the road as much as he could without sinking into the soft mud. The last thing they needed was to be run over by a road train or bogged in wet bull dust mire and have to dig themselves out. Neither was a great option.

Rory had caught snatches of conversation for the last half hour and had an idea things had progressed in Lucy's labour. They were still an hour out from the next stop but he'd been thinking along the lines of pulling off the track and down one of the side roads because they were 'near' one of the larger cattle stations.

A detour of maybe fifty kilometres would see them at a place that had facilities and an airstrip for when the sky cleared.

Kate pulled the privacy curtain while she attended to Lucy and Rory reached for a map from the seat beside him to see exactly where they were. The last crossing had been about sixty kilometres back so that made them near the turn off to Rainbow's End Station.

It wasn't a tourist facility like the high-end Xanadu they'd passed two hours ago, but he remembered the McRoberts family from the camel races when he was a kid. They'd certainly have no problem in an emergency like this.

But maybe it was quicker to keep rolling towards Derby and meet up with the ambulance coming the other way. He'd see what Kate wanted as soon as she was ready to tell him what was going on.

'Rory! I need you.' A calm voice but with that hint of urgency that had him jerk aside the curtain and heave himself in beside Kate without any hesitation.

He glanced at Lucy and blinked. The girl's whole body shuddered as the seizure took control and her half closed eyes stared vacantly at some point over Kate's left shoulder as her body shook the stretcher in jerking movements.

Rory slipped the oxygen mask over her face as Lucy's skin paled to alabaster. During the fit her body would use up the oxygen faster than she breathed it in and the tinge of blue around her lips deepened. Rory could feel his own heart gallop like the baby's heart rate had through the Doppler earlier.

Kate was focused and in control, which boded well for Lucy. Rory glanced at Lucy's stomach, which seemed to be heaving with a life of its own, and his fear for her baby mounted. He was so glad he wasn't the only person here.

'It's okay, Lucy,' Kate repeated. 'It's nearly over. We're here with you. It's okay.' Kate's soft voice repeated the litany until, after what seemed an hour but was probably less than two minutes, Lucy's body slowly settled and then lay still.

A deep dragging breath from Lucy was echoed by the one Rory pulled in for himself as he glanced at Kate before he wiped Lucy's face. He knew about fits. He'd dealt with epilepsy often but not with a pregnant woman and all he could think about was the lack of oxygen for Lucy's baby.

'The first eclamptic fit,' Kate said as she reached for the medication roll. He didn't like the sound of that.

'You expecting more?' He hoped she'd say no but of course it was likely. She handed him an ampoule and syringe and Rory busied himself with drawing up the medication while Kate checked Lucy's blood pressure.

'Her blood pressure's shot up. And we'll probably have to put some Magnesium Sulphate up in a drip to lower her cerebral irritability as well.' Kate reached into another side pocket and removed an intravenous fluid flask to add drugs for slow infusion. 'But we'll start with more hydralazine for her blood pressure. After you draw up I'll grab that satellite phone of yours, please.'

They worked seamlessly. Rory prepared the drugs, Kate checked and then injected them. Rory loaded the flask. He'd work with her on the road ambulance any day. No fluster or indecision—just how he liked it, his partner calm and the patient prioritised efficiently. She made everything easy, which was usually his job.

It was strange to remember that this was his Kate. The young woman he'd known years ago would have looked to him to save her. That time had certainly passed. He didn't know how he felt about that but there'd be time to think about it later.

'I thought her blood pressure was down.' Rory looked at Lucy who, while still pale, breathed normally now.

Kate sighed and nodded as she rechecked the blood pressure on Lucy's arm. 'So did I. Obviously not enough for Lucy's seizure threshold. Some people seize with an almost normal blood pressure, just like some babies can have febrile convulsions with only low temperatures.' She shrugged. 'If that's how their make-up is. Lucy's mother fitted. Either way, we need help.'

But what collateral damage? Rory thought. 'And her baby?'

Kate spared him an understanding glance. 'Will be fine. So far. The oxygen supply to the uterus was only decreased for a minute or two. As long as Lucy doesn't have long fits or do something nasty like separate her placenta with a haemorrhage, the baby will rest like Lucy and then recover. Babies are designed to take some stress.'

He knew he looked unconvinced as Kate elaborated. 'Lucy's out for the count but her labour will probably progress more rapidly now.'

Rory winced down at his chart, where he recorded the drugs and time given. 'More excitement to come, then.'

Kate flashed a smile back at him. 'After this, I'll be much happier when this baby is out.'

Happy? He was far from that. 'As long as one of us is happy.'

Lucy moaned and shifted her head from side to side but still didn't open her eyes.

Kate frowned and ran her hand over Lucy's abdomen. 'I'm not *that* happy.' She bent closer to Lucy's ear. 'Your uterus is contracting strongly now, Lucy. That's what the pain is. Soon.'

'Do you want me to head to Rainbow's End Station? It's less than an hour away. At least we'd have facilities and an airstrip.'

Kate had the Doppler out to check the baby's heartbeat. The clop, clop was marginally slower and very regular but Kate couldn't hear any slowing after the contractions. She stared at him for a moment and then nodded. 'I'll check with Derby but that sounds great. Let's do it.'

Rory nodded and he could hear the baby's heartbeat follow him as he climbed back through to the front, where he grabbed the satellite phone and passed it back before he started the engine.

Kate's voice echoed around his head. This Kate was a new woman, so much more independent and bolshy than the one he'd loved with every ounce of his adolescent heart and she seemed quite capable of handling any situation. She certainly didn't need him.

Kate, the person who had given his life meaning all those years ago, then had taken it away on a whim, leaving him a driven man. It amazed him to see her so gentle and calm as she talked to the semi-conscious girl and he was just as affected. Even though she was not part of his future, he could still feel proud of the woman she'd become.

Kate loosened her shoulders and took her own deep breath. Well, that was the first fit out of the way. Thank goodness Rory had been here. She'd have hated to try and cope with Charlie or Bob at the wheel.

Hopefully, Lucy wouldn't have any more fits before the drugs kicked in. 'It's okay, Lucy.' Kate stroked the girl's arm. 'You'll start to feel better when baby's born and the placenta that's causing all this trouble has gone.'

She checked Lucy's BP again and then picked up the phone. Lucy moaned and Kate slipped her other hand down to feel the contraction at the top of

Lucy's uterus. 'Your baby's fine and looks like he or she is determined to come soon.'

Kate dialled the number for Derby that she'd kept since the last stop. As she waited to be transferred through to the obstetrician on call she peered out of the window. 'Is it my imagination or is the sky becoming lighter?'

Rory started to answer but Kate said, 'I hope so,' before he could. He remembered she'd had a habit of that. The memory drew an unwilling smile.

'The storm seems to be concentrated more over the way we've come,' he said quietly, then stopped as she lifted her head when they answered.

'Hello? Yes, Doctor, it's Kate Onslow again.' She waited. Then, 'Lucy's just had one eclamptic episode lasting two minutes and her BP's now one sixty over a hundred.'

She listened. 'Foetal heart rate one hundred and fifteen,' and then nodded her head. 'We've given the Hydralazine. Start the Magnesium Sulphate? Sure. I've got the protocol. No problem.' She looked across at Rory and he waved the prepared flask.

'She's in established labour and we'd like to divert to Rainbow's End Station for the birth.' She paused, then, 'About an hour. We'd wait there until RFDS can come and get them both. How's the weather at your end?'

She smiled and Rory smiled too. It lifted his spirits to see that Kate again. So, good weather report, he gathered.

'Our weather isn't quite that here yet, but good news. So you'll ring Rainbow's End and tell them we're coming. Great. We'll see the plane there, then. Thanks.'

Kate put the phone down on the ledge and took the loaded flask from Rory and this time she gave him the full-blown grin that he'd give his brand new, fully equipped, supercharged Range Rover for. 'We work pretty well together, don't we?'

'Funny, that,' he said dryly. Maybe that's because we should have been together ten years ago, he thought with a tinge of bitterness. 'The weather's clearing and I'm guessing they'll get back to us with an arrival time?'

She nodded and turned to speak softly into Lucy's ear. 'Rory's going to take us to Rainbow's End Station and we'll wait for the plane. Just rest as much as you can, Lucy.'

The track to Rainbow's End seemed to take forever but he doubted Kate would have noticed. Things were hotting up in the back.

Lucy began to moan every few minutes and Rory realised his own shoulders had begun to tense just before the next contraction was due.

'You okay, Rory?' Kate moved up near his seat for a moment and he had the almost irresistible urge to reach back for her hand. A bit of personal comfort wouldn't have gone astray.

Instead, he said, 'I think you have enough to worry about apart from me, Kate.'

'Just to let you know, when Lucy moans it's because she's listening to her body, not because she wants us to do anything.'

He could feel himself frown. 'You're telling me she's not in pain?'

To his surprise, there was even a smile in her voice. 'Oh, it hurts all right. I'm telling you she's not scared of the pain. So don't feel you're failing her by not taking it away. Her own body is dealing with the pain by releasing endorphins. If it was overwhelming her it would be different. Okay?'

'Okay.' He didn't understand but he had to believe Kate. And, now he thought about it, Lucy didn't sound frantic or in a panic. She sounded almost drugged already. 'Thanks, Kate. It was bothering me she was upset.'

He felt her hand lightly on his shoulder and then she was gone. He only just heard her quiet, 'Thought so,' as she sat back down again next to Lucy.

The rest of the drive didn't seem as bad. Rory sighed once to relieve the tension in his shoulders and focused his concentration on the conditions.

Soon he barely heard Lucy because the road was half covered by water in places and it was his job to get them to the station without mishap.

Finally the lights of the homestead could be seen on the hill ahead. Lucy had become more agitated in the last five minutes and Rory had begun to doubt Kate's pain theory.

'Stop here, Rory!' That quiet yet immediate voice again from Kate.

Rory pulled over and by the time he stopped he could hear the sound he'd heard twice before in the back of an ambulance—the sound of a mother easing her child out into the world. And he could hear Kate's voice as he climbed through.

'Beautiful, Lucy. Nice and slow. Just breathe your baby out with the pains and relax between.'

'What do you need?' Rory whispered as he looked around, but it seemed Kate had everything ready.

'Just that towel when I ask for it. We'll dry baby before laying him or her on Lucy's skin, and if you check Lucy's BP as soon as it's over that would be great.'

'Baby on her skin?'

Kate's voice was barely audible and he had the feeling she didn't want to distract Lucy from her thoughts. 'Lucy's a natural born heater. Best place for a newborn is on mother's chest.'

He'd been thinking airways and resuscitation. Wrapping in space blankets. Apparently, that was out too for newborns. He leant over and spoke into Kate's ear. 'Breathing-wise?'

Kate shook her head and frowned but she glanced at the neonatal bag and mask she had ready. 'The heart rate is great. There's no reason to think baby won't be fine. You always give them thirty seconds if the heart rate's good before you interfere. If smaller than I expect, I'll wrap his or her body up without drying in that roll of cling wrap there, and then onto Lucy's skin to keep warm. Just dry the head and pop that little cap on.'

'Cling wrap? Plastic sandwich wrap?'

He saw the flash of her teeth. 'Neat, eh? Little babies get really cold from draughts and thin plastic wrap keeps air off wet skin. When the team arrives, if they want to access an arm or leg they just make a hole in the wrap for that part of the body. Keeps baby insulated.'

'We have all the mod cons in this ambulance.'

'Actually, I brought it with me but feel free to add it to your list when you go back.'

When you go back! The words were like a bucket of ice over the warmth he'd been feeling as he shared this moment with Kate and Lucy. He shook the thought off but some of the excitement had been diluted by reality.

'It's coming,' Lucy said on an exhaled breath and Rory stopped talking. He saw Lucy's hand clenching on the sheet and he slipped his hand over hers. She grabbed his fingers gratefully and he cursed himself for not thinking of it sooner.

'You're doing a great job, Lucy,' he whispered in her ear and squeezed her hand back gently.

Kate was down the business end. 'Here comes baby, Lucy. Nice and slow.' There was a pause and then the rest of the head appeared, then, strangely, baby's face turned as if to look the other way. Rory looked up at Kate with a question.

'Restitution,' she said quietly. 'Untwisting of the neck that happens as the head is born. Baby's head is lining back up with the shoulders.'

Then, gracefully, one pale shoulder appeared and seemed to take a dive towards the bed and then the other was out and in a rush it was all over as hips and knees and feet all tumbled into Kate's waiting hands. Kate held up the baby so Lucy could see the sex of her baby.

They all waited for the first indrawn breath or cry. The little girl lay limp and still like a stunned fish in Kate's hands, dark blue eyes wide open in a tiny unmoving face—no cry, no breath.

Kate froze. Time stopped. Her breath jammed and her heart dived sickeningly in her chest to beat one slow beat after another. It was as if she'd fallen, unsuspecting, into a freezing black shaft filled with ghouls. Down and down and down into a bottomless hell. The seconds ticked with aching slowness as the shock battered her. Dead like her baby! Lucy's baby couldn't be…

'Kate?' Rory's voice shocked her back to the real world and she looked at him and then shook her head to rid it of the panic. The world sped up.

'I'm sorry.' She sucked in a breath. Lucy's baby would be fine. It was just blue and stunned. 'Towel,' she said to Rory. She even sounded calm as she rubbed the flaccid baby until it began to gasp and flex in protest.

Oblivious to those seconds of Kate's frozen moment of horror, Lucy reached down to touch her baby. 'A little girl.' Tears ran down Lucy's face. 'A shame my mum wasn't here to see.' Then she reached for her daughter and Kate passed the towel back to Rory and slipped the little girl up to her mother.

'There you go, Lucy.' Lucy closed her arms over Missy.

Kate looked at Rory and their eyes met over the new mother and her baby. She could tell Rory was euphoric at the birth, and the fact that he'd shared it with her. She just needed a hug.

She didn't even want to think about what might have happened if he hadn't been here. How long would she have stayed frozen?

'This is the needle I spoke about to help separate the placenta, Lucy.' Kate slid the needle in Lucy's thigh but Lucy didn't seem to notice, then Rory watched Kate clamp and cut the cord.

He wanted to hug Kate. All these things she had to remember. He murmured a saying he'd once heard. 'The midwife, methodical through the beginning of life.'

Rory was back in that warm place of sharing; his throat felt tight from emotion and he looked at Kate and then Lucy with wonder, and maybe even a tear in his eye. 'You are amazing, Lucy. Congratulations on your beautiful daughter.' He pumped the blood pressure cuff up as he spoke.

'Thank you.' Lucy smiled up at him shyly. 'And thanks for holding my hand.'

'My privilege.' Rory watched the meter as he let the cuff down and winced at the height of Lucy's blood pressure. 'One eighty on one ten.' He shifted back out of the way.

Kate nodded and tucked the blankets around mother and baby so that Kate's daughter was chest to chest with her mother's skin and her little head was bonneted and turned to face Kate. 'I expected that. I'll give another dose of Hydralazine now the placenta is delivered.' She smiled a wooden smile at Lucy. 'The good news is your daughter looks great. She's tiny, probably about four pounds, but perfect. She was just a little stunned at birth and will be looking for a real feed because she's smaller than she should be. I think she's not too prem, just very hungry from the placenta shutting down. See, her ears are perfectly formed.'

Kate took the Hydralazine from Rory and slowly injected it into Lucy's second drip line.

When she'd finished, Rory gave her the saline flush to clear the line, then said, 'I'll get us up to the house,' and he crawled back through to the front of the vehicle.

Within seconds they were making their way up the driveway. All the lights were on and the door flew open as they arrived.

The next half hour blurred as Lucy was transferred from the vehicle to a comfortable bed. Mrs McRoberts had been a theatre sister before her marriage and she insisted that Kate and Rory relax after their adventures for 'five minutes at least' with a cup of tea while she watched Lucy and her baby.

It had been a stressful couple of hours and Rory was happy to take advantage of the offer. He wasn't sure about Kate, who was circling the table as if she couldn't bear to sit down. She stopped with her back to him and faced the paddocks.

Rory hesitated and then crossed to stand behind her. When he touched her shoulder she flinched so violently his hand flew up in the air. 'Hey,' he said and deliberately put both his hands firmly onto her shoulders and eased her back against his body. 'Take a couple of those deep breaths you keep recommending everyone else takes.'

To his relief, she did, her shoulders rising and falling beneath his hands. After an initial stiffness, she relaxed enough to lean into him a little, then inexplicably she pulled away and sat down. Rory let his hands fall through the empty air and turned to look at her where she sat.

He didn't get this woman at all—which would be fine if it didn't feel as if he'd just been kicked in the gut every time she shut him out—so he shrugged and sat down himself.

When she spoke it was as if nothing had happened between them and Rory decided to drink his tea. He had to find a way to stop her messing with his head.

'Apparently, after the storm left here it seems to have headed Jabiru way,' she said. 'No chance they'll have planes landing on the strip there.' The way she avoided his eyes and spoke reminded him of this morning, before they'd left, and he felt as if he were riding a roller coaster of emotions. One minute she was fine, the next she'd retreated so far he could barely see the real Kate.

She poured more tea and then glanced at her watch. 'Mrs McRoberts said the plane's only half an hour away from here. We can head back after that.'

Something was going on and he had no idea where her thoughts were. He watched her face. 'So you're not going to go with Lucy to Derby?'

She shook her head. 'No. She's had her baby now, and they're both fine.' She shut her mouth with a snap and he almost missed the moment when she started to shake with reaction. The shudders grew until her whole body shook the chair. Almost like Lucy's fit, only with such anguish on her face he could no more not go to her than not breathe.

Rory pushed his chair out and dropped to the ground to kneel beside her chair. He pulled her head down onto his chest and held her. 'It's okay, baby. Everything's fine. You did wonderfully.'

She stared straight through him and for a moment a horrifying feeling hit him that he'd lost her to some place he couldn't go.

'Kate? Honey? You okay?' She didn't move and he tilted her chin and looked into her face. Eyes tightly shut, she leaned into him and her arms crept round his chest, drawing comfort as if she couldn't help herself. They sat like that, him rocking her, for what seemed to Rory like forever.

After a few minutes she sighed and sucked in a shuddering breath before she rested her forehead against his chest. When she leaned back her eyes opened and she blinked at him. She glanced away and then back. 'I'm sorry. I don't know why I did that. Thank you.'

He smiled and brushed her cheek with his finger before he sat back on his heels. Ignored her deliberate distance as if it wasn't there. 'You're welcome. It's been a pretty big day.' He brushed the hair away from her eyes so he could see her face. 'You okay now?'

She drew another erratic breath. 'When the baby was born…' Kate shook her head at the memory. 'I had a brain freeze. I thought the baby was going to die. I've never done anything like that before in my life.'

He stroked her hair. 'I didn't see that. It must have been quick because we didn't notice. I thought you were just waiting for the baby to breathe by herself. It was only seconds until you dried her.'

She frowned. 'I shouldn't be here. It's all been too much.'

'You've had a lot of responsibility with Lucy.'

'Not just Lucy.' She shook her head again. 'My father, you coming back…' she paused '…and the past.' She shook her head. 'I don't want to talk about it. I can't.' He watched her emotions shut off from him like a roller door closing until there was nothing. No connection at all.

The last thing he wanted to do was upset her again. 'Fine.' He stood up and moved back to his chair as if he'd done something mundane like picking a napkin off the floor. He moved the topic on to what he hoped was safer ground. 'So Lucy will go on from here without us?'

He watched Kate sit back in her chair and compose herself more. She took a sip of tea, a couple of breaths and even offered a false smile before she nodded. 'The flight nurses are excellent and her aunt's at the other end. Her aunt will stay with her until Mary can come. I need to get back to town and eventually back to Jabiru Station and my father.'

Rory didn't want to think about Kate's father, what the man had done to his parents, and his own issues with him. Or what he'd done to Kate to have her wound up like this. The return part of the trip would be hard going enough without broaching the subject of Lyle Onslow. Not yet. Maybe never.

He scouted for a safer topic. 'Lucy's daughter is a cute baby. Missy's a cute name. What do you reckon she weighs?'

Kate looked away towards the room where Lucy lay cosseted by Mrs McRoberts and she smiled for real this time. 'Nearly four and a half pounds on the kitchen scales. She looks almost term, good creases on her feet and hands. So her tiny size is because she's been having it harsh in there with Lucy's blood pressure. Hypertension plays havoc with transfer of food and oxygen from the placenta. Our baby's got a bit of catch-up feeding to do.'

The expression made him smile. 'Our baby. I like the sound of that.' Rory repeated the words without thinking but he was unprepared for the absolute devastation in Kate's face.

He could only blink in disbelief as Kate pushed her chair out and turned away. 'I've got to go.'

'Kate? What's wrong?'

'Nothing. Leave it.' He could hear the anguish in her voice and Rory felt the waves of despair radiating from her as she put her hand up to ward off any questions. She hurried away to Lucy and he stood and stared after her as his brain tried scenarios to explain what had just happened.

He looked back at the table with the two half-finished cups and he shook his head. His eyes narrowed. He didn't understand but he would. Later, when the plane had gone.

He picked up the cups and headed through to the kitchen to thank the housekeeper. The rain had stopped. He'd tidy the truck and refuel and when the RFDS arrived he and Kate would run Lucy out to the airstrip and say goodbye. Then all this would be settled.

CHAPTER FIVE

THIS WAS EXACTLY why she'd known seeing Rory was a bad idea. Not once since that dreadful morning when they'd said her child had died had she spoken about her loss.

Ten years ago she'd been confused, isolated from anyone she knew and told to pretend it had all been a bad dream. She'd spent the next six weeks physically healing and mentally bricking up what had happened behind an impenetrable barrier.

Until Rory. The one person she couldn't hide from.

How was she going to get through the return trip? He was going to ask, in that caring, genuine way of his, about something he more than anyone had the right to ask. Did she have the right not to tell him?

Kate felt like throwing herself off the veranda and running into the hills so that Rory wouldn't find her but of course she couldn't. No wonder she'd decided emotions were better left out of the equation and her life.

The time for her to be alone with Rory drew closer and the tension inside her built until she was sure she'd explode. Finally, Rory and Kate stood together beside the truck out on the dirt airstrip. They waved to Lucy as she was loaded onto the small aircraft with her baby for the flight.

Her eyes slid sideways as Rory shaded his eyes to watch the door close. Shame Rory hadn't taken that plane back to Derby, Kate thought. Then she wouldn't have to go through this. 'You should have gone with them, Rory. You could have made connections and been in Perth tonight.'

They watched the RFDS taxi off down the runway under the heavy sky and Kate chewed her lip as she wished she'd decided to go with Lucy.

'That would defeat the purpose of my trip.' Rory looked at her. 'Wouldn't it?' He frowned. 'Have you forgotten why I'm here?'

As if she could. 'I'm quite able to drive the truck back myself.'

Rory examined her lovely but stubborn profile as she watched the plane. 'I'm sure you could manage the truck beautifully. But it's not happening.' He turned away. 'It's later than we anticipated. Do you want to stay here the night or leave now?'

His gut instinct said to stay the night here and not risk the trip back to Jabiru on the slim off chance they'd get through but he knew Kate wanted to get home. Either way, he planned to get her alone and find out what it was that had changed her from the young woman he'd left behind ten years ago.

Still she didn't look at him. 'My patient's gone. I'd prefer to leave now but it's your call.'

He sighed. 'It's after four. It would be very late if we did make Jabiru tonight. But if we leave tomorrow to cross the larger rivers there's less chance the crossings will be passable at all.'

'Then leave now.' Still that monotone from Kate that had him frowning down at her.

'I think we should freshen up as long as we're quick. They've offered late lunch and a hamper for the road. It seems sensible to take advantage of the hospitality.'

'You can't do both, Rory. Make up your mind.'

'Sure we can. We'll eat quick and I've already fuelled the truck.'

Kate looked through him. 'You've decided, then. Why ask me?'

He shook his head. Women. She'd changed since that incident earlier. Her face looked drawn and closed and he could barely picture her smiling in the back of the truck during the drive.

It was a battle he wasn't going to win at this moment. The RFDS plane was in the air now. 'Let's go, then.'

They were on the road within half an hour and Rory picked up the speed a bit because he had no patient to be bounced around in the back and Kate safely beside him in the front.

She hadn't spoken a word since she'd buckled her seat belt and he had things to think about too. Like why she'd had such a crisis and been angry with him when he'd done nothing that he could see to cause her displeasure. He took a stab in the dark, which seemed appropriate because the sky had suddenly become grey with threatened rain.

'Have you had a bad experience with a patient's baby in the past, Kate?' He glanced across at her and then back at the road. 'Is that why you were upset at the homestead?' It was all he could think of.

At first he thought she wasn't going to answer but grudgingly the words came at the same time as a gust of wind rocked the truck. 'You could say that.'

He tightened his hands on the wheel to keep the wheels in a straight line as he thought about her choice of words.

He knew all about bad cases at work. Emotional debris from other people's lives and disasters. Especially the good people it seemed to happen to. Maybe this was what'd changed her. He could understand that. 'Can you talk about it?'

She turned to look at him and he could see she'd erected a sheer wall like the steep-sided gorges that ran with water at the side of the road. The gorges had taken millions of years to form. He wondered how long that wall had taken to evolve in Kate.

She sighed and began, but her lack of expression was as eerie as the strange light they were driving through. 'The baby's mother had pregnancy induced hypertension the same as Lucy. Our dash with Lucy brought it all back to me.'

He nodded. 'I can understand that. Want to tell me about it?'

'No.' She stared at the road in front and he bit back a sigh. And waited. After a few minutes' silence he deliberately didn't break she did begin. 'They flew the mother out to Perth...' her voice trailed off '...but it was too late for the baby in the end. The placenta separated, she bled and the baby died.'

Rory could tell she needed to talk about it. He'd learnt that over the years in his job. The hard way. 'So did you go all the way with them? What happened to the mother?'

'Oh, I was there.' He thought for a moment she was going to cry and he had the urge to stop her from telling more. Protect her from the grief she'd bottled up, but maybe she'd never get over it if she didn't speak about it now.

Maybe he was the only person she could tell. His voice was only loud enough so she could hear over the wind. 'Go on if you can.'

'She was young like Lucy and quite sick for the next week. You know what they did? They never showed her the baby. By the time she was well enough to realise what had happened it was too late and she never saw her baby. They told her to forget it ever happened.'

'Monsters,' he muttered, and Kate nodded and he realised he must have said it out loud.

'You'd hate that happening to any patient,' he said and tried to imagine the ramifications for the young mother. 'No wonder you were upset.'

Kate nodded again and he saw the shine of tears in her eyes before she turned away. He'd bet there was more. The case had obviously affected Kate heavily. He knew ambulance personnel who'd had a series of similar cases that built up inside and then one last bad one could paralyse with grief and regret.

'And that's why you agreed to transfer Lucy? Because you were scared that would happen again?'

'To make sure it didn't happen again.' She flicked a glance at him and he winced at the hunted expression in her eyes. 'I don't want to talk about it any more.'

He wasn't satisfied but backed off and then they rounded a corner and suddenly the world intruded again. It seemed it had a habit of doing that.

They nearly ploughed into a long-wheelbase luxury camper that had skidded and come to rest diagonally across the road in front of them. With their side of the road blocked and reluctant to brake too heavily in the greasy conditions, Rory aimed for the gap on the other side of the road.

He steered between the rock of the mountain they were circling, careered past the vehicle before he could slow the truck enough to stop without skidding, then pulled back onto their side of the road and slid to a halt.

He looked across at Kate to make sure she was safe and for the first time in a long time there was an animated expression on her face.

'Not bad, sir. Maybe I'm glad I'm not driving.'

'High praise indeed from you.' He grinned at her and she grinned back and the sudden rush of joy that blossomed inside him warned of danger and he tried to damp it down. Then the smile ran away from her face and he was sad to see it go because he'd felt as if they'd bonded briefly in that moment of relief.

Then again, that way lay pain and he'd have to stop putting himself out there for the hits. He looked away to the camper. 'Let's see if they're okay.'

Kate slid from the truck onto the muddy roadside and it felt as if she'd just escaped from prison. She couldn't believe she'd started to talk about her loss, even if she'd hidden behind her fictitious patient.

The mire sucked at her boots as she crossed the road and she realised the driver of the van was knee-deep in mud behind the bus. The rear wheels were buried as he tried to manoeuvre what looked like plastic planks down to drive out over. His face was covered in smears and stripes of red slimy soil, as were most of his clothes. He didn't look too happy about it.

Kate mentally shrugged. He would have been more unhappy if they'd hit him. A little mud wouldn't kill him.

'I'm sorry,' the man said. 'I asked her to stand at the corner and wave people down but she was too busy telling me how stupid I am.' He glared at the open door of the Winnebago before he looked back at them. 'I can't do anything with her.'

Kate turned to see a diminutive brunette, beautifully dressed and made-up, poke her head out of the door. The woman limped theatrically onto the top step with her red-tipped fingernails resting on her hips and waited for maximum effect before she stepped gingerly down another rung. Still safe above the layer of plebeian mud, she bestowed an overjoyed smile on Rory. 'Well, if it isn't Rory McIver.'

'Oh, Lord.' Kate heard Rory's muttered comment as she turned to look at him but his face was bland. He avoided Kate's unspoken question by looking at the other woman. 'Hello, Sybil,' he said.

Sybil's appearance was so incongruous—she was dressed for a shopping expedition rather than a bush road trip—followed by Sybil's tone of voice when she'd addressed Rory, that Kate couldn't think of a thing to say. It shouldn't matter that Rory knew this woman or that he wasn't comfortable with meeting her here; what mattered was that some other vehicle didn't career around the corner and collect the lot of them.

Kate shook her head at the delay. 'We've hazard signs in the ambulance. I'll put them out on each corner and hopefully nobody else will have to steer for their life.'

With a narrow look at Rory, which confirmed that he actually seemed relieved she was going, Kate squelched her way in disgust to the rear of their vehicle and opened the back. Now who the heck was Sybil? And just how well did she know Rory McIver?

Kate ground her teeth. Well, what did she expect? She hadn't seen him since he'd left Jabiru ten years ago and just because she'd been miserable didn't mean he had to be the same. As far as he was concerned, he hadn't lost a baby and had to claw himself back to sanity.

Rory watched Kate yank the signs from the back of the truck and sighed.

He turned back to the job at hand. The sooner they were out of here the better, for lots of reasons.

'Why couldn't you be sensible like that lady?' the man said peevishly.

Sybil laughed. 'Don't be silly, Philip. Look at the cost. She's filthy like you already.'

Rory flicked a glance at Sybil before he made his way over to Philip. 'Watch it, Sybil. Kate and I can easily drive away and leave you.'

'But I need you to look at my ankle, and you wouldn't do that, Rory. I *know* you.' There was a world of meaning in her words and Rory couldn't help glancing to see if Kate had heard. His heart sank when he saw her toss her hair as she stomped up the road with a sign. Yep. Explanations later, though.

Rory declined to answer Sybil and glanced at the dark sky. At least it had stopped raining for the moment. 'So what's your plan? Philip, is it? I'm Rory.' Rory held out his hand and Philip wiped his palm on a reasonably clean piece of shirt and shook Rory's hand ruefully.

'I was going to use these board things I found in the back. Apparently they're the best thing out for this, but if you've ideas I'm happy to listen. This whole trip—' he glared at the door Sybil had disappeared through '—was a bad idea.'

'Not your idea, I gather?'

'We're supposed to be going to the diamond mines. I wanted to fly but she wanted to drive through some town called Jabiru on the way. I was pretty happy up until an hour ago when she turned into a petulant witch.'

'That's Sybil for you.' Rory turned and measured with a glance the distance to the other side of the road and the logistics of the ambulance simply pulling them out. 'There isn't enough room for us to pull you forward, though if we slew sideways we might leave you worse off. Your vehicle's heavy.'

He rubbed the back of his neck as he thought. 'We'll winch you forward from one of the trees across the road; that's the safest. The problem is you'll be facing the wrong way when we finish. You'll have to turn around up the road if you want to come back this way.'

'I'm happy to head back to Derby and Broome. I don't suppose the road gets better this way?'

'Only worse with river crossings.'

'Let's do what you suggest.' Philip narrowed his eyes at the camper. 'She's not getting her pink diamond now, anyway.'

'If you'll take some advice, don't tell her that until Broome or your trip will be hell.'

Phillip laughed. 'You really do know her.'

Rory raised his eyebrows. 'I've paid my dues.'

Kate came back and helped with the reversing and soon the whole road was churned by their efforts. Kate could feel her tenuous hold on her temper begin to slip. At the edge of her vision Sybil limped dramatically on the dry side of the road as she tried to distract Rory. Everything seemed to be taking forever.

Kate didn't want a night beside the road with Rory, was terrified of it, in fact, yet the afternoon was slipping away.

Finally they managed to winch the vehicle free but by the time they were finished everyone, except Sybil, was covered in mud.

'Now can you look at my ankle, Rory?' Sybil's plaintive voice broke into the feeling of accomplishment the workers were finally savouring.

Kate turned her back so she didn't have to watch. She squashed down the ignoble voice that suggested she whisper to Rory not to wash his hands first. Why should she care about Rory looking after a woman from his past? She was glad he'd had a life. She should've had one herself.

Ten minutes later Rory and Kate were back on the road. 'How was poor Sybil's dreadful ankle?' Kate said and she didn't even care that her sarcasm made Rory raise his eyebrows.

'Only slightly swollen.'

'What a surprise.' Kate was steaming. 'And they've made us even later. It's almost dark.'

Rory wondered if her irritation was even a little out of proportion to the crime. The thought made him smile. 'We couldn't leave them stranded.'

Kate shook her head in disgust. 'She could have done something to help.'

'Some people are purely decorative. That's Sybil.' His sanity-saving mistake from the past.

Kate stared as if she didn't know him and she jammed one hand on her hip as she turned. 'How handy for decorative people. Wish I'd thought to be purely decorative.'

'You were pretty decorative ten years ago.'

She tossed her hair. 'I've changed, thank goodness.' She glared out of the front of the vehicle as they drove along. 'So where do you know her from?'

'Sybil? From Sydney, more than a few years ago. She helped me when I was having a bad time.' Like not long after I'd been dumped by you. 'I worked in a nightclub on my days off and she was going out with the owner. Then she looked me up again in Perth.'

'How nice for both of you. Spending quality time together. Well, it seems she was going to look you up in Jabiru. You must have made an impression on her.'

Knowing Sybil, she was much more devious than that, he thought. What would Kate think when he told her? There was a lot at stake here and she didn't see it. He'd been so in love with Kate he couldn't contemplate a relationship with another woman. Had told Sybil so. And, being a woman, she'd dragged a few details out of him. She'd always had a knack for remembering the wrong things. What would Kate say? Especially as she seemed to have taken an instant dislike to the other woman.

'Actually, I think she was looking for you.'

Kate turned a startled face towards him. 'Why on earth would she do that?'

So Kate was still oblivious to the damage she'd caused him. It shouldn't hurt after all this time but it did. He'd meant so little to her. He really didn't want to have to spell it out.

He forced a smile and chose diversion in the ridiculous. 'You're not jealous, are you, Kate?'

Her lip practically curled. 'Spare me.'

He really did have to laugh at her disgust. He'd known she wasn't, of course, but no harm in wishing. He went on to explain. 'When I first met Sybil I may have used you as the excuse for not being married already.' To hell with it; he'd just say it. 'I said I'd left my heart in Jabiru. I didn't mention your name.'

He waited for her to comment on that, say she was sorry, even laugh at the idea, but she didn't say anything and he wasn't sure if that was good or bad so he concentrated on the road ahead and tried to forget he'd mentioned it.

After a few minutes when she still didn't offer any comment he looked across briefly at this militant woman who bore so little resemblance to the young girl he'd left ten years ago. Consciously he moved on from his own neediness. 'So what's your excuse?'

Now she looked at him. 'What do you mean?'

'Why aren't you married, Kate? Why are you still single and childless when obviously you were born to be a wife and mother?'

She didn't even look at him. 'I'm afraid that's none of your business.'

He could have ground his teeth in frustration. How could she say that?

Rory turned to look at her profile. 'On the contrary, once it was very much my business.'

Unfortunately he'd had his eyes off the road far too long and when he glanced back he realised the evening shadows had hidden a muddy section deeply scored from previous vehicles.

He veered heavily to the left so that the ambulance swung towards the edge of the road and even climbed a little up the bank. For a moment he thought they were going to make it around the quagmire but the truck slid off the bank with a slurp, stabbed the thick tyre with a lethally pointed branch on the way and then the wheels inevitably slowed in the wet bull dust mire until the truck sank to the axles and stopped.

They wouldn't get out of this in a hurry. Bloody hell.

'Oh, that's great,' Kate said and crossed her arms with a pained sigh.

Strangely, her ill humour repaired his own. Actually, he'd done pretty well to avoid tipping the truck over. He looked at her for a moment and then said, 'Thrilled about it, myself. Looks like you've got my company longer than you anticipated.' Her behaviour reminded him of a much younger Kate and, despite her obvious irritation, the possibilities were in fact quite intriguing now he thought about it.

'Hmmph,' Kate said. 'You're just lucky you're not stuck here with Princess Sybil.'

'I'd much rather be here with you,' he said, tongue stuck firmly in cheek. Kate glared at him and opened her door and he watched her jump down and stomp off.

CHAPTER SIX

RORY CLIMBED OUT and surveyed their predicament, then started to whistle just to annoy her. He'd been in worse spots and the old Kate had never sulked long. That was another of the things he'd loved about her.

The road was a challenge but, well-equipped as they were, it would only take time. Something they didn't have much of before dark. He glanced around for a good place to camp.

A few minutes later Kate sidled up to him and she didn't quite meet his eyes. 'I'm sorry, Rory. I'm a cow.'

He grinned down at her. He remembered this Kate. Always brave enough to say when she'd been wrong. 'Well, Daisy,' he drawled—Daisy had been the house cow's name when they were kids—'we'd best winch our way out of this and set up camp back off the road. I'll change tyres in the morning.'

Kate smiled warily back and Rory felt the lightest he'd felt all day. Just one smile and she had him. He was as weak as water when it came to resisting Kate. Not much had changed.

They worked steadily for the next forty minutes as the light slipped away around them. Finally they'd extricated the truck and shifted onto higher ground on the bank so they wouldn't endanger any of the infrequent night travellers.

'You did well not to tip over when we hit the mud.' Kate shook her head as she watched him open the door to get out. She glanced at the offending wheel. 'And that's one flat tyre.'

Rory jumped down. 'Only on the bottom,' he said facetiously and glanced around. 'I'll fix it tomorrow. Let's wash up and get the camp sorted.'

'I've set up a basin and the water bag on that log. If you want to wash I'll grab some wood for a fire.'

He raised his brows and looked her up and down. 'So you're not just decorative.'

She narrowed her eyes at him with the comparison to Sybil. 'You feel like living dangerously, McIver? Don't start me. And I'll have the stretcher in the back tonight in case it rains.' She raised her eyebrows at him. 'You can have it tomorrow night.'

He opened his eyes wide. 'Gee. Thanks. We'll be back in Jabiru by then.' She shrugged, unsympathetic, so he pretended to sigh. 'I'll guess I'll shake my swag out, then.'

She nodded and began to scoop up kindling and he watched her for a moment as she bent to pick up another twig. She seemed more settled since her mini-tantrum when they'd stopped. More relaxed and he didn't know why. But there was no doubt he was pleased to see it.

He glanced up at the sky; the clouds were breaking up a little for the moment. Hopefully, it wouldn't rain tonight.

Half an hour later they had the campfire set like a crackling little tepee in the middle of a clearing. Kate sat on the ground on top of Rory's swag with her knees drawn up and rested her back up against a blanket-covered log. Rory surveyed their campsite from where he leaned on a tree. They munched thick-cut cold beef sandwiches with homemade horseradish from Rainbow's End Station against a big fat boab tree.

'Mmm, mmm.' Kate couldn't remember when she'd last enjoyed food so much. The night air was cool, the fire crackled with orange flames and a few early stars twinkled in the gaps between the cloud cover now that it was dark. They were alone, the sky was enormous, and it brought back her deep love of the top end.

She glanced across at Rory; flashes of light from the fire illuminated the dark planes of his face. He was watching her. She realised he had been for a while and suddenly it wasn't so good they were alone.

She didn't want to talk about today and especially not about what had upset her. 'So tell me about your rapid rise to fame, Mr McIver. How does a country man like you make it so big in the cut-throat world of the city?'

Rory didn't say anything immediately and for a moment she thought he was going to demand they talk about her. The seconds stretched and the crickets and frogs seemed to turn up the volume of the night while she waited.

When he spoke she realised how tensely she'd waited and forced herself to relax.

'I decided early on that if I stayed in the Ambulance I'd have a big say in how things were run in the service.' He looked at her. 'So when I got your letter—' He paused, and Kate watched him look away from her and she had the first inklings of how deeply she'd wounded him.

He went on, 'I was gutted, couldn't get back to Jabiru to talk to you, couldn't get you on the phone, was trapped without holidays for another year and no money. I wrote letter after letter and when you didn't write back I pushed myself to succeed and didn't stop until I got there.'

So her father hadn't forwarded them on. She wasn't astonished, just sorry that she couldn't have made it easier for Rory. 'I didn't get any letters.'

'If you weren't there it's not surprising your father didn't forward them on.'

Kate remembered the day before he'd left and the demoralising ridicule her father had heaped on him. She'd forgotten about that too, with all that had happened after Rory had left. Would it have made a difference in her choices if she'd remembered earlier—and more of the reasons why Rory had left?

'I'm sorry you were hurt. Go on.'

Rory brushed that away. 'Not much to tell. I worked non-stop, applied for every course. I took every overtime shift, every relief senior position offered, even if they were way out in the bush, while I did other correspondence courses.' He shrugged.

That amount of work wouldn't have left much time for play. In fact, it sounded a lot like her. She'd taken little time to enjoy her life as well. She looked away. 'As I said before, it sounds driven.'

'Guess I was.'

She looked up at him and shaded her eyes from the brightness of the fire so she could see his face. 'So why are you here now?'

His voice dropped. 'Because I've come to a point where I need to clear what was between us before I can go any further.'

Kate balled the paper she'd unwrapped from her sandwiches and threw it in the fire. The silence between them stretched and she watched the flames curl around and blacken it until suddenly the paper burst into flame and was consumed. That was what would happen to her if she allowed Rory to expose her emotions.

'I'll ask again.' Rory's voice drifted from across the fire. 'Why aren't you married, Kate?'

She looked away and said the first thing that came into her mind. 'I never found the right man.'

She heard Rory suck his breath in. 'I was there.' He stood up and shifted until he loomed above her, staring down; she could feel his gaze without looking. Then he edged in beside her and moved along until his hip nudged hers. The heat from Rory's thigh against hers was even more flammable than the paper she'd just burned.

She reached forward for another stick and when she sat back she made sure there was a small gap between them; suddenly she could breathe again.

He frowned at her and moved his hip deliberately back against hers with a little bump, as if to say—this is where I'm staying. 'How can you say you never found him? I was there,' he said again.

'You left.' She didn't look at him but she felt his gaze boring into her. There was no escaping from this Rory. He was onto her and she'd the feeling he wouldn't be shut down like most people were when she put up her defences.

Rory sighed. 'I left for both of us. If only it were that simple.'

She shot him a glance and then her eyes skittered away. 'It was that simple.'

The walls, the walls, Rory thought, but at least she was talking. They needed to thrash this out and clear the air so he could see the future. 'You wrote and said you didn't love me. Sent my ring back. Why was that?'

She turned her face. 'Things happened. I changed.'

What things? She was driving him insane. He shifted so he could more easily see her face. 'Do you have any idea what that letter did to me? I was studying my butt off, we'd been writing every week, then out of the blue you threw away our dreams.' He pulled his wallet from his shirt and opened the leather. 'This letter.'

He dug into the back section and eased it out. Faded and dog-eared, the yellowed paper lay in his hand accusingly, looking up at her.

He watched her put her hand out and touch it gingerly, and then she pulled her hand away. This was what he'd come back for. This answer. These reasons.

Rory sat back and tilted to face her again. His voice lowered until it was barely audible over the crackle of the fire. 'What happened, Kate? Tell me.'

She looked at him then and the same agony that had scared him at Rainbow's End Station was back in her eyes.

Rory ached to know what had affected her so deeply but he knew he had to go gently.

'I don't want to,' she said.

'Please, Kate.'

She dragged her hands through her hair and looked around with a tinge of desperation. He wanted to pull her into his arms and hold her tight to ease her pain, only he wasn't game to touch her in case he caused more damage or she jumped up and ran into the night.

Finally she began. 'Do you remember the night before you left, Rory?'

Rory nodded. He'd never forget it. He and Kate under the old tree near the Pentecost after that horrific day. He'd had to drive somewhere off her father's property to talk. Couldn't say the things he had to under Lyle Onslow's starry roof. He'd been so young then.

He hardened his heart against the desolation in her face and dug the knife into the tree to finish '4 ever'.

'I'll come back.' He meant it with every breath because their love was as grand and magnificent as the vast Outback they'd both grown up in, but just as steeped in the tragedies of a harsh environment.

He loved his Kate so much it hurt and he'd die for her but at what cost to his future and that of his own family? He thought they had a chance if he went away.

'He fired me.' Rory shook his head at the sympathy he could see in her face. 'We knew he would.' He didn't want her pity, just to get away and make a life for them, away from the poison of her father, so that one day he'd show him what Rory McIver was made of.

'Both our fathers told me never to speak to you again,' he said, 'but that's no surprise. Give me three years. I'll be back on my twenty-first birthday for you. After the first year I can finish the degree on the road so I'll save every cent for you. Wait for me. I'll be back. I promise.'

That was when he saw her realise he wouldn't change his mind and he jammed his hands against his sides to stop himself from reaching for her.

'Money isn't everything,' and she looked at him as if he'd stabbed her. 'Take me with you.'

He couldn't not touch her and cupped her chin so their eyes met and he could hold her gaze. Try to make her understand. 'I have to do this. You can't come with me until I have something I can offer. Something more than this.'

He pulled a ring from his pocket, a tiny pink diamond from the mines behind Jabiru, and slid it on her finger. No matter that her father had refused permission.

It had come in on the mail plane yesterday, cheap by her standards, and nothing like what he wanted to buy her, but he wanted that ring on her finger so at least it could be with her when he couldn't. 'Will you wear this until I come back?'

She was so young and he was sure that leaving was the right thing. 'It's because I love you I have to leave.' Kate Onslow had been the one person he could dream with and that dream included both of them.

Then she lifted her face and kissed him, and her sweetness and ardour and the thought of the months away from her helped drag him down under the tree and when she kissed him with a desperation he hadn't been prepared for things had got a little out of control. Actually, a lot out of control. 'Take me with you,' she said again.

In retrospect, he should have.

'I remember everything,' he said.

Kate lifted her head. Her beautiful eyes, filled with the darkest shadows from the past, stared into his. 'All right, Rory. Maybe it is time. But you asked for it.'

She stared at him for a long moment and then she said it, so quietly he almost didn't hear her, 'Seven months later I lost our baby.'

Rory blinked. 'What baby?'

She chewed her lip. 'Ours!' She glanced at him briefly to see if he understood and then away. 'Yours and mine. The one we made after our last night.'

He stared at her, unable to take it in. He'd taken precautions, or thought he had, but it had been his first time too.

'The son I didn't tell anyone about, just like Lucy, until it was too late and I was too sick.'

Rory felt the shock hit him like a hammer in the gut. Kate had had a baby? First he was cold, then hot and then he stopped thinking about himself and the fruitless dreams that it would be too painful to think of right now, and thought of Kate.

His Kate had been pregnant at sixteen and he'd left her to face it on her own. With Lyle Onslow. Cold sweat beaded as he thought of how her father would have treated her. 'You should have told me.'

Her voice was flat. 'Father flew me out to Perth to a private convalescent hospital. I didn't know anyone and our baby was born by Caesarean section. Alone.'

The bastard. He dreaded the next question.

'The baby?'

She sighed. 'As I said before, I was very sick for a week and when I woke up it was too late. My baby was gone.' She turned stricken eyes to him. 'If I'd told my father earlier, maybe things would have been different but I was too much of a coward. My baby might have lived.'

Kate was the young girl she'd talked about. Not an unconnected case at all, but herself. Poor young, defenceless Kate and he hadn't been there. He tried to imagine the scenario. 'Who told you he'd died?'

'Some nurse. I'll never forget when that awful woman came in. She said it was just as well as I was so young. Earlier there'd been another, younger and kinder midwife, who'd said I could hold him but she didn't come back.' Her voice dropped even lower. 'She said she'd take a photo, a lock of hair and a handprint, but I think they stopped her.'

She drew a breath and went on more strongly, 'The awful one said he'd died from complications of prematurity and the separated placenta. I never even saw him.'

She looked at Rory with pure agony in her eyes. A devastation she'd carried bottled up for ten years. Rory wanted to kill someone for doing this to his Kate.

'I never saw who our baby looked like. What colour his hair was. The shape of his ears or hands—nothing.' She gazed into the fire. 'I think I could have borne it better if I'd said goodbye.'

Rory struggled with the monsterlike actions of a man who should have looked after her. 'Your father had no right to leave you to face that alone.'

She shrugged and rolled her shoulders to loosen the tension in her neck. 'For a long time I pleaded for information on what had happened. He kept saying, "Nothing happened. Forget it. There never was a baby."' She shook her head at the concept.

'By the time I'd left boarding school I was strong enough to stand up to him and I demanded the address of the funeral home. I even hoped faintly that the baby hadn't died, maybe he'd adopted him out, but I searched Perth, found Fairmont Gardens and there was a plaque. I'd found him. Baby of Kate Onslow. Lived for a day, and the date.'

Rory felt sick with self disgust. 'What date, Kate?'

She stared into the fire. 'The third of August. He'd been eight weeks premature and I'd never had a chance to name him.'

Rory looked at Kate and didn't know what to do—or say. She'd never forgive him for this. No wonder she hated him. 'I'm so sorry.'

'I don't blame you.' But her voice was flat and broken with memories and his heart ached for this woman who'd meant the world to him—still meant the world to him.

He tried to imagine what a young girl without a mother, or anyone to hug her, could do in the beginning to ease that pain. He guessed there wasn't much she could do without support except brick it up and try not to think about it. 'Did you go home at all?'

'No.' She shook her head vehemently. 'Why would I? I boarded in Perth and studied every minute to give myself choices. That's when I decided I'd stay for uni and do my midwifery. I'd be there for young mums.' She looked at him. 'This is the first time I've been back to Jabiru and you had to turn up.'

Rory couldn't grasp that she'd shut him out when she'd most needed him. 'It's been ten years. What about later? You never told me.'

She looked at him but there was no expression on her face. After what she'd just said. No expression. That scared him most of all.

'What was I supposed to do? Write to you and say—by the way, guess what happened? Ruin your life too?'

He needed to reach her. 'My life was ruined when you wrote to me and told me never to come back.'

She shook her head. Not wanting to hear that. 'I was scared. Scared what my father would do to you. He warned me he'd ruin you if I contacted you. Ruin your family, who still worked for him. And I was scared that, if I told you, you'd never do the things you wanted to do. I know how important moving up in life was for you, Rory. I didn't want your bitterness and disappointment to be my fault if you'd come back to look after me.' She looked away. 'Then it was too late. I didn't want to talk about it. I still don't.'

'You were more important than my career.' It was his turn to deny. But, in all honesty, would he have had that clarity in his youth? 'I would never have blamed you. We would have made it somehow.' He reached out his hand to her. 'Kate, I would have been there for you. I'm here now.'

She ignored it. 'It's too late for us, Rory. I don't want a husband. When my father dies I'll sell Jabiru Station and go back to Perth. It's time to go back. I'll open a refuge for pregnant women, plaster its availability everywhere, give young women options that they might not otherwise get.'

It couldn't end this way. 'You can do that and still see me.'

She shook her head at him like he was a child. Like the child he was beginning to feel against her implacable wisdom. 'You're still in love with someone who doesn't exist, Rory. The sixteen-year-old girl you left. I'm not that girl. I never will be again.'

This couldn't be it. After the glimmer of hope when he'd found out she'd never married. After the rapport they'd shared in flashes only today. There could be more of those. 'I could love the woman she's become.'

One decisive shake of her head. 'I don't think so.' Then she lifted her chin and said the saddest thing yet. 'Because if I can't love myself how can you?'

Oh, Kate. What had he done? 'You were too young to cope with that on your own. I was careless and unprepared for what happened that afternoon but I should have come back to check you were all right. I'm sorry I let you down, Kate.'

'I don't want to talk about it any more, Rory. Just know…' here she paused, and Rory knew he wasn't going to like what was coming '…I've been powerless. I've been excluded in consultation on what affects me and, worst of all, unable to keep myself or my child safe, and I won't ever be like that again. I am in charge of my own destiny.' She turned her face to look into the fire. 'I'm going to run my own life and nothing or no one is going to change that.'

That finality struck into his heart like a shard of ice.

But it pricked his anger as well. That wasn't fair. Rory frowned. 'I'm not trying to change you, Kate, but I'm not a nobody, harassing you. I'm your friend, the man who wanted to marry you, someone who knows you inside and out—or did—ten years ago. I loved you, Kate, as you were, and I could love you as you are now. I'm just trying to be here for you.'

He took her hand and, when she didn't respond, he slipped his arm around her and drew her close. 'I'm not going to pressure you. Ever. Though maybe we could call a truce. Share some grief that affects both of us.'

After the initial stiffness she did slightly relax against him as she thought about it. It did affect both of them. It was a new concept that maybe she'd been too buried in her own misery to think about before.

She hadn't given in, but truce was a good word and sharing the memories of that time with Rory, the only person she had ever shared them with, was painful but strangely healing. She thought for the first time of Rory as her baby's other parent. And for her possibly selfish assumption that it wouldn't matter to him if he didn't know. Maybe she did owe him an apology.

'Kate—' he squeezed her hand '—is it too late to give our son a name? It's so sad we can't call him anything. Acknowledge our baby as a real person who will always be a part of our lives, no matter how fleeting.'

The sting of tears Rory's comment caused made Kate blink and she wished just once she could turn towards him and sob in his arms. Why couldn't she cry?

A name? For their son who flew away ten years ago. She looked at Rory, in his eyes such concern that she realised he worried his question hurt her. The ice inside melted a little more. 'I always liked Cameron,' she said softly, and squeezed his hand back.

'Cameron Onslow-McIver.' He lifted her fingers to his mouth and turned her hand to kiss her palm. The gentlest benediction. 'Our son.'

So they sat there as the fire died, occasionally talking but mostly just leaning into each other and Kate could feel the easing of the burden she'd carried for so many lonely years. That pain would never go but Rory had not done the one thing she'd feared above everything. He hadn't said her baby didn't matter.

CHAPTER SEVEN

IT WAS SIX A.M. and the sun was dusting the horizon pink when Rory woke. He doubted Kate had slept well because the stretcher bed had creaked all night and he'd bet she wished she'd swapped places with him in his quiet swag.

He rolled over onto his back and stared at the tree branches lacing the sky at the edge of his vision. He needed to find a way to keep open the chink in Kate's barriers against him. Maybe then he could also ease the burden that Kate had carried for so long.

He could almost deal with the fact she didn't want to spend the rest of her life with him. Almost.

What he couldn't deal with was the memory of that despair in Kate's face and the realisation that she'd done it alone when he should have been there. No wonder she hadn't wanted to see him again.

He'd made decisions that had affected her without thinking of her choices. No matter that leaving to make his fortune for her had been in her best interests.

He sighed. Had it really been, though? Rory wondered sardonically to himself, not for the first time since he'd returned to the Kimberley. Hadn't it all been about him feeling inferior to Kate's family and needing to prove he could be bigger and better than they were? Were those goals—top man in the state, paramedic extraordinaire, independently wealthy to equal the Onslows—really for Kate or his own gratification?

It wasn't a very nice picture he'd just painted and he doubted an apology would cut for what Kate had been through.

No wonder she hadn't wanted to tell him about what had happened. He had to break down that reserve and it had better be before they got back to Jabiru or he'd never reach her. Because one thing was clear after last night—he still wanted Kate—and he wanted all of her.

Rory rose and rolled his swag. Kate was up before he'd poked the fire back into life for a mug of tea. 'Sleep well?'

'Hmm, no,' she mumbled as she walked past him into the scrub. He smiled to himself. So his Kate still wasn't a morning person.

They sipped tea and ate fruit before he tackled the truck. They jacked it up and Kate rolled the spare across to him, passing tools and clearing up when she wasn't needed. Not a bad team, Rory thought, and they smiled with less tension between them as they went about their tasks. The truck was rolling within the hour.

Kate glanced at her watch. 'You still think we'll get home today?'

'We'll give it our best shot and as long as it hasn't rained somewhere we don't know about.'

'This truck can manage most terrain.' Kate patted the dash.

'That's my girl.' Rory smiled at her and she frowned a warning at him.

'Figure of speech,' he said and Kate just shook her head. But he suspected there may have been a tiny smile there. It was a start. They used to laugh a lot together.

One thing he didn't understand. 'So if you hate your father so much, how can you stand to come back now?'

She huffed a sigh. 'Why do we have to talk about me all the time? Let's talk about you.'

He did understand her reluctance but this was important. 'I'd really like to know, Kate. I'll probably fly out of here as soon as the weather settles. Never bother you again, if that's what you want.' Lord, he hoped not. 'But you can't change that I do care about you. Or that I have some right to know why you cut me out of your life.'

She wouldn't meet his eyes. 'You do?'

'You knew the letter you sent me was a lie and yet you let your father back in.'

She flicked a stray hair out of her face. 'Don't start again. I don't need your opinion on what I do.'

'I think you do.' He glanced at her. 'Besides, with that mean and nasty attitude you have, there can't be too many people who love you.'

She smothered a laugh and Rory smiled with her. He'd been the only one who'd dared to poke fun at her and he'd bet that hadn't changed much.

She screwed her face up at him and grudgingly considered his question. 'Why did I come back?' She shrugged. 'Because he's my father and he asked me to come home. And he's dying. And maybe I need to lay some of my own ghosts—' she looked at him '—like you did.'

That was a start. 'Fair enough.' He met her eyes and then looked back at the road. 'So why are you working at Jabiru Township?'

She shrugged again and he could tell she wanted this conversation finished. 'There's a need there. The clinic is my statement that I do my own thing. My father doesn't control me but I'll still see him.' She glared at the windscreen as if her father were on the other side.

She went on, 'As we're dissecting my emotions, I think that being there for Lucy yesterday could help a lot with closure, especially as there's a good outcome.'

Thank you, God, for brief windows of enlightenment, Rory thought, but he had so much more to fathom. He wanted to ask questions but she'd slipped into a reverie. He didn't want to disturb the flow of her thoughts as he tried to grasp what was important to this new Kate.

As he'd hoped, she went on. 'Lucy made the same mistakes as me but she was more fortunate. Does that make me a bad mother because my baby died and Lucy's didn't?' She turned to Rory and he saw the moment she allowed herself to consider some absolution. She shook her head with relief. 'Thank goodness Lucy's baby is okay.'

Rory continued the concept she only seemed to be grasping now. 'We both know that young mums and toxaemia happen pretty fast, sometimes with devastating results, but you couldn't have known that when you were sixteen. Of course you were unlucky.'

Rory went on, 'You made a good call for Lucy, Kate. Leaving Jabiru, not waiting until the weather set in; it would have been easy to hold off a decision until too late.'

Kate chewed her lip as she remembered. 'I was so scared for Lucy and her baby.'

'Well, you didn't show it. Despite your own doubts. I thought you were amazing during the birth.'

She squeezed her eyes shut for a moment, as if to block out the memory. 'I lost it for a second.' She shook her head and shuddered. 'It all flashed back at me, you know, I've never had that before and, although everything was okay in the end, I never want to have those feelings again.'

'Maybe you needed that moment to move on. I think you're still too hard on yourself.'

'Maybe. Maybe not.' She shook her head. 'I know birth is run by nature. Without interference, it's designed to run smoothly and that's what happened to Lucy. Lucky Lucy.'

'Lucky Lucy to have you.'

She frowned as if the thought remained unpalatable and brushed his comment away. 'Flattery. You're wasting your time because compliments mean nothing. And you're still not invading my life.'

'Damn.' He felt like a spy peering over the top of the wall into a forbidden city and he couldn't help but smile at her back-pedalling. 'I thought I was doing well there.'

Too well, Kate thought, *that's the problem,* and she turned to look out of the window. She needed to keep some barriers up and Rory was systematically lowering them one by one. She wasn't throwing away ten years of stoicism and independence because of a few kind words but it was hard not to slip back into that old security of his presence.

Rory slowed the truck and she looked ahead as they approached the first of the river crossings. This had been the deeper one on the way with Lucy and the river height had gained another six inches. As a cemented causeway it wasn't as treacherous as a riverbank crossing but still the flow was much faster than before.

He pulled up and turned the engine off and they both climbed out to look. At least the rain had stopped and the weather was heading towards a mild day shrouded in cloud.

The roar of the water at the rapids further down almost drowned out the flow in front of them across the causeway. Rory knelt to pull off his riding boots and roll his trousers while Kate chewed her lip.

Past the causeway in the deeper part of the river the water looked to have a strong current in the middle and wild eddies down the side that swooped under overhanging trees.

Any other time it would be pleasant under those trees when not in flood but at the moment the branches swept the water and tangled anything that floated. With the amount of water that gushed past, it would relentlessly bombard anything, or anybody, washed into the branches with tons of never-ending water.

'You sure you want to wade across there?'

Rory looked up at her from under his brows. 'You just watch for crocs, though this crossing's not as bad as the Pentecost for salties.'

'The water looks fast.' My word, it did, thought Kate, as she scanned the riverbank for movement and then followed a piece of bark that scooted past her and twirled around as if unseen hands under the water were spinning it in a game.

'If I can't walk the causeway, I won't drive it,' he said, 'but I want to get closer to home than this. Don't you?'

Kate agreed but it was more difficult than she'd expected to watch Rory prepare to take that risk.

They both looked downstream where the river widened and shallowed and the trees poked out of the riverbed near the rushing middle.

Rory smiled reassuringly but Kate wasn't feeling reassured and something he must have seen in her face made his eyes narrow. 'I'm not planning to, but if I do get swept away I'll be able to get out down there.' He pointed. 'I'll be fine.' He held her gaze. 'Do not come to save me if I slide down.'

Kate had seen the clearer area he'd indicated but it still flowed too fast for comfort. The real rapids came after that and the thunder from them was what they could hear. Then, if he didn't manage to stop himself, there was a fifty foot waterfall that plunged into the gorge to look forward to.

The images were far too graphic for Kate. 'Let's not play that game.'

There was an edge to his voice. 'Promise you'll stay out of the water, Kate.'

In all the years she'd known him, the only time she'd ever seen Rory really angry had been when she'd put herself in danger. The way he said it reminded her of a time she'd always blushed to remember.

That night Rory told her not to follow him out to the shed to save the duck she'd befriended from the chopping block.

Rory was so nearly caught by Kate's father, except Kate slipped into the shed and turned out the lights and he was able to get away. Her father never was sure if a dingo had got the duck or Kate had been responsible but Rory was livid she'd put herself at risk. He flayed her with his anger so fiercely that she almost wished he'd shaken her instead; he didn't speak to her for days. But she would have done it again if she'd needed to.

Today was like that. She couldn't guarantee it.

'Well, don't get washed away.'

Rory grinned at her. 'Kate. You really do care.'

Grrr. Typical man, laughing at danger. If men took fewer risks there'd be less danger. They were so stupid sometimes. 'Oh, I care, but then I'd care if you were an animal.' She pretended to ponder it. 'Probably more.'

Rory looked suitably dashed. 'Gee, thanks.'

He gave up his attempt to roll his jeans high enough and moved back to the truck, where he shucked them down and threw them on the driver's seat.

'Now do you care?' He posed, hands on the strongly muscled thighs of his tanned legs, elbows bent like a male model as Kate tried not to see the whipcord body beneath his black boxers and shirt tails. Rory had certainly grown up.

She shrugged and looked away to hide her eyes. 'Maybe. I'd probably care as much as an animal. Now, stop stressing me and move it,' Kate said and turned her back. Actually, it was for her own protection because Rory looked far too sexy and dangerous, and too dear to lose. Yet, despite their predicament, she was beginning to wish he'd taken off his shirt as well as his jeans so she could see what she couldn't help imagining. What she should be thinking instead was how she could save him if he needed help.

'Enough joking,' he said and Kate felt her heart rate pick up with a thump in her chest as Rory turned to enter the water. Her palms truly began to sweat.

'Be careful, Rory.' She had a bad feeling about this.

He approached the edge. 'Yes, ma'am.' He looked back at her once more as he entered the water. 'Do watch for mysterious logs with eyes.'

'Absolutely.' Kate was deadly serious—they both were—and she scanned the banks again before she watched him wade in.

Rory edged across, one step at a time. The water attempted to sweep him sideways but he leaned into it, strong thighs braced against the torrent. Once he stumbled slightly when his foot slipped into a crumbled section and Kate stifled a scream but he recovered well. He threw her a one-eyebrow-raised glance and continued on.

Kate rested her hand over the pulse in her throat—she could feel the beat against her fingers—and took shallow sips of air until Rory finally emerged on the other side.

The causeway was deep but the truck would handle it. Rory started back and Kate watched his every step, which was why she didn't see the branch until it was too late.

'Watch the log, Rory,' she yelled and he twisted to see, maybe even thinking it was a crocodile, and lost his footing and the branch collided with his legs as he tried to regain his balance.

Rory was skittled into the water like a tenpin by a ball and Kate screamed his name as his head bobbed under the water and then resurfaced.

The speed of the water carried him swiftly down the swirling river and Kate scrambled along the side of the bank as she desperately tried to keep up with him through the scrub.

Her heart pounded in her ears and she couldn't see where he'd gone until she climbed out onto a fallen tree that overhung the river. The trunk stretched a third of the way across the torrent but where it dipped into the water she couldn't keep her balance and she had to sit down to edge along the trunk so she could peer out over the river.

Rory was hooked on a tree root that curled around him like an arthritic hand out of the bed of the river. It tangled his shirt as the water flowed over his face and head and he disappeared under the water. Then he reappeared, shook his head to clear it and glanced up to where Kate was overhanging the torrent.

He saw what she was about to do almost before she knew herself and she only just heard his distant, 'No, Kate!' as she launched herself into the dark water and struck out across the current towards Rory's wooden island.

The cold water took her breath as she fought to stay upright and the occasional rounded boulder in the bed thudded into her knees and buttocks as she bounced down the river. She'd be a mass of bruises tomorrow if they lived to tell the tale.

The current's strength gave her little say about direction and she tried to grasp the rocks she passed to steer towards Rory and only succeeded in breaking off her nails. When she looked towards him he'd lost his shirt, was free of entrapment and had managed to stand against the torrent with his back against the mid-section of the root.

She had about three seconds to get closer to him or she was going to shoot past and end up down the rapids and over the waterfall herself. A quiet space in her brain was tutting and saying that she should have listened to Rory and waited for him to get himself out.

She didn't know where Rory's arm came from but his hand fastened onto her shoulder like a vice and he heaved her across to him and into his arms as if she were a floating twig until they were both flattened face to face against the root with the force of the water.

He hugged her so tightly against him she almost couldn't breathe. 'If we don't die here I am going to kill you,' he ground out, and his mouth crushed down on hers with no gentleness at all, a plunging ravishment that tumbled her into more of a maelstrom than the water around her. Then he turned her in his arms and pulled her back against him again as her head swam.

Her teeth chattered with the shock of her near miss and the feel of Rory's warm, solid strength behind her made her realise how close she'd been to shooting past. But most of all there was the imprint of Rory's mouth—hot and dangerous—and the livid emotion she'd seen in his eyes that warned he wasn't done yet.

'Move where I move,' he snapped out and, still stunned by the bruising kiss, she nodded and did what she was told for the first time in a lot of years.

Rory braced like a standing stone behind her, solid and immovable to lean on, as she pulled each thigh sideways against the swirling strength of the water, step by exhausting step, until the water became shallower and she could just stand on her own. The fear of being washed away had been gradually replaced each step closer to the bank by the awareness that Rory was a thundercloud behind her and he hadn't loosened his iron grip on her shoulder.

He turned her, none too gently, to face him again and she could see his lips compressed together as he struggled for control.

'Just once!' He shook her and she could feel the barely leashed fury that struggled to be free. 'Do what you're told!'

She looked away from this hard-faced man she barely knew and yes, she'd got it wrong, she should have listened. She tried bravado and glared back at him. 'I had to do what my instinct told me to.'

Not a good choice. Rory looked more incensed than before. 'Instinct? Instinct?' He shook her again. 'You could have died. Your instinct is to do whatever I say is a bad idea.'

'I'm sorry I didn't listen to you, Rory.' She looked into his face, searching for some glimmer of the Rory who would hug her to him and say it was all right.

Rory stared down at her. 'You could have died.' He shook his head and she saw what she had done to him and she couldn't stop the sting of tears that gathered but didn't fall.

'I'm sorry,' she whispered and she leaned up and kissed his cold, hard lips that would not respond. She tried again, pushing her mouth against his, moulding the chiselled edges of his mouth with her own and still he remained immovable. She lifted her arms and pulled the back of his head towards hers, ran her hands down his cheeks to their joined mouths, as if drawing all the emotion to their lips, until eventually he shuddered and gathered her fiercely into his arms and kissed her back, not quite as fiercely as he had out in the water but powerfully, and in a way that left her in no doubt that he would like to do more than just kiss her—and not in the way the Rory of ten years ago had kissed her. This man knew what response he wanted and how to draw it from her. Kate felt as if she'd been swept into a raging torrent again, only this time she didn't want to be rescued. She wanted to drown!

When he finally lifted his mouth away she could barely stand.

He gave her another hug and she closed her eyes as she wrapped her arms around his solid strength and hugged him back to regain strength in her limbs. 'Let's not do that again.'

'The river or the kiss?' His voice still held many undercurrents but he put her away from him with some semblance of control. 'Come on. Before the river comes up any higher.' Rory's fingers cradled the small of her back in a protective gesture that was almost an apology for the harshness of the kiss and she realised he was panting a little.

The fact that Rory had acted so out of character showed her, as little else could have, just how much he cared. Still. The implications of that were too huge but for the moment she'd just be glad they were both safe.

They pushed through the scrub at the side of the river until they made it back to the truck, where she handed him a towel and took one herself as she turned her back, for her own protection, while he shucked off his boxers. He must have dried off and pulled his jeans on quickly because he was back in the truck when Kate turned around.

'Let's get this crossing over with,' he said, 'and then you can change.'

As soon as Kate was in the truck Rory let out the clutch and they crawled down into the causeway and chugged with remarkable ease through the water. A bow wave surged in front of the bonnet, Kate lifted her feet above the wash that came through the doors to ankle height, then they both opened their doors to let the water out as the wheels of the truck climbed up the other side.

Rory whistled. 'Very close. Wouldn't want to be much deeper than that.' He pulled over and she slid out and exchanged her wet clothes for a dry shirt and shorts she had in her overnight pack.

When she climbed back in she was glad he didn't mention their recent session in the river. She didn't think she could talk about it just yet without shivering. Probably shock. She fought to keep her voice steady. 'Doesn't look good for the Pentecost.'

Kate began to realise they would have to camp again tonight if the river was flooded. And what would happen between them after the high emotions of the past half an hour she had no idea and not a little trepidation.

They were talking, fairly naturally now, considering, and neither mentioned their close escape or the events afterwards and she hoped her concern and relief for Rory's safety hadn't made him think she was easy prey. Because she wasn't, or wouldn't be by the time they stopped this evening, would she?

CHAPTER EIGHT

IT HAD TO be ten minutes since they'd last spoken and Kate's imagination made her squirm. Surely Rory might be reliving her stupidity in his mind again. The more she thought about it, the more she cringed. What had she expected to achieve by jumping in?

The sensible thing would have been to stay on dry land like she'd been told—that sanctimonious voice in her head had to repeat—she could have thrown him a rope or even got help if he'd been too hurt to move and not set herself up for a last trip down the river.

Suddenly she couldn't stand her own one-sided dialogue of his disapproval or the silence in the truck any longer. 'I'm sorry, Rory.'

He seemed intent on the road ahead and when he didn't reply she cringed even more and changed the subject. She went on quietly, 'How long now until the Pentecost?'

'Still about two hours. The rain's coming down again so it depends on the creeks we have to cross.' There was no hint of censure in Rory's voice when he answered so he must have been concentrating on the road which, she had to admit, was pretty churned up. Not the only thing churned up, she thought ruefully. She really needed to get a grip.

He went on, 'After that little adventure I'm not driving across waterways in the dark.'

She'd drink to that. 'So do you think we'll have to camp again?'

He looked at her and smiled, and suddenly her world was back the right way. She didn't want to think about how much she'd come to depend on Rory's unfailing good humour.

'Not necessarily,' he said. 'If you want to do something radical we could take another ten mile detour to Xanadu and stay the night at the high-end resort up there.'

She'd agree to almost anything if it meant he'd forgiven her—but Xanadu? She'd read about that. 'It costs the price of a small car to stay there for one night.'

'True. But we haven't stayed anywhere together, so if you divide it by ten years it isn't much to spend for a couple.' He had a smile in his eyes because he knew she'd bite.

That was taking it too far. 'We're not a couple.'

'So we camp or split it.'

Rory grinned to himself. She hadn't expected him to offer to split it. Not that he needed her money. He'd made some very shrewd investment decisions before Perth had taken off as a real estate boom town, but it amused him that he had her off balance, which was a big turnaround from the back foot he'd been on since before their adventure.

They needed a little light relief after the recent events. He still shuddered to remember the sight of Kate launching herself into the river to save him. He couldn't remember when he had ever been more frightened—or more angry.

Imagine if he hadn't been able to reach her as she'd gone past. The idea brought the nausea to his throat again and he dragged his thoughts away from that scenario. For himself to fall in it had been a bloody nuisance, but the degree of danger Kate had been in made his blood run cold.

It seemed she'd forgiven him for the angry kiss he'd punished her with but it had been that or he'd have paddled her behind as soon as he hit dry land—something he would never believe he'd want to do to Kate.

And she knew it. He'd actually like some time to think about the expression on her face as she'd looked when they'd both finally got out of the river. Stuff of dreams. And that fierce hug. He could still feel her arms around him and it felt damn good.

She nodded slowly. 'If you can afford it. Or we could do the tent cabins, which are cheaper.'

He was glad to think of other things. It was sweet of her to be concerned for the cost and he was tempted to tell her she needn't worry but he kept his mouth shut.

He frowned. Obviously he still had some inferiority issues he needed to work through. He was finding out a lot about himself today.

Kate went on, 'Hang the expense. I never spend anything and haven't spoilt myself for years.' She frowned. 'What if they're booked out?'

He patted the phone on the dash. 'We could find out.'

Kate glanced out at the deepening gloom as the day edged towards another night. 'Hot showers. Hot food.' She glanced at him with a smug expression. 'Separate rooms.'

Separate rooms? Rory thought. Now, that's a shame. There'd be less chance of her throwing herself into his arms and he couldn't deny he'd desperately love to sit with Kate in his arms, even if only to soak in the fact that she was fine. It had been a long eventful day with some potential for more than emotional fallout.

Kate smiled at him. 'Let's do it. Sounds too good to miss.'

'Good.' He looked across and then back at the road. 'I was thinking if we stayed until after lunch tomorrow we could do a spot of bush walking. Check out the gorges and waterfalls because after the rain they'll be spectacular. That'd give the Pentecost more time to go down and we'd still be back to Jabiru before dark.'

She chewed her lip and he wanted to put his hand out and stop her. Not those beautiful lips—lips that he wanted to do better things with now that he'd had a recent taste. Finally she stopped biting. 'Maybe we could have a few hours before we leave tomorrow morning.'

Kate rifled through the glovebox and came up with directions and phone numbers of all the stations and refuelling stops along the road. She found Xanadu. 'Here's the number.'

She dialled and, after a few quick sentences, it was done. 'Should take us about an hour to get there.

He thought she was finding it easier to talk to him. At least she'd stopped twisting her hands. Maybe the emotions of the last few hours had put things in a different perspective for her too. He hoped so.

'Time to kill while we get there,' she said. 'Want to enlarge on the ten years between then and now, on your side for a change, Rory?'

Did he? Not really. What had he done? Not much else except work. His job had been a strange one but had suited him by blocking out his loss of Kate.

'It's been absorbing,' he said. 'The best parts are the good friends. You need them to face the tragedies, so they're a saving grace. But even mates can't stop the human emotion from taking its toll.' Nothing would.

'Though lately that camaraderie's been lost with my move to administration and away from road work. The price of rapid advancement up the ranks, I guess, so I miss that.'

He sighed, and pondered, to nut it out as much for himself as for her. 'Work was work. There pretty well every day and most nights.'

She raised her eyebrows. 'It sounds like you were on a mission.'

He looked at her. She still didn't get it. 'Funny, that.'

'You must have had some fun.' She frowned and he wondered if the frown was because he'd had little fun or because of the little he'd had. It amused him that she could be even slightly jealous.

He raised his eyebrows. 'Brief snatches.'

'Like Sybil?'

He'd been right. He nodded and squashed the urge to laugh. 'I did wonder if we'd get back to Sybil.'

She gazed out of the window nonchalantly; her turned shoulder said she didn't care if he answered. He held off until she couldn't resist. 'So?' she said.

Serious now, he stopped teasing her. 'Like a lot of other professions, there's mental wear and tear, those moments of despair at the useless loss of life.' Lost faces that tore at him at night, alone in his bed, until he'd gone out searching for anything to blot out the pictures he couldn't rid. On top of the loss of the love of his life.

'For a while, Sybil helped.' Come upon in a moment of weakness, and so difficult to extricate himself from.

Best not talk about Sybil. 'But there were delightful patients who popped up in the most unexpected places who made everything we did seem worthwhile.' He turned to look at her. Deliberately blotting those they'd lost with different images.

'I like the mix of people I come into contact with as a health worker. Young kids are hard work but satisfying because they're so frightened and we can help that, then there's old men with dry-as-a-stick humour who downplay their illnesses so you have to watch them pretty closely. Sweet old ladies are so apologetic for calling when in fact they should have called hours ago. Then a week later they'll drop into the ambulance station to say thank you with home-made scones and real jam.'

He could see she was absorbed in his stories while he considered it all pretty normal. He smiled and shook his head. 'I love old ladies.'

She laughed. 'I think there's a name for that.' She raised her eyebrows suggestively.

'Be nice.' He pretended to glare at her and she giggled. Something he'd thought he'd never hear his Kate do again.

'And the occasional birth,' she prompted.

'Trust a midwife to ask that.' He thought of Lucy's birth. 'Babies too.'

Kate tilted her head. 'So what was all this in aid of, Rory? Where did you see yourself going when you finally made it? Did you sock away all your money to fund some elusive dream?'

'Maybe.' The thought struck him. Good grief. Had he? Suddenly everything was clear. That was what he'd been planning and he hadn't even known it. Jabiru Station?

His head was spinning; he needed time to think that all through again. Like about a week. Certainly not now.

He steered the conversation away to safer topics. 'Enough about me. Tell me about your midwifery. You said you went to uni. Where did you work when you finished?'

She frowned at the switch of topic but answered him. 'Still Perth.'

He shook his head at the idea of both of them never passing at some hospital or other. 'I was there, too.'

'And Sybil.' Kate looked out of the window again.

They didn't need complications that didn't exist. 'Sybil again?'

She laughed. 'Just teasing.'

'I'm happy to share if you're interested.' He didn't want lies between them. 'Sybil was in my life for a brief while. She's a hothouse flower, our Sybil. Likes to sway along, bask in the sun, have new petals supplied by men who fancy her. It didn't last long, but there was a while there where she saved my sanity.'

'Then I forgive her.'

It was a joking comment, but something in the tone of Kate's voice had nothing to do with Sybil. It had to do with knowing what feeling really down was about. About using anything and anyone to get out of that hole and see the light again. Surviving.

It was coming home to him just how much Kate had survived. His voice dropped. 'I guess we're both survivors.'

'Hope those people up there are too!' Kate had looked ahead and seen the rolled vehicle before Rory. He bit back a frustrated sigh and focused on what the scenario could be. Would this trip never end? He braked and stopped as they came upon the wreckage. It didn't look too bad but you never knew.

In fact, maybe it had been time to shut down the conversation they were in. He opened his door and sprinted through the rain to peer into the front window of the Jeep as it lay on its side.

'You okay in here?'

'Yeah.' The young man poked his head out of the window like a jack-in-the-box. 'I'm waiting for the rain to clear before I try winching it back onto its wheels.'

Rory peered through into the vehicle. 'Anyone in the back?'

'Nah. Just me. Embarrassed. Swerved for a bullock and flipped it in the mud.'

Rory nodded. 'Want a hand?'

'I'd appreciate it.' The driver climbed out awkwardly and Kate could see he was younger than her but laconic in his predicament. Rory tilted his head and watched the way the young man held his arm tight against his chest.

'I'm Rory. This is Kate.'

'Leslie.' He held out his good arm and Rory shook it. He nodded at Kate.

Rory pointed at his injury. 'Hurt your arm, have you, Leslie? Do you mind if I have a look?'

Leslie winced as he lifted it. 'Banged it on the wheel when we went over.'

Rory ran his fingers lightly over the swelling in the forearm. 'I'd say you're lucky you didn't have it out the window, mate.'

Leslie waggled his fingers without too much effort but couldn't move his forearm from in front of his chest.

Rory raised his eyebrows at Kate and she nodded and opened the back of the ambulance. When she returned with a triangular bandage Rory carefully lifted Leslie's arm and between them they supported the arm in a makeshift sling.

'I'd say you've broken one of those bones in your forearm.'

'Thought so.' Leslie shrugged and then winced as his shoulder moved. 'It's my right arm so I can still change gears. I'll survive.'

'Where're you heading?'

'I'm a ringer at Xanadu. Camp's about three miles this side of the resort.'

They could help. 'When we get your Jeep on its feet we'll give you a lift, if you like. We're heading that way. Kate can drive the ambulance and we'll follow in yours.'

'Don't want to be any trouble.'

Kate laughed. 'We can see that. Just humour us, okay. So, tell me, you allergic to anything, Leslie?'

'Not that I know of.'

She smiled. 'Then here's two painkillers. Tell me if your injured hand goes colder than the other one.' She gave him the pills, which he put in his mouth, and then she handed him a bottle of water to sip. She turned to the Jeep. 'What do you want me to do, Rory?'

'I'll connect the winch and watch the pull if you take the ambulance back slowly in low range.'

'Done.'

A few minutes later, Leslie's old vehicle was back on its wheels, Rory had Leslie tucked in beside him and Kate followed behind until they turned off on the Xanadu Road.

Fifteen minutes later they handed Leslie over to the foreman at the camp and Kate drove the rest of the way in the last of the fading light.

As they passed through the resort gateway Rory stretched his arms over his head as much as the roof allowed. 'This has been a very busy two days,' he groaned and Kate smiled.

'True. But the company's been great.'

Was that a positive comment? 'Shucks. You're just saying that.'

She actually grinned at him. 'Yep. I'm hoping you'll buy me dinner.'

He tossed his head. 'Who's the heiress?'

She shrugged. 'So what do you make, Mr Hotshot?'

He raised his eyebrows suggestively. 'Enough for dinner.'

She nodded, as if something had been confirmed. 'Then you're on. But we share the cost of the rooms.' Kate sighed at the thought. 'Right after a hot bath.'

They pulled up under the portico and the concierge greeted them like royalty and indicated that their ambulance would be cared for like the Rolls-Royce it wasn't.

Kate smothered a laugh as she pulled the duffel bag of spare clothes out of the back of the truck. The bag was whisked from her arms to be carried by another assistant and she could do nothing but join Rory as they walked up the stairs, where they were met by the manager.

Within what seemed like seconds they were registered and personally escorted to their suites.

Kate hung back a little and whispered to Rory, 'I think we should have stayed in the tent section. I'm feeling a little underdressed.'

'I bet they can cater for that.' He smiled across at her. 'But you look gorgeous to me.'

'Don't go there, Rory. And I mean it. This is too elegant for an overnight stay.'

He held up his hands. 'Fine. But just relax. Soak in your bath and we'll meet in an hour. We can eat on a private veranda if you want.'

Which was all very well, Kate thought an hour later, admittedly more relaxed and glowing pink from the hot water, but her khaki trousers and white shirt just didn't do it for her.

When she heard the knock on the door, she glanced once more at the mirror and shrugged. It was only one night.

It wasn't Rory at the door. A young girl stood there, beautifully made-up and wearing the resort staff cheongsam. She held a fuchsia-pink silk sheath in her arms. 'From Mr McIver, Miss Onslow.'

Kate opened her mouth to say wrong room when she heard her name. She'd kill him. What was she supposed to do? Good manners won. 'Thank you,' she said. Serve him right if it cost him a month's salary. She took the dress from the girl and shut the door.

It was beautiful. She rested the material against her cheek and slid it back and forth like a whisper. She'd never been one for fancy clothes and still refused any money from her father.

She looked in the mirror. She could wear her pride or this. She looked again. That was ridiculous.

The dress won.

When Kate opened her door Rory forgot to breathe. Dark swathes of velvet hair were loose around her shoulders, the first time he'd seen her hair out in ten years, and he hoped not the last. Her mouth pouted sexily in fuchsia like the dress, and then the dress...

No bra. He sucked the breath in because light-headedness was no way to handle the next couple of hours—but my Lord. Rory gulped.

'Come in, Rory,' she said and directed him in with her hand, her mind obviously elsewhere as she searched for her key.

'I like your dress.' He looked around the room, out of the door to the magnificent view of the gorge below, at the huge king-sized bed and quickly away, anywhere except at the fuchsia silk outline of her alert nipples.

'The room's lovely, isn't it?'

'Very.' Monosyllables might be all he could manage at the moment.

'Oh, here it is!' She held the key up triumphantly. Then she looked at him and he still must have been staring. 'Thank you for the dress. I hope you've left enough in your wallet for dinner.' Obviously she'd come to peace with his presumption in buying it.

'Luckily dinner's included in the room rate. Table d'hôte gourmet and open bar. Served where you want. Any preferences?'

She blinked. 'Wow. They didn't have anything like this around when we grew up here.'

'That's the high-end market for you.'

'You seem to know a lot about it.'

'If I'd ever been here I would have looked you up and maybe discovered you were in Perth.'

The heat from the gaze he ran over her was enough to have Kate wishing she hadn't been so silly as to put on the dress or send for the matching lippy. And leave off her sensible bra.

She looked him up and down. He had a white jacket over a black shirt and black trousers, very debonair for a boy from the Outback. She'd bet that hadn't been in the duffel bag either. Maybe he was more financially secure than she'd thought.

She cleared her throat. 'We could eat in the open air part of the restaurant.' Might be safer, she thought, and she had the feeling he could read her mind. Somehow the balance had shifted again.

'Fine,' he said. 'I understand the view is magnificent.' She'd swear he was laughing at her.

Kate's enormous room was suddenly stifling despite the breeze wafting the curtains. 'Let's go, then.'

They chose to sit on the veranda outside the restaurant with its glass roof showcasing the stars that looked down on them. Rory pulled her chair out, much to the chagrin of the maître d', but at least he smiled at the man. 'I'm sorry. I wanted to do that.'

Kate dipped her head to examine the menu and hide the blush from Rory's comment. This was getting out of hand but a tiny part of her found the danger intoxicating.

'Champagne?' Rory raised those wicked eyebrows of his and Kate shook her head.

I'm heady enough, she thought. 'I'd prefer to keep my wits about me.'

'Perhaps sparkling apple juice?' the waiter suggested, and Kate nodded.

'The same.' Rory wasn't to be outdone. 'Though we may decide on a wine later with dessert.'

The waiter left as they dawdled over the menus. Kate looked around and shook her head. 'This place is incredible.'

'I'm glad we came. It's totally different from where we would have slept.'

'It's different from where you were going to sleep. I was going to have the comfortable stretcher in the back again.'

'Weren't we going to toss for it?'

She shook her head. 'Heads or tails, it was mine.'

He smiled. 'You've become quite assertive, Miss Kate.'

'Survival.'

He lifted his glass and the ping of fine crystal made them both smile. Then his smile fell away. 'To survivors,' Rory said soberly.

By the time they'd finished the meal and enjoyed one glass of the smoothest port Rory had ever tasted, he was thinking of sitting on his hands to keep them under control.

Kate had relaxed enough to laugh and, when she did, his heart felt as if it was going to shatter into a million pieces like the stars through the glass above his head.

No wonder he hadn't settled in his life when that much feeling was tied up in one woman. And he hadn't even realised.

'Let's walk,' he said abruptly and he had Kate out of her chair before the waiter made it halfway across the room.

With his hand resting in the small of her back and her hair brushing his shoulder, it was as if the floodgates had opened and all the years of striving for fulfilment meant nothing. This was what he wanted—Kate with him, side by side as they walked along the gravel-strewn paths along the clifftop. Her tiny hand in his, and how the hell that had happened he didn't know, but he savoured every squeeze of her fingers.

Lush tropical foliage bathed in moonlight—moonlight that cascaded into the gorge below like the waterfall they could hear in the distance, and Kate, giggling beside him as he recited a sweet old lady story from his repertoire.

What was she thinking? What was she feeling? Could she see how good they were together and how they must be able to work things out? This was all too good to throw away.

They stopped in unison and turned. He looked down at her, bathed in silver with her precious face turned up to his and her eyes dark pools of invitation.

She seemed to sway slightly towards him so he kissed her gently, just to taste the promise. Her lips parted and suddenly she was pressing herself against him and her tongue fluttered against his so he kissed her with all the need of his own for the last ten years without Kate.

Then he kissed her for the letter, the return of his ring, and finally for the fact that he had her in his arms at this moment.

Kate had known Rory was going to kiss her tonight. She'd been aware since they'd first sat down in the restaurant hours ago. Aware that this place out of time was the only chance they had to celebrate the past before they went their separate ways in the future.

She lifted her arms and it felt amazing just to reach up and clasp her hands behind his strong neck. To feel his arms go around her back and gather her closer, with his muscular chest solid and broad against her softness. This night had to last her a long time.

She looked up and he stared down, intent, sombre, questioning until his face moved closer; she couldn't help but sway towards him again and their lips rejoined as she closed her eyes.

Who needed vision when there was nothing she couldn't see with Rory's face there, his lips, his breath mingling with hers in that intricate dance that was solely theirs?

Homecoming yet not—the kiss had changed, they'd both grown up and this was no boy-girl kiss.

This was all man meets woman in paradise.

The kiss deepened, softened, deepened, and Kate began to lose the definition between the two. She strained closer and tightened her hold on his neck. He crushed her against him and she revelled in his long, strong hardness until Rory eased back.

For a brief moment in time there was almost a gap between them except for another quick sip and then he pulled away to grab her hand and, laughing, they ran six steps before they turned and kissed again. Moonlight madness consumed them both as they broke apart and ran another six before they stopped again. Kate could never remember feeling like this. Behaving like this. By the time they were almost back at her room, they were heaving gasps of cool evening air laden with the scent of night flowers and the taste of lust.

Just a few steps more and they were in the hallway outside her door, where

Kate crazily fumbled for her key in her door and then they were through, lips still fused, hands flying.

The first time was up against the wall, hiked dress, dropped trousers, insatiable and way too fast, though still time for Rory to protect her, yet, in some elemental way, not fast enough, and then it was over. Rory lifted her and carried her to the bed, where they lay together, wrapped in each other's arms.

They breathed in. Breathed out. Looked at each other and smiled. Then reached for each other again. Just to hold.

A little while later Rory led her to the huge shower with twin ceiling roses but they only needed one as the water streamed over her shoulders and he soaped her. This time was for slow discovery. Carefully loving her, totally rapt in his thorough task as he worshipped her and she put her face up to the water and let the years of drought wash away. Then she washed him, but after that he couldn't help but take her so they made love under the shower and then again back on the bed.

They slept entwined, or Kate slept. Rory stared at her dark head on his chest and stroked her shoulder. How had they wasted so much time? He still didn't know.

Had what they'd shared been too intense? Why did he feel the desperation in Kate that boded ill for their future when she'd just given him everything?

Did she finally understand they were meant to be together?

Kate woke with Rory sleeping beside her. So this was what she'd been missing all these years. No wonder she hadn't had the strength to fight without him all those years ago. She felt adored, protected, safe.

Then she pulled back as reality awoke. This was an interval in life, not a beginning.

That way lay weakness. Vulnerability. She only had to think of what they'd done last night to see how little control she had over herself when mixed with the headiness of being with Rory.

CHAPTER NINE

BREAKFAST WAS TROPICAL splendour on the balcony. Kate was quiet compared to last night but he remembered she wasn't a morning person. Though she'd been showered and dressed when he'd woken. Which was a damn shame.

There was a lot about Kate he didn't know and some he did. But he wanted to know a whole more before they left this place. Like when could he make love with her again?

The rain had stopped through the night, there were gaps for the sun and it was hot, but the clouds were still heavy in the valleys and over the mountains.

They walked to Golden Gorge for a swim, only a few hundred metres from the resort, and it was cool as they climbed down the leafy hundred steps to the deserted rock pool at the bottom.

The huge palm fronds and pandanus dipped over the turquoise waterhole and butterflies skimmed the water.

Rory looked around and then at his Kate, here in paradise. 'I'd forgotten how much I love the top country. There's nowhere like the gorges here.'

Kate nodded. 'I'm glad we stayed on today for a while. We might never get a chance to do this again.'

Rory shot a glance at her. 'I don't want to think that.'

She avoided his eyes. 'For this morning we won't.' She pulled off her T-shirt. 'Last in's a dirty dog.'

There was a mad flurry of discarded clothes and two simultaneous splashes as they hit the pool together but they surfaced apart. Kate shook the hair out of her eyes and swam with leisurely strokes towards the big rock at the edge, where she climbed out again, all long legs and curved arms and delicious sway of her hips and breasts. His mouth tightened for a moment as he saw the long bruise on her thigh from her rush down the river yesterday but he shook the ice away.

Rory wanted her then and there but he could see she had other thoughts so he trod water as he went back over her words with a feeling of sadness. She'd said they might never get this chance again!

It seemed last night hadn't changed anything except maybe helped a little towards Kate's healing process. He couldn't regret it if that was all this trip had accomplished—it had been worth it, though it had not been without cost to his own heart. But he guessed that was a small price to pay for what Kate had been through. But the concept of leaving Kate was too huge to contemplate here.

Kate dived in again and swam under the waterfall that fell into the pool. She stood in it, letting the water pour over her shoulders like a freshwater mermaid and he allowed the future to float away as he soaked in the sight.

When she'd had enough she dived back towards him and grabbed his ankle as she swam under him. He allowed himself to be pulled along before she let go to surface and he swam after her.

She shook her head and the water splashed in his face. 'So, you wanna play tag, do you?'

Kate grinned at him. 'I was always a better swimmer than you.'

'Try me now!' He dared her with one eye-brow raised and she turned to swim away. He easily caught her. 'Try again?'

She wiped the water from her eyes. 'Of course.'

This time he gave her a bigger head start but then easily caught her again.

She frowned. 'Been working out, McIver?'

'Could have.' He swam closer. 'Come here.'

She eyed him warily. 'Why?'

'I always wanted to kiss underwater. I need a volunteer.'

'Who says I'm a volunteer?'

'Everyone else stepped back.' His arms slid around her and she didn't pull away. Their eyes met and held and then they sank below the surface, eyes wide open as their lips came together. It wasn't quite perfect but Rory was happy to practice. They floated back to the surface.

'That could take a rehearsal.' Kate looked a little breathless.

'Yeah,' Rory said, 'you're a buoyant little thing,' and he could feel the tilt of his mouth as he smiled. 'Let's practice.'

She frowned at him. 'One more, no more.'

This time they kissed before they went under, and Rory side swam with her in his arms to the edge. When his hip hit the bottom he pulled her over so she floated above him and he could look up at her through the water. He could quite happily drown here. Her face moved away as she sat up.

'Enough. We should think about going.'

'The next time you fly over here, will you remember us?'

Remember, Kate thought, and she felt like clutching her chest. This had all been a bad, bad idea.

Rory tried to establish some return to the rapport as they left Xanadu but Kate wasn't playing and he couldn't find any way through her silence.

All he could think was that she was regretting last night and this morning. He wondered if it would have helped if he'd slowed down and let her get used to the idea that he was back in her life. And wanted to be for good!

They were close to the Pentecost. Kate stared unseeingly out of the window as she thought about what had happened last night.

She'd invited, no, dragged Rory into her room as she'd caught glimpses of the adored and carefree girl she'd been all those years ago. Stupid woman.

Who was she kidding? She had baggage with a capital B and was too screwed up for any sort of relationship. And she needed to concentrate on finding common ground with her father before it was too late.

Rory had his career. Plus he was carrying a few issues himself. She just needed to get the hell out of his arms and back to the real world.

The Pentecost was an anticlimax. The rush had been through and the river was no deeper than on their way out. The next two hours passed slowly but with no more incidents and finally they drove up the last stretch before Jabiru Township.

Kate looked at the mud at the side of the road. 'I guess you're stuck here until the RFDS can land on the strip.'

Rory frowned. 'Won't you be? Your plane is grounded too.'

She lifted her head. 'I'll drive home. As soon as we get back.'

He tried to control his disappointment. 'Don't go on my account.'

'Why not?'

How could she be so cold after last night? 'It doesn't have to be like this, Kate.'

Her eyes didn't meet his, looked anywhere but his way, just like when he'd first seen her two days ago.

'Yes. It does, Rory.'

He could feel it all slipping away and the panic fluttered like the spinifex at the side of the road as they drove past. Rory ran his hand through his hair. 'You can't deny we shared something special back there at Xanadu.'

Her fingers spread and pressed down on her legs, as if to push away that thought. Still she didn't look at him.

'It's over. Has been for a long time. I'm sorry if I've hurt you, Rory, but I don't want you to come back.'

Those same words from the letter he'd carried all those years. The hurt stirred anger. 'I wish I'd never come back.'

'So do I,' she said quietly.

Rory couldn't give up. He felt that same desolation he'd felt ten years ago. He'd stayed the one night he couldn't avoid in town after Kate had left. Had dinner with Smiley and Sophie, dug for what background they had, and then caught a lift to Derby on a road train early the next morning, like all those years ago, so he could make a flight back from there. Then he drove home from Perth Airport and, without unpacking, he switched on his computer.

He needed to find Fairmont Gardens and a commemorative inscription. Kate needed to grieve and maybe he could get some clue how to help by just seeing where the remains of his son lay.

The next day was a cool autumn day and the Fairmont Gardens were deserted. He crossed the freshly mown grass to the commemorative wall that curved around an enormous bed of roses and the scent was almost heady in its power.

He drew a deep breath and held it, as if imprinting the scent on his memory.

He was standing here for both of them. He didn't know what to expect. How it would affect him. Just knew he had to do this to gain insight into the journey Kate had travelled on her own.

He looked down at the paper printout the custodian had given him with the directions he sought.

Third row down, twenty-six across from the left; his eyes scanned as he counted. Then he saw it.

The plaque, tarnished bronze, six inches by four inches, with raised lettering. *Baby son of Kate Onslow. Lived for a day, 3rd August.*

His son. Rory hadn't expected the rush of sadness that overwhelmed him. Sadness for the little boy who hadn't had the chance to be held by his mother before he'd died. Or his father. He winced at the pain from such a tiny fragment of grief compared to what Kate had had to bury for ten years.

'I'm sorry I wasn't there for you, Cameron.' The quiet words floated up into the branches of the leafy tree overhead.

He turned and gazed over the beautiful gardens, the reminders of other lives that had been and gone, the place that families came to grieve and say goodbye. Then he slid the end of the tiny bouquet he'd brought with him into the slot below.

He thought about Kate—so young, so sick, heartbroken and alone. Kate sending him a letter that must have hurt so much to write and the noble but mistaken reasons she had.

He thought of the day he'd received it and his disbelief. How he'd phoned the housekeeper at Jabiru Station and she'd said Kate wasn't taking calls. And all his letters he'd written that she was destined never to receive.

His parents, working at a new station, the reason for their move now explained, hadn't been able to offer any information on Kate. They had enough trouble of their own trying to adjust.

So he'd stayed, had decided to achieve what he'd set out to do and more, much more. Driven, as Kate said, and for what? To hide the pain that needed Kate. He should have searched for her. Ten years of pain for Kate and him, wasted. He knew that now. And he wasn't wasting any more. He knew where he belonged. What he needed to do.

The card on the bouquet floated in the breeze and he brushed it gently with his finger as he read the words, *With love from Mum and Dad,* and he took a photograph to add to the ones the midwife had confirmed were in the medical records, the grieving parent pack that hospitals kept for years if mementos were refused, not sure if he'd done right to ask.

It was a choice Kate hadn't been given. The hospital had agreed to contact her and ask.

Then he allowed the anguish for everything to float away, to keep the memories—release the pain; their baby, ten years he'd lost with Kate, his sadness and guilt over his parents' early misfortune and, most of all, for Kate's lonely journey.

He understood. He would be there for her and this time she wouldn't turn him away.

It was time to make things happen. He walked away to lay the foundations for his new life. He would give Kate time to come to the same conclusion—he had to believe that time would come—but if it didn't he would make it happen.

Kate drove straight home to Jabiru Homestead after dropping Rory at the Hilton and couldn't help but wonder if she was the same woman who'd left less than forty-eight hours ago. For the first time she considered not selling her family's land after her father died.

Maybe she did deserve a fuller life. She could take over the reins from her father, make changes for the better, maybe some time in the future start a new dynasty of caring and integrity for Jabiru Station and the township.

But first she had to care for the old dynasty.

'Hello, Father.' She looked at him, lying back in the chair overlooking the house yard, a big man brought down by infirmity, his thick white hair still cut short in the military style he preferred and his bushy white brows beetling up at her as he pretended he wasn't in any pain.

'So you're back! Hmmph.' He turned his head away.

'Yes, I am.' She crossed the veranda and picked up his pain relief tablets. 'You haven't taken any pills in two days.'

He glared at her. 'Makes me fuzzy and I don't see what's going on.'

Typical despot. Her voice remained mild. 'There's nothing going on that's worth suffering for.'

He stuck his chin out. 'You can't make me take them.'

'Nope.' Kate shook her head. 'Your choice.' She left that battle but knew he would take them now she was home. He had this thing about the 'family' being alert to what the workers did. And Kate being home meant he could sleep.

She hoped she'd never be that paranoid. 'I went as far as Rainbow's End. They flew Lucy Bolton out from there.'

He thought about that. 'You took long enough, then.'

'The road over the Pentecost was flooded.' She paused and then said deliberately, 'I went with Rory McIver.'

That made him sit up and she saw the agony cross his face with the movement and she felt a moment's regret that she'd startled him. Her father. He must have had some redeeming features when her mother had fallen in love with him but he'd never shown Kate much tenderness.

He pulled himself up, trying not to wince, until he sat straight in the chair. 'That young cockerel. Did he make a pass at you?'

Now that was funny. 'No.' As if her father should worry about that, after all these years.

He sagged a little. 'Good.'

'I made one at him.' Lyle's head snapped up. 'And I told him about the baby.'

'Fool!' He looked away. 'Now, why would you do that? Give him pretensions to glory, knocking up an Onslow.'

Kate winced at the denigration in the comment. This was the only time she could remember when she'd had an equal part in a conversation with her father. And his last comment incensed her. 'If it hadn't been for Rory and his family I'd have known no love at all after Mother died.'

It was all starting to make sense, though. 'Is that what happened? Did Mother have to marry you? Because of me?'

He poked his finger at her, stabbing the air with each word. 'Your mother was too easy with her ways and then wasn't strong enough to survive out here. She lost my son.'

She shook her head, suddenly sorry for this sad old man she'd never connected with. 'My mother needed more than a roof over her head to live here. And you didn't have a loving bone in your body.'

He sagged back in the chair. 'Too late now.'

Did it have to be? Was there any hope they could salvage something before he was gone?

'Maybe it's not for us. We don't have to fight all the time. It would be handy to have some nice memories of you.'

She came around and crouched down beside him so that he had to look at her. 'Were you ever happy?'

He lifted his head. 'When I thought I'd have a son to carry on with.'

She threw up her hands. 'Get over it.' She stared at him. 'Rory could have been that son but you blew it.'

'That camp trash? I'd rather leave it to a dogs' home.'

She glared right into his face. 'I might sell it to a dogs' home.'

'You're no child of mine.' It was more of a mutter than a statement and they both knew it wasn't true.

She sat back, her humour restored. 'Unfortunately, I do have a stubborn and determined side that I've inherited from you, but you're too bitter and twisted to see it.'

He didn't say anything. His mouth moved but didn't open to speak. She gave him another few seconds but he turned away.

She sighed. 'Goodnight, Father. I'll send John in to help you to bed, then I'll bring the rest of your medications.'

The next morning, Kate opened her eyes and stared at the familiar plaster rose on the ceiling above her bed. Since she'd first arrived back to nurse her father, despite her determination to sell, she couldn't help her feeling of belonging to Jabiru.

Yet this morning it was not the same. Her father had never really cared for her—it was out in plain words, lost in his all enveloping grief at not having a son to inherit. Well, he deserved that she wanted to sell.

But she didn't know what she wanted. The idea of waking every morning, like today, alone in the middle of this vastness, wasn't that different from waking alone in a big city like Perth.

At least here she could be useful to people like Lucy, and the Aboriginal women who sometimes needed help to birth, or the man with the croc bite.

She'd be an orphan, no relatives that she knew of, no friends her own age except Sophie and Smiley. Was that what she wanted?

At breakfast her father looked more subdued but without that patina of pain he'd worn yesterday, so he was taking his tablets. He seemed to have thawed slightly towards her and she wondered if anything she'd said yesterday had perhaps made him think.

'You said you're determined and stubborn,' he growled, 'I'm guessing you'd have to be to put up with me.' He looked at her from under his brows. 'And why do you?'

She half laughed. 'Because that's what family do.'

'How would you know?' He sniffed.

'I read about it.' She looked him over. 'How are you today?'

He glared at her. 'Old.'

She raised her eyebrows. 'Here's the good news—it doesn't last for ever.'

He gave a bark of laughter and she nearly fell off her chair in surprise. 'You should have stuck up for yourself years ago. I like you better.'

Okay for him because he was old and able to say what he thought. 'It would have been helpful if you'd given me a hint.'

'Hmmph.'

She looked at him for a moment, fleetingly sad for the impending loss of this tiny rapport. 'I'll see you later. I have to go to work.'

He narrowed his eyes and then shook his head angrily, once. 'Why? They can get other people to do that menial stuff you do.'

He really didn't get it. She'd fight every day against ever becoming that selfish. 'The menial stuff I do saved a baby and mother's life. If there had been someone around when I was Lucy's age you'd have had a grandson to leave your precious station to.' She stood up. 'I'll be back tonight.'

As she walked away she accepted that they might talk a little more civilly to each other, and even on a rare occasion have a laugh over some incident on the station, but it was never going to be warm and fuzzy.

In Kate's mind, as well, there was always going to be a rift from his unfeeling stand over her pregnancy.

Over the next few weeks Kate flew between Jabiru Station and the township and each day she settled more into the idea of staying in the Kimberley.

On the Friday, three weeks after she'd left, Lucy Bolton and her mother returned with her baby and came to visit Kate.

The young woman glowed with health and her tiny baby already was filling out into the cutest cherub.

'How's it all going, Lucy?' Kate said, but she could see everything was going well.

'Cool. Missy eats a lot but she sleeps straight after so that's easy.'

Kate checked Lucy's blood pressure and the readings had returned to normal. 'We'll still have to watch you if you decide on more children.'

Lucy laughed. 'Not just yet, thanks.'

'Congratulations on being a nana, Mary.' Kate smiled at the older woman. 'You look like you're loving it.'

Mary smoothed Missy's hair. 'I'm very lucky. And how's that Rory McIver? I nearly fell over when I saw he was your driver. Hasn't he turned into a handsome man?'

Kate plastered a smile on her face. 'He's back in Perth in his high profile job for the Ambulance. He even sent the clinic a satellite phone, though technically I'm not supposed to know it was him.' She pretended to whisper. 'They told me at the post office it was from him. So I guess he's still thinking of Jabiru.'

That wasn't all he'd sent. He'd sent a letter to say he'd been to see their baby's grave and a photo and, a day later, a short letter from the hospital had arrived. It had taken her days to ring for the grieving parent package to be sent. Still she waited.

Mary gave Kate a tiny nudge and Kate blinked and remembered where she was.

'It must have been nice to see him after all these years,' Mary said and Kate tried not to see the wink. 'You two still in contact, then?'

'Mum!' Lucy nudged her mother out of the way and frowned her to silence. 'That's between Kate and Rory,' and she took Kate's hand in both of hers. 'Thank you for everything, Kate. You were wonderful and I would have been terrified if you hadn't been here for me.' Lucy hugged her and went on, 'They said in Derby I could have lost my darling Missy if I'd got much worse.'

Kate hugged her back. 'You're so welcome and I'm glad Missy is fine. Drop in and see me any time.'

'So you're staying on at Jabiru?' Mary asked.

'For a while.' Kate thought about it. She had decided. 'Yes. For a long while.'

After work Kate called in again to the post office and this time the postmistress handed her a package. Kate thanked her carefully, because suddenly her mouth wasn't working too well. Her body felt as if it were covered in thin ice and she stumbled stiffly out of the tiny shop like an old woman as she clutched the large white envelope to her breast.

She walked blindly to her car but when she reached it she had to turn her face up to catch the afternoon sun to warm her cheeks. 'How ridiculous. To be cold when the day's hitting thirty-seven degrees,' she admonished herself, needing the sound of her own voice and the heat to soak into her skin and into her heart before she unlocked the car door to climb in.

She leant back on the seat and the package lay in her lap, bulky yet light. She had a fair idea what it would contain because she'd prepared just such packages for other broken-hearted families in her midwifery training.

She didn't open it—couldn't open it—and a tiny voice inside her head suggested that there was someone else who should be there when she did.

Instead, she opened her overnight bag that she kept for emergencies and slipped the package in amongst her clothes. Maybe later.

Her father was worse when she got home and she put the envelope away for a time when she had emotions to spare.

There was an improvement in rapport between Kate and her father as Lyle became weaker and more resigned to eternal rest.

Kate could feel the ball of resentment she'd held against him slowly unravelling as he talked to her more.

'Your mother was a beautiful woman,' he said one morning, 'and you're not bad yourself.'

'I'll try not to let your effusive compliments go to my head,' Kate said, straight-faced, and he shot a look at her before he actually laughed out loud. Then he sucked his breath in as the pain bit.

When he had his breathing under control again Kate asked the questions she'd always wanted to ask. 'Why were you so cold to me?'

He avoided her eyes. 'Was I? Don't know any different,' he said. 'My own mother died when I was two. That's how I was brought up. When my son died with your mother I knew you needed to be tough to run this place. No room for namby-pamby cry babies.'

Kate shook her head. 'This place is a well-oiled machine and kindness isn't a weakness.' She looked him in the eye. 'It's a strength.'

For once he didn't bluster. 'Maybe I got it wrong but that's all I knew. It might have been different if your mother had lived.'

'Maybe you should have married again.'

'Hmmph. I don't have to. It's your job to ensure the succession.'

She gathered their plates. 'You might have blown it there. I'm not looking for a husband. Are there any cousins or relatives anywhere?'

'You'd better sell it to the dogs' home.' He was watching her like a hawk and she doubted he missed her frown. No, she didn't think she could do that now. Every day she felt more like she belonged, except for the emptiness at night, but she guessed that would never go away.

CHAPTER TEN

A MONTH AFTER Rory had left, Kate landed on the strip of her father's property and saw a dust-covered Range Rover waiting beside her own farm vehicle. Somehow she knew it was Rory.

In that moment she panicked and looked at the fuel gauge. All she wanted to do was dip the wing into a turn and circle back the way she'd come, to run, hide, but the sensible pilot inside her head disagreed. Land, the pilot said.

There was fuel to spare, but not much, and Kate always listened to the pilot. As she touched down the roaring of the engine echoed in her head and she tried to block out the questions.

Why had he come back? Why now, when her father was so ill? What should she do? How should she act? She'd be caught in the middle again.

The plane taxied to a stop and she looked across as the propeller began to wind down. At least he was on his own and she didn't have to pretend it wasn't a shock to see him. And he looked amazing.

Damn. It wasn't fair. She was dishevelled, exhausted from the broken sleeps with her father as he became more ill, and wretched.

The wind blew his shirt against his muscular chest, the one she wanted to rest her head against, and he lifted his hand to hold his Akubra firmly on his head, hiding the thick dark hair she loved.

Loved! The truth crashed into her as if she'd landed her plane into a fence instead of kissing the airstrip and parking normally. She'd been miserable because she'd missed Rory. Because Rory's presence was life and promise and the future—her future—and she'd been too stubborn and frightened to take the risk when he'd come back after all these years and she'd thought that chance was gone.

It should have been her landing at his back door to say she'd got it wrong. Should have been her asking for forgiveness. Her explaining she loved Rory as much, if not more than ten years ago and would he please never leave her again.

All the fruitless mental discussion of how it was better she'd seen him and could forget the past. The exhaustion and misery of the last month.

What a fool she'd been.

It was all dirt and lies and bull dust. She loved Rory McIver with all her heart and soul and always would. She just needed the guts to tell him!

She shaded her eyes as she climbed out and then jumped down to the ground in front of him.

'How are you, Kate?' He saw beneath her bravado to the young woman within and suddenly her bravery was gone.

She couldn't do it. What if it was too late? Tiredness hit her like a tsunami, flattened her, bowled her off her feet so in her mind she bobbed with indecision. She didn't look at him as she walked to her vehicle. 'Tired.' Such a small, spineless voice. She disgusted herself. 'How are you, Rory? Have you been to the house?'

'Yes.' His quiet, gravelly voice, low with compassion.

That pulled her up. 'Spoken with my father?'

'Yes.'

This time she looked straight into his face. Questioning. Dreading the answer. 'And you're both still alive?'

'He was when I left him.' His voice lowered. 'Just.'

She sagged. She didn't know how she was going to get through that either. 'I know. He hasn't long. He's just an old man who's made some wrong choices along the way and he has to live, and die, with those choices.' Like she did. She looked at Rory. 'In the last month I've come to terms with that. He's still my father.'

Rory smiled at her. Undemanding. Empathetic. Her Rory. 'I'm glad. I'm here because I'd like to stay with you until the end, Kate. Be here for you. Like I wasn't before. When Cameron died.'

She felt the tears build behind her eyes and they felt heavier than usual. But she never cried.

That was why he'd come back. How had he known she'd dreaded being alone when it happened? Technically, though, she'd have people around her—the housekeeper she'd only met two months ago, who didn't normally live-in, the manager, the yard man, John, the stockmen, the drivers and overseers. Not on her own—but alone.

He wouldn't stay. He had his important position to go back to.

'How long have you got?'

'As long as you need me.' That calm, reassuring Rory voice.

Fine words. 'What about your high-powered job?'

He shook his head. 'You're my family. As long as you need me.'

He'd do that for her? Risk everything he'd worked for to hold her hand? Be with her at the end and comfort her? No one else had ever worried about her like Rory.

And she couldn't even risk saying she loved him?

It was as if the sky cleared and the dark clouds of the last few weeks were blown away from over her head. Maybe forgiving her father had helped. Maybe knowing there was a time in the not too distant future when she could meet her lost son—if only on paper. But suddenly those restraining shackles had gone. This was all about her and Rory. So what was she going to do?

Was she going to pretend she hadn't just had the biggest brain snap in history and wait for him to decide their fate?

Or was she going to take her future in her own hands and lift her head and meet his eyes and tell him she loved him more than she could believe was possible for one woman to love a man?

It was a terrifying thought, but not as terrifying as him walking away without the truth leaving her lips.

She looked into Rory's caring eyes, this tall and straight, fabulous man of her dreams, who had never forgotten her and she spoke the truth. 'I love you, Rory McIver. With all my heart. I always will. Thank you for coming back to be with me.'

Kate felt the tears sting and then they welled. She struggled to hold them back and then realised she didn't have to. Amazingly, dampness spilled over onto her cheeks. For the first time in ten years, Kate Onslow cried. She stepped into Rory's open arms and he lifted her to him and kissed her cheeks before he set her down to cradle her against his chest.

She cried great gulping, soul-freeing sobs, and she cried quiet, whispering weeps until his shirt was sticking to her face with dampness and then she pulled away and gave him the first of many watery smiles.

She wiped her cheeks with her fingers until he pushed her hands aside and patted the tear trails himself with the big white handkerchief he'd tried to give her.

'I bet—' she sniffed '—you didn't expect that tropical storm,' and she snatched the handkerchief from him and inelegantly blew her nose before she crumpled the wet cloth into a ball and jammed it into her khaki trousers.

'I'd say it's about time.' Then he kissed her. Inexpertly at first because she hadn't expected it and then perfectly, amazingly, healingly until there was no doubt that her own revelation in the plane was matched by his.

His words caressed her as he spoke into her ear. 'I love you, Kate. I'm here for you. Always.'

Once started, she couldn't stop. It was time to open herself to the love he promised.

'I love you, too,' she said. 'I was a fool to push you away when you came back. I've missed you so much this last month, but goodness knows how long it would have taken me to be brave enough to come and tell you. Thank you for taking that risk.'

'Again,' he teased.

'Again.' She wiped her eyes.

He squeezed her shoulders. 'Have I ever told you everything would work out fine?'

She looked up at him. Her hero. 'For years.'

'And that's how long I'll be here. For years and years and years.' He captured her hand and kissed her palm. 'For ever. My darling Kate, I've always loved you, never more than now.'

He pulled a tiny box from his pocket and it sat there in his palm, daring her to open the lid. 'Will you marry me? This time?'

She looked at him and then the box and, as he had so many years ago, he took the ring and slid it on her finger.

The most exquisite pink Argyle diamond ring; the size of the central stone took her breath away, but it was the much smaller diamond beside it that brought more tears to her eyes. 'My original stone from the ring you gave me? You kept it?'

She looked from the ring to Rory. This man she'd cut from her life so many years ago had never given up and she shuddered to think of how close she'd been to losing that chance.

* * *

Later that night, when Kate had seen to her father's comfort and most of the lights were out in the homestead, she found Rory on the swing on the veranda watching the night sky as he waited for her. Still waiting.

He made room beside him and slid his arm around her shoulders as they sat hip to hip in the dark. The moon shone from behind a cloud and the sound of a night bird echoed eerily over the silver paddocks.

'How are you?' he asked quietly.

She snuggled in against him. 'So much better now you're here.'

He stroked her arm. 'I'm not going anywhere.'

She pouted but he couldn't see so she patted his leg. 'I was thinking we could go to bed.'

'Are you trying to seduce me again? Under your father's roof?' She could hear the smile in his voice.

A flicker of heat curled in her stomach. 'Serve him right.'

'I think not,' came the measured voice of her beloved from the darkness beside her.

'Rory McIver!' She couldn't believe he'd refused her offer. She'd been fantasising about him all day. Had watched his mouth as he talked, the way he held his head as he walked, and stared at the sprinkling of dark hairs in the vee of his shirt so much she could have plotted their pattern. Had waited, very impatiently, to relive those magic hours they'd shared at Xanadu.

'No, my wanton little midwife. I want to marry you first this time. Tonight I want to dance with you in the moonlight. Hold you under the same stars that I held you all those years ago. Then fall asleep, just holding you until you are my wife. Does that sound so bad?'

The wedding was intimate, beautiful, and held at Jabiru Homestead very quickly. Smiley and Sophie were attendants and even the bedridden Lyle seemed resigned to their marriage.

Kate never knew what Rory had told him but she'd seen the grudging respect her father paid to Rory now.

Her world was in harmony. That night Kate slept, sated, and with a soft smile curving her lips. Safe and finally at peace in the place she belonged—in Rory's arms.

When Lyle Onslow died he was put to rest beside his wife and infant son, in the family plot on the hill above the homestead.

Beside him stood a tiny angel, in memory of Cameron Onslow-McIver, 3rd August.

Kate stood in the windswept paddock and gazed out at the land she loved, at the land Lyle had taught her to love, and thought, this is right.

Forgiveness came from loving. Forgiveness was healing all on its own and her love had come full circle.

Life could move on.

One year later

'You said you'd never ask me to do something I didn't want to.' Kate tossed her head against the plastic-covered pillow in the shower. 'I can't do it. I want to go home.'

If they'd been anywhere but here, the birthing centre at Perth General, Rory would have given in, plucked her up into his arms and carried her all the way back to Jabiru.

But she'd told him about this. The end of the first stage of labour. Transition. He said what he'd been told to.

'I know. I love you. You're doing beautifully.' And he kissed her and held her hand and she ground her wedding ring into his already painful fingers until suddenly her eyes opened wide, startled yet intent.

'I have to push.'

'Hallelujah,' he said under his breath because he'd been ready to scream for a transfer to a labour ward and an epidural, anything to stop the pain for the love of his life.

'Oh, my,' she said as the sensations took over.

'Remember the breathing. Calm breathing.' He couldn't believe he was saying this, but then again he was doing it too, and the breathing had been the only thing that had got him through this. He'd been breathing his heart out for what seemed like forever.

His feet ached in his new leather boots, both boots as soaking wet as the bottoms of his jeans, but Kate had needed the shower as soon as they'd arrived and he hadn't had time to change.

The steam from the shower had Kate's hair sticking to her forehead and he reached over and offered her a sip of water through the straw.

Kate sipped urgently and then spat the straw out as the next contraction started and hastily he put the cup down. He still found labour very stressful.

The midwife watched them both and smiled. She didn't say much, this old bird, he thought fleetingly as he smiled back, but she'd been just like Kate had been when Lucy had birthed. Calm, unflappable, unlike the way he was feeling.

Oh, my God, he could see the baby's head. The midwife put the Doppler low over Kate's stomach and the clop, clop of his baby's heart rate filled the bathroom. Soon—very soon—he would meet their child.

'Nice and gentle,' Rory said because he remembered Kate had said that to Lucy all that time ago and nobody else said anything. He looked around.

With only the three of them here it was suddenly incredibly peaceful. Kate was totally focused on the job at hand now, with the warm shower water cascading over her shoulders like that day at Xanadu and the waterfalls in the gorge.

The midwife was prepared and patient and he was the only one talking now. It seemed he couldn't keep his mouth shut. He clamped his lips together and realised their song from their teenage years was playing in the background.

Then slowly, crease by wrinkled forehead skin crease, their baby began to birth until a thick mop of damp hair and a squashed little face spun to stare at him.

'Rest one hand under the bottom shoulder as it comes out and put your other hand on the top shoulder,' the midwife said quietly.

He was holding it. He looked up at Kate and she was staring through him as she concentrated.

Suddenly he was holding all of him...her...he didn't know which...and the baby was as slippery as a little eel and he juggled and skidded it up Kate's belly until her hands closed around it and she searched for his face. His. Her husband. Rory's.

'Oh, my stars,' she breathed out. 'Hello, baby. A boy or a girl? What is it?' Kate was still looking at him, unable to believe it was over and she held their baby in her arms between her breasts.

'It's a...' Rory lifted one leg and tried to see but it was all too hard to peer through the tears in his eyes and the baby skidded and folded up like a puppy. The midwife's hands came in and she tilted the baby so he could look properly.

His heart swelled. 'We have a daughter. Jasmine.' He looked at Kate and tears ran down his face. 'She's incredibly beautiful, like her mother.'

* * * * *

Keep reading for an excerpt of
Dark Side Of The River
by B.J. Daniels.
Find it in the
Dark Side Of The River anthology,
out now!

CHAPTER ONE

OAKLEY STAFFORD SPURRED her horse as she came bursting out of the ravine headed for the safety of the river bottom. Behind her she could hear the thunder of hooves, pounding as hard as her own blood. Only one rider, but he apparently was determined to catch her, to stop her. She knew that on horseback she could outrun him. That single rider, a cowboy who'd fallen in behind her as she came out of the ravine, wasn't who she was worried about.

The real trouble was in the sky behind her. The sound of a small-plane engine growing closer made her heart race. They were coming after her, determined to stop her at all costs. She was outnumbered and they had all the advantages. She could no longer hear the horse and rider behind her, but the sound of the plane's engine was getting louder. It was flying low, coming up fast behind her.

If it was the Piper Cub she'd seen earlier, one of the men had been shooting at coyotes from the open window behind the pilot. She knew she would make a much bigger target than a coyote. She was now easy prey.

The dirt ahead of her was suddenly pocked as a bullet struck it. Dust rose next to her horse, making it shy to the right. Ahead she could see the cover of the thick cottonwoods that lined each side of the Powder River. Once under that dark canopy, at the least the pilot and his passenger wouldn't have a clear shot at her. If they were the ones who'd just fired on her.

But the cowboy on the horse behind her was also armed—and maybe even more dangerous. She'd seen him as she'd come racing out of the ravine, getting only a glimpse before she'd heard him shoot. Her only chance was to make it past the trees and the river to the county road…

Spurring her horse, she leaned forward, urging the mare to go faster, desperate to reach the grove of cottonwoods. She heard the plane pull up and begin to circle, drowning out the sound of hooves behind her. But she knew he was still back there, determined to stop her.

She couldn't let him or the others catch her. They would kill her. She knew too much.

COOPER MCKENNA RESTED his arm out the open pickup window as he drove down the familiar county road. After being away this long, he was in no hurry to reach home. The late-June heat blew in along with grasshoppers that flew around the cab. Ahead, huge cottonwoods crowded both sides of the dirt road, making a shaded dark green tunnel. The sun pierced the green leaves to throw shadows across his path as he drove beneath them, the air in here cooler.

Overhead, puffy white clouds floated in a sea of deep blue above the treetops. He caught only glimpses of the river that began in Wyoming and traveled more than one hundred and fifty miles to empty into the Yellowstone.

Many claimed that the Powder River was a mile wide, an inch deep and ran uphill. The running joke was that it was too thick to drink and too thin to plow. Captain Clark of the Lewis and Clark Expedition had named it Redstone River. But the

Native Americans called it Powder River because the black shores reminded them of gunpowder, and that had stuck.

The river, the lifeblood of those who lived here, passed right through the heart of the McKenna Ranch. Just the sight of it felt like home. This was where he'd left his heart. After two years of being away, he'd shaken off the dust of the places he'd been, this country calling him home like a migrating bird after a long winter. He'd felt an ache for the familiar, yearning for the rocky bluffs, the spring green of the grasslands and, of course, the river that ran through it.

He'd passed the ranch sign five miles back and still had another ten miles to go to reach the ranch house. The McKenna Ranch stretched as far as the eye could see, the county road cutting through the heart of it. His eyes were on the road ahead, but his thoughts were as dark as the shadows lurking in the trees.

The deep ache in his chest wasn't just for the land or for what he'd lost here. This place had broken his heart. Yet here he was, coming back. He smiled ruefully, knowing what kind of homecoming it could be. He was the middle son of Holden McKenna, a threat to his older brother, Treyton, the self-proclaimed rightful heir of the ranching empire the Holdens had built.

Cooper was the black sheep, the rebel cowboy everyone believed was a killer. The worst part was, he thought they might be right.

With a start, he caught movement out of the corner of his eye an instant before the horse and rider came flying out of the cottonwoods. The rider tumbled from the horse, going down hard in the middle of the road in front of the pickup.

Standing on the brake, Cooper was terrified he wouldn't get stopped quickly enough on the narrow dirt road. As the pickup shuddered to a stop, he let out the breath he'd been holding before throwing the truck into Park and jumping out.

Rounding the front of the pickup, he was relieved to see that he hadn't hit the rider, who was lying on the ground just inches from his bumper, back to him. The horse, wild-eyed and spooked, had run up the road and stopped to look back.

He spotted the brand. *Stafford Ranch?* What the hell was the rider doing on McKenna property with the bad blood between the families?

"That was a nasty spill you took," he said as the rider groaned. He knelt down, not adding that it had been a dumb-ass thing to do, riding out of the woods like that onto the county road. Picking up the fallen cowboy's hat, he asked, "You all right?"

He'd seen his share of cowboys hit the dirt, thrown from their horses for all kinds of reasons. He'd certainly had his share of unexpected dismounts. Cowboys usually just dusted themselves off, limped off to retrieve their horses and were on their way again.

Another groan. This one had hit the ground pretty hard and wasn't getting up. Cooper hoped he wasn't too badly injured. As he leaned over the cowboy, shock rocketed through him as he saw the rider's face.

Oakley Stafford? He swore under his breath. He'd just assumed it was a cowboy who'd come busting out of the trees riding way too fast. He'd known Oakley and her older sister, Tilly, all of his life—even though their families had been feuding for years.

So what the hell had she been doing riding a horse like that—let alone trespassing on the McKenna Ranch? There was no need for trespassing signs. Everyone knew the last place you wanted to get caught was on the McKenna or Stafford ranches without written permission.

As far back as Cooper could remember, there had been a war going on between their two families. The only thing worse than finding a Stafford on the ranch was for a McKenna to be caught on Stafford land—the equally large ranch that bordered theirs.

Oakley let out another groan of pain and rolled toward him. He'd been sure that she'd taken worse falls from a horse, so he hadn't been too concerned that her injuries were serious—until he saw that she was bleeding.

"Easy, take it easy," he said as he tried to see where the blood was coming from without moving her too much. "How badly are you hurt?"

Her eyelids fluttered. "Buttercup," she managed to whisper as she grimaced in pain.

He assumed that must be her horse. "Buttercup's fine," he assured her. "Where are you injured?"

"No." She tried to get up, letting out a cry before falling back in obvious agony. He realized she was hurt much worse than he'd originally thought. He couldn't tell where the blood was coming from, but it had soaked into the front side of her shirt on through to her denim jacket. All he could think was that she must have hit something in the road when she'd fallen.

"No. *Buttercup.*" She said it as if he just wasn't getting it. He wasn't. Her eyelids fluttered again, then closed, her head falling to the side.

"Oakley? *Oakley?*" He pulled out his phone to call 911. As he did, he leaned over farther to see that even the back of her denim jacket was soaked with blood. Startled, he saw a perfectly round hole in the denim. He stared in shock. It made no sense, no sense at all. Oakley hadn't gotten hurt falling off her horse.

She'd been shot.